GHO$T TRAD€R

An epic for the age of finance
by
Jeremy Cook

**In reality the illusion of wealth,
in dream the illusion of reality**

GHO$T TRAD€R

Part One
New Dawn

"All financial disasters are the same.
First there's the new dawn,
as some discovery seems to offer opportunity and wealth."

"She's an enigma. I couldn't for the life of me decide
whether I was talking to a latter-day Robin Hood
or the most consummate liar I've ever met.
I still can't decide."
His eyes twinkled as never before.
"I wish you joy of her."

Chapter One : Bank Run

September 15th 2007 began like any other Saturday. Up by eight, two mugs of *Arabica* on the balcony whilst I skimmed *Le Monde* in my sweats. No sugar. Keeping up with the financial news reassured me that I wasn't the only failure in the world, and that financial crises were still in fashion. The current one was going to be the worst, but as journalists always say things like this, I missed the significance of the small piece on bank queues. Very orderly and British. I read the piece with the wry detachment in which it had been written. So detached, I missed the name of the bank. The journalist took for granted that I would enjoy a little Anglo-Saxon suffering, knowing that my French savings, however paltry, were better protected.

I was more concerned with psyching myself up for my hero's run. The weather was ideal, sunny with a light breeze. Not that rain or snow would have held me back, but I was no masochist. Just a creature of habit. Occupation kept me from brooding, which ten years ago had ruined my waking hours and plagued my sleep with nightmares.

That was when I lost my business and my home. The business I'd built from nothing to a 50-strong consultancy in Covent Garden, thriving before the area became a tourist trap; the house was a mansion overlooking Primrose Hill, which Amy had transformed from bed-sits into a home fit for entertaining and child-rearing. Even though the sales had been forced upon us, the profit had been substantial. Yet none of it had accrued to me, and very little to Amy. But my French neighbours had been more than *sympa*, and acquaintance had blossomed into friendship, especially with René, the local doctor, and Sidonie, the developer of the chalet complex in which I now lived. All of them, but these two especially, had taught me to rebuild my shattered ego.

As a result, I had long been adjusted to living alone in my *deux pièces* on the eastern shore of Lake Annecy. As for my ex-wife, Amy occupied what our son Jake called the dower doss: the basement of his house, in that part of Stoke Newington which has pretensions to Islington. For the last year, she'd also enjoyed helping Miriam, our daughter-in-law, to look after Jake junior, and the dower doss had been promoted to the rank of granny flat.

I'd once owned the largest apartment in the complex, and it was open house year round. Amy loved entertaining, and our friends enjoyed sailing and swimming in the lake, skiing in La Clusaz. That apartment had also had to be sold, and I now occupied the smallest. My bedroom had a velux, my living room balcony was a dug-out in the roof. But I liked the sloping ceilings, and the views of the castle. From the window of the galley, on my one vertical wall, I could just see the lake. It was a great spot in which to act out being happy.

In the days of success, Amy and Jake had spent the summers here, whilst I was a weekly commuter: last flight to Geneva Friday, first flight back Monday, when I could get away. Nowadays, I was chairman of the co-owners of the complex, my business acumen devoted to making sure the grass was mown, the shrubbery trimmed and the buildings maintained for the best price. In this, my neighbours now trusted me entirely, the only Anglo-Saxon in their midst, because I'd dared to stand up to the management company who'd overcharged and underserved us. This had led at first to a falling-out with Sidonie, until my one-man management had proved its worth, and she – ever the pragmatist – had forgiven me. As for the rest, my neighbours assiduously attended the legally required AGMs, where I kept grumbling to a minimum by feeding them well, buffet style, as I presented the accounts and the plans for the coming year with all the flair which I had once devoted to the boards of multinationals.

It helped that I was dark enough to pass for a native and spoke *sans accent*. Not like Amy. As fair-skinned as a real blonde, she had the tall, angular figure of the true Anglo-Saxon. Her French might have grated on my ears, but my neighbours, especially the males, found it charming. Amy was proudly English, and unselfconsciously beautiful. Or should I say handsome, now that we're divorced and officially no longer in love? Strange how financial ruin can destroy the one thing that is assumed to be above such considerations.

But enough of brooding! *C'est à bannir*. Coffee drunk, paper read, and running shoes laced, I was ready to go. Across the grass, already in need of a trim – I made a mental note to chase the garden contractors – down the path that zigzagged between allotments and orchards, across the main road, down the Rue de la Plage. Good pace, breathing steady. Wooden jetties ran out into the lake, and tarpaulin-covered boats bobbed in the dimpling water. Inland were gardens and chalets, many shuttered now that summer was over. Some were abandoned, their dark walls hidden behind elms and cedars run wild.

4

I passed the ferry stop with its *art nouveau* roof, and then the grand edifice of the *Hôtel du Lac*. The name was prosaic, but its backdrop was dramatic: the *Roc de Chère*, a vast wooded knoll whose granite face fell sheer into the water. The road climbed behind the hotel, then diminished into a track as it steepened. I wound my upward way between mossy stones. Silvery birch bark twinkled between oaks and thickets of dark holly. I was heading for the highest point, where a rocky outcrop broke through the trees and offered an uninterrupted vista of the lake. Until I reached it, the water was invisible, and silent. This early, there were few boats to disturb its peaceful surface.

Breathing hard, I surveyed the misty outlines of Annecy to the north, and the reedy game reserve of *Bout du Lac* to the south. On the far side, the ridge of *Semnoz* basked its limbs like a gigantic dinosaur.

Boosted by the effort and uplifted by the views, I turned for home: downhill all the way, the only hazard the uneven footing that could twist an ankle. Back at the chalet, I took the steps to my front door two at a time, just for the joy of it. My telephone was ringing.

In the old days I left telephone answering to my p.a. and to Amy, who loved phones far more than I. Now I was dehydrated and I needed a shower: good reasons for letting it ring itself out. The last thing I wanted was to be arguing over an invoice or refusing a timeshare in Corsica. But it might have been a new client. Even on a Saturday. As for bad news, better to get it over with. So I compromised, waiting until I'd drunk some water before answering.

To my surprise, it was Amy. We hardly spoke these days, and when we did, she called very early if she needed my attention, or very late if she couldn't sleep. My pulse raced, far more than it had on the *Roc de Chère*. She still had that effect on me.

"Clem! I've been queuing outside Northern Rock all morning."

"Whatever for?" This wasn't *rapprochement*. Anything but.

"Haven't you been following the news?"

"Not the English news." The last thing I wanted was daily gloom from the British media. By now I was scrabbling through *Le Monde* for the small item I'd glanced at over my breakfast coffee. The bank had indeed been Northern Rock. Trust Amy to have chosen it. "Did you get your money out?" I tried to be patient and sympathetic.

She choked back a sob. "I was ten back when they closed."

Runs on British banks were unprecedented, and I ought to have been horrified for her. But I was still thirsty, and I didn't see what I could do to help. "What does Jake say?"

I hadn't seen Jake since he and Miriam had stayed last year, when Jake junior was only months old. I'd held him in my arms, the same way I'd once held Jake. His brow had furrowed, as he'd studied me with huge solemn eyes, as though he couldn't believe I should be any part of his life. Not like Granny Amy, whom he adored, or so they said, and whom he saw every day. It was to Jake Amy should agitate.

"He said I should speak to you, of course."

Trust Jake to pass the buck. "Don't worry." I tried to sound all-knowing again, in the manner that had once been second nature. "The Government will have to step in."

"They didn't before, did they?" She meant they hadn't stepped in to save me from ruin, but then I hadn't expected them to. We investors in the venerable insurance society of Lloyd's – Names as we were known – were supposed to be rich enough to look after ourselves. Nor were there enough of us to swing an election, even if we'd been united. Small savers ought to be different. "It's all very well for you," she continued, "This is all I've got." She could have added "thanks to you", but she didn't need to. She'd said it often enough.

"The Government will have to step in. As soon as they guarantee savings, the runs will stop." That's what the journo in *Le Monde* had hinted, anyway. "If the bank gets taken over, or goes bust, shareholders and bondholders will be the losers." Just like Names. "Not you."

"So that's your advice, is it? Do nothing?" Her voice rose. "Look where it got us before."

"I seem to remember I was very active in defence of my assets."

"Active!" She snorted. "All you did was punch Wormsley on the nose." She was referring to the Lloyd's chief debt collector. "You made things worse." I hardly needed reminding. According to Wormsley, I would owe Lloyd's until the day I died: then he'd seize my estate. Earning peanuts in France was how I kept below his radar.

"Ambrose was there too," I reminded her. "He said I was a hero."

The two-timing bastard had praised me to the sky, after we'd staggered back to Primrose Hill, triumphantly drunk after the punch-up, but it was he alone who had won Amy's admiration. If I'd realised what was coming, I'd have broken Ambrose's neck, never mind Wormsley's nose. But how could I have realised? Ambrose had been my friend and a fellow Name. Neither his self-effacing manner nor his academic appearance, still less the unnerving way he brought those staring eyes up close when talking, suggested a wife-stealer. At least she had the decency to choke at the mention of his name.

I fought to get my emotions under control. Losing my temper with Amy had never worked since she'd hardened herself against tears. "It's either do nothing or start queuing again Monday." I knew for a fact she hated queuing. Ten minutes waiting for a chair lift at La Clusaz on a busy Sunday was about as long as her patience would stand. The fact that she'd queued for a whole morning outside Northern Rock spoke far more for her worries than her words.

"On your head be it, then." She sounded calmer, too. Perhaps she still trusted me on serious matters, after all. Or else she was glad she could put the blame on me if it all went wrong. Easier to scream at me than at a ring-fence of call centres and legal departments.

It was only under the soothing jet of the shower that I began to sympathise with Amy's agitation. It was easy for the financial journalist on *Le Monde* to be detached because it wasn't his readers' savings at stake, but I really ought to have shown more understanding. There are ways of being right – always assuming I were right, of course – and smugness wasn't one of them. As I assembled my late lunch of *pâté* and *crudités* and poured the glass of *Chignin* my exercise had earned, I debated whether to call Amy back to apologise. By the time I'd stacked the dishwasher, I'd decided against. When humility and understanding were necessary, the telephone was the worst method of communication, especially when the recipient was my former wife, who could nowadays be so prickly, even at the best of times.

I brooded instead. Governments did not always behave to order. Neither I nor *Le Monde* had any insight into the mindset of the British Treasury. I foolishly finished the *Chignin* with my dinner, so I shouldn't have been surprised to find myself that night in a horrible dream. Ten years ago, I'd often dreamt that Wormsley had flown through my window like a vampire to suck me dry, whilst Amy and Ambrose had beckoned me to join them in lewd and naked dances. But those dreams had been short and fragmentary. The dream I found myself in now was so vivid in its detail that it went beyond wild imaginings. This was more like prophecy.

I stood in a doorway, facing a long queue, three and four abreast. Coats buttoned against the cold, they stared at me from pinched faces, their flesh so wasted I could make out the skulls beneath. They didn't speak, but their breathing was scratchy, as though dry leaves were tumbling across the pavement. Then a man at the front began to cough, discreetly at first, but rising inexorably into paroxysm. He collapsed at my feet. Rag and bone falling upon his spewed-out lungs.

More began to cough and fall. Each face was individual in detail, like the terracotta warriors, and I experienced the pain of each as if it were my own. In particular, there was a tall, angular woman a few rows back, huddled into her coat, which hung off her wasted shoulders. "Do something, can't you?" A stranger daring to order me about.

The door was a heavy slab of plate glass. There were no handles, merely a metal panel for pushing. But the harder I pushed, the more it resisted. Inside, all was warm and neat, with smartly dressed young men and women sitting at desks, or shouting at screens. Before each desk there was an empty chair awaiting us customers. But to the extent that those inside noticed the queue, they found us amusing.

"You're pathetic," the woman shouted at me. Though her once luxuriant hair straggled in lank strands, and her emaciated figure retained only mocking echoes of its former allure, the stranger had become Amy, mocking me for my failure now just as she had mocked me long ago over Lloyd's. She'd linked arms with the man next to her, as if to say that even this thin, pathetic creature was preferable to me. "I don't know why I ever trusted you."

They were all belittling me now. The men and women jeered from the other side of the door, and the remainder of the queue smirked behind their hands. I rushed for her. Releasing her companion, she stood as proudly and as uprightly as she could. Beautiful in her pitiable defiance. I raised my fist, but she did not flinch. My head boiled with a rage that threatened to tear me apart. I closed my eyes to contain it and to shut them all out. Her especially.

When I opened my eyes again, she was sprawled in the gutter, face down. I had no memory of hitting her, but how else could she have fallen? Choking back tears of remorse, I turned her over as gently as I could. But the face this revealed was totally unfamiliar. A strong face, in which I could discern intelligence and humour, even though one cheekbone was disfigured by a terrible bruise, and her forehead was bleeding. The kerb, against which she must have fallen, was streaked with blood. Dark eyes glittered beneath the lashes of half-opened lids. A world away from Amy's cornflower blue. Amy or a stranger? Amy *and* a stranger. The madness of dreams.

The dream repeated itself on Sunday night, in the same grisly detail, though the woman in the queue was more the stranger and less like Amy, and the sense of guilt and foreboding was more intense. On Monday morning the real queues were round the block at every branch of Northern Rock, under the full scrutiny of the media. Yet the faces on my TV screen seemed less precise and less involving than the agonised

8

phantoms of my dream. Not that this inhibited the French commentators. Unfettered Anglo-Saxon capitalism – light-touch regulation as the British called it – was about to reap the whirlwind it had sowed. Amy called me mid-morning to demand whether I'd changed my mind. I did my best to assure her that I hadn't, though after two bad nights I was trying to convince myself as much as her.

"You realise I'm sitting on my arse, whilst the rest of the world is getting its money out?"

"Aren't you at work?"

"Of course I'm at work. I can't afford not to be, can I?"

Amy ran the accounts for a small restaurant chain, her earnings safe even from Wormsley, since she had never been a Name. They had five outlets scattered around North London, and were planning to open another in Windsor. The owners were enthusiastic and hard-working, but clueless about profit and loss. Amy's ability to control cash-flow amazed them as much as her pedantry over figures amused them. But they were grateful that she kept suppliers happy and staff paid, that she dealt with VAT officers and health inspectors, and best of all that she could spot when managers were cheating them. They underpaid her, of course, but she was delighted to be irreplaceable. So I sensed that her devotion to duty was as important a reason for not queuing as my recommendation. It was my only consolation.

Fortunately, *Le Monde* had been right. An hour after Northern Rock branches closed for the night, the Chancellor of the Exchequer announced that he was standing behind savers. Amy called the moment he stopped speaking. "You were right, Clem. I should never have doubted you." This was generosity like the old days. "Saul's taking me out to celebrate. Nothing flash. Such a pity you can't join us." My pleasure immediately dashed, I forced myself not to ask who Saul was. "I'll introduce you sometime. I know you'll like each other."

"If you say so." In Saul's shoes, Amy's ex would be the last person I'd want to meet, but then I wasn't Saul, and I might be leaping to wild conclusions. After so long, it was strange that one name, so lightly nuanced with the warmth of possession, could prick my jealousy.

"He's just a friend." Amy was still sensitive to my vibes, and her tone did its best to be reassuring. But the sub-text was so clear, she might as well have admitted they were lovers. My mood sank from its usual apathy to misery. Until this moment, I had nursed, or at least failed to dismiss, the delusion that sometime or other Amy and I would get back together. "I'm sorry I got silly before. I was really worried. I hope you didn't mind too much." Her voice was soft, almost as soft as it used to be. But I knew now she was only trying to be kind.

Amy, Amy! I had fled to France to escape Wormsley, but I needn't have chosen the same village, nor the same chalet complex. I didn't have to shop in the same *pâtisserie*, drink in the same bar, nor swim from the same beach, except that I'd shared them with Amy in the days of happiness. Here all memories and reminders of Amy were joyful. It was London that was tainted with sorrow and defeat. It would be impossible for me now to stroll through Covent Garden like a carefree tourist, or to run to the pinnacle of Primrose Hill for its vistas of the City. As for the City itself, that meant only Lime Street and the Richard Roger's tower of steel and glass that was the Lloyd's building and the symbol of my disgrace.

Here by the lake it was possible to believe that Amy would one day come back to me. The thing with Ambrose had been an aberration, driven by fear and fury. She had warned me against Lloyd's, and I had ignored her. Her gut instinct had been right: I the self-styled expert was wrong. She'd seen me as pig-headed, Ambrose as guileless. Because he'd been duped, he'd deserved the consolation of her bed: because I'd duped myself, I deserved nothing. But if succour for him had been brief, surely my punishment needn't be permanent? Except that now there was Saul, the just-a-friend with whom she was celebrating.

Jake confirmed my fears during his fortnightly duty call a few days later. After I'd reassured him that I was well, and he'd told me that his architectural practice remained solvent; once I knew that my grandson had taken his first steps only yesterday, and had added considerably and more or less comprehensibly to his vocabulary, we got onto Amy.

"Is your mother over her scare with Northern Rock?"

Rarely at a loss for words, he faltered. "She's OK. Really."

"Has she moved her money out?" I demanded.

"It's not up to me." There was no hesitation, just bitterness.

"She relies on Saul, is that it?" There was a sigh, but no answer. "Who is he, by the way?"

"Her new friend." He didn't sound happy. "She said she'd told you."

"She mentioned him, that's all. What's the problem?"

"He's one of these up-himself Americans. But she seems happy."

Jake had coped with our divorce by withdrawing more and more into himself. He had always been a quiet boy and an over-serious teenager, like his mother in looks, but with nothing of her vivacity. He'd only once intervened, just after I'd confronted Amy over Ambrose, and he'd convinced himself that my rage would get the better of me. Then he'd hauled me away with a strength I never knew he possessed. I could only flounce out of the house, and for a long time we were strangers to each other. Even now, he treated me more like a distant uncle than his father, whilst his instinct to protect his mother from me morphed into a desire to control every aspect of her life. "He fusses over me like I was his teenage child," Amy had once confided, in a rare moment of criticism. Usually Jake could do no wrong.

"What does Saul do?" I asked.

"He's an investment advisor to charities and pension funds."

Jake's tone rang alarm bells, but I tried to sound casual. "Your mother's neither, or does he make an exception for his friends?"

My son took the point. "He only deals in serious money."

"But you don't approve?"

"He makes out he's some kind of philanthropist, when all he's really doing is raising money for a fat commission." He made an effort to laugh. "Maybe it's his American way. Don't take any notice of me. Mum can look after herself." He sounded less than convinced.

"Let's hope so."

"I mean it, Dad. There's nothing to worry about." I could sense my son striding up and down his living room with the phone in his ear, waving his arms to convince himself as much as me. Probably to the amusement of toddler Jake. Trying to be fair, but equally jealous of Saul. "His contacts in New York are impeccable. One of the main funds he tries to put his clients on is run by an ex-chairman of the NASDAQ. Believe me, Saul's kosher."

"So he's in with the great and the good." When I signed up, Lloyd's credentials had been impeccable too. "Just tell me you trust him."

There was a sigh. "Yes, I trust him. I just don't like him."

For Amy, I was reassured. Jake would never let his prejudice colour his judgement, but nor would he place his trust where there was doubt. I must accept that Amy was committing herself into safer and richer hands than mine. That my heart sank was entirely down to my own feelings. From little purpose, my life seemed now to have none.

But I paid even more attention to the financial news. To my practised eye the parallels with the near collapse of Lloyd's were all too apparent, though they seemed to have been ignored by every financial practitioner and economic commentator. The only difference was one of scale. Lloyd's was the first financial crisis to have made losses in billions commonplace; now, the talk was all of trillions. But there was nothing practical I could do.

11

So I started to brood again, and with brooding came more bad dreams. A new nightmare alternated with the first, just as vivid in its detail and every bit as foreboding. I was on the upper deck of a ferry. It seemed to be the Staten Island Ferry with the Statue of Liberty slipping past. The orb of the setting sun, blood red and ominously engorged, hung behind the statue, so that not only her torch, but her whole body seemed to be on fire. Yet when I turned to the Manhattan skyline, all I could see were the white cliffs of Dover.

The deck was deserted, except for one man. His face was turned away, yet he was known to me. He was thin, and rather distinguished: an academic, or a lawyer – even a banker. His demeanour said "trust me", yet far from trusting him, I was filled with disgust. He was sitting astride the rail, one leg dangling down towards the deck, his polished loafer not quite reaching it, and the other leg out over the water. But I was no longer alone. Amy, or that dream-like amalgam of Amy and a complete stranger, took my arm.

Her cheek was still disfigured by the bruise, there was still a smudge of blood on her forehead, but her eyes were sharp and focused. Grimly and with all humour suppressed, she propelled me towards the rail. The man turned. His face had once been strong, and he retained a large forehead under receding silver hair. His eyes flamed as they caught the sun. But his prominent nose seemed to droop with his cheeks, a mournful prow above a wide, fleshy mouth. As he turned, his eyes lost the sun, and seemed to recede into his skull. It was an expression I had seen all too often at Lloyd's action group meetings. This was a man staring upon ruin. He roused himself, nonetheless, offering a hand to Amy, a salesman's smile to me.

"I trusted you." Her voice was as cold and unyielding as ice.

His shrug was wide and theatrical, and it almost tipped him into the water. "He cheated me, too." His accent was pure New Jersey. "You believe me, Clem, don't you?"

"That's what they all say." My disgust had turned to anger. He stood for the Lloyd's underwriters whose greed had blinded them to risk, for the oversight directors who'd turned blind or conniving eyes to the ruin of those in their care. And now it was happening again. This smarmy scoundrel, who had stolen my wife and her money, was even now denying responsibility. As I lunged, he raised an arm to protect himself.

"It wasn't me," he shouted.

He hit the water just beyond the wash and sank from sight. When he came up again, he was some metres back, yet his face filled my vision. "Help me." He swam desperately towards me. But other heads were bobbing round him. It was the people from the bank queue. All of them, even the ones who had died, their faces still more gaunt but no less recognisable in the filthy water. They closed around the desperate swimmer and tried to drag him under. He was stronger than them, and it looked as though he might fight them off. He even gained the side of the ferry and reached up with an elongated arm for one of its fenders of knotted rope. But there were too many of them. Thin arms wrapped around him, and bony fingers prised his grip from the fender. He was right beneath me as he sank for the last time.

His final cry – half scream, half gurgle – reverberated around my bedroom. Then I heard a car door slam and the splutter of a diesel engine: Sidonie's husband, Armand, always the first of my neighbours to leave for work. As the room fell silent, I slowly took in the familiar surroundings: the sloping wood of the roof, the velux with its almost light-proof blind, my bedside table with its lamp and alarm clock. There in the corner, next to the wardrobe, was my trouser press with my jacket on its hanger, and the pile of pictures for which I had no hanging space. No queues, no bank and no drowning. Just my humble possessions. Wiping cold sweat from my brow, I knew I was safe for another day.

Chapter Two : Excess of Loss

"You're looking pale, Clem," said Sidonie, her hand on my forearm. I shrugged, to show that it was nothing. She appealed to René. "Don't you think Clem looks under the weather?"

"I'm here as your guest, not in an official capacity. Diagnosis is for the surgery." René's dark stubble made his frown far sterner than the twinkle in his eye suggested. "But I will say, one friend to another," his frown was now all for me, "that I haven't seen you running lately."

"You see?" She ran her hand over my stomach. "You'll get fat."

"Hardly in a few weeks. Besides, I watch what I eat. Just like you."

Even if I had not known her so well, her slender frame would have told me that she was very disciplined about her weight, as in everything else. This *soirée* was not mere entertainment, it was a business event. Most of the guests spilling onto the balcony were prospects. Even René's wife, Céline, was here in her role of *agente immobilière.*

What had once been my holiday place, economically kitted out, was now Sidonie's office and home. Her heavy, traditional furniture clashed a little with the architectural drawings and property advertisements on the walls. But her personal ensemble was well chosen to suit her latest project. A linen shift floated around pencil-slim trousers, and her short, fair hair was coiffed just enough to look both casual and business-like: matching the bold style of her illustrations, which promised lucky investors a cable-car view of Talloires and its circular bay, the lake's prettiest according to *Michelin.*

Her daughter, Marie-Sainte, and the girl's boyfriend, Andréa , had been co-opted to serve drinks; her husband, Armand, was expected, as a *notaire*, to handle legal questions as well as to lend gravitas to proceedings, a task for which his deep, slow delivery and his air of old-fashioned authority made him eminently fitted. A man who made platitudes seem like insight.

Marie-Sainte was a natural hostess, with her elfin face, her honey-coloured hair and a figure that managed to look both elegant and weightless. I watched admiringly as she glided between the guests, always ready with a top-up and a smile. She had the kind of prettiness that made the men feel protective and the women charmed. I wondered how many of the business guests realised that she had achieved one of the highest *baccalauréat* results in the whole of *Savoie*, and was taking a highly technical degree in computer science.

As for Andréa, he would have been my last choice for waiter duties. Sardonic and cynical, he hoped to be a journalist, but his outspokenness offended mainstream editors, and his income was sporadic: occasional articles for *Le Canard Enchainé* and *Time Out*. But he seemed to be taking his waiting duties seriously. His torn jeans, in-your-face tee-shirts and *sous-chef* shoes had been substituted for neat trousers, clean shirt, and polished loafers. His locks had been brushed into submission, and only those who knew him as well as I would spot the ironic slant to his eyebrows. Though his long apron was a little over the top.

I had been one of Sidonie's first customers. In those days, before Marie-Sainte was born, she'd lived in an old house in Annecy. By the time I came to France permanently, her daughter was eight or nine, and Sidonie too was in the midst of divorce. The smallest apartment, right above mine, was for re-sale, and she bought it as a stop-gap. It was too small for them both, so I offered them the freedom of mine.

It started when Sidonie had an on-site appointment she couldn't break just when Marie-Sainte was due from school. Normally, the child could have gone to a friend's, but there was a complication, I forget what, so I offered to be the stand-in. After that they were in and out of my apartment more or less as they chose. We even had an intercom, so that Marie-Sainte could go to bed safely if Sidonie was with me.

In their different ways they were very self-contained, and we would often sit in companionable silence: me with my newspaper, Sidonie with her plans, and Marie-Sainte with her *devoirs*. I made sure I had plenty of juice and iced tea, and became adept at making *tartines* with chocolate-hazelnut spread on *pain complet*. Of the two, Marie-Sainte was the chattier, and she would consult me over her homework, inveigle me into a card game, or introduce me to one of the innumerable TV cartoons.

"Are you going to be my new Papa?" she asked one day, fixing me with her clear hazel eyes as she dealt the cards. Her hair was brushed back in a pony tail, giving me full benefit of her guileless expression, from which it was hard to tell whether she was asking the first question to pop into her head, making a statement under the guise of a question – a subtlety of which she well capable – or making a wish. I glanced at Sidonie, but all she offered was an amused shrug.

"That's up to your mother."

"Don't ask silly questions," Sidonie said, without rancour.

"It's not silly. Anne-Sophie's getting one, and Laure's got one," Marie-Sainte replied with some force. "We went to the wedding."

Sidonie shrugged again, this time meaning that the actions of other mothers were nothing to do with her. She also shook her finger, forbidding Marie-Sainte to ask further questions. But after dinner, when Sidonie had put Marie-Sainte to bed, she poured us another glass of wine, and sat beside me on the sofa, which was ornate, not very comfortable and too large for the room. But it had belonged to her family, and could never be disposed of. She rested her head on my shoulder. "Do you want to be Marie-Sainte's father?"

Sidonie would never dream of asking me whether I loved her, still less of expressing her own feelings. Effectively, she was asking me whether I wanted the responsibility of being Marie-Sainte's father without actually telling me whether the job of being her husband was on offer. Yet, after life on the edge with Amy, where everything tended to extremes, I found Sidonie's manner strangely reassuring. "I don't know if I'm ready for new responsibilities."

"That makes two of us." Her hand found my neck and she drew me into a kiss. She didn't come on strong like Amy, but she was full of quiet affection. Take me as you find me, I make no demands. But after a while, she took me by the hand, and led me to my apartment.

Long ago, before Marie-Sainte was born, Sidonie had been my one lapse from marital fidelity. With meetings in Geneva, I'd used the apartment as a base for two days, and she'd been in and out of the complex, arranging completion details with the customers who would soon be my neighbours and friends. She'd emerged from the *trois pièces* by my steps just as I was returning. She'd looked exhausted, so I'd offered an *aperitif*. Her husband, she'd explained, had been summoned to his head office in Paris. Detecting an undercurrent of anger or disappointment, I'd suggested dinner, during which we'd confined our conversation to the vicissitudes of business. Then over coffee she'd asked if I would mind if she stayed the night.

As a married man, I ought to have refused, or offered the spare room. But those clear hazel eyes – that Marie-Sainte would one day inherit – had not been asking for the spare room. I'd known she wasn't the kind of woman who sought casual sex, or who found the idea of seducing a married man amusing. She wasn't even a flirt. So I'd agreed.

Sidonie enjoyed her pleasures quietly, with none of Amy's joy and spontaneity, whilst I'd been inhibited by guilt. We'd been strangers sharing the same bed, joined but far from united. Afterwards, in my dreams, I'd tried but failed to make love to Amy, who'd laughed and said that these things happened, even to the best of men. In the morning, Sidonie had gravely thanked me for my understanding, as though she were a client approving my handling of a tricky meeting. Then we'd hurried away to our appointments.

Back home in Primrose Hill, my dream had come true: I'd been unable to make love. Convinced my guilt was obvious, I'd been on the point of confessing, when Amy had smiled. "These things happen, even to the best of men. No big deal." I'd felt so relieved, my prowess returned. "Ye-es!" she'd shouted at the moment of truth.

When I moved to France, there were many repeat encounters, but the night of Marie-Sainte's question was the last. With no reason for guilt, I was always full of enthusiasm. Yet there was still that disconnect, and we both knew it. "*Je t'aime bien*, Clem," Sidonie said afterwards, meaning, in one of those curious linguistic reversals, not that she loved me to bits, but only that she liked me.

"You'd better get back, or we'll give Marie-Sainte the wrong idea."

"Come for breakfast," she replied with a kiss, "I've got a business proposition for you."

Her proposition was that we should swap apartments, with a suitable cash adjustment. "We'll open a joint account," she explained, "so Lloyd's won't be able to touch your profit. That's if they ever find out. I'll pass on any mail they send you."

The extra cash was necessary, of course, but the prospect of cheating Wormsley was the clincher. The offer was Sidonie's diplomatic way of saying no to any ideas of marriage. Armand was the *notaire* who drew up our contracts, and that, too, was a pointer to Sidonie and Marie-Sainte's future. With his legal knowledge and his maturity, he was more useful to Sidonie than I. But I had no complaints. He was a good man, and a conscientious step-father, and far from embargoing my friendship with his wife and step-daughter, he encouraged it.

"Monsieur Clem!" Andréa roused me from my reverie. He was holding a bottle of champagne over my glass, frozen in the act of being about to pour. "You were miles away."

"Don't waste your time on him. He's been uncommunicative all evening." Sidonie sounded almost cross, and I realised guiltily that my introspections could be interpreted as boredom. She swept on to other more promising guests, as Andréa poured.

"It's not going well." He rolled his eyes. "Nobody wants to take risks." Half-admiring the outright wickedness of capitalists, he saved his contempt for the pusillanimous *bourgeoisie*. But me, as a ruined man, he treated as one of his own. If success were measured in volume of conversation, the event was going well, but I knew that bonhomie was no guarantee of commitment. *Le Monde* offering its readers a little *schadenfreude* at the expense of Anglo-Saxons was temporary relief only from the financial cloud that was hanging over every country.

I found Sidonie, to apologise. "I'd better go. I don't want to put a dampener on proceedings." Her eyes filled with concern. "Don't worry. Just an attack of the blues. They happen."

"Go and see René, and stop being stubborn." She slapped my shoulder and let me go.

It was a pleasant October evening, and I felt restless. Better a brisk stroll down to the lake than brooding at home. I strode down the path, with the forced jollity of Sidonie's party ringing mockingly in my ears. In my current mood, I was better out of it. I crossed the road and followed the Rue de la Plage down to the lake. The water gleamed like polished jet as I followed the shoreline towards the lights of the *Hôtel du Lac*. I thought I had the road to myself until I reached the ferry stop. Then I heard an English voice from under its roof.

"If it was just me, I'd short them like a shot…" In deep shadow, she was hunched over her mobile. "I can't face another Enron." As I drew closer, a street lamp enabled me to see that she was dressed in a donkey jacket, brown cords and matching boots. What she was hearing was not to her liking, and she rose angrily to her feet. "You know what the members will say. They're investors not gamblers." She listened some more. "That's not what they think we're about. Whoever gets screwed, it won't be the banks. That's what they'll say."

Suddenly aware of my presence, she turned, and the light fell on her face. Her features were strong, with good cheekbones no longer disfigured by a bruise. There was no sign of bleeding on her forehead, which was in full view, not at all hidden by her rich, dark hair. Her nose was narrow and regular, but beginning to flare with anger, and her expressive mouth looked anything but humorous. In the poor light, her eyes, under their long lashes, looked almost black, but there was no doubting their displeasure. She did not take well to my staring.

But I was rooted to the path. This was the woman of my dreams: the woman who doubled as Amy until I rolled her over in the gutter, the woman who'd pushed me across the deck towards Saul. It was impossible. Dreaming of Amy was understandable, but how could my brain, however demented, dream of a woman I had never met?

It was too early for skiing, and too late for bathing, so she was unlikely to be a tourist. Yet I was sure she did not live in the village. She was too striking to be easily forgotten. Even if I *had* seen her before, why would my unconscious mind remember her, when my conscious memory held no trace of any such encounter? Until this moment, my dreams had been bearable. Just. But if they were now invading reality, that surely was a sign of madness.

"Monsieur, are you OK?" Her annoyance softened to concern.

The shock had drained my face of colour, so her question was understandable. But I wanted no contact with her. Muttering that I was fine, I forced my legs into action, almost running towards the *Hôtel du Lac*, and back to the main road. As I reached my steps, the party was breaking up, and I almost collided with René and Céline.

"Clem! You look as if you've seen a ghost." Céline was a true local, born and bred in the mountains, who seemed not to care that her once dark hair was now grey. I mumbled that I was fine, but with a shake of the head she appealed to her husband. He pursed his lips.

"I've a slot 9:15, as it happens." I was too shaken to argue.

That night I had a new nightmare. It began as the guilty, post-coital dream I'd dreamt after that first night with Sidonie. Once again I was trying and failing to make love to Amy; once again she laughed and said it could happen to any man, even the best. But now the dream continued. I was making love to her again. Successfully, wonderfully. But as I looked down, the eyes that gazed into mine weren't Amy's any more. It was the ghost woman, with no bruise and no blood, her face ablaze with joy. "Ye-es!" Even as she laughed, her features blanked. Blood trickled from her temple; a livid bruise disfigured her cheek. Glittering from under drooping lashes, her eyes registered nothing.

René and Céline had an ivy-clad chalet on the main road. It was a clear morning, and sunlight streamed through his surgery windows onto his cabinet, which was stuffed with old surgical jars and instruments, as though he were a curator not a medic. But his computer was state of the art, and, unlike my London doctor, who seemed to think every minute with me was a minute wasted, René was courteous and patient.

"I'm not sleeping. As for last night, maybe I did see a ghost."

"You look tired, and tiredness can make ghosts out of anything."

It was a promising start. He wasn't going to dismiss me as mad. Instead, he examined me with his usual thoroughness, and declared me as healthy as my age allowed. "So tell me about your ghost." He sat back on his sleek office chair, his expression impassive, his recently-shaved jaw unthreatening. I took a slow breath: something he'd taught me, when the pain of losing Amy had shredded my nerves. I was damned if I would stumble incoherently. I had come about my dreams, and now I must describe them – apart perhaps from the last.

19

He listened until I had finished. "If you expect me to analyse your dreams, I'm going to disappoint you. The latest thinking is a long way from Freud." He tapped his keyboard. "Think of the brain as a computer, instead of a hotbed of unconscious fantasies. Dreams show the brain cleaning up after a hard day: defragmentation, to use the jargon. As memory fragments are shifted around, they may make a coherent story, which we remember as a dream."

"I don't have any memories of coughing and dying to defragment."

"The mind interprets. Dying's more vivid than an empty account."

"Fine. But why do I keep coming back to the same fragments?"

"Amy's queuing reminded you of your old problems. Like a computer stuck in a loop."

"Can you unstick it?" I had to admire his ability to cut to the chase.

"I could of course refer you to a specialist, but you might prefer simpler remedies first." He consulted his screen. "A sedative perhaps, plus a mild antidepressant, and a course of multivitamins. And I'd advise getting back to your exercise. You're not a sedentary man."

"None of this explains the woman I saw last night."

"Ah, the ghost!" He smiled, irritating in his certainty, yet somehow reassuring too. "There's no need to over-dramatise. It was dark, the only illumination was a street lamp…"

"The light was poor in the dreams, too. It was definitely her."

"You say she's impressive. So impressive, perhaps, that you've reinterpreted the stranger in your dreams as her." He spread his hands judiciously. "An extreme form of *déjà vu.*"

"Then why the Staten Island ferry? Why not the ferry here?"

"You said this Saul is American. So why not an American ferry?"

"So you don't think I'm going to kill him?"

"Even the wilder fringes of Anglo-Saxon psychiatry rarely see dreams as predictive nowadays. We don't have to take the musical of Joseph and his dream-coat as a piece of history." His smile was both charming and mocking. "Whether you choose to kill him or not is up to you. You least of all will ever be the helpless victim of your subconscious. That you are jealous of this man is understandable, and jealousy often produces violent fantasies."

"If he screws up her savings, there's no saying what I won't do."

"Look here." He summoned a website, "Citigroup losing $40 billion; Merrill Lynch $50 billion, even UBS – so Swiss and so prudent – writing down over $10 billion. Amy's friend could be the saint of prudence, and still she could lose her savings. I'd suggest a French bank, except they too are catching the mark-to-market virus. When they all do that, the world will be worthless. It's the modern Black Death." It was like listening to a clinical prognosis.

"At least I'm broke already." I tried to sound light-hearted and philosophical. "As for you, the world always needs good doctors."

He handed me my prescription, and shook my hand. "Away with you to the pharmacy. And when I cycle up to Bluffy this evening, I expect to pass you in your running gear."

The consultation had done so much to reassure me that I took his advice about running. The road to Bluffy climbs steeply past the castle, whose floodlights guided me between tall, brooding trees. I had almost reached the Route de Thones before René passed me on his racing machine. "You're out of condition," he called. I shook my fist. "Call Amy if you're worried about her." He was already visible only by his rear light. "She'll listen, I'm sure."

Perhaps it was the exercise, perhaps it was the sedative, perhaps, even, it was the multivitamins, but that night was dreamless. The next night, too. The relief was palpable. So much so that I called Amy. I chose office hours, so that I could be sure of getting her alone.

"Clem! What's got into you?" She sounded happy. Too happy.

"I've been worrying about your savings," I said.

"That's so sweet of you. I might have known you'd start worrying about me." It was almost like the old days. Almost, but not quite. She was remembering, not rekindling.

"So where's your money now? Somewhere safe, I hope."

"Don't worry. Saul's got me into his best fund. Half of New York would kill to be where I am. New Jersey, too… and Florida."

"Spare me the sales pitch. What fund? Who runs it?"

She giggled. "I'm not supposed to say. Saul really had to wangle it."

I thought of the ferry dream. "There's a big financial crisis brewing," I said sternly. "You need to know what you're getting into."

"I do know. It's a special fund. Earns 10% every year, and I can take money out anytime. Lots of charities and pension funds are in it."

She almost had me convinced. "Is it some kind of hedge fund?"

"It doesn't charge like one. And they won't let you take money out."

"But how can it guarantee 10%? What if markets go belly up?"

"He uses something called Split Strike Conversion."

"What the hell's that?"

She laughed. "You may well ask, but it's quite simple in principle. Whenever he buys stock – that's shares to you and me – he hedges with an option, then he hedges the hedge the other way. Saul showed me lots of analysis: it's practically foolproof."

"Reinsurance and retrocession," I said. "It didn't help Lloyd's."

"I don't know what you're talking about." There was now an edge to her voice. "We are talking blue chip stocks that everybody trades, not the kind of nonsense Lloyd's insured."

I realised too late that my irresistible analogy with Lloyd's was a mistake. It would be useless now to point out that the insurance claims which had ruined so many of us Names had all been made by blue chip companies. "So why can't you tell me who the fund manager is?"

"Oh, you know what Americans are like. They're terrified that if they let anything slip, half a dozen lawyers will jump out of the woodwork. To be honest, I don't know what all the secrecy is about. Perhaps he doesn't want flak from those who don't get on. I'm really too small, but Saul wangled it, if I kept it quiet. It's all rather silly, isn't it? But I don't mind telling you, if you promise to be discreet."

"I'm in France. Who am I going to tell?"

"Right!" She giggled again. "Bernie Madoff. He's well known over there. He used to be chairman of the NASDAQ."

The name meant nothing to me, so I Googled him. Not only had he been chairman, he had been instrumental in turning the NASDAQ into a major exchange, as well as being a pioneer in automated trading. His current company was used by large hedge funds and banks for their share trading and clearing. Everything I read about him suggested the safest of safe hands. But I could find nothing about any fund. His secrecy in that regard was certainly very effective. Should I be worried, or was I just being silly? The pining ex, with nothing to go on but his jealousy. Jealous not of Madoff, but of Saul. Ten per cent was not the absurd promise you might expect from a real con-man. A hedge fund could do much better – or much worse.

I did not sleep well that night, despite the sedative, but nor did I dream. I was too restless over Amy. But as December wore on, and the village put up its Christmas lights, I began to relax. If financial Armageddon were nigh, it was far beyond my control.

It helped, too, that throughout December the weather was perfect for exercise. Snow fell on the *Dents des Lanfins*, the mountain above the castle, and bleached the tops of all the hills around the lake. But down in the village, there was only morning frost. The air was generally still, so that the water lay as smooth as gunmetal. Now that I was running regularly, my weight was down, and my breathing strong. It was time to tackle the hero's run again.

All went well, and I made good progress to the foot of the final ascent, where the bare rock of the summit reared forbiddingly before me. Ignoring the less precipitous zigzag path, I went straight up, trying to avoid treacherous roots and slips on the bare earth, until I rejoined the zigzag just below the iron bench that marked the summit. I glanced up, wondering if I had enough puff for the last culvert. The bench was occupied. I recognised the donkey jacket and the cords immediately. It was her again: the ghost woman of my dreams. I stopped dead.

The air was so still I could hear her faultless French clearly. "Of course S&P are threatening to downgrade the monolines. Now do you accept I was right to pull us out of MBIA?... Well thank you, it's nice to be appreciated." She ended the call, and dialled another.

"Hi," she said, this time in English. "For once, L'Esprit is happy. He's even invited me to lunch on New Year's Day. At the *Hôtel du Lac*, no less. It's all down to you, of course, but I had to take the credit. So thanks." She turned as she spoke, and saw me standing on the path, still panting and still in shock. She turned angrily away, and dropped her voice, but not so much that I couldn't hear. "I've got to go. There's some Frog stalker on the path."

The injustice of her remark stung me into action. I would have flung myself up the culvert to remonstrate with her, but for the likelihood of an ignominious slip. Instead, I sprinted up the track and into the safety of the woods. But I seethed all the way home. What right had she, one of the financial breed, to pass ill judgement on me? My only consolation was that, now I had seen her in broad daylight, there could be no doubt that she was the woman in my dreams, nor that she was entirely real. An extreme case of *déjà vu*, as René had diagnosed.

It was Christmas Eve when I saw her next, as I was dropping into the *Bar de la Fontaine*. At the heart of the village, the bar had pool, bar football and a flat-screen TV permanently tuned to every variety of extreme sport. In summer the *Place* outside was crammed with metal tables, and even today, taking advantage of December warmth, the landlord had put out a few of them. And there she was, half hidden by the sparkling waters of the fountain, her dark hair softened to golden brown as it caught the sun. She was studying the financial pages of *Le Monde* with the aid of a notebook and a propelling pencil. An espresso and a shot of clear spirit lay untouched. The chair opposite her was empty, and I pulled it out noisily.

"*Bonjour, Madame.*" She dropped her paper a fraction. "For your information, I'm not a stalker. I live here." Then I added in English, "Nor am I a Frog, as you insultingly choose to call my neighbours."

"You do startle me in unexpected places, don't you?" A smile played over her lips, the first time I'd seen her look remotely friendly.

"Now I can see you're harmless. Just a bit of a prat." Her eyes sparkled mischievously. "Merry Christmas to you." She raised her glass.

The landlord came for my order, giving me a moment to reflect. Though her words were unflattering, it was difficult to take offence. "You don't live round here, do you?"

"No," she agreed. "Do I need permission to be in your village?"

I found myself smiling. "Seeing as it's Christmas, I'm prepared to make an exception."

She picked up her cup, and frowned. "I always let it go cold."

"Let me get you another," I offered.

"A waste of your money." Then she finished her glass. "But I could use another *genepé*."

Smiling at what he interpreted as my good fortune, the landlord gathered up her empties, and was back so fast with our drinks that neither of us had managed to think of anything further to say. She filled the silence by scribbling a note against one of the share entries.

The arrival of her drink allowed me to raise mine. "*Salut!* You must be a fund manager."

"You've listened to my phone calls enough. So what are you, a regulator in plain clothes?"

"I didn't know regulators had a uniform." Humour, it seemed, would serve us very well.

"Dull suits, bad tailoring. You can spot 'em a mile off."

I laughed, but I couldn't avoid a furtive glance at my cuffs.

"Don't worry," she continued. "You dress like a Frenchman. Your disguise is perfect."

"I'm not a regulator," I told her. "But sometimes I wish I was."

"Fearlessly, you'd bring the banks to heel. I know the feeling." She smiled at my surprise. "If I remember rightly, the first time you overhead me, I was being rude about banks."

"Why just banks?" I demanded rudely. "I tend to think the entire financial sector is guilty until proven innocent."

I expected her to be defensive, but she merely nodded. "So what was your particular bad experience: the tech bubble, Equitable Life, Enron?" I shook my head. "Surely not CDOs?"

I had to laugh. "I'm not rich enough for CDOs. Not any more."

"Ah." Her tone became warmer. "Your bank foreclosed on you."

The last thing I wanted her to think was that my business had failed. "Not at all," I said firmly. "The bank never foreclosed, they simply handed everything I owned to Lloyd's of London."

I didn't often talk about Lloyd's because there were usually two reactions only: *schadenfreude* or a diatribe against global capitalism. But if she played the markets for her clients she was unlikely to be anti-capital. I waited instead for the superior smile. But her face paled and she closed her eyes. "I'm sorry." It sounded almost like an apology.

"There's no need to be." Her response was so unexpected and so spontaneous that I was almost overcome. "My ex-wife says it was my own fault. Nobody made me join, after all."

She ignored the *mea culpa*. "Which syndicates were you on?"

"Wu was my worst, but I copped it all: asbestosis, pollution, catastrophe re-insurance: if it lost big-time, I was on it. Yet my agent said everything was safe for widows and orphans."

"You weren't rescued by R & R?"

"R & R was a joke."

Reconstruction and Renewal had been Lloyd's way of ring-fencing its toxic debts. The main beneficiaries were those Names able to trade on; the victims were those whose losses had already forced them out. We sacrificial lambs lost our assets *and* the means to recoup them.

"It was rough justice, but without it, *everyone* would have tanked."

"You think I care!" The suppressed anger came surging back.

"You didn't try to settle with them?"

I banged my glass down. "Settle with those crooks? Never!"

Her eyes seemed to sadden. "Not everybody there was bad."

"I'll grant they weren't all corrupt: some were merely incompetent." It was a cheap retort, but I was flushed by the release of anger long repressed. "Anyway, how would you know?"

She shrugged. "Let's just say I knew people working there."

"Nobody I would have known, I suppose?"

"Not unless..." She hesitated. "Not unless you were on Tonbridge."

Despite my foolish investment in Lloyd's, I'd avoided the Tonbridge syndicate. But Ambrose had been heavily exposed. Rex Tonbridge was the underwriter whose syndicate had been the most catastrophic of the London Excess of Loss (LMX) spiral: foolhardiness on an epic scale. So epic, he'd shot himself rather than face his Names.

"The only underwriter to do the decent thing," I said bitterly. One look at the pain in her face told me that I had reawakened some terrible sense of bereavement, long suppressed. It was horrible to watch such a self-confident woman fighting to bring her anguish back under control. My anger dissipated. "I'm sorry," I apologised. "I didn't think."

"You couldn't have known." She found a tissue in her bag and blew her nose. "And you're right," she continued bravely, "Rex was an honourable man. It was all too much for him."

Before the LMX market had spiralled out of control, Rex Tonbridge had been the coming man at Lloyd's, a flamboyant player in a market where underwriters were stars. Before the crash, Names were as desperate to be on the Tonbridge syndicate as women were to be in the Tonbridge bed. If this woman, so attractive now in her maturity, had been the starry-eyed *ingénue* then, she would have been irresistible to an alpha male such as Tonbridge.

"I ought to be going." Smiling bravely, she held out her hand. "It was nice talking to you."

"Will I see you again?" All remnants of dislike vanished at the idea of her disappearing.

"I expect so." Her composure almost restored, she offered me an encouraging smile. I handed her my card. At first she was disinclined to take it. *"Clem Holden, Marketing Consultant."* She read my name slowly and deliberately, as if it ought to mean something to her. Then she grinned. "Pity I don't need marketing advice."

"Maybe I need financial advice," I said, anxious not to lose her.

She pulled a card from her bag. "I specialise in investing for ex-Names. In memory of Rex. Pity our paths didn't cross long ago."

Then, before I had time to glance at it, she planted a lightning kiss on my cheek and hurried away. My face, where her lips had touched, tingled as though she were charged. I ordered another beer, and studied her card. On one side was her name, *Mallory M Stellenbourg*, a mobile number and a wanadoo email address. On the other was a logo: *Ghost Trader*. But no postal address or website. For lack of information, she was up there with Madoff. But I had permission to call.

Chapter Three : Incurred but Not Reported

Now that we'd met, my fear that Mallory Stellenbourg was a ghostly emanation of my tortured dreams had transmuted into fascination. She might be blunt, but she was also sensitive; she might be quick to anger, but her sense of humour was in tune with mine; she might be self-contained and over-confident, yet she'd revealed her vulnerability. Though her loss had been the greater, Lloyd's had scarred and shaped us both. Lloyd's had robbed her of the man she loved, yet she had put her skills to the service of its other victims. She was the embodiment of what I used to preach to my clients, but had never managed to apply to myself: that they should see loss as opportunity, that they should transform setback into success.

The only ghost was in her logo, and that only added to the intrigue. I supposed at first that Ghost Trader was a tribute to the late Rex Tonbridge as well as an apology to those whose fortunes he had destroyed. Though in life he had failed his Names, in spirit he would restore them to financial health through the offices of his lover. But there was more to it than that. Not only did Ghost Trader publish no website, it was unknown to the search engines. Her only email address was a public service, the French answer to Yahoo or Hotmail. However Ghost Trader operated, it was invisible to prying eyes. When she'd asked me if I were a regulator, I'd assumed she'd been joking. But she might genuinely have had something to hide.

She could be seeking restitution for straightened Names by prudent investment, as the snippets of overheard conversation would suggest; but by operating under the radar of the internet, she could be up to any or all of the tricks that regulators were there to police.

She had gone from insulting me to apologising for what Lloyd's had done to me. She had even offered to help me. Though it was too late to turn my paltry savings into serious money, I was all for revenge. If not on Lloyd's, then I'd settle for those who had tried to ruin Amy. Whether Mallory Stellenbourg was a saint or a Robin Hood, her kiss tingled still on my cheek and I was desperate to see her again.

I sent her a text on Christmas Day: "Happy Xmas. Do you ski? A few of us are going to La Clusaz, New Year's Eve." I was enjoying my second breakfast coffee next morning when she called back.

"I really wish I could come." Her voice was full of regret. "Unfortunately, I'm off to Aix for *St Silvestre*."

"Pity." I feigned indifference. "The forecast's for sun and powder."

"Don't tempt me. Aix is more business than pleasure."

"I'll be the only unattached male in the party."

"Tough," she fired back, "I'll be the only unattached female in Aix."

"So when are you free?"

"We'd better make it before the seventh. Before the markets go frantic." She paused for so long I thought she'd hung up. "What about the second? Total dead time."

"Good enough for a prat, then?"

She laughed. "Sorry about that. I only half meant it."

"Let's hope you won't mean it at all after the second."

"That remains to be seen. Will you ski down to Les Confins?"

"That's certainly the plan. They've got the best restaurants."

"You may see one of my clients then. He's a *ski de fond* fanatic."

"Shall I give him your regards?"

"Just tell him not to forget our lunch on New Year's Day."

Remembering the telephone conversations I'd overheard on *Roc de Chère*, I guessed this must be L'Esprit. How could anyone be called The Spirit? "How will I recognise him?"

"He'll be the most elegant fitness freak on the tracks. About your age. As for his wife, she makes like she's a countess." Then her voice became serious. "On second thoughts, don't speak to him. He'd be furious if he thought I was giving out client names."

The overheard calls had suggested a prickly character, and I promised her that I would not do anything to spoil client relations. "I had plenty of awkward clients, too," I assured her.

"Thanks. Enjoy your skiing, and see you Friday. Same place."

"Before you go," I cut in, for the pleasure of keeping her talking. "Are you English or French? You've got an English first name, a French surname, and you're bilingual."

"The surname's *alsacien*, my mother's a Brit, and I've lived all over. As for you, Monsieur Holden, you're very observant and far too inquisitive." With that she rang off. Until her last sentence, we had spoken in English: at the end, she had not only switched to French, but had used the formal *vous*. But for the lightness of her tone, it would have been a terrible put-down. I couldn't wait to see her again. In the meantime, I would keep a lookout for the elegant Monsieur L'Esprit, in the hopes that his demeanour would tell me more about her.

The 31st dawned dimly with cloud down to the castle. But when I checked the *metéo*, all was well: all the slopes were above the cloud, and the forecast remained optimistic: clear sunshine all day. I drove up with René and Céline behind Armand's Renault *Espace*, which was chock full of our gear as well as Sidonie, Marie-Sainte and Andréa.

"I gather Sidonie hasn't had any bites, yet," I observed, repeating what she'd told me over Christmas dinner, to which I was always invited, just as if I were family.

"The locals aren't buying any more," Céline confirmed gloomily. "If it weren't for the English, last year would have been dismal. Now it seems they won't be buying either."

"I'm sorry to let you down," I said.

"You English drove prices too high for us locals." As always before a day of serious exercise René hadn't shaved, so his jaw was particularly menacing. He punched the steering wheel for emphasis. "The country's full of foreigners mopping up property and jobs. The EU was all very well before we let everybody join."

"You should read the British press," I countered. "They claim the EU exists solely for the benefit of France."

He snorted, but Céline gave me a sympathetic smile. "I always think of you as practically one of us. No one is blaming you, of course."

"I'm too poor to be responsible for property prices. But if I ever do come into the money again, I promise to buy one of Sidonie's developments through you."

"If only they were all like you, Clem. Local solidarity and loyalty are very important." She pointed to Armand's *Espace*, just ahead of us. "They're really worried that those two will never find proper jobs." She meant Marie-Sainte and Andréa.

"Or any jobs at all," René added.

"With their English, they should become ski instructors."

Céline shook her head. "Tourism's down. Lots of empty chalets and hotel rooms. La Clusaz used to be a boom town. Not any more."

But the car park at La Balme was almost full. "This is just locals," she insisted, as we unloaded our skis. "They don't spend as much as the weekly boarders." Sure enough, nearly all the licence plates ended in the 74 of *Haute Savoie*, our local department. I glanced at the youngsters, as they adjusted their boots. They were in a world of their own, oblivious to the concerns of their elders on their behalf. All they wanted for the moment was to hit the snow. Conditions indeed looked perfect. The snow was deep and so white it might have been airbrushed by some celestial graphic artist. Already, the first skiers were coming down off-piste, almost up to their waists in powder, and knocking snow off the tops of bushes as they passed.

The cable cars were continuous, and we did not have to wait long before we were on our way. The economy was forgotten as we congratulated ourselves on the perfection of the day, as though the weather were a force under our control. "You mustn't go too fast, Clem," Sidonie chided me. "We want to enjoy the ambience."

"I'll be struggling to keep up – especially with these two." I pointed to the two youngsters, nuzzling each other over the tops of their snowboards. I doubt they even heard me.

From the mid-station there was a much longer wait for the chair to the top, but the mood of the queue was happy. At the top, there was a small flat area, more a platform than a plateau, between sharp peaks. On one side was a sheer drop of at least a thousand metres, on the other was the round bowl of the *piste*, which was merely precipitous. The drop was the result of the peculiar shape of the *Aravis*, the local range, where the mountains were like waves frozen in the act of breaking. Standing on the crest to admire the vista of the Alps beyond was an unnerving experience, despite the safety netting. We could see nothing of the rock face that curved inwards below our feet. Armand was anxious that his step-daughter should not go too close to the net, but he needn't have worried. She stood with Andréa on the edge of the *piste*, impatiently waiting for us seniors to stop wasting time.

We weren't, in fact, very long, but the quality of the light that day made a short pause worthwhile. Each peak stood out against the clear sky with a clarity that was unreal. Here was grandeur on a massive scale; beauty that was impervious to the petty troubles of the miniscule figures who troubled to admire it.

We warmed up down the groomed red run, before we tackled the black that would take us to the bottom again. Ungroomed, it ran down between dark cliffs, lowering reminders that mountains were dangerous as well as pleasurable. I doubted this was the ambience Sidonie had in mind, and I noted that she concentrated on the snow ahead and scarcely gave the stark rocks a glance. Even when we paused for breath, she pointed with her ski pole to the softer features of Grand Bornand in the distance. "You're skiing well," she said politely.

"He takes my advice about exercise." René slapped my shoulder.

"I've never felt better," I assured them. Not that I could hope to do more than trail inelegantly in their wake. The four of them hardly disturbed the snow, their skis glued together. As for the youngsters, they were already exchanging kisses at the foot of the drop we had yet to negotiate. But none of them could accuse me of caution.

At the end of the run, it was back to the top. Then we were ready for the serious stuff. After we'd come down the bowl, we left the groomed *piste* along a narrow track that crossed an ungroomed, but marked, mogul field. Then we were truly off *piste*, following the tracks of those who had gone before us, or cutting silently through virgin powder. We rounded a huge buttress, and we were in the next valley. Far below us, lay the *ski de fond* trails of Les Confins. Tiny wisps of smoke rose from the wood fires of the two restaurants, one either side of a frozen lake. From where we stood it looked no larger than a dinner plate.

The valley of our descent was nothing but tumbled rocks, visible in summer, but all of them now hidden beneath deep snow. We must trust that it was deep enough. I felt the knots tightening in my stomach as we discussed the best route down, comforting myself that none of the ski and snowboard tracks ended suddenly with a splayed body.

The first part was wide enough to be relatively safe, provided you didn't mind the dizzying steepness of the descent. The grip of the powder slowed the turns, but this was oddly unnerving, keeping me on the fall line for much longer than the cautious part of my brain would wish. But the difficult stretch was yet to come. About half-way down, and just before the valley opened out into wide pastures, the mountain played its last trick. Huge ridges reared out of the valley floor like the ruined ramparts of a citadel. We had to shimmy through the narrow gaps – steep corridors between sheer rock, that from here looked no wider than a mountain goat – and rely on the wideness beyond to reduce our headlong plunge.

Marie-Sainte and Andréa were under strict instructions from Armand to avoid the narrowest, but they ignored him. Sidonie chased after them in vain pursuit, and out of some mad sense of duty I followed behind. The others headed for one of the easier routes. The kids seemed to have no nerves at all, and shot down the narrow culvert as it if it didn't exist, then whooped loudly as they carved long arcs in the pasture beyond. Sidonie shot through a moment or two later; then it was my turn.

The corridor between the rocks seemed almost sheer, though I tried to reassure myself that this was impossible, otherwise it would not be carpeted in snow. It was more or less straight, which is to say that there was a straight line through, but to follow it, my left shoulder would almost be scraping one side, before the right would be hard against the other. Though it had looked short when the others had gone through, now it seemed impossibly long.

It was wide enough to sideslip, just, but only a wimp would contemplate such ignominy. Knowing the prospect would get no better, I gritted my teeth and launched myself into the cutting. There was a blur of black rock, a surge of adrenalin, and then I was through. The pasture, though almost as steep as the valley above, was a lot flatter than the pipe down which I had hurtled, and the sudden change in gradient almost drove my knees into my chin. But it was smooth and wide, and I managed a long, slithering turn to draw alongside the others. Céline and René with Armand in the rear were just coming through a wider and less precipitous gap. "You see," said Marie-Sainte sweetly, as they joined us, "No problem."

"Even for Monsieur Clem," said Andréa cheekily.

"Absolutely nothing to it," I lied, realising that his purpose was to avert remonstrations from Armand. He frowned, but allowed Sidonie to give his arm a placating hug. After that, the run seemed tame, but it was pleasant to glide smoothly through the deepest powder so far encountered. In summer, the pasture would be dotted with cows, and the air full of the chimes of their bells; now it lay several metres below our skis, and the silence was immense.

Such had been the speed of our descent that we were too early for lunch, so we sat on the terrace in the sun, ordered coffee, and watched the cross-country skiers as they glided round the lake. It was good exercise, and I enjoyed coming here every so often to enjoy a good workout on the long, narrow skis and in the light boots of *ski de fond*. René was also a fan, and often accompanied me; Céline and Sidonie were neutral, whilst Armand thought it was too much like hard work. The youngsters dismissed it as a pastime for old fogeys.

Across the terrace, I noticed a striking couple. About my age, he looked like a 1930s golfer, with white sporting cap, silk cravat, cashmere sweater and check knee-breeches. I half expected his cross-country boots to be black and white with cookie-cutter tongues. A least ten years younger, but no chicken, she wore white salopettes and a silky shirt of delicate blue. A white blouson was neatly draped over the back of the vacant chair beside her. Small, tasteful jewellery flashed at her wrists and neck. Her hair was improbably golden and secured by a hair-band that matched her shirt. "The most elegant fitness fanatic, with a wife who looks like a countess": surely this must be L'Esprit. They were conversing so softly their lips barely moved. His mouth was full-lipped; hers was small and disapproving, even when she smiled, a gesture which never lit up her eyes. If he was a difficult client, she must be his inspiration.

Watching them, from a safe distance, was a lone skier. He was still wearing his sunglasses, and his ski-hat was pulled so well down that half his face as well as his eyebrows were hidden. I could only tell that he was watching them from the intent way in which he faced their table, never shifting his head to glance at other customers or the waitresses. He was wearing an old black anorak that hung off his gaunt frame, and dark trousers, tucked baggily into his socks, rather as if he were wearing old-fashioned bicycle clips. Elegant, he was not.

"*On y va, chérie*," said the man I took to be L'Esprit, suddenly.

His wife nodded, and he snapped his fingers. One of the waitresses sprang anxiously to his summons, and practically bowed when he presented her with a 20 euro note and waved away his expectation of any change. He could have been any one of a dozen of my least favourite ex-clients. They rose majestically to their feet, and he made a great show of assisting *la comtesse* L'Esprit into her immaculate white blouson. Then, as they pulled on well-fitting leather gloves, they marched from the terrace to retrieve their skis.

Hardly had they gone, before the strange man in the black anorak also took his leave. He did not summon a waitress, and I wondered for a moment if he might have skipped off without paying. Then I saw that there was neither glass nor cup on the table. I wondered how he had persuaded the waitresses to allow him to sit without ordering.

His gait was shambling and awkward, as though his body were dragging his legs forwards, rather than the other way about. He looked vaguely familiar, in the way that people I hadn't seen for ages could flicker in that no-man's land between acquaintance and stranger, but I couldn't see enough of him to examine him properly. "Strange fellow," I mused to René, who was curious as to the direction of my gaze.

He shook his head. "I saw nobody."

"He followed that splendid couple."

"Oh, them! They ought to be in Megève, not here."

"Not this fellow," I laughed. "Obviously you couldn't keep your eyes off *la comtesse*, or you'd have noticed him for sure." He shrugged, as if to say that he would never waste an eye on men when there were women to be observed. Even battleaxes of a certain age.

Armand summoned the waitress, who arrived promptly, if not as instantly as L'Esprit would have expected, and we ordered lunch. An hour into eating, the youngsters got bored, and said they would take the paths back to the centre of La Clusaz, and its snow park. As the rest of

33

us ordered desserts, we saw two *gardiens des pistes*, in their purple outfits, jump onto a skidoo and cut across the tracks at full speed. They were towing a blood wagon behind them: a stretcher on sledge runners. We watched them reach the steep slope of the ridge, which separated Les Confins from the resort of Grand Bornand, and roar their way up into the trees, the blood wagon bouncing behind.

"There's been an accident." Céline glanced at her husband.

"I'm off duty," he said, though I knew he'd never duck a crisis.

As we watched, skiers came down the same slope, then gathered at the bottom. There was much gesticulating with ski poles. Shortly afterwards, the skidoo returned, now going quite slowly. The blood wagon was empty, but there was a woman sitting behind the driver, a blanket round her shoulders. The other *gardien* skied behind.

"Doesn't look too serious," said Céline. Yet there was something in the manner of the onlookers that did not bear out her words. A strange hush descended, as more and more skiers stopped in their tracks, either watching the skidoo or gazing up at the ridge as though they expected some ghastly apparition. René rose to his feet.

"I'm sure they can cope, but perhaps I ought to take a look."

Like me, he assumed the skidoo would head for the small chapel that was the focal point of the area, where all the runs began and ended. Instead, it parked as close to the road as possible, and then the two *gardiens* accompanied the woman towards the restaurant. Her face was sickly white, and she was trembling so much they almost had to carry her. They rushed her into the interior and sat her down at the nearest table. Brandy was ordered and brought.

René strode inside, and I rushed to follow. Normally, such a thing would have been none of my business, but I recognised the pale blue headband and the white blouson. The woman was *la comtesse*, and I felt compelled to find out what had happened.

One of the *gardiens* had his hand on her shoulder, the other was talking into his phone. "The helicopter will be here in the next few minutes, Madame," he said, ending his call. "Then we'll get you straight over to Grand Bornand."

"What about the ambulance?" she asked, through chattering teeth.

"On its way, Madame, I assure you."

The other *gardien* recognised René. "She's in shock." Confirming the diagnosis, my friend ordered coffee with plenty of sugar.

Then he knelt in front of the woman, and gently took her hands. "I'm a doctor. You'll be fine." She stared at him as if he were mad.

"My husband was pushed off a cliff. Just find the perpetrator."

"The police have been informed, Madame," said a *gardien*.

"Where are they then?" she demanded querulously. As she spoke, we heard a distant police siren, as well as the thump of helicopter blades. "He was English," she added.

"How do you know?" René's eyebrows cast me an upward flick.

"Everything about him." Her voice was acid with contempt.

"Did he speak to you, then?"

The questions were having their effect, and her shock was turning to anger. "Some nonsense. I couldn't make it out. But the accent was absolutely English. *Execrable!*"

"I have an English friend here. He may be able to translate."

His words were almost drowned by the helicopter as it touched down just beyond the chapel. The swirl of its blades blasted snow from its roof. The pilot remained at the controls, but his colleague rushed across the road. As he reached the restaurant door, the police car arrived, and two *policiers* in blousons and caps followed him in.

The co-pilot wanted to take the woman straight off to find her husband, the policemen insisted they must question her first. An inevitable altercation ensued, which was only increased by René. "This lady is a patient first. If she wishes to learn the fate of her husband, she must be allowed to, for the good of her health. I must insist."

The policemen, who were young and local, were not unsympathetic, but explained that they too had duties to perform. "We understand there may be a crime involved."

"Of course!" the woman shouted. "It was plain murder."

"Where is your husband, Madame?" the slightly older of the *policiers* asked patiently.

"He was pushed off the ridge." She turned on the *gardiens*. "You should have a net. This *commune* is responsible, too."

At this point Armand joined us, explaining that he was at their disposal in his capacity as a *notaire*. Whilst he joined the jurisdictional debate, I worked out what must have happened.

On the ridge there's a circuit of ski tracks, and for a short stretch the *piste* runs along the top of a cliff. To make matters worse, one set of the twin tracks that traditional cross country skiers push along runs close to the edge. It had startled me the first time. Why there was no net, I couldn't understand, given that the drop was several hundred metres into thick woodland above the ski tracks of Grand Bornand. But when they are flat, ski paths are deemed too safe to merit netting. Alpine skiers may lose control on steep slopes, but neither they nor responsible cross-country skiers take to pushing each other over cliffs.

35

"Are you sure he was pushed?" Armand's natural authority seemed to have asserted itself, and he was now asking the questions. "Are you absolutely sure that it wasn't an accident?"

"Do you take me for an idiot? Of course I'm sure. I was there." She pushed the blankets from her shoulders and jumped to her feet. "Look, I'll tell you exactly what I saw."

The older policeman produced a notebook and pen from his jacket, and Armand gently but firmly made the woman sit again. "They have their procedures," he explained.

"The police in Grand Bornand are going to the scene," said the younger policeman. "It may be better that you are not the first to arrive," he added. I shuddered. A body that had fallen several hundred metres into trees was unlikely to be a pretty sight.

Inconsequentially I thought of Mallory Stellenbourg hurrying back from Aix with a hangover only to discover that her lunch at the *Hôtel du Lac* had been aborted. Always supposing, of course, that the man who had fallen was indeed L'Esprit.

"My husband and I had just got onto the ridge," she explained.

"You were doing traditional-style on the tracks or skating?" Armand asked pedantically.

"On the tracks, of course. On the side nearest the cliff."

"Who was in front?" The older policeman tried to regain command.

"My husband." She threw up her hands at the impertinence of these interruptions. "Then this madman, this Englishman, skated past us. Very badly, I may say. He almost caught my stick. Then when he was alongside my husband, he shouted at him, and started to push him. My husband tried to shove him away, but he was too late. He went straight over." She choked on her last sentence, and a mascara-stained tear rolled down her cheek.

"An Englishman?" Armand boomed. "Are you sure?"

"Of course I'm sure."

"He said something," René put in, "but she didn't catch it."

"I heard it perfectly," she contradicted him. "It made no sense."

"My friend here is English," René said. "As I was saying as the police were arriving, if you would repeat what the man said as best you can, he may be able to translate."

Armand turned to me, but the policeman ignored him. "Did anyone else see this man?"

The *gardiens* shook their heads, and shrugged for good measure.

"I'm not making him up!" The woman's voice rose dangerously. "He was wearing a black ski hat, pulled right down, a black anorak, very untidy, and disgusting trousers. Also black."

I could restrain myself no longer. "I saw him," I said. All eyes turned on me. "We were having coffee on the terrace, and I noticed this man staring at you and your husband." In the interests of protocol, I ought to have addressed the policeman, or else Armand, but I felt that this distraught lady deserved corroboration from somebody. "He left as soon as you did. I didn't hear him speak, but I agree that he looked English. You can often tell."

"You don't look English," the policeman frowned. "Or sound it."

"I've lived here for ten years, and I worked in Paris long ago."

Armand nodded authoritatively. "It can be said that Monsieur Holden has gone native."

"Did you see this other man, then?" The younger policeman appealed to René.

"I'm afraid not," René said. "Why should I?" Armand concurred with a judicious shrug.

The woman was studying me carefully, as if trying to decide if she could trust me. "What he said was *Aie bi ain aa.*" She pulled a face. "That's as best as I can pronounce it."

"IBNR," I repeated, my heart suddenly beating hard.

She nodded vigorously. "Exactly, Monsieur. That's what he said."

"Does it mean anything to you?" asked both policemen at once. Even Armand gestured them to defer to my knowledge.

I took a deep breath. There was one more question I needed to ask before I was certain of my facts. "Madame, was your husband ever a member of Lloyd's of London?"

Her eyebrows shot up. "Ten years ago, yes. How did you know?"

I eyed the half-finished glass of brandy on the table longingly. "IBNR is a Lloyd's term. It's short for Incurred But Not Reported." I wrote it down for the policeman on his pad. "It's a technical term, describing an insurance claim that's expected, because the catastrophe, or whatever, has happened but hasn't been formally claimed. I don't know the French equivalent; it's something like *encouru mais pas signalé* or *encouru mais pas encore revendiqué.*"

"Then you might know this man?" She stared at me pleadingly.

"England's a big place, and I haven't been there in years, but if this man knows IBNR, he must be an old Lloyd's member, too. In my day, there were about 30,000 of us."

"More likely, Madame, that you might know the man, if he was a member of the same group as your husband," Armand suggested before either policeman could speak.

"We weren't yet married then. Nor have we been in the habit of discussing his business interests since." Her voice cracked as it came to her that the habit would not be broken now.

Just then, the younger policeman's phone rang, and he listened in incredulous silence for a minute or more. Then he stared helplessly at his colleague before turning to the lady. "That was the Grand Bornand police. They can't find him." He shrugged helplessly. "It's a big area, lots of snow, and lots of pines. But it's just possible he survived and is wandering around with concussion." I stared at René. Surely nobody could survive such a fall? Then I remembered a story about an RAF bomber pilot whose parachute had failed to open, yet who had survived because his fall was broken by snow-covered trees. The policeman continued: "They'd like you to fly over, Madame, as you are the most likely to recognise him."

The co-pilot, who had stood in a fury of impatience, needed no second urging. The older policeman waved them away, but ordered his colleague to accompany them. The co-pilot started to object, but when Armand spoke authoritatively about the necessity of everybody conforming to the proper protocols, he conceded, and ushered his two passengers towards the helicopter. Once more the rotors swirled, and snow blew across the road. Then tail up, and nose down, like a dragonfly on heat, the helicopter jumped into the sky, roared over the ridge, then dropped down into the valley of the River Borne.

The older policeman turned towards me. "Is there anything more you can tell us?" he asked. I shook my head. "We may need to contact you again." I gave him my card.

"He's my neighbour," Armand said, which settled the matter.

The policeman returned to his car, and the *gardiens* to their *piste* duties. Then Armand suggested "We should rejoin the ladies." Once we'd explained what had happened to Sidonie and Céline, none of us felt in the mood for more skiing. So it was agreed that we should collect Marie-Sainte and Andréa from the snow park, and head for home as rapidly as we could.

"I hope you're all still on for *St Silvestre*," Sidonie said anxiously.

"Indeed, my dear, we cannot let the New Year pass unnoticed," Armand observed with all the conviction he could muster. "Who knows, after all? There may yet be a happy ending."

It was beyond even Armand to convince us, but we took some comfort from his calm. Yet I could not help but shudder for *la comtesse* L'Esprit. To see her husband pushed to his death must have been horror enough, without the need to raise false hopes. But I could understand that Sidonie would not want to waste her preparations, whilst the others looked in need of jollity. It was not their tragedy, after all. My own thoughts I kept to myself, and I said even less on the return journey than my companions, subdued though they were.

As soon as I'd shut the door of my apartment, I called Amy. She answered immediately. I cut through her protestations that two calls from me in two months were unprecedented. "Look, I'm sorry to ask, but do you know where Ambrose is at the moment?" Her only response was a sharp intake of breath. "I wouldn't ask if it weren't vital."

"I meant to tell you." Her voice was so tight I hardly knew it.

"You mean he's in France? Right here in *Haute Savoie*?"

I must be right. As soon as *la comtesse* confirmed that she'd heard the phrase IBNR, I realised why I'd half-recognised the skier in black. He was my old *bête noire*, Ambrose Hanter, the man who'd stolen Amy from me. The awkward gait, the gaunt look: they had suddenly fitted Ambrose exactly. If not the Ambrose of ten years ago, the older, sadder and more ruined man that Ambrose must have become. With a father the son of *émigrés*, Ambrose could pass for French, if he chose, but his mannerisms were entirely English.

IBNR had been the clincher. It had become his rallying cry against the machinations of Lloyd's, that he'd repeated endlessly to whomever he could persuade to listen. "We Names incurred losses which were never reported to us at the time. We were set up. They incurred the losses, then we were signed up to pay for them."

"Of course he's not in France," Amy said. "He never got so far."

"Oh, yes he did. Unless I'm very much mistaken, I've just seen him. In La Clusaz." Then I told her quickly what had happened.

"You're completely wrong. I'd have told you, only I didn't know how you'd react. Then there was Northern Rock. Ambrose is dead. He jumped off a Channel ferry mid-September."

Chapter Four : Rota for Last Cufflinks

I first met Ambrose Hanter at our Rota session, the prosaic name given to the ceremony at which newly recruited investors were formally inducted into the mysteries of Lloyd's. Founded in the 17th century at the coffee house of Edward Lloyd, the society had slowly transformed from an informal gathering of ship owners and traders, offering mutual insurance for their cargoes, into an electronic bourse, run by professional underwriters, fed by brokers and agents, and supported by an army of investors. Lloyd's was such an old institution that it pre-dated the limited liability company by nearly 200 years. The liability of its backers was limited only to the extent of their wealth, down to their last cufflinks, as it was put in the humour of a male establishment.

When Lloyd's was founded, ships relied on wind, and Governments waged unofficial war by privateering. A voyage to the Far East or the Americas took so long that a ship was not presumed lost until three years had passed. To this day, Lloyd's syndicates do not close trading years until two and a half years later. Names must commit to the next before they know that the year just gone has traded profitably.

Lloyd's began as a club of merchant adventurers, but by the late 1980s, the number of its backers had grown to 30,000. The first backers insured each other's ships, voyage by voyage. But as the Society grew, so it expanded into every kind of insurance from clippers to tankers, from tankers to refineries and drilling rigs, from refineries to trucks and railroads, from trucks to private cars and aircraft, from aircraft to space satellites. Thanks to Lloyd's, San Francisco rose again from the ashes of the earthquake and fire that devastated it in 1906. From things, Lloyd's diversified into people via professional indemnity insurance, and from primary insurance into reinsurance and retrocession.

The first Lloyd's members were wealthy men who could afford to cover the risks that they underwrote. Besides, it was in their interests to do so. Tomorrow or next year, it might be their cargo that rotted as their ship lay becalmed in the Tropics, or their ship that foundered in a Biscay storm. But by the time the number of its backers had climbed from hundreds into thousands and tens of thousands, the swashbucklers had dwindled into people like Ambrose Hanter and me: little more than

Names, as we were now known. Whilst, all the time, the potential losses grew with sub-prime stealth to staggering proportions.

Our Rota was held in the old Lloyd's building, a traditional City castle with a heavy stone façade and an interior of brown marble and dark wood, heavily suggestive of probity and security. There were several groups of us, mostly men in their best suits, with here and there a lady in a resplendent hat, each group accompanied by a smooth young agent. None of us neophytes seemed to be whiz kids or fat cats, just ordinary citizens who normally went soberly about their business, but today were venturing into the world of unimaginable wealth. Most were older than Ambrose and me, which is why I noticed him.

We were in our mid-thirties then. With his tall, slightly stooping stance, he looked more like a French intellectual than a businessman, though – as he explained to me later – he ran a small, but quite successful, packaging company. He'd inherited it as a loss-maker from his father, himself the son of wartime *émigrés*, and turned it around. The dogged attention to detail that this had required suited Ambrose perfectly, and he had not only returned the business to profit, but just sold the factory that made plastic bottles to Tetra Pak.

The profits from that he had ploughed into his other two divisions: one making plastic rubbish bags, the other carton-board boxes. His bags came in every size, from industrial monsters you could lose a car in to dainty white models for bathroom pedal bins. He offered handles and drawstrings, and every thickness from bullet-proof to diaphanous. He even had a military contract for body bags. His cartons were more specialised: he had developed a shiny laminate that was far cheaper to produce than it looked, and which made him the darling of chocolatiers and luxury goods manufacturers. His was a business that would never excite the tabloids or the Sunday supplements; even his shares were too few to interest any but the more arcane financial journals.

Like me, he was asset rich but cash poor, and Lloyd's was the classic way to make your assets work twice, first to support your business and your life, second to underwrite Lloyd's insurances in return for the annual cheque. Though you had to deposit a third of the value that you underwrote, this could be done with a bank guarantee, secured on your house at less than 1%. It seemed a no-brainer.

The room where we waited was mutedly ornate, like a sepia print. Chandeliers hung from a high ceiling, whose mouldings were as intricate as the frames on the portraits that lined the walls. Ambrose stood by one of the long windows, gazing down at the crawling traffic in the street below. He seemed to be part of a bevy of Names, and yet

41

detached. Whilst the rest chatted happily with their agent, Ambrose seemed nervous and ill at ease. Several times, he bit his lip and sucked in his cheeks, then frowned at the traffic as if it held the key to some vital question. Since I knew none of my fellow joiners, and had become bored by my agent's platitudes, I found myself drawn to the only man of my own age in the room.

"We could have done this faster by letter," I observed.

He pursed his lips pensively. "I think it's meant to impress us."

I shrugged. "They're not going to tell us anything new."

"I suppose not." He waved a long hand around the room. "But this gives off an air of grandeur, don't you think? Reminds us how long the institution has survived. Safe as Lloyd's, isn't that what they say?" I smiled to show him that I was not really taken in. But he was right. The show was impressive, and I had not failed to heed the signals.

"I suppose we're doing the right thing," he continued. "My accountant seems to think so."

"Accountants love the tax angles. Mine's the same."

That didn't seem to be the answer he wanted, and he sucked in his cheeks once more. "This is the last chance to back out." He had sandy hair, slightly receding, which added to the air of academia, and prominent brown eyes. Though to me he seemed unassuming, I later learned that these eyes were very appealing to women, whilst his outbursts of diffidence made them want to mother him.

"Do you want to back out?" I asked, slightly surprised by his attitude so late in the day.

"No." But his tone belied the simple word. "It's just... well, the formality of it all set me thinking. Made me realise we're putting everything at risk. Everything."

"In theory, yes. But not in practice."

"How can you be so sure?"

"Like you said: the place has survived for so long."

"I suppose so," he acknowledged, with a brief smile. The ready upward twitch of his lips revealed a sudden and attractive bonhomie. "But don't the financial ads say that investments can go down as well as up, and the past is not a reliable guide to the future?"

"That's just to cover their backsides. If everyone really believed that, business would be impossible. Not to mention life in general."

"Let's hope next year's light on catastrophe, then."

"On the contrary," I pronounced loftily. "Catastrophes drive up premiums. Losses take time to bite: the higher premiums are invested for immediate profit." At least that was the theory.

"Ah, I see you're a bit of an expert." Though he was taller than me, his stoop seemed to bring those large, penetrating eyes down to my level. It was briefly unnerving.

"I've done my homework." In my business, it did no harm to seem expert in all things.

"Are you on Outhewaite?" he asked. I shook my head. "Me neither." Outhewaite was one of the star underwriters of the time, though his syndicate would be one of the first to crash.

"Widows and orphans stuff for me. Nothing too exciting," I explained. "And yourself?"

"Brabazon, Micklewright, Pargetter, Tonbridge and Wu." He rattled them off like a nursery rhyme. "They're mainly marine," he added, as if that made them safer. Then he held out his hand. "Ambrose Hanter." His expression was friendly, but his grip was limp.

"Clem Holden." I crushed his fingers in manly fashion. "We have the Wu syndicate in common."

"My agent says they've never had to ask anyone for money."

"Insurance is like gambling," I told him. "Only we're supporting the bookies not the punters. Have you ever seen a poor bookie?"

"Actually, I have." He stooped lower, as though he didn't want to be overheard. "One of my old school friends, but he never laid off his bets properly." He sucked in his cheeks judiciously. "On the other hand, I never heard of a casino going bust."

"So which is Lloyd's?" I asked lightly. "Bookmaker or casino?"

Before he could reply, his agent was calling him over. He nodded quickly. "Catch up with you later, perhaps." Then he was gone.

I stared down at the traffic, a scrum of taxis, messenger bikes and security vans. Taken as a whole, Lloyd's was much like a casino. Its trading floor, the Room, where each underwriter sat at the workspace they called a box, was laid out like one. All it lacked were the cocktail waitresses. Unlike a casino, each syndicate was a separate enterprise, and each Name was a sole trader. It was as though Las Vegas rented out every crap table, every roulette wheel and every blackjack pit to a separate business. Its supporters claimed that Lloyd's blend of small and large was the source of its strength; its detractors, though vociferous only later, said it was too cumbersome for the modern world; that a gentleman's club could never compete with modern corporations in Zurich or Bermuda. As I waited my turn at the Rota, I was definitely a supporter, convinced that this was an enterprise that should never and could never fail. Ever.

Ambrose was out again within minutes. He gave me a small thumbs up. "It's all quite painless."

Then it was my turn. Flanked by my members' agent, I was ushered through a heavy door, across the expensively nondescript carpet to a group of silver-haired men seated at a huge polished table, beneath muted chandeliers. Their dark worsted suits matched the heavy curtains behind them; their collars and cuffs were saintly white; whilst the rich silk of their ties hinted at the wealth that they were prepared to share with me, their newest recruit.

It was a catechism: did I realise the nature of the Society into which I was entering? Did I understand that I would be one of a band of sole traders, severally but not jointly entitled to a share of the profits, and similarly liable for any losses? Did I understand, in regard to losses, that I pledged all my wealth, not simply my underwriting deposit?

I noticed the chairman's chunky gold cufflinks, winking under the lights of the chandeliers above us. I was supposed to murmur "Yes", as I had to all the previous questions, but this time I couldn't resist the knowing quip. "I understood you left me my last cufflinks."

Aware that I had said something out of the ordinary, the chairman glanced left and right, but his colleagues were smiling. "Yes," those smiles seemed to say, "we too are men of the world. We know and you know that that kind of catastrophic loss just won't happen, but we have to warn you. It's just a formality, don't worry about a thing." And I didn't, any more than first communicants worry about hellfire. "We're all at risk ourselves," the chairman explained, as if that proved the point. "Even more than you," said a voice down the table. "For the moment," said a third. Ah, yes! As each profitable year passed, I might increase my underwriting line, until who knew what I could make.

To my surprise Ambrose was waiting for me. "Fancy a drink?" I glanced at my watch. In my business, time was money, and I resented the loss of any of it. On the other hand, my Rota session had taken less time than I had allowed for. So why not?

He led me to a small wine bar in Leadenhall, London's former game and poultry market. Specialty food shops, gentlemen's shirt makers, and bars now occupied the spaces that had once been hung with goose and pheasant, venison and boar. Where porters had pushed their barrows amidst a throng of ruddy farmers and sharp-faced wholesalers, there now strolled the men and women of the City. The hush of money had replaced the noise of the market.

"So you went through with it?" I asked, as we sipped beers.

He considered this. "You know when they got to unlimited liability? I was going to say I'd only accept loss if they weren't negligent. I mean that's normal in business, isn't it?"

I tried to imagine how all those silky directors would have responded to such a challenge. Would they have smiled soothingly, or would they have spluttered with outrage? Either would have been a sight to see. "Why didn't you?" He shrugged shyly. "Ten of them to one of you." Enough to be intimidating. "Anyway, you're in now."

"For better or for worse." He ordered another round. "It's a bit like a marriage, isn't it?"

I laughed, accepting the second half. "Except divorce from Lloyd's is more difficult. Imagine a divorce court saying you had to live with your estranged wife for another three years at least, and that she had total access to your bank account in the meantime?"

"Are you divorced, then?" He leaned towards me with that unnerving intimacy of his.

"Not yet." I don't know why I put it that way: it was no premonition. Amy and I were still very happy together, despite her reservations about Lloyd's. "What about you?"

His mouth turned down. "Oh, yes, I'm divorced."

I couldn't tell if he were saddened by the memory of his loss, or angry with my question. "I'm sorry."

A smile contested the frown across his lips. "She was always searching for new horizons. That's life, I suppose. And life rarely plays fair." As I was to discover, Ambrose had an issue with fairness. It was the iron principle behind his way of doing business, and he expected the same in return. "I called her Mai, you know, even though it was her second name. It seemed to make our relationship that bit special." He shook his head bravely. "Seems I was wrong."

The detail could only possibly have been of interest to him, but he said it with such wistfulness that I felt his loss.

"Mai sounds Scandinavian," I said to break the unease.

"No, she's half English. May is hawthorn, you know. It's bad luck to bring may into your house." He sighed. "Do you have kids?"

"A boy. He's eight. A nice age." I felt bad to throw my joy in his face, but he actually laughed.

"I know it well. My daughter's nearly ten now."

"She must be a consolation." I hoped this was the right response.

"She is." This time his smile was decided. "Business is too time-consuming for full-time fatherhood, but I get the access I want."

45

With that opening I was glad to switch to the safer topic of what we did for a living. With a stranger, it was so much easier to discuss the intricacies of planning and finance, the ups and downs of profit and loss, than to poke into the intimate recesses of his private life. Amy, of course, would have had Ambrose's entire love life out of him in five minutes, but I lacked her empathic skills. Given a management to restructure or a new business opportunity to exploit, I was in my element; but I never pried into what my clients did outside their offices. So it wasn't long before Ambrose was regaling me with the details of his company. It probably sounded dull to the barman, but I find all business fascinating. The nature of enterprise was my bread and butter, and any businessman was a potential client.

I could tell that Ambrose was my kind of client. There's a misconception that the best entrepreneurs are flashy robber barons who terrorise their staff and make their money in breathtaking deals. In the real economy, attention to detail counts for more than histrionics. Ambrose was small, but he cared about what he did and he did it well. A small project would be profitable and fun, and might lead to bigger things. Like selling his glossy carton business. Schmoozing prospects was time well spent, and I'd decided to schmooze Ambrose.

That he was the owner of his company made it all the better. I aimed to deal only with CEOs, though I often had to settle for the marketing directors of large multinationals, and console myself that their irritating brand managers, handled right, would one day bring me their business when they made it to the top.

I suggested we tried a small Lebanese restaurant which I'd spotted off Fenchurch Street. As I'd hoped, he hadn't a clue about Middle Eastern cuisine, so I could talk him through the intricacies of *meze*. He was an appreciative guest, and after a sip or two of *Château Muzah*, a Lebanese red, I broached the idea of advising his business.

"I couldn't afford you," he apologised. "Everybody hates paying for packs and wraps. They'd complain if I gave the stuff away." All clients say things like this; it's part of negotiation, and the fact that he sounded disappointed was a good sign. "Anyway," he added, "There's nothing sexy about us; nothing to interest a consultancy like yours."

I spent most of my time at dinner parties dispelling to Amy's friends their misconception that mundane products must be equally boring to produce. "Fancy grown men worrying about things like cat food," as one of them put it to me, with a smirk on her delectable lips.

"The mechanics of production are the same for everything," I told her. "I don't suppose the sweated labour that knocked up your designer dress thought, 'wow, this is a Versace'."

"I don't mean the shop floor," she protested. "Management."

"Cat food, fashion. It's all the same. Costing and presentation."

"My husband's in venture capital. That's something else."

"It's only a matter of scale. Your husband buys and sells companies, my clients keep those companies up and running by selling what they sell. He needs them; they don't need him."

It was her smug assumption that strings of noughts confer nobility on otherwise mundane transactions that got to me. It was the evening I finally decided to join Lloyd's.

Put-downs were part of the dinner party game, but it was surprising to hear Ambrose – an actual entrepreneur – running down his own business. "Anyway," he continued, "In our humble way, we run a tight ship. Do you think you could improve that?" This was better, because it showed that underneath the diffident manner he had the perverse pride of the details man. He negotiated, not by flash and fervour, but with the same care that he gave to his manufacturing processes.

"It's a misconception that only badly run companies need advice: in my experience, it's only good companies like yours who are sensible enough to realise when they need help, and who don't treat us as a threat to their egos. Admit it, you spend more time fighting fires than thinking about the long-term. It's inevitable. I'm always committing the same mistake with my own outfit."

"This wine's strong." He studied his glass. "I'll think about it."

"Think of all those nice Lloyd's profits to invest."

This was a joke too far. "Let's not count our chickens." His manner was suddenly severe. "I meant it about being in two minds. My instinct told me 'get out of here!' But then you reassured me."

I'd always liked to think of myself as persuasive, but the idea that a few casual remarks could have made such a difference amazed even me. With another man, I'd have assumed he was joking, but I'd already decided that Ambrose was too literal for irony. "Glad to be of service." I raised my glass. "Just don't blame me if it all goes pear-shaped."

He smiled, but continued to fix me with that intimate stare.

The same stare, I now realised, with which he must have fixed L'Esprit from behind those impenetrable sunglasses.

Except that Ambrose was dead. Officially, on the say-so of a British coroner. According to Amy, the suicide had made the inner pages of the nationals under such headlines as *Fatal Ferry Fall* and *Bankrupt's Last*

47

Dive. His note, stuck under the windscreen wipers and addressed to the captain, apologised for any inconvenience, then explained that Ambrose had nothing left to live on or to look forward to.

Yet he'd used a borrowed car, and it had taken two weeks to track down his identity, which to my mind were the hallmarks of a man trying to disappear. Yet the coroner had concurred with his jury.

"You simply made a mistake," Amy had said. "This man in the black anorak looked like Ambrose, but it couldn't have been."

"How do you account for IBNR, then? It was his battle cry."

"I don't have to. It wasn't Ambrose. That's all there is to it."

"Tell me about the ferry."

"There's nothing to tell. He jumped."

"But he was a good swimmer..." This was the bit that really freaked me. Ambrose was more than good: he did the annual Swimathon, 5,000 metres of his local pool for charity, and he'd twice persuaded me to do it with him. It was incredible that Ambrose, always so precise in his methods, would have chosen death by drowning. "Once you can swim, you do it instinctively." It would have taken hours in filthy water before exhaustion overcame him. "Did they ever find him?"

"The Channel currents are very strong, so they wouldn't expect to find a body. They only realised because he didn't collect his car."

"So nobody saw him jump?"

"There were a couple of drunks on the upper deck. They saw Ambrose up there by the rail. And much later they heard a splash. But they didn't put two and two together."

"So he could have faked it."

"That's a horrible thing to say," she protested. "I know you didn't like him in the end, but even you can't think him capable of murder. If you can't believe me, you ought to believe the coroner." I ought, but I didn't. Ambrose might be the last person to spring to mind as a murder suspect, but if he *had* decided to commit murder, faking suicide in advance was totally in keeping with his attention to detail.

A dead man would always be in the clear. Yet faking death was an extreme step, even for Ambrose. His lack of funds must have turned his mind, if not enough for self-destruction, enough for murder.

I might, as Amy charged, be letting my feelings get the better of me, if it weren't for IBNR. It was not a phrase a Frenchwoman was likely to invent; and who else but Ambrose would shout it? Though most ex-Names half-suspected that Lloyd's had knowingly recruited us in order that we should pay for losses they'd failed to disclose, there was little unanimity as to how to exploit the suspicion. Conspiracy is difficult to prove, and even those who passionately believed in it had not warmed to IBNR as their rallying cry. It resonated only with Ambrose.

Ambrose had not befriended fellow ruined Names any more than I had. We had joined action groups, to be sure, but that had been strictly business. Comparing losses had been competitive not sympathetic, as each strove to prove that he or she had been uniquely mistreated.

But between Ambrose and L'Esprit, there was another link. L'Esprit was an ex-Name and a Mallory Stellenbourg client. Almost certainly, he'd been a Tonbridge victim; so it was likely that Ambrose, like him, had transferred whatever assets he had left into Ghost Trader. That would also explain why I'd never heard of Ghost Trader; after his fling with Amy, I was the last person to whom he would have confided his investment plans. If my speculations were right, Mallory Stellenbourg ought to know why Ambrose and L'Esprit had quarrelled.

I had to speak to her. It was only kind, anyway, to warn her that the client with whom she expected to have lunch would not be coming. Better to hear it from me than on the news, or from a policeman. All I got was her answering service. No doubt she was now in Aix, perhaps winding up the business part of her trip, or chatting over pre-dinner drinks. "Clem again. Please call when you get this. It's urgent."

After that there was nothing more to do except get ready. I had rarely felt less like jollifications, but nor did I relish pacing my apartment in a fever of uncertainty. Despite Amy, I had no more wish to believe Ambrose a murderer than she. I kept telling myself that I must be wrong, that Ambrose was merely another, if sadder, victim of financial malpractice, a lonely man driven to a desperate suicide. Yet every fact pointed the other way. The coroner's jury had had no cadaver to support their verdict; they had taken the suicide note at face value; and they had accepted the advice of experts as to the ease with which bodies in the Channel could disappear. Unlike me, they had not known that Ambrose was an excellent swimmer, nor had they known how methodical he could be. IBNR... The initials haunted me.

To celebrate *St Silvestre* – France's answer to Hogmanay – Armand and Sidonie had transformed my old apartment into a magical grotto of flickering candles and silvered fir cones. A thickset Father Christmas figure climbed one of the French windows, whilst a ragged chimney sweep nimbly pursued his sooty-cheeked Columbine across the other. On the dining table was a huge platter of oysters; into my hand, Armand pressed an icy flute of champagne.

René was the last to arrive, having sent Céline on ahead. As he explained, he had been talking to his friend the *gardien des pistes*.

"There's still no news from Grand Bornand. The body caused a small avalanche, it seems. It may take all night to dig through it."

"At least they know he's dead." Céline shuddered. "Poor woman."

"They don't know anything for certain until they've found him."

I heartily wished that the coroner had had the same attitude.

"Any sign of the man in black?" Andréa grinned. "The Englishman."

"No," said René, "Nor do they expect one." We were all ears, and he relished being the only person in the know. "The police found two more witnesses. They were further along the ridge, but facing the right way. They both saw the man going over the edge…"

"So what are they saying, that she pushed her own husband?"

He shook his head. "Not at all. They said she tried to save him."

"So it was an accident?" Marie-Sainte gripped Andréa's arm.

"Exactly. The man seemed to stagger, and swerve. But there was no skater in black." He paused reflectively. "There were other skiers but none fitting Madame's description."

"But why would his wife invent him?" I demanded. "And don't forget I saw him, too."

"Only in the restaurant." René shrugged, to remind me that he too had failed to see the man. "The woman was distraught."

Armand nodded in solemn agreement.

"They'll have to put up a net now," said Sidonie.

René laughed grimly. "Now we enter the realm of politics. The *gardiens* believe the wife. A mystery suspect in black is much more to their liking than one of their customers having an accident. The police, on the other hand, want to avoid a costly man-hunt for an unknown Englishman. Foreign suspects always create complications."

"But surely they can't not investigate?" Céline asked.

"Oh, they'll investigate," he replied. "But if you want my opinion, when they find the body, they'll conclude that the unfortunate man suffered a heart attack. No more and no less."

"Then nobody would be to blame," Andréa sneered. "How typical!"

Chapter Five : A Debt Collector Served

By one o'clock we had all had enough. Sidonie and Armand had done us proud, and we had done justice to their efforts. Replete with food, and fuzzy with wine, I stumbled up the steps to my apartment. My brain buzzed with everything I had seen and heard that day. Nothing made sense. However cunningly Ambrose might have plotted to kill L'Esprit, he could hardly have arranged to be invisible to witnesses; if he had been able to achieve such a feat, he would not have needed the desperate cover of a faked suicide; nor would he have failed to be invisible to L'Esprit's wife, the nearest of the witnesses. Yet if his fall had been nothing but an accident, why had she invented a murderer, and with a description that fitted Ambrose better than anybody else: the only Englishman in a French ski resort likely to shout "IBNR"?

In an effort to clear my brain, I wrenched open my French window and stepped onto the balcony. The cloud was long gone, the night clear and cold. My breath rose like incense and blurred the outlines of the castle. Its narrow turrets took on the macabre appearance of headstones, and the pines on the *Dents des Lanfins* beyond huddled under their white shrouds like a platoon of ghosts. I shivered in the silence.

The weirdness of the scene only fuelled the fever of my thoughts, so that it was some time before I noticed that my mobile was ringing. The number was withheld, and it rang off just as I was about to answer. I stared angrily at the handset. It must be Mallory Stellenbourg, I thought, but if it were not, it was unreasonable to call her now. Either she would be in bed, or she would be enjoying her party.

My phone rang again. This time it was Amy. She sounded slightly drunk. "Clem, darling, I just wanted to say Happy New Year."

It was the first cheerful moment of 2008. Downstairs had been the obsequies for 2007. "Thank you, and bless you," I said.

"It's not as if I don't ring every New Year."

This was true, but we'd spoken just hours ago. "So what's new with you, apart from 2008?" I asked.

"Just so you don't accuse me of keeping things from you." Her voice turned solemn. "Your old nemesis Wormsley popped his clogs."

Wormsley! The Lloyd's debt collector who had orchestrated my ruin with such fanatical relish. A man who had seemed so much larger

51

than life then, that the idea of his being dead now was incredible. Even ten years later. Miracles like that just didn't happen.

"When?" It was all I could manage.

"Boxing Day. He was throwing this big shindig. Evening dress, champagne, party hats: the whole caboodle. Still revelling in his ill-gotten gains…" I'd never realised that Amy must have hated Wormsley as much as I did. All her anger at the time had been heaped on me. Perhaps she'd learned to hate Wormsley from Ambrose.

"What he took from us didn't go to him." Not that I meant to excuse him. It takes a special mind-set deliberately and methodically to reduce fellow human beings to penury in the line of duty. Had he acted purely selfishly, I would have found his actions more understandable.

"I thought you'd be over the moon," she said, a little sulkily.

Of course, she was right. The way Wormsley had treated us, I ought to be as delighted at the news of his death as Amy expected me to be. But all that had been so long ago, and I'd done my best to put it behind me; the sudden reminder was too painful for joy. To gloat would make me no better than my tormentor. "So what happened?" I asked.

"It was right on the stroke of midnight. Wormsley was opening his French windows so they could go out on the patio for a toast. All his guests were behind him. Then down he went. Bang! Life and soul one second, dead as a doornail the next. Everyone rushed forward, of course, and his wife tried to loosen his collar. But there was nothing anyone could do. Massive coronary, apparently. Completely out of the blue. No medical history, no warnings at all. Everyone was shocked rigid." Her words slurred with relish.

"Nice for him, though," I said. "Going out on a high." He who had caused such lasting pain to his victims had been spared any for himself. The suffering he had left to his wife.

"Not necessarily." Amy was positively gloating. "All the guests said it was like he'd seen a ghost. He went as white as a sheet before he fell. His eyes were popping out of his skull."

"How do you know all this?" Surely Wormsley was too obscure, and a coronary too commonplace, to have made the tabloids. Yet who else would have reported such macabre detail?

"A friend of a friend of Saul's was there."

It figured. The financial sector, in all its ramifications, is quite small, its capacity to wreak havoc out of all proportion to its numbers.

In return, I brought Amy up to date on what René had learned. "So it looks like an accident, too. Maybe even another heart attack."

"There you are then. Let Ambrose R.I.P." On that we agreed.

As she rang off, my phone bleeped that I had a message. I hurriedly opened it in the hopes this might at last be Mallory Stellenbourg. "Involved But Not Responsible? It doesn't work, and the guilty should know." No name, and when I tried the number, no answer.

I sat down heavily in my one recliner and closed my eyes. It seemed the only way to shut out the confusion of images and emotions that tormented my brain. Deliberately, I tried to relax each of my muscles, the way René had taught me, and to slow and deepen my breathing. To begin with it seemed hopeless, but I persisted, determined to empty my brain of everything that disturbed it. Breathe in... breathe out...

To see a woman distraught by the fall and almost certain death of her husband, a man I had myself seen just before, was bad enough; but for that death probably to have been caused by Ambrose, when Ambrose himself was supposed to be dead, was infinitely worse.

Then Wormsley. I could hardly rejoice at the death of my old enemy, when reliable witnesses sought to explain it by his seeing a ghost. And what ghost could be more shocking than that of an old victim driven to suicide? I had no idea what Ambrose had against L'Esprit, but he had hated Wormsley even more than I. To fake suicide in order to get away with one murder was perhaps extreme, but for two, it made more sense; even better sense if he could turn the mere sight of himself, revenant from the dead, to lethal effect. And why stop at two?

If shouting "IBNR" pointed to Ambrose, its reinterpretation in the text was conclusive. If anyone challenged his IBNR accusation, he'd said that "Involved But Not Responsible" was no defence. "Everyone can accept small losses, but losing 500% is negligence by definition!" It was as close as he ever came to shouting. So there was nobody but Ambrose who could have sent this message to me. But why?

Was it possible that he held me responsible for my reassuring words at the Rota; that nothing but my persuasion had prevented him from pulling out? It was absurd. But I had not seen Ambrose in 10 years; I had no idea the extent to which his sense of grievance might have unbalanced his mind. It was all too probable that he had recognised me at the restaurant in Les Confins. Unlike him, I had removed my sun goggles and ski hat. So he might be warning me to keep quiet. Either possibility was scary. The Ambrose I had once known had been the opposite of scary, but a deranged Ambrose was something else.

Yet it was all so fantastical. Nothing added up. I could be jumping to wild conclusions on weak evidence, relying like Amy on intuition. But intuition wasn't my *forte*; in business I had always prided myself on strict analysis, never making a recommendation that wasn't rooted in all the facts. But at least the effort of being logically intuitive was calming. My fingers relaxed against the comforting texture of the chair's arms, and my breathing sounded less as though I'd been running to the viewpoint on *Roc de Chère*.

The quiet discipline of recent years began slowly to reassert itself. After a minute or two, I headed for the fridge to pour myself a shot of *marc*. Mine was a fiery moonshine from an old mountain man, an acquaintance of René, who lived near Les Confins. "It's cheaper than central heating," René had told me, "And a lot more enjoyable."

My apartment was compact, with kitchen, living and dining areas all occupying different corners of one room. It took no more than six strides to get from my chair to the fridge, and another one to the cupboard where I kept crockery and glasses. Returning to the recliner, I sipped the *marc* and closed my eyes.

I suppose I fell asleep, except the jump was so sudden, I had no sense of time passing. One moment I was sitting comfortably indoors, the next I was standing outside in a place I'd never seen in my life.

The garden was large, surrounded on either side by dense hedges of holly, each as black as a wall. The night sky was studded with stars, not diamond sharp as they were here near the mountains, but soft like tiny pearls. The damp of the lawn penetrated my shoes, and the moist cold seemed to creep up my legs. All was quiet, except for an owl.

A large, white house with big Georgian windows lay in front of me. Two rampant stone lions marked the top of the steps onto the patio, and, as my shoes scraped on the brick, their eyes glared at my intrusion, as though they would roar a warning to the household if only they had breath in their moss-streaked bodies. The French windows faced me, flat and dark, until suddenly light sprang from the dining room beyond, as its double doors were thrust open. A large man stood in dramatic silhouette, whilst behind him there was a confusion of bare-shouldered women with champagne flutes and men in party hats.

The man flung the French windows apart. He had aged certainly. His hair had receded and silvered, and his jowl was heavier. The pockets of loose skin under his eyes were slacker, and his back had a slight stoop which it had never had before. But in every other respect this was Wormsley. For his age, the picture of vigour and health. Anger knotted my fists, and brought a sour taste to my mouth. I stepped forward out of the shadows until we stood face to face. Such had been his speed, that his guests were still fanned out behind him, and their laughter was merely background noise, an irrelevance.

54

He was a big man, with the broad shoulders of the rugby forward he once had been, and the heavy jaw of the bully. My instinct should have been to fall back in a gesture of appeasement. But anger conquered fear. Had I not broken his nose at an action group meeting, the first against Wu, my worst syndicate? As then, so now. Except that instead of hitting him, I spoke. Not angrily, but with the sonorous tone of authority. "IBNR," I said. The four letters came out just right, awful and measured, the tone of a judge, not the rant of an accuser.

The blood drained from his face as though I had pulled a plug in his feet. Then he pitched forwards so violently, against one of the windows, that a pane came loose and shattered on the flags. There was a surge of guests trying to reach the stricken figure. I saw them with such clarity that I could tell which of the men had tailored dinner suits and which wore off-the-peg; which of the jewellery their wives sported was in taste and which was bling; as well as the cut and stuff of their dresses. I'd done a project for a fashion house once, so I knew my silks from my tulles, and good cut from the merely ostentatious.

Yet they took no notice of me. When I stepped forward, there was no resistance, as though I had walked right through them. There was a woman bending over Wormsley, presumably his wife, pulling so hard at his collar and bowtie that the studs popped from his shirt. "Call an ambulance!" There was a general scrabble in pockets for phones. Not that there was anything any paramedic could do for him. The expression on Wormsley's face was such that I would never wish to see again. Yet I could describe to this day every droplet of spittle on his chin, the exact contortions of his rictus, and the protrusion of his crazy, staring eyes with the accuracy of the pathologist who must later have noted such things at the morgue. Had I been him, I would have concluded without doubt that Wormsley had seen a ghost.

Chapter Six : Claimable Events

I woke shivering with cold. In my agitation after the text message, I had left the balcony window slightly open. I closed it, and crawled off to bed. When next I woke – with a stiff neck and a headache – it was nearly 10:45. But at least my time in bed had been dreamless, probably thanks to the moonshine. Wincing at the strength of the sunlight that poured through the velux – I had also forgotten to pull down the blind – I groped my way to the kitchen area and prepared strong coffee. Against a cloudless sky, the pointy towers of the castle and the peaks of the *Dents des Lanfins* stood out in agonisingly white focus.

I stretched my arms and rolled my neck. Yesterday's events and last night's dream had faded into the shadowy recesses of my sluggish brain. To keep them there I needed exercise, and the day was perfect for it. Fortified with a mug of coffee, I went to my bedroom to change. Back in the kitchen, in my leggings and sweats, I sat on the floor to lace up my running shoes. Not too loose, not too tight. The concentration required kept my mind off unpleasant thoughts.

It was 11:40 by the time I was ready. I was just making for the door, when I heard two ambulances on the main road. Their sirens rose in unison to such a crescendo that I feared they would burst through my front door. Their noise became so unbearable I had to cover my ears. Then they stopped. The silence that followed was scarily eerie.

I started for the door, but my legs refused to obey me. The features of the room, normally so familiar, seemed hard-edged and strange, as if some celestial joker were fiddling with brightness and contrast settings. I thought I was going to faint, and I clung to the recliner to stay upright. The leather felt clammy. I shook my head. This was ridiculous. As hangovers went, mine was nothing. I continued determinedly if unsteadily to the door, fearing some terrible carnage had been visited upon the parking bays. But there was nothing. The neighbours' cars slumbered in their accustomed places. No ambulances had joined them, and no paramedics were rushing to our doors. I felt an immediate surge of relief. None of my friends was in danger. My nerve steadied.

I glanced at my watch again, so that I could time my run. To my surprise, it registered 12:40. Surely my panic attack, or whatever it had been, could not have lasted a whole hour. More likely I had misread the numbers first time round. Shaking my head, I set off down the zigzag path between the allotments and the orchards to the main road.

Once across the main road, I would have a choice: to take the Rue de la Plage towards the *Hôtel du Lac* and then over the *Roc de Chère*, or to take the continuation of my path down to the Route des Vignes, which offered continuous lake views: the heroic cross-country route in the woods versus the speed run. I was still undecided when I saw flashing blue lights ahead, where the path was interrupted by the road.

I guessed immediately what must have happened. The corner of the Rue de la Plage was obscured by a high wall and an overhanging tree, which Armand had often described as an accident waiting to happen, although in all the time I had lived here, the worst had been a minor shunt during the holiday season, when a car from the beach had dented the wing of a commuter driving home. I slowed to a walk, queasy at the thought of what I might see, yet morbidly compelled to look. But before I reached the ambulance, its siren burst into life and the vehicle sped away. Its departure brought the other ambulance into view.

Three *policiers* were directing traffic, which was backed up in both directions. There was a car slewed across the road with a huge dent in its bonnet and its windscreen crazed and buckled in. The ambulance doors were open and the paramedics were bending over and obscuring a figure lying against the kerb. They were moving cautiously so as not to disturb the victim until they had assessed the injuries. Watching them intently was a lone man.

Tall and stooping with greying hair almost hidden under a black beret, he was not from the village, so I took him for the car driver, until I noticed another man sitting on the pavement beyond with a blanket round his shoulders. Uninjured, but clearly in shock. If the stooping man was not the driver, I thought his interest intrusive, and I was surprised that the nearest policeman did not move him along. As if sensing my resentment, the stooping man glanced up. Our eyes met for only a moment, before he hurried away. It was Ambrose. No sunglasses obscured his face, so that I was in no doubt. Aged and haggard he might be, his eyes more sunken, but he was perfectly familiar.

Not only that, I had seen a flash of recognition in his eyes: the guilty anger of a man who was anxious not to be spotted. His every movement from his loping stride to his furtive manner was unmistakable. As he reached the policeman, who stood with his back to him and blocked the pavement, the panic returned with tenfold force, and I had to reach for the wall to steady myself. When I focused again, Ambrose had disappeared. The policeman, quite unperturbed, was stepping into the road to wave traffic through.

I wrenched my eyes back to the paramedics. In the act of lifting the victim onto the stretcher, they moved with great care. I could see that it was a woman, but nothing of her face.

A hand gripped my arm. "Clem! Thank God." It was Sidonie, shaken and obviously glad to see me.

"What happened?" I demanded.

"She ran into the road. A runner tried to save her. He threw himself between her and the car." The words tumbled from her. "I really thought it was you." She hugged me fiercely as if to make sure. "They just took him away." I had never seen her so shaken.

Slowly the stretcher was lifted towards the ambulance, so that the woman lay briefly at an angle, and I could now see her clearly. Her face was ashen except for a livid bruise on her cheek and there was a horrible stillness about her. It was Mallory Stellenbourg, not as I had recently seen her, but as she had appeared in my dreams.

She stirred, and her eyelids fluttered open. Our eyes met. It was as if a bolt of lightning jumped between us. Her lips moved, as though pleading for my help, but if there were words I could not hear them for the ticking engines of the waiting traffic. Then the paramedics slid the stretcher inside the ambulance, and it was on its way.

The police enlisted some of us to help push the wrecked car into the Rue de la Plage, and in a few minutes the traffic was flowing again, whilst the driver had sufficiently recovered his composure to give the senior policeman his account of what had happened.

The activity of moving the car helped to dissipate my shock. If only I had been that runner, I could have saved her. Instead of feeling sorry for the man, I cursed his ineptitude. Taking my leave of Sidonie as quickly as I could, I took the Route des Vignes, determined to run to Annecy hospital. If Mallory was dying, she wouldn't die alone.

To my right was a narrow strip between Route des Vignes and the main road. Once it had been vineyards, but the only vines now decorated the gardens of the houses which had been built in recent times. To my left the ground fell steeply to the lake. With vast sloping gardens, the houses were substantial, two developed by Sidonie.

A breeze stirred the water, which reflected the pale winter sun in a myriad points. A perfect mirror of season and weather, the lake could be sombre and mysterious, as smooth as a sheet of glass or rough with choppy waves. But whatever its mood, it was always beautiful. Even now, it spurred my pace, urging me to reach the hospital in time.

In half an hour, I reached the outskirts of Veyrier, the next village. Breathing hard as I crested a sharp incline, I saw a man ahead. Walking slowly and disjointedly, he was scrutinising a small wood to his left as though he were searching for something. It was Ambrose! The intense scrutiny, and the awkward gait were unmistakeable.

Yet it was impossible. Surely? I had set out no more than five minutes after he had walked away, and he was still walking. No way could he have outpaced me. Such was my shock and confusion, I almost stopped running. But my desire to reach the hospital drove me on. There was nothing for it, but to ignore him completely. But he had heard the slap of my running feet, and he turned. His eyes flared and his lips curled back, more like a beast at bay than a man. Then he lurched right across me, his arms spread as if to seize me.

With the advantage of speed, I swerved towards the verge, and managed to avoid his arm. All I had to do now was sprint and there was no way he could catch me. Fear and instinct took over, and I surged forward. I ought to have swerved back into the centre of the road again, where the surface was smooth, but I was intent on putting as much distance between him and me in the shortest possible time. I ran straight. Right beside the verge.

My second mistake was to glance back to see if he was following. So I missed the break in the road surface. Striking soft earth instead of tarmac, my foot slid sideways and down. Pain seared my ankle, and I fell heavily. My hands and forearm scraped along the tarmac, and my face banged into something hard in the grassy verge. I lay stunned.

By the time I was capable of looking around, Ambrose had vanished. Which didn't seem possible, as the road was fenced on either side. But I was too relieved to care how he had disappeared. All that mattered was that he had gone. The mild Ambrose I once had known seemed transformed into a madman, a madman capable of murder and given to gloating over accident victims. Shuddering, I sat up slowly. My whole body ached, and I felt weak and uncoordinated. I supposed it was shock. I struggled to my feet, though I could scarcely bear to put weight on the ankle. Yet I must reach the hospital, and soon.

In a fury of indecision, I looked around and saw the path. I must have run past the little wood many times without a glance. It was a dense coppice of birch and cypress, the silvery birch breaking up the density of the evergreens. Two cypresses obscured a small opening in the fence, and beyond the opening was a path, which must lead to the lake, in whose icy water I could bathe my ankle. If that did not reduce the swelling, it might anaesthetise the pain enough for me to continue.

It was worth a try. I hopped forwards. Once in the trees, using branches and trunks for support, I made slow but steady progress. The path meandered this way and that. A deep quiet enfolded me. No traffic noise from the main road penetrated here, nor any boat sounds from the lake. Above me the sky was lost in a haze of green amidst a skein of leafless silver. I felt cocooned in peace and eternity.

My progress was inevitably slow, and the path seemed in no hurry to arrive anywhere, so I don't know how long it took me to reach the gate. It was made of rusty iron bars, and looked as though it had hung open for a long time. The hinges were coated in lichen, and its bottom corner, instead of swinging free, was buried in loose earth and long grass. Even so, it made me hesitate. It suggested the wood was private, and it reminded me that Ambrose might have come down here before me. How else could he have disappeared so quickly?

But to do so would have required his stepping around me or over me, and I had no memory of his even coming near me after I had fallen. I shrugged. If I hadn't seen the entrance to the wood before, there were doubtless gates and pathways on the other side of the road which I had never noticed either. More importantly, I was losing valuable time.

The ground levelled, and the trees thinned out. But instead of water, all I could see was a featureless wall rendered in grey roughcast. It was part of a single-story building. Its roof was the usual chalet-style, deep-pitched and overhanging. The path led round the side to a door. Though the path was well-trodden, the building had an air of neglect and dilapidation. The door's paint was peeling, but the lock was new.

It was a boathouse, with jetty and boat bay. Judging by the graffiti adorning the wall on this side, and the peeling shutter on its window, it had been abandoned. Two old tyres were suspended from bollards into the water on rusty chains. The water danced invitingly, and I sat down on the jetty with my back against the wall and started to unlace my shoe. Both shoe and sock came off with difficulty, and I winced loudly several times before I was able to inspect the ankle properly. Swollen to twice its normal size, its skin was taut and red.

The jetty was too high above the water for me simply to dangle my feet. I had to grab a bollard and a chain, then work my bottom out beyond the edge. At last my throbbing ankle hit water. The cold was enough to ice my brain, but I gritted my teeth, and forced myself to keep the ankle immersed for a full minute. Then I repeated the exercise, and cried aloud with grim relish.

There was a sudden noise behind me. Fearing Ambrose, I rotated on my bottom in time to see the shutter swing open. I had a brief view of a lit bulb beneath a plain shade, before it was obscured by the head and shoulders of a woman. Far from being abandoned, the building was occupied, and the occupier was about to berate my trespass.

Apology died on my lips. The occupier was none other than Mallory Stellenbourg. Confusion fought with joy, and joy soon won. I had seen her too often to be mistaken. The accident victim had been only briefly visible. Shock had turned resemblance into identity. Sad as I was for the victim, nothing could take away my delight at being wrong.

"Thank God you're OK," I cried. Now I knew exactly how Sidonie must have felt on seeing me.

At first Mallory's eyes had narrowed with anger; now they widened with surprise. "You!" she exclaimed. "Why wouldn't I be OK? Or is that stalker talk?" She didn't appear to be joking.

"There was an accident up the road. I honestly thought it was you."

"Sorry to disappoint you." Her brow furrowed. "That doesn't explain how you found me."

"Disappointed! I'm delighted," I protested. "As for the intrusion, I twisted my ankle. I hoped the water would reduce the swelling."

"You're shivering," she said. "You'd better come in."

In my relief at seeing her alive, I had forgotten my injuries. Now my cheek throbbed anew, and my ankle, though partially anaesthetised by the water, twinged agonisingly as I put weight on it. And my teeth were indeed chattering. I hopped to the door just as she opened it.

She was smartly if austerely dressed in a black trouser suit and cream blouse, and her hair was formally pinned back. The room into which she led me was similarly austere, though its furnishings were much cheaper than her clothes. I had a quick impression of a plain sofa, pine table and chairs and bare walls before I was led into the former boat bay. Now it provided a bathroom, a kitchen and her bedroom. With a steadying arm, she helped me to sit on the bed, which was prettified by a multi-coloured throw. Apart from a simple dressing table and an old wardrobe, the rest of the room was a work-station, built around several large computer screens. This was an office in which she slept more than a bedroom in which she worked.

"You have been in the wars. I'd better get you a plaster as well." Her fingers brushed my cheek, before she was off to the bathroom. She was back in a moment with bathrobe, towels, antiseptic, sticking plaster and cotton buds. "I never realised running was so dangerous."

"It isn't. But there was some idiot on the road who veered into me. Not looking where he was going." For the moment that was enough. I wasn't ready to pick her brains on Ambrose.

"Get out of your wet things. Then I'll attend to your cheek."

I took the bathrobe and towels from her. "I can manage."

"Help yourself to the shower." Then she was gone, leaving behind a faint aroma of alpine flowers. Slowly I peeled off my damp gear, and pulled on the bathrobe. It was comforting as well as warm, and my shivering subsided. Kneeling on the bed, I peered out of the window. Right in the arch of the former boat bay, I had the impression of floating on the lake. Even the blank computer screens threw off dim reflections of the water. It all added to my sense of unreality. That she was alive and not the victim of a terrible accident was wonderful, yet my confusing her with the real victim, as well as Sidonie's mistaking me for the other, compounded the confusions of the past 24 hours. I seemed to be as adrift in dream and fantasy as I now seemed adrift in the lake; no more anchored in reality than I seemed to be to land.

I hobbled to the bathroom, and peered at my cheek. It looked as though it had caved in. Closer inspection showed this to be an illusion of dried blood. The shower cubicle was compact, but the water was hot, and with warmth came a sense of perspective. To be sure there had been a dreadful accident, but the victims were strangers, to be lamented but not mourned. Neither I, as Sidonie had thought, nor Mallory, as I had feared, had been involved. The malign presence of Ambrose had yet to be explained, but I wasn't ready to think about him.

As I emerged from the bathroom, I found Mallory in the kitchen putting together salads and *charcuterie*. "You're lucky my lunch was called off, or you really would have had to crawl home. I take it you haven't eaten." I shook my head, and she pointed to a baguette and a bread board. "If you wouldn't mind cutting."

It was like being with Amy, and I fell readily to the various simple tasks of preparation Mallory gave me. As we worked, I wondered how best to raise the matter of L'Esprit. That her lunch had been called off confirmed my belief that it had indeed been L'Esprit who had fallen, but she moved around the tiny kitchen with such concentration that I decided to say nothing until we were eating. For all I knew, her concentration was her means of keeping her emotions under control. Instead, I told her something of the accident up the road.

We ate in the living room, which was a muted symphony of browns, from the russet of the floor tiles to the fawn of the walls. There were no books or magazines, or even a bookshelf, and the only picture was a sepia print of a mock-gothic *château*. A forbidding nineteenth century pile, perched on a rocky outcrop above a lake, clearly not this one. There was none of the domestic clutter in which I lived. Yet the room was airy, and the closeness of the water provided such a sense of peace that the rest of the world and its troubles seemed far away.

"I should have guessed the path was private," I said, over coffee.

"I should have fixed the gate. But you're the first person to find it since I've been here."

"Plus the odd graffitist."

"Before my time. The rent's ludicrous, the view's unparalleled. And I enjoy my privacy."

"I'm sorry I disturbed it. How long have you lived here?"

"Not long." She said it with a finality that forbade probing.

Now was the perfect time to broach L'Esprit, but in the companionable quiet of that bare yet pleasant room, I felt restrained. My quandary must have shown in my face, because she smiled. "How was the skiing?" Her manner was casual, the graceful hostess keeping the conversation flowing. Unless she were a brilliant actress, she could not know anything about L'Esprit's fall. I took a deep breath. I could delay no longer. I had decided last night that she ought to hear the news first from me. "You got my text?"

She shook her head. "I haven't checked my messages since last night. Was it important?"

"It was about your lunch," I said. "I knew it would be cancelled."

"You spoke to L'Esprit?" Her brow darkened ominously. "When I asked you not to." Under the circumstances, it seemed strange to be focusing on whether I had broken an agreement. But there was no doubting her annoyance, or how quickly it had been aroused.

"Of course not," I said. "But I was there. I heard what happened."

"What happened?" She repeated my words with puzzlement. Yet how could she know her lunch had been called off but not why?

"Would your client have been wearing check plus-fours? Has his wife got white salopettes and golden hair, probably dyed?"

She shrugged. "I wouldn't put it past them. Why?"

"I'm afraid he's had an accident… a bad one."

"An accident!" She looked thunderstruck. "But I spoke to him this morning. He told me he was up to his neck in superb powder."

It sounded like a sick joke. But hardly one L'Esprit would tell against himself, even if he could. "I'll tell you what happened." All I left out was my belief that the skier in black was known to me, or that he'd shouted "IBNR". We'd get to Ambrose later.

When I'd finished, she sat in stunned silence. "All very strange," she agreed at last. "Obviously your man wasn't L'Esprit."

"He fits your description." And he'd once been a Name.

"Lots of men could fit that description. Ditto snooty wives with dyed hair." Her voice grew in confidence.

Even if L'Esprit had miraculously survived, he would hardly call next morning as if nothing had happened. Unless the shock had blanked his memory. "Suppose he's in hospital with concussion. You thought he was skiing in powder; he might have meant it more literally."

"He sounded perfectly normal. Men with concussion don't. Anyway, no hospital would let him make silly phone calls." She patted my hand. "You've had a nasty shock two days in a row. If you could mistake me for the accident victim up the road, you can be forgiven for thinking the man who went off the ridge was L'Esprit."

It was difficult to fault her reasoning, and I wanted to agree with her. If it weren't for Ambrose. Who was not only in France, but nearby, and looking quite likely for further targets. Including me. Or Mallory.

"What if it wasn't L'Esprit," I suggested carefully. "What if it was the man in black pretending to be him?"

"Impossible. He'd have to be an actor, not an obvious Englishman."

Or he'd have to be half-French, as I knew Ambrose to be. If he'd rehearsed what to say, he could have fooled a woman with no reason to be suspicious. As for his Englishness, it was likely that Ambrose had wanted L'Esprit to know who was pushing him and why.

"There's something I haven't told you. According to the wife, the man in black shouted 'IBNR' just as he was pushing her husband." Her eyebrows shot up like the ears of a startled rabbit. "Incurred But Not Reported. It's a Lloyd's term, isn't it?"

"It's an insurance term." Her eyes took on a shuttered look, as though she were watching me and hiding from me all at once. "I don't know that Lloyd's have an exclusive on it."

"There's one Name who used it a lot. He was on Tonbridge." At the mention of Tonbridge her expression froze. "Ambrose Hanter. I'm guessing he's one of your clients."

She went so white I thought she would faint. But she recovered quickly. "You're not a regulator, you're a bloody policeman."

Taken aback by her vehemence, I assured her I wasn't even a private detective. "So why the interest in Ambrose?"

I explained how the phrase IBNR had clinched my half-recognition of the man in black; I described my text message, explaining how nobody but Ambrose had reinterpreted the letters. Finally, I described his ghoulish interest in the accident, and our clash at the roadside. "He was really peering into the wood. Perhaps he's after you, too."

She shuddered. Then she shook her head. "It's a good story, but it won't wash." She eyeballed me fiercely. "Ambrose is dead."

"I think he faked the suicide."

"That's impossible!" It came out as a hoarse whisper.

"Nobody saw him jump, did they?"

"So how did he get off the ferry?"

"He could have walked off with the foot passengers, he could have cadged a lift from one of the other cars. All the passport and ticket checks would have been done in Dover."

"There were witnesses who heard a splash."

"He swam too well to drown. We did the Swimathon together."

Her fingers drummed the table. "He was a friend of yours, then?"

"Until he made off with my wife. After that we lost touch."

"You're Amy's husband!" She stared at me awestruck. "I should have realised from your card." My cheek and ankle began to throb, and I felt suddenly drained. "Now I understand the interest in Ambrose." She seized my wrists. "For your own good, let him be. Otherwise, he'll drive you mad." She seemed to speak from knowledge.

"What about you?" I asked. "What's he got against you?"

"Ambrose is dead. Let's leave it at that. I really, really don't want to talk about him."

Chapter Seven : Duty of Care

"We're praying for you, Monsieur Clem." I half-opened my eyes. "You see, he heard me. His eyes flickered." I could just make her out through a blur of lashes. It was Marie-Sainte sitting at my bedside with Andréa. The fearless snowboarders with no job prospects. Long ago she'd seemed happy for me to become her step-father; now she nestled her head against her boyfriend's shoulder, and gazed adoringly into his eyes. "Say something, Andréa."

"*Andréa pas André. Moi, je suis un vrai Savoyard,*" he'd proclaimed, when first we met. "We should be independent: *L'Etat Souverain de Savoie.* In 1860, our only choice was France or Italy." He insisted that alone *Savoie* could have kept out of the current crisis.

"Maybe he blinked." He leaned towards me. Like Marie-Sainte, he was slim, but whereas she was fair like her mother, he was dark and angular. His sharp nose came quite close to my face. "But don't worry, Monsieur Clem, we are indeed praying for you. Not that we are believers, you understand, but because it does no harm, and just might do some good." He sat back with a wicked smile. "You've heard of Pascal's wager, of course. A no-brainer to bet that God exists. If He doesn't, so what? but if He does, you make it to Heaven."

Marie-Sainte kissed him on the cheek. "That's silly," she said. "What kind of God would accept you on those terms? Any worthwhile God would prefer honest disbelief to hedging."

"Then all financiers will go to Hell. They hedge all the time."

"And look where it gets them, even here on Earth!"

"No! Look where it gets *us*. They play silly games with our money, and we're the losers, never them."

"*Our* money. As if we had any. Ignore him. We *do* pray for you, Monsieur Clem. I do, at any rate."

"Of course we do," Andréa conceded. "God knows I'm a charlatan on His terms, but He won't take it out on you. I can pray for *you* with a clear conscience." He shrugged. "For all we know, the honest prayers of an atheist might really make Him sit up and take notice." He patted my hand, which was lying on top of the covers. "I think of you as the embodiment of the economy. You look dead, but you're only sleeping.

When you wake, the green shoots will appear, and things will look up. Think of that as you slumber. We're counting on you."

Marie-Sainte actually took my hand and squeezed it. "We're not just counting on you. We want you to recover for your own sake." Her smile would have made any step-father proud.

"At least you're not one of those French who act so superior and cock everything up," Andréa said with mock solemnity, as though he'd been taking lessons from René. I nearly laughed. Really it was very pleasant lying there and listening to them chatter. To the youngsters, especially. I had never realised that I meant so much to them; Marie-Sainte might have looked up to me when she was a child, but she was a student now, whilst Andréa was such a cynic. Yet they were amongst my most regular visitors. It brought a lump to my throat.

Everything was done for me. There was a drip in my arm, and tubes up my nose and out of my bottom. As for peeing, I wasn't sure, but it was difficult to keep track of everything. There was a screen next to my head, that played out my heartbeat and my brain activity. Armand, who was a bit of a dabbler on the stock market, said it reminded him of the *Bloomberg* financial channel. Whenever he dropped by, usually on his way home from his office in the town centre by the *Palais de Justice*, he'd stare at the screen, then laugh ponderously as he sat down. "Well, Clem, markets trading within a tight range; zero volatility."

Sidonie came the most, and she made a point always of kissing me on the forehead. Then she would sit mostly in silence, her clear eyes watching me gravely. As usual, her emotions were hard to interpret, though I sensed that she found it difficult to talk to a comatose man. Only once did she let herself go, on her second or third visit. "Trust you to be the hero. Trying to rescue a strange woman, when you leave your friends to suffer." Then she smiled an odd little smile that could almost have been a frown. "My dear, sweet fool."

On another occasion she told me not to worry about the management of the complex. "Armand's standing in for you. He scares the contractors almost as much as you do."

Sometimes she came with Céline, who always apologised that René would have come, except he feared the hospital would think he was interfering. If only I could have told her that he often came on his own, to regale me with droll stories about the doings of the village.

Even Amy came. The nurses made a big fuss, and referred to her as Madame Holden, even though she was on Saul's arm. They assumed I wouldn't notice. Amy looked wonderful, once she'd got over the initial shock, with her hair fair and up, the way I liked it, and resplendent in a fur-trimmed coat. She was looking brave and cheerful for my benefit, but she needn't have bothered. In my vegetative way, I was quite content. I also saw that underneath the tension over me she was truly happier than I'd seen her in a long time.

For that, I had Saul to thank. He looked better than the man who'd fallen off the Staten Island ferry. Or had I pushed him? It hardly mattered, because here he was alive and prosperous-looking, with a mane of silvery hair and a mouthful of American dentistry. He reminded me of Ambrose in the days of his prime: Ambrose as he might have looked if he'd been brought up in Tenafly, New Jersey. His smile was broad and easy, and he gave me its full benefit. "She's in good hands, Clem, I tell you. Be darned sure I'll look after her."

"You don't mind, do you, darling?" She stroked my brow. It was hard to say whether I minded or not, and I certainly didn't want to confuse them. Saul didn't look like a man who coped well with subtlety. So let them interpret my feelings as they chose. "They've nationalised Northern Rock," she continued brightly. "Just like you predicted." Since I had predicted no such thing, I thought it nice of her to make me sound so prescient to Saul.

"It's a dangerous thing, governments being involved," he declared in the gnomic tone Americans find so easy. "Banks shouldn't be rescued. Nobody's too big to fail. I'm sure Clem knows that, being an entrepreneur himself." He made it rhyme with manure.

"Don't speak too soon," Amy laughed. "If this crisis gets any worse, even Uncle Sam will have to step in. You mark my words." He placed an indulgent hand on her shoulder. His cuffs were immaculate, and his cufflinks twice the size of those worn by the chairman of Lloyd's at my Rota. Compared with now, Lloyd's had been small beer.

"If the Democrats take the presidency, anything could happen," Saul conceded graciously. I had the feeling he was a Republican. Though with Americans, you can't always tell.

My least expected visitor was Max Carstairs, my accountant. Senior partner in a City firm, and passionate to retain his independence, he had made himself expert in the needs of small companies. He was tough with Revenue and Customs, but he never stepped across the fuzzy line that distinguished avoidance from evasion. He came so soon after New Year that I assumed, rather uncharitably, that he'd come to judge for himself how quickly he would have to wind up my estate, whilst Wormsley's successor circled vulture-like from afar.

In fact, he was skiing with family and a friend in La Clusaz. "White-out, today," he said in his calm voice, more suited to summarising facts than small talk. "So I thought I'd take a look." He explained that his friend was a liquidation specialist, currently unravelling the affairs of a collapsed hedge fund in Geneva. "He helped to wind up all the failed Lloyd's syndicates. Amazing the stuff he uncovered." Then he treated me to a monologue of slush funds and off-shore deposits, false accounting and plain theft, but it was nothing that hadn't done the rounds of every gathering of angry Names. Poor Max, he was doing his best, but his tone was too dull, his stories too stale. The last word I heard was Tonbridge, which ought to have roused me, but I was in such torpor that I was past caring. I didn't even remember his going.

Jake came too, with his wife and my grandson. Jake junior was now perfectly steady on his feet, and raced round the room, skilfully avoiding his parents' attempts to restrain him. By a miracle, he didn't interfere with any of my equipment either. Like Armand, he was impressed by the screen, but couldn't understand why it wasn't possible to change channels. I only wished I could oblige him by transforming my brain patterns into Bugs Bunny.

"Quite frankly, Dad, you're well out it," Jake informed me. "I've had two projects cancelled, and one suspended. It'll be part-time working or worse if things don't improve. At least Mum seems to have fallen on her feet." He tried to look pleased for her.

"We can manage," said Miriam bravely. "We can always let the basement." Then she bit her lip as if she'd said too much. I'd always found her a bundle of nerves, but this was more than her usual disquiet. Whether that was down to shock over my condition, Amy's departure from the granny flat or the threat to Jake's practice I could not tell. Perhaps it was all of them.

I woke as usual to the dawn chorus of diesel engines, as my neighbours set off for work. The comatose scenario was my new recurring dream, and it was so frequent that it soon ceased to disturb me. On the contrary, I was always impressed by its detail, and rather looked forward to how the events in my waking life found their way with perfect logic into my dream world.

The dream had begun as soon as I went to bed on New Year's Day. My shivering had started in earnest after Mallory had refused to talk any more about Ambrose. Then she'd insisted on driving me home, and refused to leave until I'd collapsed into bed with an extra blanket to sweat the fever off. In fact, she didn't leave at all.

When I woke the next morning, I was still weak and disorientated. So much so that when I heard a female voice singing in the next room, I thought it was one of the nurses out in the corridor. It was the aroma of fresh coffee that brought me back to reality, and when Mallory appeared a few moments later with two steaming mugs, I was surprised only that she was still here, and not that she wasn't a nurse. "I thought you could use some coffee," she said as she set one of the mugs down on my bedside table. "How are you feeling?"

I flexed my legs experimentally, then I managed to sit up. There was a dull ache in my head, and I felt utterly weak, but I was delighted to realise that I was not in hospital, and that my body essentially worked as I wanted it to. "I'm much better," I said, gratefully taking the mug from the table. "You didn't have to stay the night on my account."

"I was quite worried about you," she answered briskly, as though missing a night's sleep in her own bed on behalf of a semi-stranger was perfectly normal. "We're supposed to be meeting today anyway." Of course. We'd arranged no more than a week ago to meet January the second, which was indeed today. Making the arrangement seemed more like a lifetime ago, so much had happened since. As I recalled the events of the past two days, I couldn't help but shiver again, despite the warmth of the coffee. "Where do you keep your sweaters?" She was reaching for my chest of drawers as she spoke.

"Top drawer." I pushed off the duvet and swung my legs onto the floor. But when I tried to stand, I felt so dizzy that I could only sink down onto the mattress again. At least I wasn't as useless as I'd been in my dream. She was beside me in an instant, taking my mug from me and helping me to get the sweater over my head. Her attention, and the need to focus on the placement of my arms, steadied me so much that the dizziness and shivering disappeared almost as soon as the sweater's warmth enveloped me. Hunched on the side of the bed, I drank some more coffee, before putting the mug determinedly down on the bedside table, and pushing myself upright. Compared with my usual spring-footedness, it seemed a slow and ponderous process. But I ignored the offer of her steadying hand, and made it upright on my own.

"There," I said. "Now let's see if I can walk." Distracted by my dizziness, I'd forgotten yesterday's twisted ankle, and I had to bite my lip to stop myself from yelling out, as it protested at taking my weight again. But it made me forget about the fever and the headache, and I reached the door in an ungainly hop. Compared with normal, I felt like a useless invalid, but compared with my dream, I was in reasonable working order. "Don't worry," I said, "Twisted ankles and runners go together like punctures and cyclists. I should have iced it last night." I stretched out a hand. "If you'd support me to the fridge."

She did better than that, bundling me into my dressing gown, which she'd spotted on the back of the door, and then into the living room and onto my recliner. "I'll get the ice." Her lack of fussiness forestalled any protest from me. Instead, I stretched luxuriously in the recliner and prepared to be looked after. It hadn't happened for a long time.

"I usually put the ice in a plastic bag. They're under the sink." Then I watched as she extracted two trays of ice from the fridge. "I'm sorry to be a nuisance." In fact, I was enjoying watching the easy way in which she went about the tasks of loosening the cubes and dropping them into the bag, all without losing a single one onto the floor, a feat which had always been beyond me. She also brought a towel, to encase my foot, with the ice pressed snugly around the swelling.

"I hope that's not too painful," she said, as I winced at the cold.

"No, it's wonderful."

"You're a masochist."

"Not at all. Cold is a good pain, and it soon dies down."

She refilled the trays and put them back in the ice compartment. Then she fetched my mug, and poured me another coffee. "I don't know about you," she said, "But I mainline on the stuff."

We sipped in companionable silence. Unlike Amy, who was rarely silent or still for long, Mallory was the epitome of self-containment. She lifted her mug to her lips and drew in the liquid with minimalist precision; otherwise, her hands were still. Her eyes roamed quickly around the living room, absorbing its detail without intrusive peering. When she met my gaze again, she smiled. "Nice place you've got."

"You should have seen my previous apartment."

I was apologising for the clutter, the inevitable result of cramming too much of my old life into a far smaller space. Sidonie had had enough of her own stuff to need none of mine, so I'd sold as much as I could, but still kept more than I needed. Even the most ordinary things have sentimental value, and I had been less disciplined than I needed to have been. I didn't need a coffee table and a dining table, even if the latter folded, and the bookshelf took up far too much wall, so that I'd had to screw some of my pictures to the sloping ceiling, and cram the rest into my hall and bedroom. Another stack of them propped up the wardrobe. Not that I was any kind of connoisseur, but Amy and I had been in the habit of picking up things that took our fancy in antique markets, mostly watercolours by unknown artists of places we had visited: remote farms, stark valleys, and misty lakes, with here and there a *château*, a town square, or a village carnival. It was all a far cry from the Spartan emptiness of Mallory's boathouse.

71

I told her about the swap with Sidonie, and much of what had led up to it. That is, I told her nothing about sharing my bed with Sidonie, something about Amy – how we had fallen rapidly in love and more insidiously out of it – and a lot about my business: how I had built it from nothing to flourishing, only to lose it all to Lloyd's.

"A business is a separate entity. How could Lloyd's take it?"

"I had to sell. If I'd worked on, they'd have had my earnings."

"Didn't Amy have shares?"

I hesitated. This had always been a sore subject. "I put half my shares in Amy's name as I was joining Lloyd's, then I transferred the rest when the losses started mounting. They argued these were an improper attempt to distance myself from my assets."

"*Both*?" She frowned. "The second perhaps; surely not the first?"

"They got me on a technicality. I signed up early September, but the share transfers weren't confirmed until mid-September. So even though I didn't start underwriting until the following January, I was 'at risk' when the transfers happened." I shrugged, as my years in France had taught me. "Amy's never let me forget how stupid I was."

Mallory, in contrast, was sympathetic. "Hadn't your accountant heard of Gibraltar trusts?"

"What's special about Gibraltar?" I asked, grateful how she'd shifted the blame onto Max Carstairs, though I doubted Amy would have accepted his ignorance as an excuse for me.

"Trusts registered there are hard to break. If your accountant was prepared to let you loose in Lloyd's, he ought to have known."

"I'm sure Lloyd's would have cracked them."

"Not necessarily. Who was their chief debt collector? He died recently." I told her Wormsley, surprised that she would know him. "Of course! His name was on the tip of my tongue. Now there was a realist. Let him have something, and he backed off Gibraltar." The idea of Wormsley backing away from hidden funds seemed preposterous, and my scepticism must have showed. "You're forgetting Ghost Trader." She smiled so knowingly she almost winked. "I had my ups and downs with Wormsley, but I learned how to get round him."

Of course! If all her clients had been Names, it was more than likely that she'd had to fight Wormsley for the money they'd been attempting to invest with her. I would have loved to see his bullying founder against her steely charm. I also determined to challenge Max Carstairs on the subject of Gibraltar trusts. I could forgive him for being ignorant of an obscure procedure, but if he'd known about it all along, he had some serious explaining to do.

As I ruminated, she consulted her watch. "If you don't mind, I've been in the same clothes since yesterday "I'd like to slip home for a shower and a change." She threw me a sidelong glance, as she rose to her feet. "I could pick up some brunch... that's if you're up to it."

The ice, the coffee and the company of this reserved but intriguing woman had all but banished the fever, and I was as delighted with her suggestion as I'd been disappointed by her desire to go. "Don't get up," she urged, as I extricated my foot from the towel and the bag of ice. But I was determined not to seem an invalid a moment longer, and I led her firmly, if gingerly, to the front door. "I'll be an hour at most. In the meantime you can read your paper." She gathered up the copy of *Le Monde* that was lying on my doormat. I explained that Armand, Sidonie and I had an agreement that whichever of us made it to the newsagent first collected the other's paper. She smiled wistfully. "What good neighbours you have."

The fatal fall into Grand Bornand had not made the front page, but there was a small item in the financial section: "Tragic skiing accident not to delay London flotation". A spokesman for Linberger & Cie assured readers that the tragic death of his chairman, Jean-Michel Linberger, on New Year's Eve would not delay the company's London flotation by so much as a day. I skipped to the end of the piece, where interested readers were referred to page 6 of the main paper.

Here, his distraught widow accepted that her husband had fallen off the ridge as the result of a heart attack, and apologised for claiming in her agitation and confusion that he had been pushed. Far from deliberately pushing her husband, the skier in black had swerved to avoid him, as he'd staggered under the first onslaught of his heart attack. Unnerved, the skier had sworn and raced ahead. The piste, according to two witnesses, had been full of skiers in front of *les Linberger*. Seeing nothing of what was unfolding behind them, few had stopped. Neither witness remembered a skier in black, though both described Madame as making a desperate lunge to save her husband. "If she'd caught him, they'd both have been over."

At first I couldn't believe it. *La comtesse* had certainly been distraught, but her description had been precise and lucid. But as I reread the article, I came round to it. Extreme shock had convinced the poor woman that her husband could only have been taken from her by another's hand. In the horror of the moment, she had turned the skier in black's proximity into intent, and her disapproval of his appearance had turned him from oddball into murderer.

All I had achieved was the reinforcement of her delusion, if only temporarily. So much for IBNR, and so much for murder. Despite my fears, it seemed it really had been L'Esprit who'd called Mallory, not Ambrose disguising his voice. Being up to his neck in powder had been L'Esprit's hyperbole not Ambrose's sick humour. The skier in black had not been Ambrose, and nor had the man I'd seen yesterday.

My own delusions made Madame Linberger's all the easier to accept, as hers helped to justify mine. Whatever had been shouted at the fatal moment had not been IBNR. I sank into the recliner as my stunned disbelief transfigured into elation. My fever fled.

As good as her word, Mallory was back in 58 minutes. If I was surprised, it was because Amy had been a poor timekeeper, and proud of it. Mallory, it seemed, was like me, treating time as a valuable commodity. She now wore the same cords and donkey jacket in which I had first seen her, clothes chosen more for their comfort than their *éclat*, though they suited her perfectly, especially with her hair loose. She looked happy and relaxed and I pushed the paper aside, determined that the subject of Ambrose would not spoil a second meal.

She had bought a spit-roasted chicken, an array of local cheeses, and a *tarte aux myrtilles*, together with two half bottles. "A *Riesling* and a *Gewürztraminer*. I hope you don't object."

"Why would I object?" I asked, amused at her defensiveness.

She shrugged. "The French can be so parochial. Take my landlord. He knows his wine, but he won't touch any from Alsace."

I laughed. "Is that the English part of you speaking?"

"Half Anglo-Saxon, and the other half is almost German."

"You should meet my young friend Andréa, then. He wants all of *Savoie* to be independent of France."

As we were chattering, she laid out the food, and I laid the table. I was now recovered enough to feel hungry, and we soon fell to eating, a task we both took seriously enough not to exchange more than pleasantries on the excellence of what we were consuming.

"Is there no trading today?" I asked as we were finishing the tart.

"Europe's still on holiday, and Wall Street's counting its bonuses." She smiled. "You're not keeping me from anything important."

"You were going to tell me about Ghost Trader."

"Was I?" Her face tightened, her expression became guarded.

"I thought you'd accepted I'm not a snooping regulator," I said teasingly, yet surprised by a reticence that bordered on hostility.

"You ask questions like one." She tried to smile, but the defensiveness had not gone.

"I'm a busted Name, remember. I only wish I'd met you before Wormsley got his hands on my assets."

"Ghost Trader's a club," she explained, her voice softening. "I couldn't just sign you up; you'd have to be proposed and seconded. Names never approached me out of the blue."

"It sounds more like the Masons."

She bristled, then laughed. "I suppose it is, a bit." She paused, considering her next statement. I was already learning that she rarely spoke unthinkingly. How unlike Amy, who couldn't even conceal her unfaithfulness. "And just like the Masons, it's all in a good cause."

"I'm not sure how to take that." According to your prejudice, the Masons were either a shadowy self-help organisation for members only or a generous charity for good causes.

"If you think I'd have helped you to hide all your wealth from Lloyd's, forget it. I always encouraged Names to co-operate. Give some to keep some. I'd have told you the same."

"And what would you have said to Wormsley?"

"What I always told him. Whatever Names brought to me was their business, and I had no intention of divulging anything without their permission. Then I'd tell him that I always encouraged them to co-operate, because Lloyd's had a legal obligation to settle all legitimate insurance claims, and Names' quarrels with their syndicates did not and never could invalidate the legitimacy of those claims." She reeled it off pat like a much rehearsed speech.

As I tried to grasp the import of what she was telling me, I took a reflective sip of *Gewürztraminer*. Its subtle intertwining of spiciness with fruitiness seemed to match the convolutions of her diplomacy. "Let me get this straight. You were encouraging Names to set up Gibraltar trusts, but to give Wormsley a few crumbs to keep him happy, whilst you were telling Wormsley you were persuading Names to pay whatever they legitimately owed. Did he buy it?"

Once again her eyelids came down like protective veils. "Like I told you, he was a realist." Then she raised her glass, which distorted her smile. "What, may I ask, did you tell him?"

"I was a lot less tactful." I laughed awkwardly. "I told him Lloyd's was a mixture of thieves, liars and incompetents, any of which invalidated any contract I'd entered into." In the cold light of January 2nd 2008, my words of over 10 years ago sounded as crass as old anger always did. "I see that I should have been more devious."

"I think the word is diplomatic." She said resentfully.

"Come on, I'm on your side. I only wish you'd advertised yourself."

75

"The last thing Ghost Trader needed was too much publicity."

"The only Name I knew well was Ambrose," I sighed, "and I was the last person he was going to tell. As for action groups, I thought most of them were a waste of time." After I'd punched Wormsley on the nose, I became *persona non grata* at action group meetings, especially Wu. Though Names had taken vicarious pleasure in the incident, most soon decided that I'd made Wormsley meaner, that I was a trouble-maker whom action groups could do without. The charge had stung, and I'd long ago wished the incident had never occurred. But I didn't yet know her well enough for confession.

At the mention of Ambrose, she paled. "These things are always messy." Her voice sank almost to a whisper, as though she were talking to herself. "A lot of Names were misled... but tell that to hurricane victims without a roof over their heads... or thirsty citizens whose reservoirs have been polluted... or the victims of asbestosis. While Names were suing Lloyd's, they were suffering and dying."

We both fell silent, but this time there was no sense of easy companionship. She had succeeded in making me feel guilty for trying to protect my assets, as well as stupid for not making a better job of it. Worse, she had inadvertently reminded me that breaking Wormsley's nose had made other Names' struggles with him all the harder. As for her, I could only guess her thoughts: probably that I was a heedless fool, perhaps that she'd been too Machiavellian in protecting Names whilst seeming to support Wormsley's aims. How else was I to understand her plea for the plight of disaster victims, if not as an admission that she too had worked to cheat them? It was a disturbing thought and I was far from ready to go there.

"Amy was a victim, too," I said, in an attempt to break our gloomy introspection. "She didn't want me to join, but she didn't have any evidence against. Just her instinct. I thought I'd done my homework, so I didn't listen. If I had, she'd still be a wealthy woman."

"A man who cares for his ex! I should be so lucky."

"You were married?" Naively, I'd seen her only as Rex's lover.

"Like your Amy, I'm afraid, I was the unfaithful one."

"You mean with Rex?" I asked tentatively, unsure how she'd react.

"I'd have married him, too..." Her voice faltered.

At least Amy had never loved Ambrose. "How did you meet?" I asked gently. If she were prepared to speak about Rex, that might mean she wanted to tell me more. Then I'd understand her better.

"I was his junior underwriter." She said it reluctantly, as well she might, having listened to my diatribes against Lloyd's. "So which am I: a thief, a liar, or just plain incompetent?"

I was too taken aback to say anything. I saw too late that I ought to have guessed. What better way to fall in love with Rex Tonbridge than to work for him? Yet I couldn't simply dismiss her as one of the enemy. No typical insider would have set up Ghost Trader.

She drummed the table with her fingers, one of her few nervous habits. "If it makes you feel better, I did very little underwriting. My real job was investment. Rex used to leave that to the syndicate's bank, but they were useless at everything except charging high fees." She managed a brittle laugh. "I made more investing the premiums than Rex with the underwriting. He said I kept him afloat." Her lip quavered. "Until he was beyond any kind of rescue."

"Then you started Ghost Trader?" I asked, softened by her distress.

She nodded. "It was the least I could do for our Names."

"It can't have been easy persuading them to trust you."

"I went to the action group meetings," she explained carefully. "Rex had told them about my investment role, so they knew I had the experience. I said litigation was up to them, but I doubted Rex's estate would have much for them. I offered to invest whatever they had left." She hesitated again. "As well as some money to start them off."

"You offered them money! That must have been a first for the world of finance." I could hardly contain my delight. "How did they react?"

She shrugged as if it were nothing. "They were suspicious, naturally. But I was lucky to get early support from L'Esprit and another French Name, Le Baigneur. That broke the ice. They also persuaded me to offer membership to all losing Names, not just Rex's."

"How many members are there?"

She thought before answering. "About 2,000."

"How does it work?" I'd asked once and been rebuffed, but there was no harm in a re-try. This time she relented a little.

"Technically, it's a hedge fund, but the ethos is very different. I do the trading, but the members have the power of veto. I have to get their agreement to large or unusual trades. They can inspect Ghost Trader activity on-line whenever they like, and there's an on-line forum where they make their pleasure or displeasure known. It's very active, believe me. Think investment co-operative, more than typical hedge fund."

"A tough brief!" Herding cats would have been easier than keeping sweet a bunch of loss-hardened ex-Names with the power of veto.

"It is. But the members have stuck with me." Again that shuttered look. "All but one. There's always one, I suppose. And before you ask, I don't want to talk about him."

I'd have been delighted to have kept all members bar one loyal. But there was no point in pursuing the issue. "Otherwise you've been successful," I suggested soothingly.

"I like to think so," she assented, but with a note of caution.

Was she being modest, or was she fearful of weathering the credit crunch? I doubted it was worth pressing her. "Dare I ask what the fund's worth?" I enquired instead.

Even this failed to elicit a precise answer. "Let's say we're small by hedge fund standards, but very good for a bunch of near-bankrupts, as nearly all of them were." She allowed herself a brief note of pride. "I can assure you they aren't bankrupts now."

"I'm amazed you took it on." I resisted reminding her of the truism that leopards never changed their spots. Despite discovering that she had been part of the organisation that ruined me, I preferred to harbour another truism, in the hope that Mallory was the exception that proved the rule about the rapaciousness of the financial world.

"It was the least I could do for Rex."

That her desire had been to atone for her lover was touching. A passionate human being is always more attractive than a cold-hearted saint. A saint would not have encouraged Names to hide their assets from Wormsley, whilst pretending to him that she was doing the opposite. Nor would a saint be so guarded. But a passionate and determined human being could lie and cheat to any extent that suited them. I was hooked, but only, I told myself, up to a point.

Chapter Eight : Off the Record

"Poor Clem," said Céline, as she smoothed the sheet under my arm. "You did yourself no favours trying to save that woman. I've just seen her daughter. So charming , and she speaks almost as well as you." She meant French. Céline was no expert on English. "Her mother's in a coma, the same as you. But she thanks you all the same. But for you, her mother would be dead. She's convinced her mother will recover when she's ready. It's an absolute article of faith." She patted my forearm encouragingly. "Of course, we feel the same about you. Even my husband, and you know what pessimists medical men are."

I woke to the sound of Armand's *Espace*, he being the first to leave. Even after several weeks of waking from the comatose dream, it was a relief to find that I could move again. Yet, as I went to wash, I had an unnerving feeling that *this* was the dream: that getting out of bed and taking a shower were but wistful memories of my active past.

The dream-world was life as it might have been if Mallory and I had really been the accident victims. Within it, Céline had just praised Mallory's daughter, for whose existence in the waking world I had no evidence. I'd seen Mallory once since the 2nd, when we'd dined in one of Veyrier's unpretentious restaurants, but she'd never mentioned a daughter. Not that I'd said much about Jake. What was there to say with relations so distant? But I had acknowledged his existence.

I'd also done more of the talking, so that Mallory now knew far more about me than I about her, despite her half-serious accusations that I was a regulator or a policeman. Whereas I had no objection to talking about myself, Mallory often mistook my curiosity for intrusion. Not that I'd expected her to bare her soul. As always, I'd been happier to talk about my business than my personal life, but compared with her I was as open as a well-thumbed guide book. Good company as she was, she was expert at deflecting questions that pushed too far, especially when I probed her choice of the boathouse.

"There's something I don't understand about you," I'd begun.

"Only one? That's a relief."

This was deflection by teasing, but I wasn't to be deflected.

"You're a hedge fund manager," I pointed out teasingly."Where's the office in Mayfair, the champagne lifestyle?"

"Sorry to disappoint you." Her smile became a little forced.

"I enjoyed success," I fired back. "And I resented losing it."

"You deserved to enjoy it." Her face softened. "I'm sorry Lloyd's screwed it up for you."

"You're a success now," I said. "Don't you deserve to enjoy it?"

"I thought I was successful then. As for now, who knows?"

"Not if you're careful, surely? Things might be tight for a bit…"

"I hope you're right." Her tone anything but hopeful.

"I'm no expert, but aren't there ways to profit from downturns?"

"Sometimes." Then she turned the conversation to blander topics.

By now I'd told her how to operate a business such as mine, but I still knew next to nothing about hers. The collapse of the syndicate and the resulting death of her lover must have scarred her so deeply that she preferred plain to high living. Yet it seemed incredible that she'd lived in the boathouse since Rex's death. Indeed, I remembered that one of her curt and forestalling answers had been that she hadn't lived there long. She'd also told me that she'd lived all over the place, though I'd thought at the time she was referring to her childhood.

These reflections took me through my coffee, and the preparations for my run, my first attempt since I'd twisted my ankle. Regular icing had done the trick, and it was now back to its normal size, and I was looking forward to being active again. I took the Route des Vignes, since it offered the smoothest surface. Apart from the odd twinge at the beginning, the ankle was fine, and by the time I crested the incline before the wood, I was moving confidently.

Last time this way, I'd still been in shock over the accident, and terrified that Mallory would die before I reached the hospital. Even now I half expected to find Ambrose barring my way once more. But the road was deserted, and the parking bay beyond the wood was empty of cars. But I knew she'd gone. When I'd asked, as we left the restaurant, when we'd meet again, she'd been unsure. "I'm all over the place for weeks." I must have looked disappointed, because her parting embrace had been warm. "Business before pleasure, I'm afraid."

All over the place. It summed up the little she'd told me. The anonymity of her personal life matched the secrecy of Ghost Trader, and I couldn't help wondering whether she were hiding from more than the past. And what of her daughter? If indeed she had one. Not that a child was unlikely, given she'd been married. Probably Mallory emanated subtle vibes that an unhappy father could tune into, and these had been crystallised by the Céline of my dreams.

Sure now the daughter must exist, I wondered if she had inherited the same defensive secrecy as her mother, and whether she offset it with the same balancing of humour with seriousness, anger with charm. But of course she might take more after her father, whoever he was. All I knew about Mallory's husband was that she had been unfaithful to him. Was he even the father, or had Rex Tonbridge not only cuckolded him but sired his wife's child? "I'd have married him, too." I'd taken that as a sad affirmation of love, but perhaps she meant that she needed marriage to the true father for the sake of her baby.

Telling myself that this was idle speculation, I concentrated for the return half on running, pushing myself as punishment for entertaining unfounded thoughts. The few facts that I had suggested a conscientious woman who wanted to do her best for her members; everything else was supposition, based on no more than her reticence to talk about herself. Such reticence was frustrating to a man who wished to know her better, but it was hardly a crime.

I was stepping into the shower, when the phone rang. Instead of cursing its timing, I ran for it, my wet feet slithering dangerously over the tiles. But it wasn't Mallory. My heart had jumped to conclusions well ahead of my brain. To bring me totally down to earth, the caller wasn't even Amy or Jake: it was Max Carstairs, my accountant.

"Just back from skiing," he said. Nowadays I was of little profit to him, but there were still annual returns from Lloyd's, and he provided the service for a nominal fee, for which he usually forgot to invoice me. He had taken my catastrophic losses almost as hard as I had myself. Yet he was only just returning my call of two weeks ago.

"Why didn't you set me up in a Gibraltar trust? Even Wormsley couldn't break them." There was a resentful silence.

"I only know two people who had one," he said at last. "Both went to jail. One for insider trading, the other for money laundering."

Ignorance I could have forgiven, but fastidiousness was absurd, given what had been at stake. "I don't care if they were crooks. So long as the trusts were unbreakable."

"Put it this way," he said carefully. "If the Revenue had had so much as a hint you were doing one of those, they'd have been all over your accounts from the year dot."

"So what? There was nothing wrong with my accounts."

"You wouldn't have wanted the hassle." He sounded flustered.

"Anything would have been better than Wormsley."

"They'd have been all over me, too. And all my other clients."

"Oh, fine! I could go bust, provided you got a quiet life." This was unfair, but I didn't want to hear anything that questioned Mallory's methods. Having no counter evidence, my only resort was anger.

"All I know is, there are plenty of Names who used Gibraltar trusts, and they're a lot better off than me," I added self-righteously.

"How come you know this, all of a sudden?" he retorted acidly.

"I've just met the person who helped them."

"In France you mean?" He made it sound as though everything was now explained; that these Names had obviously been led astray by a devious foreigner or a renegade ex-pat.

"She still looks after them," I said. "Doing all their investing."

"And what's *her* background?" he asked with heavy emphasis. "Law, finance, money-laundering, what?"

I hesitated, certain that Mallory would not want me to talk about Ghost Trader, yet determined that Max should understand her good intentions. "She used to work for one of the syndicates. She felt she owed something to ruined Names. Unlike the rest of Lloyd's."

"I see." He made it clear he saw nothing. "Which syndicate?"

"You don't need to know."

"Suit yourself." I could almost hear his brain whirring as he tried to guess Mallory's identity from the little I'd given away. "But if you want my advice, just be careful."

I swallowed an angry retort. He was still my accountant, after all, and he saw it as his job to protect me. The little I had told him, and the more I had refused to divulge, had over-excited his interest, and I felt I must divert him towards safer topics. So I asked after his business, which was doing as well as could be expected, and after his family, who appeared to be faring similarly. Then it was his turn to ask after Jake, and mine to provide a suitably anodyne reply. "Do you hear much from Amy these days?" he asked finally.

"She's met this American financial advisor Saul," I said, grateful for the opportunity to keep him away from Mallory. Then I told him about Northern Rock. "He's persuaded her to put her savings into some fund run by Bernie Madoff. She's delighted, and I hope he's right."

"Didn't he chair the NASDAQ? A smart cookie from all I've heard," he observed. I told him the little I knew about the fund. "Steady 10% return? Sounds like a Swiss private bank. Let's hope he's as careful." Finally, I told him about Split Strike Conversion. "Now you've lost me. Would you like me to ask around?" I told him I'd be grateful. "I could check out your mystery woman at the same time."

"No," I said firmly. "My interest is entirely non-financial."

"All the more reason to be careful, then," he said knowingly.

With that parting shot, he promised to get back to me as soon as he had news of Madoff. I flounced into the shower, determined to shut my mind to his innuendos. It was impossible. All I could do was tell myself over and over that if Mallory's methods did not meet with Max's approval that was his fault for being a financial prude.

I also told myself that her need for anonymity must have grown out of a natural desire – on Rex's part also – to conduct their affair discreetly; that it would have been reinforced by the collapse of the syndicate and the tragedy of his suicide. By the time she was helping to set up Gibraltar trusts, she must have been as habituated to secrecy as a spy. But the analogy with espionage was not a comfortable one. The end justifying the means was always a questionable philosophy.

It wasn't as if I were a stranger to subterfuge. As far as Max and Lloyd's were concerned, I still lived in my old apartment. Even Wormsley had drawn the line at throwing me onto the streets to pay my debts, though he'd insisted I dispose of my London property in return for being allowed to live in my French one. But if he'd had wind of further downshifting, he would have taken most of that profit, too. Far from feeling guilty, I still gloated over cheating him. Who then was I to criticise Mallory? As for Gibraltar trusts, they seemed guilty only by association with their users, not because of any intrinsic illegality.

The mechanics of my swap had been every bit as devious in its intent. With the help of Armand, Sidonie and I had formed a company to which we had transferred our apartments. From then on, which we chose to live in was our affair. Nothing we did offended French law: as to whether Lloyd's would have worn it, we chose not to test.

Yet the next two days were uncomfortable. There was no Mallory to cheer me; no hint of her presence to offset the gloomy suspicions that Max had sown. I hadn't even been able to speak to her. She never answered her mobile, and I declined to leave a message. My only consolation was running, which I did with renewed savagery.

I was lacing up my running shoes the third day, when Max called again. "I've got the gen on Madoff." His manner was calm as usual, so it was impossible to tell whether his news was good or bad. I held my breath. "His fund's huge, around $60 billion, and he relies on feeder funds for business. Saul runs a large one out of New Jersey. Most of his clients are state charities and pension funds. As for Split Strike Conversion, everybody thinks it must be salesman jargon."

"It must mean something," I protested, though his first words had almost reassured me. The fund's sheer size had to be impressive.

"In my opinion, it's meant to make hedging sound more impressive than it is. Some traders do most of their dealing in options rather than shares, plenty do a bit of both. Split Strike Conversion sounds to me like a quick way of summarising different activities. Don't forget that Americans are big on jargon. It passes for explanation."

"That's excellent news," I said. "Thanks for all the effort."

"I know you asked me not to, but I also did a bit of ferreting on Lloyd's," he continued rapidly, to prevent interruption. "There's only one lady who fits your description." My heart skipped several beats. "She was junior underwriter to Rex Tonbridge, but her real job was investing the premiums. It seems she had quite a reputation…"

"If you mean she was his mistress, she told me that herself."

"That too," he agreed. "I meant she had a reputation as a smart operator. Not that anyone seems to have known her very well. She played her cards very close to her chest." I demanded to know what point he was making. "Apparently the liquidators raised questions. Nothing could be proved, but I thought you ought to know."

"If it's idle gossip, I don't want to know." As much as anything I was infuriated by his presumption that I was in love with her.

"All the more reason why you should hear it from the horse's mouth. The liquidator in question is an old friend of mine, and right now he's just up the road from you. He's winding up a hedge fund in Geneva, and I know he'd be delighted to talk to you."

"You mean you've spoken to him already?"

"The fact is he's had a bellyful of buttoned-up Swiss."

"Can't you give me the gist?" My mind was already in ferment.

"Sorry, old man, you need to hear it from George himself."

"Not that I'm guaranteeing I'll ring him," I said, as I wrote down name and number. It seemed so underhand. Surely I knew Mallory well enough to give her the benefit of the doubt? It would anyway be more honest to challenge her directly. But even that would create distrust between us: the last thing I wanted. Despite being the dry figures man, Max was right to conclude that I was falling in love with her. I'd been alone for too long, and I ached for a loving and earth-shattering relationship. I wanted to matter to someone as I had once mattered to Amy, just as I wanted somebody to care about in return.

By now I was panting up the steep road to Bluffy. By the time I reached the top I'd made up my mind. Whether I called George Wiseman or not, Mallory was too observant not to spot immediately that something was wrong. Better to face her fury forearmed. Besides, there was always the chance that there would be nothing to worry about. Hadn't Max told me that nothing had been proved?

Liquidations were always messy affairs, and no business was scandal-free, especially a failed one. If there had been anything dodgy about the Tonbridge syndicate, over and above the negligence of its underwriting, that must have been down to Rex himself. He was the one who had committed suicide; leaving Mallory to pick up the pieces. But at least I would know the worst, and could act accordingly.

So I called George Wiseman that evening. He seemed as delighted to hear from me as Max had predicted, and offered to meet me in Annecy the very next morning. "I haven't seen the old place for years," he explained. "There's no point in my dragging you to Geneva, when I can't wait to get shot of the place, if only for a day. I'll come by train, so I can do a bit of work en route. Besides, I love trains."

He sounded boyish in his enthusiasm, and when we met at the station next morning, I found his appearance just as youthful. His face was scarcely lined, his hair was still dark, if a little receding, and he walked with a juvenile bounce. He wore a bright red scarf, wound rakishly around his neck, and his cord blouson was covered in pockets.

"Perhaps we could walk," he said, as we shook hands. "I hate sitting around." It was a bleak wintry day, with a strong hint of snow, and the few people on the streets huddled into their coats without dawdling, but this did not appear to deter George. He was shorter than me, and as he surged ahead, he seemed like an eager terrier straining at the leash. I imagined him nosing with the same tireless enthusiasm into the dark and murky corners of the collapsed enterprises that it was his job to investigate. I had arrived at the station prepared to dislike him, but it was impossible. No doubt his charm helped him in his job.

We were soon in the old town. The architecture here was more Italian than French, its narrow streets and canals threading like canyons between tall buildings. Some canals were flanked by pavements, others flowed, Venetian-style, directly between the buildings, though the steep alpine roofs and the simpler lines were a long way from the flamboyant grandeur of Venice. The water itself ran fast and clear from the lake with none of Venice's stink and scum.

As we approached the River Thiou, the central waterway of the old town, George spotted a large *traiteur*, its sumptuous display of gastronomic delights laid out under heavy stone arches. "This is where we buy lunch." His eyes alight, he plunged inside and was soon ordering a mouth-watering array of composed salads, small quiches and *pâtés en croûte*, all of which he insisted on paying for. "I've a generous subsistence allowance," he explained, as he added a half bottle of wine and a mineral water to his order. "A shame not to use of it."

We crossed the river where it was split by the fortified prow of the old prison. Ducks and swans clustered where the lake water poured over the sluice gate that controlled its flow. In summer, the bridge was festooned with geraniums, but now the boxes were bare. There were warm restaurants, snug cafés and heated bars in every direction, but George wanted nothing but to march up the steep incline to the ramparts of the castle. I thought I was fit, but I struggled to match his eager pace, which was not at all diminished by the lunch bags which he refused to let me carry. It was only at the top that he was prepared to lean against the old walls and gaze down upon the jumble of courtyards and balconies our elevation now revealed.

These were the scruffier and more intimate backs of the buildings that fronted the river, and I wondered if it was the sense of peering into what was normally hidden that attracted George enough to stop. Or else it was the width of the rampart, which served as a table for our food, since he also seemed to prefer standing to eat than sitting.

From one of his many jacket pockets, he produced a Swiss army knife, which bulged with gadgets, including a corkscrew. From another he extracted two silver tots, into which he poured first a libation of mineral water, and then, once we'd slaked our thirst, the wine. Finally, from a third pocket, came what I thought at first was a tobacco pouch, but was in fact the wrapping for a set of cutlery. "You'll have to forgive me, but I long ago learned that bankrupt firms never feed you, and I didn't like to disappear in the middle of a job in case somebody made off with the files. This way, I eat well, and I never lose time."

He certainly lost very little eating his fill, and he wasted none on talking until we had finished, and the remains of our repast had been deposited in one of the bins. Then, as we strode down the far side of the hill to the lake shore, he finally broached the purpose of his visit. "Max tells me you want the lowdown on Tonbridge." His eyes twinkled as he spoke. "Everything I say is strictly off the record, of course. Though I know you're not a journalist."

"My interest is entirely personal."

He nodded. "Max explained about Ms Stellenbourg." The twinkle strengthened. "Which is lucky for you, as Rex was dead before I got involved. Quite a character by all accounts. All his staff were in awe of him. He was their main topic of conversation. The fulcrum of their working lives. They couldn't believe what had happened. So different from most of the companies I deal with. Usually the staff can't wait to put the boot in. Mind you, no mistake he was the boss. If you made a cock-up, he let you know it in no uncertain fashion. But he always gave you a second chance, apparently, and he never bore a grudge.

"As for her, they said she was a dark horse. Polite, but you never knew what she was thinking. The astute ones said she was the brains. He was the inspiration, but he could never have managed without her. That's what they said. Everybody knew they were lovers. Staff always know things like that. But they were very discreet. Especially her, and she never made out she was more than the junior underwriter.

"In fact, she hardly underwrote at all, which was a shame. Like most underwriters then, Rex was basically a gambler. An intelligent one, but too ready to believe in his own infallibility. She was different. He gambled with risk, she controlled it.

"Syndicates were supposed to invest cautiously, and she never forgot that. She never took an unnecessary risk, yet she pulled off some amazing trades. Quick ins and outs, so that if anyone asked, she could always point to a liquid position. To the amateur, what she did was black magic, but she could unravel a balance sheet better than anyone I've ever met, and her research was meticulous.

"There were detractors, of course. There always are. Because her interpretation of risk-free investment was imaginative, to say the least, there were those who said it was her investing that must have broken the syndicate. But it wasn't, and she knew it. So did I, once I'd gone through the paperwork, and she'd talked me through her trades. Her returns were consistently good right from the start, and they got better as she became more experienced."

I listened to all this without interrupting him. By the time he'd finished, we'd walked down past the site of the old hospital and crossed the road to the yachting marina. The wind, which had been minimal under the shelter of the castle, was brisk down at lake level, and the surface was broken by steep, choppy waves, and almost empty of boats. After this paean of praise, I was starting to wonder what Max was on about. "Is that it?" I asked hopefully.

"Not quite." He fell silent, as he gathered his thoughts. We were walking between the steamer quay and the town hall before he started speaking again. "You must understand, I couldn't prove anything." He smiled ruefully. "She was too good for me." I stiffened, but I could hardly back out now. "Companies don't collapse neatly at year end. When I go in I have to look at the day book, the invoices and the orders – and usually they're a mess. Whether that's true of all companies, I wouldn't know. I only get to see the failures. Anyway, the Tonbridge books were not just in good order, they were impeccable. The staff said it was her doing: before she joined things were rather chaotic."

"What's wrong with that? It made your job easier."

"Too easy," he asserted, with a sad smile. "On the rare occasions I find apple-pie order, it's to cover something nasty."

"I thought you said you didn't find anything?"

"The other orange flag was the auditors. She had them eating out of her hand. In a way she had to, so they didn't make waves over her investments, but it went further than that. I don't say firms must hate their auditors, but there needs to be some tension, otherwise they aren't doing their job. Here there was none. Quite the reverse."

We'd passed under the graceful cedars of the park behind the town hall, and had reached the apex of the *Pont des Amants*, which crosses the canal that separates the gardens from the grassy lake-shore esplanade where the citizens promenade, and where many of the town's open-air events are staged. Today it was deserted, and the lustrous green of the grass had faded to a dull khaki. George leant on the rail of the bridge, and I had no choice but to join him, though my feelings were the opposite of loving. "Tell me what you found."

"Two things. A reinsurance policy taken out each year with a Geneva-based reinsurer, and a risk-assessment report bought each year from a firm of risk consultants in Lausanne."

"So? Syndicates are supposed to reinsure – and consult risk assessors, for all I know."

"I read the reports. You could have written one in an afternoon; all the tables were standard stuff you'd find in a library. It's an old trick. You log it in the books at £100,000, when it cost you £10,000."

Are you saying the invoices for £100,000 were fakes?"

"Nothing so crude. The invoices were real, and I spoke to the company that sent them. They were cagey, but politeness pays off in the end." Despite myself, I had to smile, as I pictured George's enthusiastic charm wearing down even the most stonewalling of Swiss. "They admitted occasional subcontracting to an outfit in Mulhouse – *Risque Alsacien* – though they wouldn't confirm or deny whether they'd subcontracted the Tonbridge reports."

"*Alsacien?*" The exclamation was out before I could stop it.

"Ah, so you know Ms Stellenbourg's from Alsace? But I'll warrant you don't know she was the founding partner of *Risque Alsacien*." He chuckled appreciatively. "You have to hand it to her. There's no law against hiring risk analysts, or in their sub-contracting the job, and there's no law against overcharging for sub-standard work. Tonbridge's auditors ought to have had something to say, but they never looked beyond the thickness of the reports."

I had to admit it didn't sound good. "What about the reinsurance?"

"Similar story. Gen-Va Re is part of the Credit & Insurance Group of Geneva & Vaud. Ms Stellenbourg began her career there on the sales side. When she joined the Tonbridge syndicate, it was only natural to steer a bit of reinsurance business the way of her old employer."

"It sounds perfectly legit to me. Where's the catch?"

"The wording of the policies was strange. There were no realistic circumstances under which they would have to pay out. For starters, the excess threshold was set way too high. Only the LMX losses came close to triggering them, but the policy wording specifically excluded claims on top of multiple reinsurance triggers."

"Are you sure it wasn't a case of Gen-Va Re being too clever for them?" I asked. "Lloyd's Names would have killed to be underwriting that kind of policy." As far as we'd been concerned Lloyd's had caved in far too readily to corporate claimants and their lawyers.

George pointed across the esplanade. "Fancy a boat trip ?"

He set off before I could protest, one end of his red scarf streaming out behind him. In spring and summer, the pontoons along the esplanade were jammed with pedalos and motor boats for hire, but it was unusual to find any of them open in February. But George was right. One hardy boatman was open for business, and in no time we were in possession of a sleek wooden launch.

"Haven't done this sort of thing for years." George's face glowed with healthy pleasure as he pointed our boat into the middle of the lake. The wind had dropped considerably, and the waves had lost their white caps, but our progress was far from smooth. Cold air whipped my face, and I pulled an old ski hat out of my overcoat pocket.

"In answer to your question," George shouted, above the rumble of the engine and the slap of the waves, "Rex Tonbridge was far too experienced an underwriter to fall for any tricks of that kind. There's no doubt in my mind that the wording was quite deliberate."

"So how did he get the money back from Gen-Va Re?"

"They took their commission, then they paid the rest to *Risque Alsacien* for consultancy work. Copy-book money laundering." He sounded almost admiring of the process.

"I can't believe Gen-Va Re volunteered this information."

"No," he agreed. "I was lucky there. I found an invoice at the bottom of Rex Tonbridge's desk. On *Risque Alsacien* notepaper, and addressed to Gen-Va Re. I think it was a draft. There were notes on it, and crossings out. Somehow it missed the shredder.

"Not that I could use it," he added sadly. "I couldn't even link it to the reinsurance. The most clueless lawyer would have had it thrown out as evidence. There's nothing illegal in a junior freelancing, or in her consulting her boss about the best wording for the invoice."

"You must have asked her, though."

He slowed down and we drifted past a reedy bird sanctuary on the western bank. A few ducks slipped in and out of the shelter of brown, lifeless bulrushes. "We went to Rex's memorial together in Clement Danes, the RAF church. His widow and two daughters were there, of course, and lots of Lloyd's dignitaries. Mallory and I had got to know each other quite well during the liquidation, and she found it easier to sit with me than with the rest of the staff. I don't know how she got through it, but she managed it beautifully. She even said the right thing to the widow. Afterwards, I took her to the Cheshire Cheese on Fleet Street. It was early, so we had an upstairs room to ourselves.

"I didn't want to put it to her then, but she seemed in the mood to talk. She told me a lot about risk and her feelings for Rex. She told me he was the love of her life. Not in so many words, but it was obvious." He smiled understandingly. "That was a long time ago. Nothing's fixed forever." He pressed the throttle gently and we nosed towards St Jorioz. The bank here was wooded, but two tall cranes stuck out above the trees, idle and forlorn. The last project around the entire lake, according to Céline. Yet on that bleak wintry day we seemed not only to have the lake to ourselves, but to be the last living people in its environs.

"Anyway, I put it to her. I think she was expecting it. 'Rex is dead,' she said, when I'd finished. 'I'm setting up a fund for ruined Names, and I'm putting my money into it. All of it.'"

"She did, too," I said eagerly, and I explained Ghost Trader.

He frowned thoughtfully down the lake. "Do you believe her?"

"Of course I believe her," I retorted angrily. "I've met her, too."

"But you're not sure?" His eyes twinkled, and for the first time, it irritated me. "If you were, you wouldn't have called me."

I pointed peremptorily across the lake. "Head over there."

Obediently he turned the boat. Ahead was the sheer face of *Roc de Chère*, as dull and cheerless as the water. The snow on the *Dents des Lanfins* offered the only relief from the unrelenting greyness of sky and water, but its whiteness was cold and forbidding. I directed him past the *Hôtel du Lac*, the ferry stop and the beach, forlorn and deserted.

"I want to show you where she lives," I said, as we nosed along the shore beneath the Route des Vignes. The windows of the houses along the slope were blank and featureless, and none revealed any signs of life within. At last we came to what I thought must be the wood, with its blend of birch and evergreen. But of the boathouse there was no sign. The trees clustered to the water's edge without interruption. From the lake, everything looked different and strange.

"I know it's around here." I said in exasperation. By now we had reached the port and beach of Veyrier. He turned the boat around without a word. But still I couldn't find it. No former boat bay thrust out into the water, there was no jetty with rubber tyres on rusty chains, whilst George was pointedly consulting his watch. "It doesn't matter. At least this proves it's small. It's a converted boathouse. Two rooms only, and she sleeps next to her screens. If she isn't investing for her members, she certainly isn't spending on herself.

"Besides," I continued, "I can name at least three members." I ticked them off on my fingers. "Ambrose Hanter." George acknowledged he'd seen the name during his searches. "Le Baigneur. All I know is he's French." George shook his head. "And L'Esprit. I nearly met him in Les Confins." I told him something of the fatal incident and all the attendant confusions. "Even if I had the wrong man, she wouldn't have mentioned him if he didn't exist."

"I don't know either of them, I'm afraid."

By now we were almost back at the pontoon, and nothing more was said until we'd tied up, and George had paid the boatman. Then, as we walked across the esplanade in the direction of the station, he announced that he'd thought of something important.

"If this investment co-operative of hers has a forum the way you say it does, then it's likely the members have on-line user names. So it's not surprising I don't recognise *L'Esprit* or *Le Baigneur*. However, I do remember there being at least two French Names in the lists I saw. One of them had quite a distinguished background. Robert de St Hippocrate, or something similar. He was from Aix-les-Bains."

"*Le Baigneur*," I said excitedly.

What better user name for the man from Aix-les-Bains than The Bather? "She went to Aix at New Year. Part business."

"The other French Name I noticed was an important man in a drinks conglomerate. All I recall was one of their brand names. Not their biggest, but their most profitable: *Spirito di San Luigi*. Electric blue, the young things in Italy love it. He could be your *L'Esprit*."

"You must have a photographic memory," I was amazed at the detail of his recall. "This corroborates her story, though, doesn't it?"

He awarded me one of his twinkling smiles. "It's a step in the right direction, but three members don't add up to an investment co-operative. They could be three co-conspirators."

"Not Ambrose," I protested. "He threw himself off a Channel ferry. Why would he do that if he was sharing in a bundle of Tonbridge money? Anyway," I continued, warming to her defence, "I overheard her once on her mobile. She was arguing with somebody about shorting the banks, and she said her members would never go for it."

"She's an enigma," he agreed. "That day in the Cheshire Cheese, I couldn't for the life of me decide whether I was talking to a latter-day Robin Hood or the most consummate liar I've ever met. I still can't decide." We had reached the station, and he removed his glove before shaking me warmly by the hand. His eyes twinkled as never before. "I wish you joy of her."

GHO$T TRAD€R

Part Two
Euphoria

"Then, as the early promise
seems to be justified,
euphoria sets in,
and experts convince us
that this time it's different."

I had never felt so alive.
Not even Amy had ever turned me over so completely.
Mallory clung to me hungrily,
and I revelled in knowing that she felt as I did.
Instinct had overpowered suspicion and innuendo.
Hypothesis had nothing on hormones.

Chapter Nine : Strictly Business

To compound my confusion, Mallory actually rang me that evening. "Sorry it's been so long." Her voice was almost caressing. "I've been frantic, what with one thing and another."

"You never answer your phone." I tried not to sound reproachful.

"You never leave a message," she replied blandly.

"But you knew I was calling," I protested.

"I'm sorry." Now she sounded suitably contrite. "Things haven't been easy…" She lapsed briefly into silence. "It was wrong of me. But I'm calling now, if you can forgive me."

"When can I see you?" George had wished me joy of her, after all.

"I should be back early March. I'll call you the moment I arrive."

With that I had to be content. But it wasn't until the 17th that she finally returned. It was a blustery Monday, I'd underestimated the wind and I'd gone shopping without sweater or gloves. Back on my porch, I fumbled painfully with raw fingers for my door key.

"Hello, Clem." It was Mallory, advancing up my steps, all smiles.

She was so much later than promised, I'd almost given her up, consoling myself that I was well rid of her. Now here she was, smart-casual, in designer jeans and a tailored tweed jacket over a cashmere sweater; yet closer to, for all her style and her apparent cheer, she was pale and her eyes were tired. I was torn between seizing her in my arms and slamming the door in her face. Instead, I embraced her stiffly. Her answering hug was much more affectionate.

It was the perfect opportunity to confront her with what George had told me, but her warmth towards me, despite an underlying sadness that she could not quite disguise, disarmed me. "You'd better come in." A scent of wild flowers teased my nostrils as she passed into the hall. "How about elevenses? Fresh from the *patisserie*."

"You know my weaknesses too well." If only, I thought.

"Please sit down." I pointed, as I reached for the coffee pot.

"So how are you, after all this time?" Instead of sitting, she had followed me to the sink. I held the pot defensively in front of me.

"As you see, I'm fine."

"Your cheek's unblemished." For a glorious moment her fingers brushed my face. I faked indifference. "No problems with the ankle?"

94

"Apart from my doctor saying I must cycle like a good Frenchman."

She laughed. "But you aren't French. Do what you like."

"I like it when they forget." I put the pot on the hob.

"They never really forget, do they?" She fingered the boxes from the *patisserie*. "Can I help?" I pushed plates towards her, and she slipped the ribbon off the boxes. "*Pains au chocolat* and *tartes aux framboises*!" Her eyes lit up. "Am I allowed a *tarte*?"

She said it so charmingly, I could hardly refuse. "I'll have one, too." Almost reverently, she transferred tarts to plates, and we were soon sitting at my dining table, sipping and nibbling in awkward silence. A moody thoughtfulness had replaced her forced cheer, and she toyed fretfully with her fork. When she looked up, her face was troubled.

"The markets must be driving you crazy," I suggested.

"I ought to be used to that." She hunted in her bag for tissues. "I've just buried my father. Before that I was back and forth to Paris, though I doubt he recognised me."

My own father had died of a heart attack, when still young enough to be invincible, and my mother had been killed ten years later by two strokes in relatively quick succession. The months in between, when she had been alert but unable to communicate, had been horrible. "I'm sorry." I didn't know Mallory well enough to offer proper comfort. "I wish I could have helped." It was meant to sound sympathetic, but it came out more like criticism. She chose not to notice.

"It's over now. For his sake, it should have been years ago."

"Is your mother still alive?" She shook her head, which I took to mean she didn't want to go into details. "That makes us orphans."

"We're a little old for that." She managed a brief smile. "But I could use some help, since you're offering." She composed herself into a business-like posture, back straight and knees together. "The thing is, I don't know what to do." She corrected herself. "I know what I'd like to do, but I don't know if I should, or how I can bring it off."

Though her words could have meant her problem was personal, she sounded more like one of my old clients come to confess a drastic loss of market share. Though flattered to think she needed my professional advice, I was disappointed nothing else was wanted. "A problem shared is a problem solved," I coaxed. Business was better than nothing. Her lips hovered between frown and smile. "If you're worried about security, I'm as secure as the confessional."

"I don't doubt it. It's whether I ought to burden you with something I need to resolve for myself." Her mood was so different from anything I'd seen before, that I could only nod encouragingly. "You remember

95

overhearing me at the ferry stop?" She didn't wait for an answer. "I said I'd short the banks with my own money…"

I was right, this was business.

"You said it was gambling; your members would never go for it."

"You've got a good memory, as I've noticed." It was the first time I'd seen her looking uncertain. "I'm thinking of doing it anyway."

"So what's changed your mind?" It really was like being back in Covent Garden with a new client. I felt the same rush of adrenalin, though no client's voice had stirred me like hers.

Most clients go round the houses. But Mallory's answer was so brief I wouldn't have understood it if I hadn't been following the news, plus the commentary from my dream visitors. "Bear Stearns."

"JP Morgan just took them over. Otherwise, they were bust."

"I'm glad you keep up with events." She nodded appreciatively. "If Bear Stearns is bankrupt, then Lehman Brothers and Merrill Lynch are zombies: dead but walking. Once they go, the whole system could implode. Then there's AIG."

"AIG?" This really startled me. AIG was the world's largest insurer, vastly bigger than Lloyd's. If they were in trouble, then I could readily understand how bad things had become.

"I lived through the LMX spiral. I saw how quick profit could blind insurers to risk."

"They're supposed to calculate for these things," I expostulated. It was my first outburst of anger since she'd arrived, and I put all the frustration of the past weeks into it.

"Our models never allowed for such a run of huge catastrophes," she said humbly. Her use of "our" showed that she'd understood how much of my anger was directed at her.

"Why on earth not?" Amazing how Lloyd's still set me off.

If it had been Rex Tonbridge opposite, I'm sure he would have blustered or matched my anger. Mallory merely shrugged. Only her eyes reflected the pain I was inflicting. "It had never happened before. The unprecedented is almost impossible to predict."

"All it takes is imagination." The bedrock of my business.

"But where do you stop? It's impossible to allow for everything unlikely. No syndicate could reserve against something like Noah's flood without going out of business."

I had to hand it to her. She had turned my righteous anger, not by denial but by explanation. I realised, too – and just in time – that she was defending Rex Tonbridge; that for her own sanity she needed to believe that he had acted honourably. I might be jealous of his hold over her, but I had to admire her loyalty. If I were going to be useful – and being useful to her was better than nothing – then I must not get embroiled in arguments about the past.

"So what unprecedented horrors have AIG failed to predict?"

"The perils of mortgage-backed CDOs. Everybody – even regulators and ratings agencies – thought mortgages were safer than they could be, and that when they were bundled together in Collateralised Debt Obligations, the small risk of default was spread so widely it was eliminated." Articulate and in command of her subject, she sounded like the most intelligent of my old clients. Much as I would have preferred intimate badinage, I was impressed by her professionalism. "They forgot that because a catastrophe's never happened doesn't mean it can't. They believed that because the entire U.S. property market had never gone down all at once, it never would. Ever."

"The Noah's flood syndrome again," I suggested. She nodded, pleased that I'd understood. "So let me guess. AIG are insuring against CDO failures as if they're low-risk or no-risk, whereas in fact they're toxic. Only the shit hasn't hit their fan yet."

"Very good. This really is Incurred But Not Reported, big time."

I laughed. "Incurred But Not even bloody Registered, you mean."

"I can see it would be fun working with you." I almost blushed. It was not only the first time she'd paid me a compliment without a barb, it was the strongest hint that we might really act in partnership. Working together might not be living together, but it would be a step in the right direction. If I wanted it. "Fifteen months ago, Bear Stearns shares were $172." she continued. "Yesterday, JP Morgan offered $2. Imagine the same for every share."

"$2 is still positive. Unlike the bottomless losses they threw at me."

"But not very nice for the pension funds and ordinary investors who trusted last week's official line of $35 plus. Compared with now, Lloyd's were pillars of prudence."

"You're saying we had it easy?" I almost splashed our refills.

"Unlimited liability was dreadful for Names. But the world could have survived the loss of Lloyd's. This time..." She shivered, despite the warmth of her refilled coffee. "The banks are leveraged anywhere between 30 and 50 to one. When that unwinds, it won't be the LMX Spiral, it'll be the Whole Earth Spiral. Instead of Names, it'll be entire countries." Her quiet tone made her words all the more chilling.

"It very nearly got Amy," I told her. "She was with Northern Rock."

Mallory grimaced in sympathy. "Is she still with them?" I told her about Saul and Madoff, and how Max had given him a clean bill of health. "As long as she can get her money out, she'll probably be OK. But even Madoff can't turn the world round on his own. Split Strike Conversion, whatever it is, won't be anywhere near enough."

I knew things were bad, but this was doom-saying on the grandest scale. "So what's your solution: cash under the mattress?"

"We must do better than that." She blew on her coffee. "The markets could be dead for decades, with inflation, currency collapse, government defaults, you name it. What my members need is a big play to double, even quadruple their money."

She'd forgotten Amy, of course. She was focused entirely on Ghost Trader. This was a business discussion, not a philanthropic debate. But at least she was thinking about her members rather than herself. Not even a consummate liar could dissemble so feelingly. Surely?

"You want to short Lehman and Merrill Lynch, plus AIG?" Our eyes met; she didn't even blink. "Isn't that about as risky as it gets?"

"A chance of life is better than certain death."

I got up and paced, as I struggled to decide whether this was on the level. I remembered all too clearly her words at the ferry stop. "You said it wouldn't be the banks who got screwed."

"Bear Stearns hadn't gone belly-up then. You can't short anything until you're sure the market will follow. I need to be ahead of the game, but only just." She grabbed my arm. "You're making me dizzy." Obediently, I sat down. Seizing my hands over the table, she squeezed my fingers. It was our first time in continuous contact, but it was anything but erotic. "Trust me, I know what I'm talking about."

Trust! I'd trusted Lloyd's and they'd taken almost everything; I'd trusted Amy, and she'd deserted me; and if George Wiseman were right, Mallory was the last person I ought to trust.

Nor was it only me. Amy had trusted Northern Rock, and they had let her down; as a consequence she had entrusted her savings to Saul, so now she had to trust Bernie Madoff. Every depositor trusted their bank not to blow their hard-earned money on absurdly risky investments. Depositor or not, everyone trusted regulators to keep a sleepless eye on what the financial sector got up to with the world's money. Trust was essential, yet so often abused.

Mallory released my hands. "We should continue this, this evening. That's if you're free." Her smile was apologetic, yet I could tell that she expected me, the putative supplier, to be available at her convenience. "I'd really value your advice. Maybe your help, too." She smiled roguishly. "I've found a new restaurant, right on the lake. My shout."

"I'll fit you in somehow," I assented, with mock severity.

"Thank you. I really appreciate it. I'll pick you up. 8:30 sharp."

Then, she kissed me on the lips. It was so rapid, it was hard to believe it had happened.

As good as her word, she arrived on the dot, dressed again in the formal trouser suit she'd worn New Year's Day, ready then, I now guessed, for her lunch with *L'Esprit*. How like a client to cry off at the last moment. I too was in business mode, in my darkest grey, set off by a white shirt and a blue silk tie. This time our embrace was formal.

Her car was an old Peugeot Six, as nondescript and as functional as her boathouse. As soon as we hit the main road, her acceleration pressed me back into my seat. I must have been too feverish to have noticed before, or else she had driven with more consideration for my then fragile state. Ahead was a lone cyclist, driving his pedals as if he were breaking away from the *peloton*; approaching fast on the other side was a pair of headlights. Mallory swung out nonetheless. She might be a mongrel to her neighbours, yet she drove like a native. But she held the wheel expertly, and kept her focus on the road.

Disinclined to talk, I felt emboldened to gaze on her. The near darkness threw her profile into relief. Her chin was strong, and the collar of her blouse did not obscure the elegant curve of her neck. Her dark hair contrasted the lightness of her skin. She might have been an enigma, as George had observed, but she was a beautiful one. Sensing my scrutiny, she threw me a sideways smile. "I've been doing my homework on you, Clem. I checked your website, and I Googled you." We squeezed past another car. "It seems you think fast and laterally, and I wouldn't disagree. I'm sorry I called you a prat."

This was the kind of things clients said when they wanted me to do something difficult for a low fee. I wondered how she'd feel when I told her I'd done my homework, too. "Don't worry," I said, content to let things ride for the moment. "Amy called me much worse."

"I'm not Amy." We slid round a sharp bend. The road dropped in steep hairpins down to Talloires, the lake's only three star village, which meant, in *Michelin*'s opinion, that it was worth a special journey. I hunkered down in my seat as Mallory, in the act of overtaking, seemed certain to collide with the upcoming traffic. Headlights washed over us, as she tucked in again. We swept past Talloires, and the road narrowed as it rejoined the shoreline. The water gleamed beside us, and at every bend I expected to be plunged into the lake or rammed.

Soon the road turned inland to skirt a promontory of trees. Mallory swung off onto a narrow track I didn't know. But I hadn't been this way since Amy and I had explored every lake-shore beach. "This one's new," Mallory reminded me. *This* was a low wooden building right at the water's edge. We parked under a huge cedar, and Mallory flicked on the interior light to check her face in the mirror. Unlike Amy, whose toilet took forever, she was done with a few touches of eyeliner and lipstick, a dab of tissue and a flicker of fingers through her hair. I reminded myself that this was a business appointment, not a date.

The restaurant was minimally lit by dimmed wall lights and a floating candle on each table, so that the faces of the customers were hard to determine. Perfect for intimacy or confidentiality. From our table we could see the lake through floor-to-ceiling plate glass. Outside was a terrace, which in warmer weather was doubtless packed with tables like ours, with glass tops in wrought iron frames. The chairs were similarly *art nouveau*, their hard surfaces softened by padded cushions. The service was quietly efficient, and we'd soon ordered the *Menu Gastronomique du Terroir* on which the choices were largely made for us. Then Mallory got down to business.

"Tell me what you know about shorting."

"The morals or the mechanics?"

"The morals can wait. Let's see if you grasp the mechanics."

"Shorting means selling shares you don't own, on the expectation the price will fall, right?" She nodded. "Then you buy them at the lower price, and pocket the difference." I paused as a waitress placed a small dish of appetisers before us. "What I don't really understand is how you go about it. I thought share trading was instantaneous."

"Imagine you're a pension fund. You're investing for the long run; provided your investments have good long-term prospects, daily and weekly fluctuations in the market don't worry you. You sit on what you've got; if the price goes down, you might even buy more. By and large, you don't sell. I, on the other hand, am a market trader. Volatility is what I thrive on. I'm buying and selling the whole time. And I need to make money on falls as much as on gains. So I make a deal with you. You loan me some of your shares, in return for a rental fee, and I sell them at the best price. Then, when the price falls, which I'm predicting it will, I buy the same number of shares back at the lower price, and hand them back to you."

"So I get my shares back, safe and sound, plus my rent, and you make your profit on the fall in price. Even if you're wrong, and the price goes up, you're taking the risk, not me. I'm safe and I'm getting my rent. It's a bit like skiing, isn't it? I'm Clearway Clem who sticks to the beautifully groomed *piste*, and you're Mogul Mallory, who loves going over the bumps. We're both enjoy doing different things, the things we like, in the name of the same sport."

"I can see why you were a good consultant," she said approvingly.

"The way you describe it sounds fine, and nobody could seriously object," I countered. "That's not what we're talking about with Lehman Brothers and AIG. You're going for the jugular."

She didn't flinch or protest. "If I'm right, those companies are dead anyway. I just don't want my members to get killed in the aftermath. They've suffered enough already."

"It's like betting the Titanic will sink."

"Lehman and Merrill Lynch are investment banks," she replied evenly. "They're not full of innocent passengers. They're a bunch of overpaid traders who loused up."

"What about AIG?" I persisted. "If they go bust, they can't pay claims, not even on ordinary insurance everybody needs."

"*If* they go bust? They *are* bust. They just don't know it." She leaned towards me conspiratorially. "Ask yourself this: would you have bet against Lloyd's if you'd had the chance?"

She had me there. I'd have done it like a shot, if I'd known how, and I wouldn't have cared about the humble settlement clerks and personal assistants who lost their jobs. Or not enough to stop me. "I suppose they'll get rescued," I mused hopefully. "Lehman will get taken over like Bear Stearns. AIG will be bailed out like Northern Rock."

"Very probably," she agreed. "And, in the long run, it'll be the rest of us who pay for the rescue. All I want is something on account and up-front for my members."

"Plenty would argue it's wrong to profit at the expense of others. It's like insider trading."

"Absolutely not!" Her denial reverberated in my ears like gunshot. "Insider trading is profiting from something nobody else could possibly know. Like the chairman selling his shares before he makes the hole in his balance sheet public. What I'm telling you is stuff anybody could work out. It's just that they haven't or they don't want to. Yet."

Our first course arrived: a confection of *langoustines* from the lake on gossamer shreds of vegetable. It was a brief distraction.

"Look at it this way." She wiped her lips delicately. "It would be lovely to share what I know with the rest of the world, but then *nobody* could profit. Nobody at all." She took up her fork again, but her eyes drilled into mine. "You can't rescue the entire world, it's impossible. But you can help those you care about. Like Amy and Jake."

"Count me out," I said, albeit reluctantly. "I don't have any money."

101

"We'll come back to that. For the moment, imagine you're a member of Ghost Trader and I'm asking for your permission in the forum: how would you vote: to short or not to short?"

Fillets of seared fish were produced in time for me to gather my thoughts. "I buy the principle," I said, as waitress and wine waiter departed. "I still need to know it's going to work."

She stiffened, and the sliver of fish on her fork slipped back onto her plate. "The members usually trust my judgement." It seemed there was to be no escaping the issue of trust.

"I'm not a member," I said, "And I'm an awkward sod. Not all my clients liked me for it, but most of them learned to appreciate it in the end." At least she seemed to have members.

"There's plenty of stuff I can show you tomorrow, and I'm sure it'll convince you as much as data ever can." She retrieved the piece of fish with some deliberation. "But it can't make the decision for you. Only you can decide if you trust me to bring this off."

She'd almost boxed me in. I was very nearly at the point of no return: where I must either accept her reasoning or challenge her with what George Wiseman had told me. "Why is my opinion so important to you? Why not ask your members like you have to?"

"You said you were as secure as the confessional." She pushed her plate aside, as if she'd had enough of distractions. "I need to tell you something confidential. Something I've never discussed with a non-member." The wine waiter approached, but she waved him away.

"I'll happily sign a confidentiality agreement, if it helps."

"If I didn't trust you, it wouldn't matter how many you signed. I wouldn't tell you a thing." Then she smiled disarmingly. "But I do trust you, and I value your opinion."

I tried to ignore the compliment. "So what do I need to know?"

We were forced to pause by a waitress come to take our plates, followed by another with our meat course. It was game of some sort, but I hardly noticed the food by now, delicious though it was. Then we had to accept the ritual of tasting the red wine. If the staff had been hired to crank up the tension, they couldn't have done it better.

"I told you the members have stuck by me, except for one."

"You also told me you didn't want to talk about it."

"I was still in two minds then. Now I'm not." She toyed with an exquisite sliver of game. "In 2001 Ghost Trader nearly fell apart, because one member was obsessed with Enron."

"The masters of the SPV. They hid their losses in Special Purpose Vehicles, so their balance sheet looked brilliant. Such a pity Lloyd's didn't think of those," I said bitterly. "They should re-invoke the law of Attainder. When one of his ministers crossed Henry VIII it wasn't just his head on the block, he was stripped of his land and his titles."

"Think of shorting as the next best thing," she retorted.

Despite everything George Wiseman had told me, I could only marvel at how well her humours matched mine. Whether I ought to trust her or not, she would undoubtedly be fun to work with.

"Anyway, this one member, he'd really done his homework, and he was convinced Enron's results were a charade. He kept on and on that we should put everything behind shorting Enron. But the members couldn't agree. Some were all for it; some liked the principle, but thought it too risky; others hated the thought of ruining Enron's shareholders, many of them innocent employees. *L'Esprit* was the leading anti, and the arguments became absurdly overheated. So I called a vote, and it was against. If I hadn't put a stop to the arguments, we'd have split apart. Which would have been such a waste."

"What about you? Where did you stand in the great debate?"

"I was against. Enron used so much smoke and so many mirrors, they fooled even me. More importantly, I thought the desire to punish Enron was a bad reason for shorting them."

"I thought you wanted to punish the banks."

"No." Furiously, she skewered another piece of game as though it were still alive. "My sole aim is to protect my members. If that screws the banks, well and good. But that's all."

"He must have really loved you, then, this Enron obsessive."

"He accused me of going against him. He said if I'd supported him, the vote would have been for. I told him I still wouldn't have done it with such a vociferous minority against."

The perils of her job were all too clear. "I guess he quit in a rage?"

"Worse than that. He tried to short Enron on his own." Her voice faltered. "He didn't have the experience; his timing was all wrong. He finished even worse off than he was after Lloyd's." She bit her lip, trying to hold in a shock that was all too fresh in her mind.

"That's terrible. But he'd only got himself to blame."

She attacked another strip of meat. "He said I'd let him down."

"Why? He was an ex-client, what could he expect?"

Her pallor was visible even in candlelight.

"He was my ex-husband."

I reached for her hand, where it had dropped like her spirits to the table, and drew it towards me. Whatever financial misdeeds George Wiseman suspected of her, she could not feel so tormented by an invented story, and I felt her sorrow at her ex-husband's foolishness, with its undertow of anger and guilt, as if it were my own. I stroked her fingers, not only to ease her pain, but to acknowledge the privilege of sharing what she normally kept well hidden.

She released my hand, but not without an affectionate pat on the knuckles. "So now you see the problem." It was hard to accept that the moment of intimacy was over, but Mallory was not a woman to wallow for long in self-pity, still less in my sympathy.

"Enron was a one-off. Now the whole world's gone mad."

"The tech bubble was bursting. The world was just as mad in 2001."

"So what are you going to do?"

She regarded me solemnly, her emotions under control once more. "That's what I'm hoping you're going to tell me." In my prime, this was where I expected exploratory conversations to lead. Yet it had never occurred to me that she wanted anything so sweeping as a plan of action. A friendly stiffening of resolve had been my expectation, even perhaps an independent check on the assumptions which had led to her shorting targets. Instead, she wanted nothing less than a bridge across the chasm in attitudes between her members and herself. "I'm not quite so arrogant as you," she added. "I know when I need advice."

Few clients had spelled out a problem so well, and none had wrung my heart in the process. Struggling to recover my poise, I played for time. "I rarely give advice for free."

She waved a dismissive hand. "I want the best, not a freebie." She was from the financial world, where nothing came free. "I'll increase your fee by however many times I increase the fund by shorting."

This was too generous. Yet I had only myself to blame. Raising the prospect of payment had been my attempt to stall; too late, I realised that she had intended to buy me all along. Truly was this a business proposition, and nothing more. "We both know shorting's a gamble," I said. "I don't want to be better placed than your members. If the gamble doesn't pay off, I'll insist my fee be reduced *pro rata*."

"Thank you," she said. "I'm glad that's settled."

Whether I liked it or not, she'd pushed me to the point of no return. To back out now was no longer an option. I knew next to nothing about the world of investing, but getting up to speed on a new business area had always been my *forte*. Besides, to be on the payroll meant I'd be seeing a lot of Mallory, putting me in the kind of proximity she had enjoyed with Rex Tonbridge. It was a tantalising prospect. But her members – those nineteen hundred and ninety-nine loyal ex-Names – were more important than either my ego or my desire.

Beyond the plate glass lay the lake, silent and still. Inside, the other diners sat around their tiny pools of candlelight, oblivious to what was at stake. Between flitted the staff, as silent as ghosts. None of them could help me. The livelihood of her members, losers like myself, depended on me. "There's something I need to ask you," I said.

She smiled, in expectation of a mundane question. "Fire away."

"That money you put into Ghost Trader. May I ask where it came from?" Her jaw tightened and her lips narrowed. At the same time, her eyes widened, as surprise and anger fought for supremacy. "I'm afraid I've been doing my homework, too."

Anger won. "You bastard," she almost screamed. Then, with terrible dignity, she recovered herself. "I suppose you had every right."

"I'd no right at all, and I wasn't looking for trouble. It started because I asked my accountant why he hadn't put my assets into a Gibraltar trust. The next I knew he was telling me I had to speak to this liquidator in Geneva, who'd wound up the failed syndicates."

"You spoke to George Wiseman!" She shook her head. "I suspected from the off you were good, but I seriously underestimated you."

"I'm just a lonely man who wants to learn all about the wonderful woman who came from nowhere to light up his life. That's all."

She closed her eyes, as if that would shut out whatever she didn't want to hear. "I won't drop Rex in the shit to make you feel better."

"I'm not asking you to." It was her involvement only that mattered.

"Lots of underwriters put money aside." She gave an angry shrug. "When the syndicate went down, we were just as broke as you."

"Except for what you'd salted away," I told her sharply. "Whose idea was it, yours or Rex's?" As if on cue, the waitresses arrived to clear our plates, and to bring the cheeseboard. Mallory dismissed it angrily. I smiled at the crestfallen staff. "We're not as hungry as we thought. But we could use some coffee and a *digestif*. Two *marcs égrappés*, if possible." Even that required some choices, but at last we were alone again with our liquid comforters.

"It was my idea." Her words came slowly and reluctantly, and each one drove a nail into my heart. At least she wasn't shirking responsibility. It would have been so easy to put the blame on the boss who was in no position to defend himself. "If Rex had a fault, it was arrogance. He was sure his syndicate would always be profitable."

"You mean he didn't know what you were doing?"

"He knew. But he didn't approve."

"So why didn't he stop you?" The idea of the imperious boss led astray by his junior didn't ring true. I could accept that the execution had been Mallory's – I felt sure she had more of an eye for the required detail – but she must, surely, have been obeying orders. Everything George had said implied that it was Rex who had to be in charge.

She clamped angry hands around her glass, glaring into the clear liquid. "We were making so much, he thought it didn't really matter. If indulging my pessimism kept me happy, he didn't see the harm." She looked up fiercely, daring me to disagree. "But he did say that if we ever were in real trouble, we'd have to give the money back."

"That destroyed the point, surely?" The more I heard, the more convinced I became that she was describing an idealised Rex – the icon she needed to believe in – and never the real man. It cheered me almost enough to forget that she had played her part willingly. There was no way that even a man as forceful as Rex Tonbridge could have coerced her, but there was every possibility that her love for him had overcome her scruples even more effectively.

She gave a tiny lift of her shoulders. "I didn't really believe him."

It made a weird kind of sense. She'd carried on investing in bogus re-insurance and spurious risk analysis, hoping that Rex would never insist on returning the money, whilst he'd assuaged his conscience by convincing himself the money would never be needed. Perhaps he really had made ritual protests to salve his conscience, knowing that she would ignore them. Perhaps he'd even planned to put the blame on her if the thing had come to light. I couldn't help wondering what he'd have done if the syndicate had remained in profit until he retired. Would he have kept their ill-gotten gains, or would he have handed them back to his Names?

"So what happened in 1991?" The year the LMX spiralled.

"We didn't talk about it. There was too much going on. We were bouncing from crisis to crisis. All that mattered was getting through each day. Rex was in a terrible state. Practically unapproachable. You can't imagine what it was like." Her face contorted. "What am I saying? You must know exactly what I mean. I'm sorry." Her lip trembled, then tears rolled slowly down her cheeks, which she caught with the backs of her hands. I could weather her anger: her sorrow was much harder to witness. Gently, I urged her to continue.

"Then things went quiet. The eye of the storm. He was almost his old self again. It was a Friday, the end of the week. We went to our favourite restaurant. I don't think it's there now. He was tender and attentive, and we didn't talk business." She smiled wistfully. "As we were finishing, he came over all serious, took both my hands, looked me in the eye. 'Promise me you'll give that money back.'

"I reminded him it was our personal reinsurance. 'Why me?'

"He told me he was going away. 'Until things settle down. Besides, you'll find the best way of doing it without fuss.' He meant without too many awkward questions being asked.

"Afterwards he drove me to my flat. But he wouldn't come in. He said he had things to settle with his family, before he went away. That was the last time I saw him alone." She sniffed her glass, pulled a face, then drained it in one. I thought she'd choke, but her mind had retreated to some remote place beyond ordinary reflexes. "He drove to his house in Sussex, and a few days later he shot himself. There *were* awkward questions, of course, but George Wiseman couldn't prove anything. Besides," she managed a strange smile, half sad, half wry, "once I told him about Ghost Trader I don't think he wanted to."

Chapter Ten : Moral Hazard

We'd agreed to meet the next morning. Mallory had insisted that she valued my opinion more than ever and, after her pitiful show of grief, I had no desire to refuse her. I reached the boathouse at 9:15 as agreed, though it was with some trepidation that I knocked on the door. She was dressed casually in jeans and a denim shirt, but her manner was formal and businesslike. She ushered me into the living room, and pointed to the sofa. "I've got catching up to do. Give me fifteen minutes, and I'm all yours." Then she was back to her screens.

They were going full blast. Of the two that I could see, in her office-cum-bedroom, one showed columns of prices endlessly changing to the beat of the markets; on the other, news flashes scrolled across top and bottom, whilst economists, chartists and sundry experts issued their strident views on split screens. Even from the living room, the voices sounded manic and the visuals were disorientating. But Mallory seemed perfectly at home.

She worked with great concentration, moving seamlessly between the virtual world of her screens and the reality of her desk. It was a pleasure to watch her, even though I was impatient to get on with our meeting. I did my best to match her calm. Like it or not, she was the client, and keeping suppliers waiting was what clients did.

But after quarter of an hour, I had to shift position. I strolled into her office and stood at her shoulder. "Please don't," she said, without looking up. I crossed to the window, and gazed over the lake. There was no wind, and the water lay as smooth and unmoving as ice. On the far side, clouds brooded over *Semnoz*. "You're in my light."

"If this is a bad time, I can always come back." I tried to keep the edge out of my voice.

"I won't be much longer. Make coffee, if you want to be useful."

Her tiny kitchen boasted an ancient stove, fuelled by a gas cylinder from under the sink. On the worktop I found a bag of fresh *pains au chocolat*, and the pine cupboard above it revealed a pack of coffee, a matt steel pot, mugs and plates. In the agitation of my first visit, I'd failed to notice how cheap and basic were the cutlery and crockery, the kind of things you would find in a holiday let, which I supposed the boathouse had once been.

As I waited for the water to heat up, I returned to the living room. At New Year, I'd found the simplicity of the room restful. Now it seemed austere. An overnight guest would have left more signs of occupation in a business hotel. With little else to look at, I studied the sepia print of the mock-gothic *château* I'd noticed previously. *Le Sanatorium de St Hippocrate*. I supposed it must belong to Robert de St Hippocrate, one of the few Names that George remembered. The print was tenuous proof of *Le Baigneur*'s importance, though whether as a co-founder of Ghost Trader or as a co-conspirator, it could not reveal.

I was roused from these thoughts by the first plop of steamy water against the top of the pot, and, as I returned to the kitchen, the room was enlivened by the aroma of coffee. I filled two mugs and put *pains au chocolat* on plates, before carrying hers into the office-cum-bedroom. "On the pad will do." Her eyes never left the screens, but she reached suddenly for a pen. Our wrists collided, and hot brown liquid spilled over my hand and dripped onto her notes. "What are you doing?" she yelled. Snatching her coffee-sodden pad, she pushed past me to the kitchen. I followed more slowly, but no less angrily.

"That hurt," I snapped, banging mug and plate down on the worktop. She was bending over the sink, dabbing her pad with a dishcloth. Her eyes flashed crossly until she saw my discomfort. Immediately she was all concern. Dropping the pad, she took my scalded hand in hers. The touch of her fingers was cool and soothing as she drew them gently over the redness. She looked up, her eyes soft with contrition.

I don't know which of us moved first. It hardly mattered. Whatever barriers there were between us dropped away as suddenly as the wind on the lake. Client and supplier became simply woman and man, and we fell into each other's arms as joyfully and unthinkingly as teenagers. Neither of us spoke. There was no way to compete with the booming experts on her screens. I had never felt so alive. Not even Amy had ever turned me over so completely. Mallory clung to me hungrily, and I revelled in knowing that she felt as I did. Instinct had overpowered suspicion and innuendo. Hypothesis had nothing on hormones.

How long we kissed in that tiny kitchen, whilst the forgotten coffee cooled, I have no idea. But at last we paused for breath. Her eyes shone into mine, but she laid a finger on my lips and extracted herself from my arms. "I'm not sure that was meant to happen."

109

"I'm glad it did." I tried to hug her again. But the magic had gone.

With a deep breath, she smoothed her hair. "I'm still hoping for your unbiased opinion." Sadly, she was right to bring us down to earth again. We were together to talk business. Nothing else.

"The coffee must be cold by now," I said, as calmly as I could. "Shall I make some more?"

She nodded. "Yes, please. I'll go and turn the sound down."

We were soon seated at the table with fresh coffee. To outward appearances the interlude of passion might never have happened, though my whole body was still in ferment. As for Mallory, I sensed, or else I hoped, that she was similarly keeping the lid on her emotions. "This is a preliminary session," I began. "We need to set down the parameters and the variables, including just how variable they are."

This opening usually went down well with clients, but the upward twitch of Mallory's eyebrows made it sound like the worst kind of consultant-speak. I cleared my throat. "The question you put to me was stark and simple: to short or not to short." This time, she nodded. I couldn't have put it more simply, and she liked that.

"From everything you've told me, not shorting isn't really an option. It's more like sticking your head in the sand and hoping the problem will go away because you can't see it any more. If so, the question really becomes not whether to short, but how to short." She leaned forward, eager for me to go on. Instead I held up my hand. "But let's stop there a moment. I still want to explore the option of not shorting." She leaned back as if in recoil. But she didn't interrupt. "Your members won't object, and if the world blows up it's hardly your fault."

"I'm supposed to think ahead, not go with the herd."

"You were wrong about Enron. Why so certain now?"

"Enron taught me a lesson."

"I don't mean about Lehman and AIG. I mean suppose you're wrong about the system imploding. If you are, there's no need to short."

"The chances of the world economy imploding are far greater than the chances of me being wrong about shorting." She spoke firmly, but evenly. "In fact, the two things are related. The more I'm right, the more imperative it is to be short."

That suggested that if she were wrong, she could be doubly wrong. But I was more than prepared to accept her macro analysis. On that, she really was going with the herd, which already included most financial commentators, as well as my neighbours and friends. Sidonie and Armand, René and Céline might not be economists or market analysts, but they were shrewd observers, as well as direct sufferers. The only way in which they differed from Mallory was that they could see no solution beyond a stoic gritting of teeth and tightening of belts. But I still needed to be sure Mallory's pro-active solution was better.

"If you did the shorting, what's the worst possible outcome?"

"We lose the lot." As simple and as stark as that.

"How likely is that?" Passion was focusing my brain nicely.

"It's not very likely at all, but I can't put an exact number on it."

"And what's the best outcome?"

"Every member is at least four times better off."

"But is that very likely? A long shot on the Grand National pays better than four to one."

"Not very, no. But it's more likely than the worst scenario." Far from being offended or defensive, she seemed to be enjoying these rapid-fire exchanges. "Anyway, it's not a case of lose everything or be four times richer. If four times isn't on, we can still come out ahead."

"OK, so what's your most likely outcome?"

"I'll double their money. I can show you the figures if you like. It's all here." She pointed at her laptop. "I wrote myself a think-piece on the subject. All the pros and cons."

"Email it to me." I was impressed that she'd answered my questions without the usual financial flannel, where the only certainty was how much they were going to charge. Even so, I wanted a little more precision. "I'll have to rely on you for the odds, but if it were me, I'd take a small number of outcomes – to keep it simple, quadruple your money, double your money, break even, halve your money or lose the lot – put a percentage on each, and add up the results. If the answer is healthily positive, I'd do it. Otherwise not."

"That sounds wonderfully scientific, until you realise I can give you whatever odds suit my argument." She leaned forward earnestly. "That's half the trouble with the financial industry. They've learned to quantify, but they haven't learned to distinguish good input from bad. Putting a number to a sheer guess doesn't make it more accurate. This isn't going to be a single punt, and at every step I'll be feeling my way. I won't get a feel for the way things are going until I start. Think of me as a jazz musician improvising with an unknown band."

"You've never done this sort of thing before?"

"Quick plays to exploit volatility. Even *L'Esprit* doesn't mind that kind of thing. But, as you pointed out yesterday, it's a different ball game when you're betting the farm the victim is terminal. I play good poker, but I've never played in the world championship before."

I stared into her eyes. She didn't flinch, and I had to admire her courage. "You've just made it impossible for me to judge you objectively. It's what we talked about last time: how to make the best judgement on something that hasn't happened before." Her face was a mask. She wasn't going to influence me. "It all boils down to trust, doesn't it? If I say 'Do it', it means I trust your judgement. But if I say 'Don't', do you trust *me* enough to go along with *my* judgement?"

"You've really put me on the spot, haven't you?" She smiled thinly. "But yes, I'll act on your judgement. Whichever way it goes."

It really was my call. Mine alone. It would be so easy to say "Don't do it". But I hadn't been briefed to provide easy answers. More importantly, I believed Mallory's analysis of the crisis to come. Doing nothing meant that Ghost Trader's accumulated value, which had saved its members from ruin, could shrink like Bear Stearns's to almost nothing. Surely Mallory's shorting had to do much better than that? She was no fool; she'd been investing for longer and probably more consistently than most of her competitors. She'd already spotted the threat to AIG. Nor had she been rushed into shorting Enron just to please her ex-husband, the likely father of her probable daughter.

Just as importantly I believed her description of Ghost Trader as a club with nearly 2,000 members, and I rejected George's pessimistic alternative that it comprised only a tiny ring of conspirators. But even if I were wrong, my conclusion would be the same. Whether Mallory was acting selflessly for 1,999 people like me or self-interestedly for herself and a few bent cronies, her drive to succeed would be the same.

Yet in compelling me to review my thoughts, she was making the dangers all too apparent, and I had to force my breathing to slow before answering. The adrenalin had not gone away, but now it was focused entirely on the matter in hand. "I trust you. You should do it."

For a long time she did not move. Then she shivered, as though everything had been drained out of her. "Thank you," she said at last. She did not elaborate. She didn't have to.

I relaxed, too. "So we're back where we started. The question is not *whether* but *how*. How we persuade your members to back us."

"You won't," she cut in sharply.

"You were against Enron. This time it's different. The shorting recommendation will come from you. That must win a majority."

"You're saying my ex-husband was right?" she demanded.

"Only in retrospect. At the time you made the best recommendation you could on the evidence available. Which is exactly my point. Last time, the members had to choose between the expert and the amateur.

They backed you then, and they'll back you now. Even if the die-hards won't back you this time, I'm sure the others will. Just present your case the way you've presented it to me."

She shook her head. "You don't know the die-hards."

"You told me the members divided into three groups: pros, don't knows, and antis – the die-hards as you call them. Suppose you get all the pros, as before, and a majority of the don't knows, now that you're recommending the scheme: won't that give you a majority?"

"It's not that simple. I need more than a narrow majority. I need nearly all the members to be behind this. As it is, the die-hards won't simply agree to an immediate vote. They'll want time to marshal their arguments, and they'll fight a tremendous rearguard. *L'Esprit* will be their leader, and he's very persuasive. There's too much of a risk that the members will divide down the middle. Even if I win the vote, the die-hards will do their best to stop me going ahead, and even if they let me, they'll be on at me to buy back too early."

"Just make it clear that a 'yes' vote gives you total discretion for however many months you need." Even as I said it, I could tell she hated the idea. To her, every degree of freedom added would scare more of the don't knows into voting against.

"The die-hards will threaten to resign."

"But when it comes to the crunch, I bet most of them won't."

"Enough will. It'll be like Enron, only ten times worse."

"Let me talk to them. Talking round the obstinates was something I often did for clients. I'm good at it. At least, I used to be."

"I'm sure you haven't lost your touch."

"I can also burnish your case to the members for you. My job is turning facts into the most persuasive argument. Email me your think piece and I'll start work on it right away."

"Yes, you ought to do that." Yet she still didn't sound happy.

"What's the matter? Do you think I've gone rusty?"

She shook her head. "I just wish we weren't so democratic."

"But that's your strength!" I protested. "It's because you've empowered your members that they've stuck by you so long. They trust you not just because you're good, but because you trust them."

More than ever, I was convinced that Ghost Trader was exactly as she'd described it to me, and exactly as George hoped it to be. Whatever his fears that she might be a consummate liar, he had wanted to believe her, and I was no different.

She reacted with a bitter smile. "Its strength at all times but now."

"All you can do is give it your best shot. On their heads be it."

"These are my members. People like you. Many of them are my friends. We've gone through everything together for over a decade. I don't want to lose any one of them."

"You don't have any alternative."

"That doesn't stop me wishing I did."

"You could always present them with a *fait accompli*," I mused. There was always a chance the members would accept an action already taken even though they might not have agreed to it in advance. "You could tell them you had to act now to ensure the best return. They might shout and scream, but at least you'd have done it."

"I did think of that." She frowned. "The snag is the die-hards would insist I bought the shares back at the first opportunity. So the profit would be negligible, at best."

"And the others would agree because you hadn't consulted them?"

"That's the trouble with shorting. There are so many stages. As soon as I tried to borrow shares, the members would raise questions in the forum; even if I managed that without them noticing, there'd be uproar as soon as I started selling. Then their nerve would never hold whilst we waited for prices to bottom. Like I said, they'd have me buying back the shares and closing out the trade far too early."

The meeting had reached that point where we would only waste time to continue with it. I needed to go away and think, and to start work on what we'd have to send to members to get them on side. My mind was already racing ahead. Precise, persuasive and terse. There was no point in swamping them with figures; just enough to see that not shorting would be dangerous, whilst shorting itself would pay handsomely. Virtually a no brainer. Except that all the members – just like me – had once felt the same about Lloyd's. Ex-Names were living proof of another truism: once bitten, twice shy.

Perhaps that's how the case should begin. "Of course you're sceptical, but this is no time to be faint-hearted…"

I rose to my feet. "I need to go away and think. Email me your think piece. Also the rules. Whatever members sign before joining."

She stood too, a little surprised at my abruptness. "I'll send you whatever you want."

"What about access to the forum?" I continued. She frowned. Surely George's pessimistic interpretation wasn't going to prove true after all? Or was she just protecting her members from outside prying? I hoped so fervently. "If I'm going to construct a watertight pitch, I need to get inside their heads. What they say, and how they say it."

"If it helps, I'll email a password. But you mustn't participate."

"Of course not." All I needed was proof of the club's existence.

At the door, there was a moment of awkwardness as we considered how best to part. We both laughed, before she kissed me very quickly on the lips. Then she stepped immediately back with a restraining hand on my chest. She might be smiling, but there was to be no further intimacy. "I just wish there was a way round the need for a vote," she said. It sounded more like an instruction than a wish.

"I'll give it some thought," I promised, as I turned up the path.

"When can you get back to me?"

"Give me today for thinking, tomorrow for writing."

"I'll expect you the day after tomorrow, then. Make it 9:45."

I walked home in a happier frame of mind than the one in which I had arrived. Whatever Mallory's original intentions, I was now convinced that she had devoted herself and the money she had taken from the syndicate to the benefit of others. I could not know for sure whether she or Rex had initiated the fraud, but I admired her for attaching all the blame to herself and none to him.

As for the onslaught of passion, I was still reeling from its effects. I felt as though I'd been roused from a long and enervating sleep, that my moribund senses had come to life again at last. Best of all, I was sure that the effect on Mallory had been equally electric. Her road to recovery from the loss of Rex might be longer than mine from Amy, but I felt that we both had taken the first step. Joyously, spontaneously, without conscious thought. That in itself was progress.

As for Mallory's challenge, I was convinced that the members could be won over, and I was keen get started. For so long, my life had lacked both the solace of loving companionship and the drive of purposeful business. Now, all at once, there was the chance to fill both voids. Even as I walked, I couldn't help smiling. Like a heroine of old, Mallory had set me a daunting challenge, and I was determined not to fail her.

As soon as I reached my apartment, I logged into my mail box. Mallory had been as good as her word, and I quickly downloaded her think piece and the club rules. Then I used the username and password she'd also sent me to log onto the Ghost Trader website.

It was well set out and easy to use. Summary portfolio, detailed portfolio, monthly reports, forum, polls and even a list of members were ready, each at a single click, for my perusal. The site might be hidden from the eyes of non-members, but once in, there were no further obstacles. I went first to the list of members, which informed me that the total number of active participants was 1,952 together with 47 deceased members whose beneficiaries had replaced them. The list itself showed members in alphabetical order of user names, with the promise of more detail for any name I cared to click on.

The first name was *Allinost*. Intrigued, I highlighted the name for details. These informed me that the username was short for All Is Not Lost, that his first name was John, that his surname, age and occupation were withheld, but that he lived in Guildford, was married, and had two grown-up children and three grandchildren. Finally it listed the Lloyd's syndicates on which he had participated, and declared that he was prepared to receive emails from other members.

I was tempted next to check out *Le Baigneur* and *L'Esprit*, but their membership was not in dispute. With so much to go through, my time was better spent checking the existence of other members. I selected nine names at random, of which *Busted Flush*, *Lost Deposit* and *Sadder & Wiser* most typified the brave irony displayed by all. The snippets on each were similar, yet too personal to have been the invention of a single hand. This was wonderful. Proof positive that Ghost Trader was a proper club with nearly 2,000 participating members.

I went next to the portfolio summary, which told me that the total value at today's prices was just over £600 million, which meant that the average member's participation was worth over £300,000. A big improvement on the state of bankruptcy in which many had started. Finally I turned to the forum. It was as active as promised.

Some comments were silly, some rude, and many were critiques of earlier comments rather than direct questions or protests to Mallory. The general tenor might best be described as informed scepticism. But the sceptics were not throwing down fundamental challenges. Usually they simply wanted reassurance that a trade they didn't understand had a proper rationale. In her replies, Mallory was conscientious, and always took the questions seriously. Particular issues might run back and forth for a week or more, but nobody was demanding a wholly different approach, or protesting that they were being ignored.

There was plenty about the credit crunch, generally concluding that Mallory should take even more care than usual in choosing what to buy and what to sell. There were also plenty of suggestions for investments, all of which Mallory had answered. But the records only went back two years, so it was impossible to go back to the Enron saga.

In three hours, I had the measure of the forum. As with most of its kind, active participants were a small proportion of the membership. To make sure, I even did a count. Over the entire two year period, fewer than 100 members had ever written anything, and of these, well under fifty made regular contributions. Interestingly, neither *Le Baigneur* nor

L'Esprit was a regular contributor, though their occasional missives were authoritative and taken seriously by the others. Doubtless they contacted Mallory directly when they felt it necessary. Either way, the forum was a dangerous guide to the entire membership, unless I were prepared to assume that the silent majority thought exactly as the forum users. Here, fortunately, I had some guidance from an annual two-question poll, taken every year from the first:

Covering the past 12 months, how satisfied are you:

Q1 With the fund's performance?

Q2 With the fund manager's performance?

Almost without variation, two-thirds of the members declared themselves "very satisfied" on both questions, and only a small minority, under 10%, said they were dissatisfied. The exception was, of course, 2001, the year of the Enron debacle. Yet even then, the dissatisfaction levels rose no higher than 25% for fund performance, and 27% for manager performance.

Both satisfied and dissatisfied members were always asked to give their reasons, and every year positive and negative reasons were mirror images. Satisfied members thought all investment opportunities had been explored, and felt well-informed by the fund manager: the dissatisfied thought opportunities had been missed, and they had not always been kept abreast of what was going on. Since so many more members were satisfied than dissatisfied, the positives always heavily outweighed the negatives, which led me to the general conclusion that dissatisfied members were over-represented in the forum.

The 2001 reasons differed only in that so many of them related overtly to Enron. Even so, the number of satisfied members reporting that the issue had been well-handled outweighed the number of dissatisfieds thinking the opposite. Most criticisms targeted other members rather than the fund manager. Only a minority bore directly on the merits or demerits of shorting. For what it was worth, the number expressing satisfaction that shorting Enron had not been attempted was larger than the number wishing it had gone ahead.

Finally, I turned to the rules to which prospective members had to assent before their membership could be confirmed. According to these, members must accept that they were long-term investors who could not withdraw more than 10% of their personal holding in any one year (unless they wished to resign). In return, members were entitled to view the fund portfolio on line and to participate, politely, in the forum at all times, provided they never divulged their username or password to outsiders. They were encouraged to put questions and suggestions, but the discretion of the fund manager was paramount.

In return, the fund manager promised to keep members informed, via the website, to act always in their best interests, and to charge no more than 1% per annum. Amazing terms for a hedge fund, yet at current value, Mallory's take would be in excess of £6 million. Allowing for the fees paid to market analysts, Mallory's net return was substantial to anyone whose frame of reference was the real economy.

The fund manager could be removed by majority vote, but to initiate such a vote required the support of at least 50 members.

It was mid-evening by the time I'd digested all this, and I was feeling exhausted. Over a sandwich and juice, I nevertheless felt pleased with my efforts. It seemed to me that the members were not as recalcitrant as Mallory had described them, and that she had more latitude to act as she saw fit. I felt confident that we could carry any vote; also that she had the authority to act unilaterally, though I was far from certain that she would, whatever I were to say. But tomorrow I would set out my recommendations.

I went to bed that night contentedly hoping that I would dream of Mallory. But it was back to my hospital room. This time my visitor was Andréa. Out of sorts, he fidgeted for a long time without speaking. The sophisticated cynic had regressed to bolshie teenager. I told myself that it was nice of him to come when he had other things on his mind.

"You've got a son, haven't you?" he said at last, then relapsed into silent study of his shoe. His shoulders slouched truculently. "Was he planned, or did he just happen? What I mean is: was he planned by you, or did she trick you?" He glared at me angrily. "Marie-Sainte comes on her own sometimes. She must have told you, asked you." He slapped his thigh hard enough to raise dust from his jeans. "Look at me. I'm a bloody labourer now. Céline took pity on me. Well, on her really. They're punishing me with hard labour. Céline's acting for the last development on the lake. Over in St Jorioz. Developer needed an extra pair of hands. I'll write a pamphlet: the exploitation of labour."

I thought back to Marie-Sainte's last visit. Had she looked pregnant? Radiant certainly, and that was a sign supposedly. Had she been rounder in the face? Perhaps. But it was hard to imagine such an elfin creature carrying another human life. I wondered why she hadn't said anything. Perhaps she thought I wouldn't approve because I was her parents' friend. Poor Armand, the so proper step-father; poor Sidonie, the mother who'd brought up her daughter to be sensible. As for Marie-Sainte herself: had she been careless, or had she planned it all?

It amazed me how much of their troubles my visitors poured out to me. I put it down to their treating me as a secular priest, who heard their confessions without criticism or penance. All except Marie-Sainte, who had so far been unable to proclaim her baby to me. But she had always been the most secretive of them all, hiding more behind her gentle smile than the supposedly more worldly ever managed.

I woke with a start. It was too early for the diesel chorus, yet I was wide awake. My dream had prompted the solution to Mallory's problem. Marie-Sainte was a computer expert in need of employment. An expert with no contacts in the financial world, who could thus work in complete anonymity on what I now wanted to propose.

Then I cursed myself for an unprincipled fool. How could I possibly expect Marie-Sainte, the girl who might have been my step-daughter, to involve herself in the deception I had in mind? Even a deception in a good cause, a deception that ought to have nothing but a happy ending. Was this how to introduce a sweet child to the world of business?

As I pondered this over coffee, it occurred to me that I had no proof that Marie-Sainte was even pregnant. Nobody had told me, except in my dream. On the other hand, my dreams had always been consistent with what was going on in my waking world. Subliminally I must have noticed that Marie-Sainte had the glow of awed pride which had suffused Amy when she'd learned she was carrying Jake.

My idea might be hare-brained, I half-hoped that Mallory would reject it as unethical, but it could not be un-thought. Nothing would be lost if I sounded out Marie-Sainte today.

Chapter Eleven : Moral Imperative

I called Sidonie after breakfast to explain that I just might have work for Marie-Sainte. "If she can spare the time, this could pay very well."

Sidonie was all enthusiasm. "Of course she'll find the time."

Marie-Sainte rang a few minutes later. "Monsieur Clem, Mama asked me to call you." She tried hard to keep the enthusiasm out of her voice, but I knew instantly that she was keen. I consoled myself with the thought that whatever happened Marie-Sainte would be rewarded, and that she would never know what I really had in mind.

"No promises, but this could be interesting for you. It's a financial project," I explained. "On-line dealing, that sort of thing. Real and virtual. Is that something you can cope with?"

"That's so lucky," she exclaimed. "The current part of my course covers exactly what you want. It's not difficult, just tricky. Lots of data streams, lots of links. It's not just instant access to the current price, you need back data, charts, all sorts of stuff. It's very easy to set up a clunky site; much harder to make one that works really smoothly."

"Just match the existing model." I was reassured by her knowledge, but fearful that the complexity was greater than I'd realised. Members made grumpy could become suspicious.

She seemed un-fazed. "I'll do my best to improve it."

The self-confidence of youth, I thought. Marie-Sainte was one of the quietest and most biddable girls you could wish to meet, yet on her subject she was certain. I could only hope that her faith in herself would live up to my trust. As for her trust in me, that depended not only on the justice of Mallory's cause but its proper execution.

Marie-Sainte was happy to fit me in over lunch, and she suggested a restaurant in Veyrier that had a pontoon over the water. "It's warm enough to sit outside." I agreed. Outside, the tables were so spaced that confidential conversations were easy. We met at 13:45, and we had the pontoon almost to ourselves. In bobble hat and quilted jacket, Marie-Sainte was equipped for all weathers, and when she arrived, she unwrapped her scarf and placed it with her gloves on the seat beside her. We both ordered the dish of the day, which was *Fritures du Lac*, and out of deference to Marie-Sainte I also ordered salad rather than potatoes. She accepted a glass of wine, but diluted to a spritzer.

As we waited for our food, I withdrew a typed and headed sheet from my briefcase. "It's a confidentiality agreement. I'll need you to sign it before we really get down to business." She smiled sweetly as her eye roamed over the paragraphs, each in English as well as French. She trusted me completely. But she read it before she signed.

"How long is this job likely to take?" she asked.

"I'm hoping you'll be able to tell me," I said. "I'm guessing two to three weeks. Then you'll need to be on stand-by for sorting out glitches. All paid, of course."

"I suppose Andréa told you." She blushed. "He said he would."

I was about to admit my knowledge, but bit it back just in time. Andréa had spoken to me only in my dream. Yet I must have known the truth in some way, unless I were to accept that I was psychic. "Told me what?" I asked innocently.

She looked confused. "Isn't that why you're offering me work?"

If I had any doubts about her, her modesty won me over. "My dear girl, I'm offering you work because I recognise your skill and care."

"I'm pregnant," she whispered. Then she smiled wickedly. "Andréa calls me *Marie-Enceinte* when we're alone. He was angry at first, but now he's pleased. He's even got himself a job, thanks to Céline." She became serious again. "You don't mind, do you? I mean, you won't stop considering me?" Her manner was so childlike, my conscience pricked me harder. But I was too committed to turn back.

"Of course I won't," I promised. Then I gave her the proposition I'd worked out. "My client's an investment club, a group of ex-Lloyd's investors. People like me. Their aim is to recoup their losses, and their trading is done by a professional. I've talked with her, so please believe me when I say she's good. Her trading name is Ghost Trader."

"Ghost Trader or Ghost Raider?" Marie-Sainte giggled at her little joke. I could only shrug. She was more perceptive than she knew.

"The members are far from passive," I continued. "They follow the trading on-line: a viewing platform, if you like, rather than a dealing platform. They also have an active forum. With so many different opinions, it's difficult to take all of them on board. What we now need is three or four viewing platforms: one will show the real trading, the others will be virtual. If a virtual strategy starts to outperform the real strategy, then we can switch around."

"I'd love to help. But why not use the outfit who set it up?"

It was a good question, but I was prepared for it. "The first rule of business," I explained with a knowing smile, "is never turn it away, unless you don't want it. If the client prefers you to somebody else, there's a good reason. Here, it's quite simple. The current outfit are making difficulties. Doing a bespoke job for Ghost Trader just isn't their idea of profitable activity. The fund may look big to you and me, but to these guys it's peanuts. So they want to sell us something ready-made. Only that isn't what we want."

She smiled that innocent smile. "You expect me be cheaper, too."

"Yes. But not because we want to rip you off. The other outfit has huge overheads; you don't. You can make more money than the hack programmer they'd put onto it, and still give us a better price. And better service." I did my best to look wise and avuncular. "I'm as keen as you that you get a fair reward for your work, and I've got a better understanding of what the market will bear. If I think you're under-quoting, I'll make sure you up your price."

"You're too good to be true, Monsieur Clem." There was no irony.

"You haven't got the job yet," I reminded her. "If you do, you'll find I'm a stickler for timing and for top quality work. You'll earn what we pay you, don't worry about that." Her face fell. "Nevertheless, most people I commission enjoy the work." I smiled reassuringly. "Do your job, and we'll get along just fine."

After we'd eaten, she pulled a notebook out of her bag. "The main thing with trading platforms is access to market data. Current prices, of course, but also back data. Active trading platforms update prices every 15 minutes. Is that what you want, or will once a day be OK?"

"It's twice a day now. Opening and closing. If you improved on that, I'm sure plenty of members would be delighted." She was sharp, and I was glad I had briefed myself well.

"What exchanges do you trade on?"

"Paris, Frankfurt, London, New York and NASDAQ. Plus small caps, but they don't need special links. They're explained monthly on the site. Ditto corporate bonds and treasuries."

"That's quite a few." Her lips pursed thoughtfully. "But, of course, this isn't a trading platform – sorry, viewing platform – for amateurs. I see why the other lot don't want it."

"Is it a problem?" Surely we weren't going to fall at the first hurdle?

She shook her head. "More to think about, that's all. But it'll take more than three weeks." I frowned non-committally. "I'll be as fast as I can." She glanced down at her notebook. "What about CDOs? Not that there's an exchange for them exactly. But there is data."

122

"We don't touch those," I assured her, delighted by her knowledge.

"Not even triple As?" When I shook my head, more in amazement at the depth of her knowledge than to dismiss triple As, she laughed. "I'm glad. They're rubbish, according to my professor. He's been showing us. You can devise computer programs to dice and slice the underlying mortgage bonds until the ratings agencies don't know whether they're coming or going. So the banks persuade them even junk is investment grade." She glowered, as if I were part of the conspiracy to bamboozle the rating agencies. "It's disgusting. When I explained it to Andréa, he couldn't believe it. You know what he said?"

She blushed as she giggled. "He said, one dog turd everyone steps round; but if you slice up ten and mix up the slices, suddenly you've got a work of art that everyone wants to buy." She turned serious again. "Then he said he'd like to go down Wall Street with a chain saw."

Uncannily, I'd had exactly the same idea about Lloyd's. "They're there in the Room," I'd shouted in the pub, after breaking Wormsley's nose at the Wu action group meeting. "I'll have the pricks off the lot of them." Ambrose had said a machine gun would be faster.

"Just make sure he doesn't. He's got responsibilities now."

"He wouldn't hurt a fly." She consulted her notebook again. "What about CDSs?"

"I don't even know what those are," I admitted.

"Credit default swaps. They're a kind of insurance. One company takes one out with another. No exchanges, and no regulators. My professor says there's enough of them, if – when – they go bad, to wipe out the wealth of the world." Her face was a wonderful display of emotions. Anger and incredulity, but also a childlike disdain. "If I'm a bank with a pile of crappy CDOs, I'd want to swap the risk away as fast as I could, but who'd take it on?"

Now it was my turn to be incredulous. Here was I, a middle-aged and supposedly experienced man, being given a lecture on the absurdities of the financial system, not by a Wall Street insider, but by a young student, with scarcely a *sou* to her name, who was studying computing rather than economics. I reminded myself that this was France, a country with deep reservations about global capitalism and a strong intellectual tradition. A tradition in which Marie-Sainte, for all her youth, was one of the brightest exemplars. "Tell me," I said.

"Suppose I'm a bank and I want to insure my CDOs…" she began.

I held up my hand. "What are you insuring them against?"

"If homeowners can't pay their mortgage, the CDOs can't pay their interest." Again that glower of fury. "The homeowners are mainly sub-prime or close, so if they lose their jobs, or their mortgage interest goes up, they're going to stop paying. They can't help it."

"Surely the banks must know this."

"Andréa says of course they know, they're just a bunch of crooks on the make." She struggled to contain her anger. "I think they blinded themselves with their own science."

"Like Andréa's artist with the dog turds, you mean? He wasn't being cynical, he genuinely believed he'd created a work of art." All the old anger that Lloyd's had provoked set the blood pounding in my cheeks. "People paid that much have no right to think that way."

"The money's too easy and far too much. Enough to tempt a saint."

I laughed grimly. "Before he sells it, the artist knows it's a heap of shit. Once somebody's agreed to give him millions of dollars for it, even he's convinced it's art. The only thing that disappoints me is that homeowners didn't see they were being conned."

"The deals were too tempting. They were offered low teaser rates, they were encouraged to lie about their income. The salesmen didn't care because they knew the mortgages would be sold on. The banks didn't care because they'd bundle the mortgages into CDOs, get most of them rated investment grade, and sell them on to unsuspecting pension funds and local authorities, the kinds of people who are only allowed to buy investment-grade stuff."

"If enough suckers take the bait, the conman is convinced he's providing a public service."

"Oh, yes. The original aim of sub-prime mortgages was to make loans cheaper for poor people. Cheaper because they were secured on their home. So they paid off their credit cards and their car loans, as well as getting a home of their own. Andréa says we're lucky we don't love credit like you Anglo-Saxons." She blushed. "Sorry."

I had to laugh. "These CDSs. Who *does* take the risk off the banks?"

"I don't know. The CDS premium's tiny compared with making good the CDO if it fails. Unless you're certain it won't fail, you're mad to take it on. But if the risk's zero, why would a bank offer to pay you to take it?" She wrinkled her nose in puzzlement and disdain.

"So if a bank wants to buy a CDS from you, you should know it's dodgy, or they wouldn't be asking?" Remembering what Mallory had said about AIG, I realised they must be the company offering the swaps. They were an insurer, just like Lloyd's, and I knew first hand what absurd risks Lloyd's had accepted. "The bank plays up the investment grade, you convince yourself low risk is no risk, that the premiums are pure profit." This was exactly the half-baked,

124

unquestioning logic which had inflicted such huge losses on Names. Shorting the charlatans and the wilfully stupid wasn't simply an investment opportunity, it was a moral imperative. Marie-Sainte, of all people, had unwittingly given me the justification I needed.

"The banks aren't looking for customers, they're looking for fools to exploit." She almost bared her teeth. *"That's* why I hate them."

Even after everything she'd said, I was staggered by her vehemence. She who had had no direct experience of the humiliation and despair that financial ruin brings in its wake was consumed by an anger every bit as fierce as my own. "You were almost defending them a minute ago," I reminded her. "Temptations to test the virtue of a saint."

"Think what a failed CDO means," she continued fiercely. "Thousands thrown out of their homes; people whose only mistake is to be poor. Never mind the organisations that buy CDOs. It's the human tragedies that matter. Neighbourhoods devastated. Hurricane Katrina over and over. And it's coming here, though we've done nothing."

Following that little outburst, I came within an ace of telling her what Mallory and I were really about. But I managed to restrain myself. I had no right to put her at risk simply because she was angry. I consoled myself that if ever she did find out, she would understand.

She was smiling again. "Is it all right if I involve my professor?"

I hesitated. Involving her professor would mean another person in the loop, a stranger, and a man of some importance. At the same time, it was sensible of Marie-Sainte to want to tap his experience, as well as honest of her to ask me. She'd probably consult him anyway. "As long as he'll sign the confidentiality agreement." From everything she'd said, he sounded an interesting man.

Chapter Twelve : Risk & Uncertainty

The duty nurse arrived with a new visitor. For a moment I thought it was Mallory, though she was wearing a gilet and sweater I'd never seen before, and her hair was shorter and several shades lighter. Then Amy had often surprised me with new outfits and hairstyles. But Amy had never managed to grow taller and slimmer. The Mallory who wasn't Mallory sat at my bedside, and stared at me gravely, without a spark of recognition. Now she was closer, I could see that her face was shorn of all the tiny lines that I already knew so well. If this was Mallory, for the likeness was uncanny, it was Mallory as she must have looked before experience and tragedy had shaped her. Mallory as Rex Tonbridge might first have seen her.

"I don't know whether you can understand me, but I hope so." She hesitated. "I've been wanting to come and see you for a long time, but I kept putting it off. Even after Jake said it would be OK. Seeing her like this cracks me up enough as it is. You absolutely saved her life, you know. At least I hope you know. I just wanted to say thank you."

Her voice was sharper than Mallory's, and her accent more decidedly English. She took my hand and shook it solemnly. "I should introduce myself properly. I'm her daughter. Hope." She pulled a face. "The name was my father's idea. To be the opposite of Mallory. It's from *malheur* – misfortune, as I'm sure you know. God knows why my grandparents chose it. I suppose they liked the sound, may their souls rest in peace. But my father looked up its meaning. He's like that. *Was*. Her name was the only thing about her he didn't like."

She sighed. "That was the awful thing: he adored her, but she never really loved him. Right until the end, what he always wanted was for my mother to take him back. The three of us to be a family again... except we'd never really been one in the first place." She tried to smile, but the effort defeated her. "It's like he wanted to turn the clock back so we could make a new beginning... things we'd never done. It was hopeless." She frowned defiantly, just the way her mother did. "I should have helped him more, but we were never that close."

She glanced around the room, and I took the opportunity to study her carefully. Now I realised who she was I could see differences from her mother. Her features were more angular, and she had a more intense way of looking at things. "If the accident spared her one thing it was having to watch her father die. That's a blessing of sorts." Her face closed up on mine, in a gesture that was strangely reminiscent of Ambrose. Awake or dreaming, it seemed that I was to be forever plagued with reminders of him. Fortunately, to be peered at close up by her was charming in a way it could never have been with him.

"I wish she'd never come back to France. But she had to get away. My father was driving her mad. They divorced long ago, but he never quite lets go. At least he didn't." She faltered, then tried to laugh it off. "But the last thing you want to hear is me going on about my troubles. I do this with her, too. Sit and talk. I think it helps. There's still brain activity. You, too. You'll make it, one of these days. Both of you. Then she can thank you for herself."

She sighed, and straightened her back. Like Mallory getting down to business. "I run a firm of market analysts. We do all the research for Ghost Trader. I wonder if you've any idea what I'm talking about." She shook her head and smiled. "It's not as if you can exactly pop into each other's rooms for a chat. It's just there has to be something between you. I imagine you communicating telepathically, or wandering into each other's dreams. I'm sure you do dream, like I'm sure you know what I'm saying. Is that foolish of me? I don't think so."

She relapsed into silence, and sat without moving. There was none of the restless fidgeting that afflicted so many of my visitors. "Jake told me all about you," she continued after a while. "It seems you qualify for Ghost Trader membership. Same as my father, until he got all fixated on Enron. Once he got an idea, he'd worry away at it. A real obsessive. But he was right. She could have made a killing over Enron. I was trying to persuade her to do it this time with the banks, but she kept saying the members wouldn't go for it. But look what's happening now. There's still time, just about. I'd do it like a shot, if I knew how to get round the members." She laughed grimly. "I do the trading now, as well as the research. But the members don't fully trust me. I'm merely the stop-gap, until she recovers. They've given me until the end of the year. In the meantime, I daren't suggest anything off the wall."

The advantage of the comatose state was the placidity with which I could face what my visitors said. It was the mention of telepathy that made the difference this time; plus the realisation that if Mallory and I really were marooned in hospital, the members could never be saved. Now that reality had violated my dream, I must break silence.

I concentrated my strength, but nothing happened. Without muscle tone, I was as powerless as a dream could make me. But I would not give up. The venture depended on my speaking. Sweat oozed from my brow, as I focused all my energy. "Talk to Marie-Sainte."

It wasn't much better than a croak, but she almost fell off her chair.

"You spoke!" Leaning right into my face, she seized my arm. "Don't go back to sleep, please don't." Then she scrambled to her feet. "I'd better fetch the nurse."

"Wait!" My voice was hoarse after so long, but it was enough to bring her back to my side. "You're right. We do communicate." Even as I started speaking, I felt my strength failing, but my will refused to give up. "She wants to short Lehman... AIG, too. You need to talk to Marie-Sainte... a student in computer science. Bright as they come... no connection with the financial industry." Then, as my voice faded to a whisper, I wheezed out what I planned to tell Mallory tomorrow, before tumbling into the black abyss of exhaustion.

The next thing I knew, the nurse was bending over me. "He definitely spoke," Hope was saying. "Perfectly lucidly, too." I felt like a drowned man rising from the deep.

The nurse smoothed my pillows. "It's a good sign. They don't just wake up all at once. It takes time. But his brain patterns are much more active than usual." She smiled at me. "You hang in there, Monsieur. We'll have the both of you up and about one of these days."

"I'll come and see him again," said Hope. She gathered up her bag, and smiled down at me. "I'll think about what you said. I promise." Then with a wave, she was gone.

"I have a solution," I told Mallory, as we started our meeting the next morning. "One that doesn't require balloting your members. But I don't know that you're going to like it."

"You intrigue me." Then she laughed. "But this doesn't sound like you. Two days ago you were the great champion of democracy." Far from being horrified, she was teasing me.

"I still am. But I've read your rules. Investment decisions rest with you; the members can question, but they can't veto, unless you hack them off so much, they vote to sack you. In return, you promise always to act in their best interests. So you'd be entirely within your rights to short Lehman, AIG and any other outfit that fits your criteria. And talking of democracies, remember that governments seek a mandate to govern: they don't ask their electorates to micro-manage the economy by voting on every decision. You have your mandate from the two-thirds of members who are 'very satisfied' with your performance each

128

year, including the last one. You have the power and the right to act: the only question is how to exercise it."

"Go on." There was already the light of excitement in her eyes. Far from being fearful that my plan was immoral, she was eager to learn its detail. The leopard had not entirely lost her spots, whilst mine were growing darker by the minute. But I was haunted by Marie-Sainte's image of blasted neighbourhoods, brought about not by the impersonal forces of nature but by the greed and stupidity of Lehman and AIG. Mallory's prime motive might be to protect her members; mine was vengeance. A bad reason for shorting, perhaps, but a powerful one for showing how, in this case, it could be done.

"What the members see is not a real trading platform. Just a place to record trades for inspection, not to execute them. Virtual, not real. Which means you could continue ostensibly trading as you are, whilst in reality you'd be shorting out of their sight."

"A complete deception, you mean?" Her brow darkened.

"Precisely why I'm not recommending it. What I want is for the members to see shorting and the current strategy going on side by side. In fact, I want to go further than that. I propose four viewing platforms: the current strategy, two conventional variants, *and* shorting. So members will see everything that reasonably could happen going on before their eyes. They'll think you're carrying on as before, but they'll see the alternatives going on in parallel."

"*Four*! Why?" She managed to look both horrified and intrigued.

I smiled like a conjuror reaching into his hat. "However we do this, we'll have to switch from the platform they see now to a new one. We can't risk the current provider getting even a hint of this. But your members won't appreciate the change unless it can be shown to be a big improvement. So you acknowledge that trading is getting tough, that there are different strategies that might be followed. Then you tell them there'll now be four viewing platforms enabling them to compare what you're actually doing with a full range of alternatives. Then you can really encourage suggestions from them."

For a long time she sat thunderstruck. For so long, I thought I'd blown it. Finally she banged the table with her fist. "So the members will think I'm still doing what I normally do, and the rest are purely for comparison. But they'll see the shorting working."

"With luck, they'll be clamouring for you to switch."

"And if it fails, they'll want my head twice over."

"It's not going to fail. You'll prove shorting was the only strategy."

She let out a long whistle. "I've accused you of being everything from a stalker to a policeman. The truth is you're a genius. A devious and twisted genius, but brilliant nonetheless." Then before I could respond, she turned to a clean sheet on her pad. "Do I take it you've got a computer outfit in mind?" I described Marie-Sainte. "Are you sure she's experienced enough?" I explained that not only was she a clever programmer, she had an experienced professor for back-up, and she was so well-versed in the ways of the financial world that she understood the difference between a CDO and a CDS. "She sounds good," Mallory conceded. "When do I meet her?"

"You don't." I explained my reasoning. "If this thing ever goes pear-shaped, she must be in the clear. So long as you brief me properly, and give her access to the site, she can work it out from there. Trust me, she's a very bright girl. One of the best."

For a long time she said nothing, her expression deadpan. Then she nodded. "Good. I can see you've thought it through. So! Take me through it step by step. Exactly what the young genius is giving me. We know what we're aiming for. I want to nip snags in the bud."

We sat for over an hour, and she covered several pages of notes. Then she opened her laptop and logged into the existing platform. "Pretend you're some awkward sod, like *L'Esprit*. Look for snags. Things the program's weak on at the moment. It's years old, after all. Your Marie-Sainte is quite right to think it can be improved."

After another hour and a half, she'd almost turned me into an investment expert, and we'd identified at least ten improvements, which she typed up and printed for me. "I've only one complaint," she said, as she handed the printed sheet to me. "You're wanting me to run four portfolios instead of one. That's four times the work."

"Twice," I corrected her. "At the very least you'd have had two: the current strategy and the shorting strategy. And the others are supposed to be variants not radical departures."

"I might just make you do the necessary research," she threatened. But she was laughing as she said it.

We stood by the window and surveyed the calm and indifferent beauty of the lake. There was no going back now. The lake had become our Rubicon and from where we stood we seemed already to have started our crossing. I slipped my arm around her waist. In response she turned to face me, arms around my neck, with an expression of regret. "You're going to think me absurdly superstitious, but I don't want any distractions until this thing is over." She shrugged as if she understood how bizarre she sounded. "This is the biggest thing I've ever tried. I can't let anything jeopardise it. Not even you." She smiled wistfully. "I'm only asking for your patience. When it's all over, you won't know what's hit you. Am I being absurd?"

I found myself laughing. It was the only way to dissipate the energy she had aroused. "I thought it was only boxers who denied themselves before a big fight. To make them meaner."

She laughed too. "Mean as Hell. That's what I need."

"You need to relax as well. This is going more than 12 rounds."

"It's hard to explain." She gave a helpless shrug. "If I'm putting the members' savings at risk, I shouldn't be enjoying myself. I'm shorting the banks, not behaving like a banker."

"Your self-denial becomes mine, too. Is that fair?" But as the words escaped my lips, I could see that she was right. I thought of Marie-Sainte, angry but innocent. I thought of all the sub-prime borrowers who had been forced to default on their mortgages. Hurricane Katrina had been an impersonal force of nature; the devastated neighbourhoods which Marie-Sainte had so graphically described were disasters of man's own making. Self-denial might help nobody, yet – given the deviousness of my plan – it was poetically just. The task ahead was all that mattered, and if that task meant putting the happiness of others at risk, it was only right that we should for the moment suspend our own. "OK," I conceded. "I accept."

Thus the great venture began. Marie-Sainte was a diligent worker who committed herself exactly as I'd hoped she would. Yet, like most new ventures, it took longer than I'd hoped: five weeks, not three. Just as impatient as my old clients, Mallory chafed at delay. I consoled myself that her frustration lacked the venom that only lovers generate. In like mode, my response was as correct as a supplier's ought to be, within the compass of my ego. Which is to say that she swore and I shouted, but we never came to blows, and we never resorted to the insults that lovers cast with such wounding precision.

I did my best to protect Marie-Sainte from all this, because she was right not to cut corners, to make sure that even a *L'Esprit* at his most awkward would have no proper cause for complaint, and every reason to be grateful. Her attention to detail matched that of Ambrose at his best, and she was far more fun to work with. Yet I could not entirely spare her, since I knew that Mallory was impatient for good reason. The markets waited for no-one.

She was especially twitchy when Bear Stearns shareholders launched a class action against JP Morgan's share offer. "This could freak the markets, and I'm not ready," she stormed.

131

"You were never going to be ready in time for this one," I pointed out. "Anyway the market's have factored it in. The shareholders have been screaming murder from day one."

"You'd better be right." We hardly spoke for the rest of that day.

I also worked on the announcement to members, which had to sell the advantages of the new scheme and give them no excuse to make difficulties. Its wording became another source of friction between Mallory and myself, as well as its timing. She wanted to announce as close to launch date possible, I wanted to announce early. I won that argument, and I was proved right. The members had time to make suggestions; thereafter, they were as anxious as we could have wished to see four viewing platforms in action. Instead of sniping, they demanded to be up and running as soon as possible.

We launched on the last day of April. I wanted to pay Marie-Sainte a thank-you bonus, but Mallory was too fraught to consider it. "No way! She's late. We're probably fucked already." But she calmed down when the members started to report their delight in the forum. There were almost no complaints, and Marie-Sainte was so quick to respond we were able to turn even these to our advantage. "All right," Mallory conceded. "She's wonderful. Pay what you like." She gave me a kiss, her first friendly gesture since the venture had begun. Yet friendly was all it was. Our only achievement so far was the ability to start. But that was something, and with that something I had to be content.

Chapter Thirteen : Gambling with Insurance

"Is there anything I can do to help with the trading?" I asked.

We were sitting in Mallory's living room over a bottle of wine. The screens were still on, but the sound had been turned down. It was a sombre evening, and thunder grumbled around the hills. Lightning from the other side of *Semnoz* lit up the undersides of the clouds, and seemed to solidify their blackness into crags and ravines of rock. Every so often, savage flurries of rain pitted the surface of the lake. Mallory's mood was similarly brooding.

"No way. There's nothing to see, and I hate being watched."

"I wouldn't get in your way. I could even monitor one of the screens. Otherwise, I'll provide refreshments."

I could feel her retreating from me. I knew she was only psyching herself up, but I feared the loneliness of exclusion. The last weeks had been fraught, but I'd never regretted her company.

She sipped her wine in silence. Then she smiled. "I will need feeding, won't I? That's if you don't mind. But I don't need my hand holding. That would drive me spare."

From accomplice, I was reduced to nursemaid. I consoled myself that keeping her healthy was just as vital. On the first morning I brought *pains au chocolat* and coffee, which we shared for breakfast, then I left her to it until mid-day, when I brought *pâté* and salads. We ate from the living room table, but she was tense and distracted, and kept returning to her screens, mobile never far from her hand.

"The moment you hear," she instructed during the first call. "Keep on it," she remonstrated in the second. "That's what I'm paying you for," she shouted, as soon as she'd taken the third. Her anxiety as the fourth call came in was painful. "You have?" She punched the air. "Brilliant. Don't let up. I need the rest. Yes, now. If not, yesterday." She paused to allow her caller to reply. "Moving mountains is what I pay for, not promises. I can't trade on promises."

She returned to the table. "Believe it or not, I hate coming heavy."

I cast my mind back to altercations I'd had in the past. "You sounded quite restrained." With my suppliers, I'd often come close to blows. "And you seemed to be making progress."

She nodded. "I'm rounding up the shares to rent. I'm pretty much there on AIG, but Lehman and the others are taking longer. I'm not the only one looking." She toyed unenthusiastically with a sliver of *pâté*. "AIG shares peaked – last October I think – at just over $70. Now they're south of $50. That's why I need to get selling a.s.a.p."

"That's quite a drop," I agreed. "Are the markets onto them?"

"There's worry out there, that's all. I'm counting on the shares going under $10, and very suddenly, too. I don't want to give my lenders time to think they ought to be selling."

"You mean if they want to sell, you have to give them back?"

"Of course. That's the deal. The shares belong to them."

"So you're relying on them being less on the ball." At last I truly grasped the hard game we were playing. Making money for her members was a proper objective; putting bad companies out of business was acceptable collateral damage. But this went further. Unsuspecting shareholders would find the stock they'd loaned was worthless.

She read my expression. "Look, they can sell whenever they want. If they don't, that's their bad judgement. At least they get rent."

"People say that shorting causes companies to fail."

"That's crazy." She startled me with her vehemence. "What would be the point of trying to short a perfectly healthy company? The market wouldn't sell and you'd lose."

"If selling drives the price down, it becomes self-fulfilling."

"Nobody's big enough for that. What's the point, anyway? Good companies are the ones you want to buy." Her mobile rang again. "Hi!" Her worry lines receded. "Sounds great. Speak to you later." She turned back to me. "I told you about Hope, didn't I?" I nodded non-committally. "She's doing the extra portfolios you talked me into. So you're off the hook."

"She does your research, right?" I wasn't sure Mallory had told me, but I doubted my dream would have invented it, any more than it had invented Marie-Sainte's pregnancy.

"It was my husband who wanted a child," she continued, as if she hadn't heard me. "He thought it would keep us together. Instead, she drove us apart. Not intentionally, poor lamb."

"I thought it was Rex who was responsible for that."

She glared. "You must think me a rotten wife and mother."

"I'm not passing judgement."

"Aren't you?" She sighed. "You and my ex are quite alike."

The last person I wanted to be compared to. "How come?"

"You want Amy back, the same as he wanted me."

"Not now," I countered, though her perceptiveness startled me.

"I grant you're more realistic. Won't she have you?"

"Not since Saul. But that's not the reason. You know it isn't."

She leaned back, her eyes hard. "Thank you," she said at last.

"Is that no thanks?" I felt more like a job applicant than a suitor.

"I can't be an Amy substitute."

"You're nothing like her." I longed to seize her in my arms, but her embargo on sex unnerved me. "You're unique. Mallory *Malheur*." The translation of her name had haunted me since my dreaming of Hope, and it slipped out before I could stop it.

For a moment she looked stunned. Then she laughed, but without much humour. "Just what my husband used to say. You are like him, whether you want to be or not."

"No way!" I protested. "He hated your name, I love it."

"Perhaps you shouldn't." She seemed unaware that I'd blurted out something I couldn't have known but for Hope's appearance in my dream. "Whatever my parents intended, I *was* well-named. I bring bad luck to relationships. If you've any sense…"

Her voice trailed away as a gust of wind stirred the lake, and water sucked uneasily under the jetty. "Bad luck happens," I pointed out firmly. "It's not a personality defect."

She glanced at her watch. "The U.S. markets will be opening." She sprang to her feet, back in trader mode. "Sorry to cut you off." Coming to my side, she ruffled my hair. "I'm going to be a pain in the arse until this thing starts to work. What's for supper?"

I returned that evening with a roast chicken, a *tarte tatin*, and a bottle of *Mondeuse*. Mallory looked tired, but upbeat. "I've sold my first AIG. $46 a share. You're spoiling me."

"Nonsense. I'm keeping the Yellow Jersey in top condition."

"I thought I was a boxer." She smiled. "But a cyclist is better." We ate companionably as the evening settled into night, and the waters of the lake became still and black. Not only was there no rain, but the sky was clear, and, by the time we'd finished eating, a quarter moon was casting its pale light across the water, and softening the ridge of *Semnoz* where it touched the velvet of the sky. "So I can look forward to this treatment every night?"

"Of course." I took her hands. "I'm here for you. Always."

Smiling an inner smile, she stroked my fingers in silence. "I seem to attract melancholy men." She spoke to herself more than me.

"*I'm* not melancholy."

She kissed a finger, then laid it gently on my lips. "Yes, you are." It was such a small gesture, yet it said so much.

It was my turn to smile. "Not any more."

The first part of the plan was soon executed. Before May was out, she had borrowed and sold shares in AIG, Lehman, Merrill Lynch, Fannie Mae and Freddy Mac, Morgan Stanley, Royal Bank of Scotland, and Halifax Bank of Scotland. "All the key suspects," she explained. "I hope that's enough of a spread. What do you think?"

"It's a bit late for my opinion now," I said. "But I suppose, even in this venture, it's right not to put all your eggs in one basket. But what happens if one of them goes wrong?"

"I don't think any of them can go absolutely wrong. But one of them might get taken over before it hits rock bottom. My main concern is that the owners will panic too early."

That night Hope said much the same in my dream. She also consulted me on her choices. "Just squeeze my hand if you think I'm wrong. It doesn't have to be hard." She took my hand lightly in hers and ran through the same list. "I checked them the same way with her. But I'm the analyst. I know this lot are heading for trouble."

Her confidence was reassuring. If she had gone through agonies of indecision, she had spared me from them. Was this the bravado of youth, that sense of certainty which experience had tempered in the rest of us; or was she on a mission for her father to achieve at the expense of Lehman and AIG what could have been achieved against Enron? She had said so little about her father that I had no idea how she felt about his losses. If she blamed her mother, she kept it well-hidden.

Only a loving daughter would visit her mother so assiduously, and only a very loving daughter could be so certain of her mother's recovery. As for her interest in me, despite my ruined state, it was very touching. She seemed genuinely pleased that I had managed to prevent her mother's death, rather than disappointed that I had failed to save her from serious injury. If Amy and I had managed to have a daughter, Hope was just the kind of young woman I would have wanted her to be. In an outburst of gratitude, my hand twitched in hers.

"Have I done something wrong?" she demanded anxiously. I tried to shake my head but nothing happened. "If you can move your hand, just do it once more to show I'm right." I concentrated all my efforts, just as I had when I'd told her about Marie-Sainte, and somehow I managed to do as she asked. It was no more than a tremor at the tips of my fingers, but she was as sensitive as the princess in the fairy story, the one who'd felt the infinitesimal disturbance of a pea to the softness of twenty mattresses. "Bless you," she said. Then she leaned right over, so that she was almost whispering in my ear. "I only wish she'd bought more credit default swaps back in 2006." How like her mother she was to return to business matters just as my thoughts were turning personal! "They're paying out now like you wouldn't believe. I'd buy more if I could, but of course the market's dried up completely."

What she said was so strange that I couldn't help but dwell on it. I couldn't see how Mallory could have insured other people's CDOs. It was as if I'd bought life insurance on a stranger, which I was sure was either illegal or heavily discouraged. Otherwise there'd be nothing to stop an unscrupulous doctor, the opposite of a René, giving a seriously ill patient a good medical, then taking out insurance on that patient's life, so that he would be the beneficiary rather than the rightful heirs. It seemed to stand the principle of insurance on its head. I was so surprised, my hand twitched again, and Hope smiled.

"I knew you'd understand. At least I'm using the profit stream as collateral." Once again she'd lost me. "Share borrowing has to be done through intermediaries, and they like to be sure you can afford to buy the shares back if the market goes the wrong way." That made sense, but it did not explain how Ghost Trader could have bought CDS insurance on somebody else's risk. On that she did not elaborate.

I was so puzzled that the issue continued to nag me after I woke up. By the time I joined the queue at the *patisserie* I was so concentrated on it that I almost missed my turn. It was only on the third, and louder, cry of "Monsieur?" that I roused myself.

"Sorry," I apologised to the baker's wife. "I was miles away," I added to the queue behind. They laughed. Monsieur Holden up to his usual eccentricities. It was a beautiful morning, full of spring fragrance. The fresh green of lawns and leaves was reflected in the surface of the lake as deep turquoise. It lightened my step, but got me no nearer to a solution. The sheer craziness of being able to insure a risk to which you weren't exposed was beyond my invention; it was yet weirder to think I was in telepathic contact with a woman I'd never met. It only hit me as I neared the gateway on the path to the boathouse.

The old gate was now entwined in convolvulus, and the burgeoning undergrowth threatened to swallow the path. Burs clung to my trouser legs, but as my progress slowed, my mind seemed to speed up. The answer of course was Marie-Sainte. At her first briefing, when she'd astounded me with her financial knowledge, she'd asked whether we dealt in CDOs – *and* CDSs. At the time, I'd been too struck by what a bad deal they were for the insurer to consider who else, apart from the owners of CDOs, might be able to buy them.

Mallory always left the boathouse unlocked, so that my arrival didn't require her being dragged from her screens. I made my way to the kitchen. She already had coffee on the go, so I transferred my croissants to plates, and poured myself a mug. "Do you want a top up?" I carried the pot and her plate to her work-station.

She glanced up with a smile. "You're looking quizzical."

I poured coffee into her mug and set the croissant successfully down beside her. Since the first occasion, we were both careful to avoid accidents. "I had this weird dream last night."

"Lucky you. I hardly ever dream." She sounded quite jealous.

I fetched my coffee. "I dreamt you'd bought CDSs."

"Late '06." She smiled warmly. "How perceptive of you."

"2006! The same year I dreamt you did." Marie-Sainte might have planted the idea of buying CDSs, but she'd said nothing about dates.

"Of course," Mallory didn't even look up. "That was the last year that CDSs were readily available. By 2007, mortgages were defaulting like crazy." It seemed I must have known that.

"How can you insure a risk that isn't yours?" I demanded.

She shrugged dismissively. "Wall Street's a casino. They don't mind which way you bet, so long as they take a percentage."

So that was it. The decent principle of insurance had been corrupted by Wall Street into mere gambling. I could see that Mallory was too absorbed by her screens to explain further, so I finished my coffee in silence, and left soon afterwards. But over lunch Mallory returned to the subject. "I'm trying to visualise a financial dream. I mean what was I doing when you dreamt I bought these CDSs?"

It was a fair question. The average financial transaction was about as exciting to an observer as watching paint dry. But to describe the dream would open a strange can of worms, and I regretted ever mentioning the subject. As I hesitated, she seemed to retreat from me. It wasn't that she did anything other than cut up her ham; rather that I saw her in a new perspective. The message of the dreams was that I was forever trapped whilst Mallory would be free. As soon as she'd expiated her guilt by enriching her members, she would feel entitled at last to break free from this nondescript boathouse, to live it up in London or Paris. No longer would she need me, the failed Name, the no-longer-necessary supplier. Even if she were to let me tag along, I could never burden her. This was the ultimate meaning of my dreams.

"What is it?" I shook my head, and tried to smile, but she wouldn't let it go. "I didn't realise it was a nightmare." She stroked my hand, the way my mother used to comfort me. "Do you want to tell me?"

I was reminded of our first encounter by the ferry stop, when her annoyance at my eavesdropping had turned to concern for my pallor. Then I had hurried away in confusion, but I could hardly do so again. Not now her eyes were gentle with anxiety, and her fingers were stroking mine. If I was to lose her anyway, what did it matter? Telling her would even make it easier for her by showing how absurd I was.

"It wasn't you in the dream," I said. "It was your daughter."

"*Hope!*" Her voice hardened. "You've never met her."

"She looks like you, doesn't she, only she's taller and fairer?"

"And younger." She sounded as if I were a stalker after all. "Do you dream of her often?"

"She visits me after she's been to see you." I described my dreams since New Year. "The first time, Hope thanked me for saving your life. Otherwise, it's all been Ghost Trader." By the time I'd finished, the U.S. markets were opening, so there was no time to pursue the matter. I couldn't tell from Mallory's expression whether she was merely puzzled or hiding her lowered opinion of me. It was with some trepidation that I arrived that evening with our food.

To my surprise, she wasn't at her screens, but sitting on the small sofa, with a bottle of wine already open and two glasses on the table. As soon as I opened the door, she sprang to her feet, and greeted me with an unusually warm hug. Then she followed me into the kitchen and helped me prepare. She was barefoot, in jeans and a tee-shirt, and her hair was loose about her shoulders. For the first time, she looked not only girlish, but vulnerable.

As we sipped our wine, she smiled over the rim of her glass. "The happenings at New Year really shook you up," she said. "I'm sorry I wasn't more understanding."

"The dreams don't bother me. In a funny way, I quite enjoy them."

She laughed. "They even give you ideas, it seems. Very biblical."

"You aren't shocked?"

"I certainly don't fancy the idea of being in a coma," she answered, her voice more serious, but still friendly. "But I don't really feature, do I?" On the second point, she sounded almost disappointed, though she covered it with an indulgent smile.

"You don't think I'm weird?" I tried not to sound too hopeful.

"Certainly not." She punched my shoulder playfully. "If I'm *compos mentis*, I'm doing the trading; if not, there's Hope's. What could be more logical? Just like the dreamer."

"You accused me of being a stalker, once," I reminded her.

"That was before I knew you. Mind you, you did look strange." She wagged an admonitory finger. "The way you stared at me. Especially the first time. As soon as I looked at you, you went all pale." She shook her head in disbelief. "It was like you'd seen a ghost."

I was amazed that she'd remembered the event so clearly. But what could I say that wouldn't sound absurd? It was so long since the old dreams that I'd almost forgotten Mallory's role in them. The last word, after all, had been René's, who'd assured me that the recognition had been merely a form of *déjà vu*. I coloured in confusion.

"For once, I've silenced you." She grinned like a schoolgirl.

"I'm sorry," I said feebly. "I wasn't feeling well at the time."

"You looked well enough until you saw me."

She was back to her teasing manner, yet her voice retained much of its former warmth, as if my explanation really mattered to her. "If I explain, you really will think I'm weird," I countered, trying to match her tone, but probably sounding only confused and foolish.

"I certainly will if you don't."

"It's silly looking back on it now," I began, "but it disturbed me at the time." Then I told her about Amy queuing outside Northern Rock, and something of the dream it had provoked.

"You still care about her, don't you?" Mallory cut in, as I described Amy's collapse into the gutter. It was a generous interpretation of why I'd hit Amy, if that's what I'd done.

"But when I rolled her over, it wasn't Amy... It was you."

"*Me!*" One hand flew to her throat, the other almost spilled her wine. "Before we'd met?" I nodded, and she shivered. "Amy I can understand. But me! That's beyond weird."

"I even went to my doctor about it." I explained his description of dreams as defragmentation. "As for recognising you, he thought I was post-fitting you to my dream memory. *Déjà vu extrême.* I'd told him you were very striking. He decided that's what did it." In retrospect, it all sounded rather feeble, but it was the only explanation I had.

Without a word, she jumped up and retreated to her office-cum-bedroom. She was back in a moment with a small leather album. It contained six photographs. "See if you can spot Hope."

The first showed a young woman in academic dress smiling with an older couple. It could have been Hope, but I saw immediately that it wasn't. "It's you," I said. "With your parents?" She was a wonderful amalgam of the two of them. Her father was tall with the same strong face and upright stance, but his features were fairer, his eyes lighter. Her dark hair and eyes she'd inherited from her mother, who must then have been a similar age to Mallory now. It was small wonder that such a couple had produced a beautiful daughter.

"It's tough when our parents, people we love, have to die," I said, trying belatedly to atone for the lack of sympathy I had shown when she'd first told me of her father's death back in March.

"If your parents were anything like mine, they really didn't approve of your divorce, did they?" Though casually thrown out as an aside, the turn in the topic took me by surprise. "Their generation just didn't approve of divorce, period. Especially with a child involved."

"Jake was an adult by then. Mother blamed Amy more than me."

"Lucky you." She gestured impatiently towards the album.

The next two photos were of a more mature but still young woman with an older man. She was closer in looks to the Hope of my dreams, but I saw right away that this too was Mallory. In one, she held the wheel of a boat as the wind whipped her hair. He had a hand on her shoulder, the other on her hip. An imperious man who enjoyed giving orders. In the next, they sat on a restaurant banquette. He smirked to camera, whilst she gazed raptly at him. The last thing I wanted to see was Rex Tonbridge basking in Mallory's adoration.

The fourth was of a dozen or so kids in party hats, eating cake and cookies from paper plates. I quickly spotted Hope. She must have been about seven, but the angular face and the intent way in which she leaned towards her neighbour were unmistakeable. Though there was less of her mother in her then, it was easy to see how this lean, self-possessed child would grow into the attractive young woman who visited me in my dreams. "That's her," I said without hesitation, amazed though I was. Mallory gestured for me to go on.

The fifth was a student group. I recognised Hope at once: the calmest and most serious amongst them. The last was of a couple: one of the male students from the group – a little older, less callow, and with an air of steely purpose – and Hope, happy in her choice of partner. The likeness was absolute. My hand shook as I pointed.

"Graham, her husband." Mallory took the folder from me. "A cynic would say you were bound to spot her if I told you she was there."

"I'm not trying to trick you. But that's the woman I saw."

"You're a strange man, Clem Holden." Curiosity fought uneasily with humour, and her expression was troubled. "I don't begin to

141

understand how you can dream about people you've never met. Your doctor must be right. You make too much of resemblances." She drew her knees defensively to her chin. "Not just in dreams. There was all that stuff about seeing Ambrose, up in Les Confins and then again on New Year's Day. Not to mention thinking I'd been run over."

It was six months since I'd apparently seen Ambrose, and received that anonymous text. Since then, there had not been so much as a hint of him. Ever since I'd read the newspaper report of the accident, in which the victim's wife had retracted her fraught accusation, I'd convinced myself that I'd been wrong. Indeed, as I thought back now, I had not immediately recognised the skier in black as Ambrose. It was only a frantic wife's belief, since retracted, that he'd shouted "IBNR" which had magnified faint recognition into certainty.

"You're right," I said humbly. "I was in a low state back then."

"Hope wasn't back then, she's now. Like all your recent dreams."

"The current ones are harmless. The violent ones were earlier."

She stood abruptly, as if to say "enough of introspection". Then she reached for my hand, and led me to the dining table. "Let's eat."

"Good choice," she said encouragingly, as she tried the *salade des langoustines*. She then chattered inconsequentially through the meal, in a manner that wasn't really like her at all. I could only assume she was trying to cheer me up, or else steering me away from questions about Hope or her parents. It wasn't until I fetched the cheese that she became serious again. "Do you have a history of dreams?"

It was a pertinent question of the sort that René might ask. Like him, she seemed to have my welfare at heart. "I've always had vivid dreams," I conceded. "But not like these."

"I don't seem to do very well in them, do I?" She sounded genuinely upset. "Are there any more? Any where you actually kill me?"

The thread of violence had not really struck me before. Even the one sexual encounter, which had begun joyfully enough, had ended in blood and death-like stillness. I shook my head firmly. No way was I going to describe that dream. "According to Hope, I saved your life," I countered instead. "Not very efficiently, but I did my best."

"At great cost to yourself. I hadn't forgotten." She smiled, as she cut a sliver of *reblochon*. "It's not that I hold your dreams against you, but I'd like to know where I stand in that vivid subconscious."

I told her about Amy's call at New Year, and how in my dream I'd arrived at Wormsley's party in time to scare him to death. "But that's easy to explain: I'd had a detailed description from Amy, and the moonshine *marc* did the rest. It was *St Silvestre* after all."

"Freud would have loved you, whatever your doctor says." She laughed as she cut herself another sliver of cheese. "Is that it?"

She seemed to think no worse of me, and I shouldn't have gone on, but the pre-dinner wine had weakened my guard. I told her about the Staten Island ferry, with Saul astride the rail. "Only the white cliffs of Dover kept showing up instead of Manhattan." I should have noticed Mallory's hand whitening around her glass.

"I was with Amy – or you. She or you accused Saul of cheating her of her savings. He appealed to me, and I lost my temper. Then he went over the side. I think I pushed him. I certainly meant to."

There was a snap. Mallory's grip had become so tight, it had broken her glass. Wine and blood dripped onto the table. But what I noticed most was her deathly pallor.

Chapter Fourteen : Proprietary Trading

Next morning she was all smiles. "I'm sorry about last night." Fortunately the glass had snapped cleanly and the cut had been straight and shallow. Fresh plaster had replaced the one I'd helped to put over the wound the previous evening. "And before you ask, I don't need to see the doctor. Your washing and disinfecting last night worked perfectly. There's not a sign of infection." She laughed. "So much for cheap wine glasses. I think I'll replace them."

"Good idea," I agreed. "I was quite worried about you."

"Just shock. I'm afraid I'm not very good with blood."

"You were fine with mine." Not that my cheek had bled copiously.

"I had you to worry about. Last night I just felt stupid."

"I thought you were going to faint." Never having seen her so shaken, I'd been convinced that she'd cut an artery. Only when that clearly wasn't the case, had I surmised that my dream had upset her. But yesterday, when cut and shock were fresh, hadn't been the time to question her. "That's the last dream you'll hear from me."

"Ah, your dream. I suppose it did set me off." She stroked the plaster. "I'm afraid it reminded me a little too much of Ambrose."

Of course. She'd known of his suicide long before I had. "It was the white cliffs," I said apologetically. "I should have thought."

"My only member to drown." She shuddered. "It gets to you."

"We won't talk about him any more," I assured her. It nagged at me, nonetheless, that I'd dreamt of pushing Saul from the ferry long before I'd known that Ambrose had killed himself. I remembered, too, how much Saul had reminded me of Ambrose when he'd visited me in my comatose dreams. Whatever dreams my brain was cooking up, they seemed to go beyond *déjà vu*. And what, after all, was *déjà vu*, other than a clever phrase? It no more explained my dreams than Split Strike Conversion explained Madoff's investment strategy.

"Can you get hold of Marie-Sainte today?" Mallory seemed anxious to switch to practical matters. "There's a glitch on Platform 2. I want it fixed before the members spot it."

I reached for my mobile. "I'll speak to her right away."

I'd hardly got back to my apartment before Marie-Sainte was knocking on my door, her laptop under her arm. "All fixed. Let me show you." I

144

ushered her in, and she set up her computer on my coffee table. She logged onto Platform 2, which was one of the conventional variants of what members assumed to be the real portfolio. She showed me what the problem had been, and demonstrated that it was now fixed. She even had me clicking for a few charts to make sure. "I checked the other platforms as well. Everything's fine."

"Can I offer you anything while you're here? Tea, coffee, a snack?"

"Iced tea would be nice." She blushed. "Maybe even a *tartine*?"

I laughed. "I think I've got some hazelnut spread in the fridge."

She followed me towards the galley area. "We're getting married. The 22nd August." She smiled proudly. "You will come, won't you?"

I gave her a warm hug. "Of course I will. I'd be delighted."

"Just a civil wedding," she said. "None of us being devout."

As we shared the iced tea and *tartines* around the coffee table, it felt almost like old times. It was strange to think that the child to whom I had briefly been like a surrogate father was now a young woman about to be married and would soon be a parent herself. She was still easy to talk to, and she was happy to tell me about her course. It seemed that her professor's interest in financial matters was encyclopaedic.

"He was telling us about the Securities & Exchange Commission, and how they're not tough enough with Wall Street. There's this big fund manager, apparently, who's had several formal complaints made about him, but the SEC won't even bother to look into it."

"Why ever not?"

"He often advises *them*, so they treat him like he's one of their own, instead of investigating him. No wonder we're all in such a mess."

"Does he have a name?"

"All I know is he was once chairman of the NASDAQ."

"Bernie Madoff!" Then I told her about Saul and Amy, and how my enquiries so far had revealed nothing untoward. "Do you know what these complaints were about?"

"Something about his results being too good for what he's invested in. One theory is he's front-running. That means he trades on behalf of his fund before he does the same trades for his other clients. His other business is routine, low-margin stuff, so he's got an incentive to get the best deals for his fund clients."

"That's nice for Amy, though, if it's true," I observed, which drew a frown from Marie-Sainte, to show that she expected better from her old friend. "Not very ethical of me, I admit, but after what I did to Amy over Lloyd's I have to think first about her."

"If the SEC did its job there'd be no dilemma," she conceded.

"I'll speak to Amy. Then it's up to her."

We'd almost finished our *tartines*, and Marie-Sainte left soon afterwards. I decided to call Amy right away. She was quite unmoved. "I've heard all this before. Saul says there are lots of jealous people out there. It all started because some advisor challenged his returns, and Bernie gave him the brush-off. He's a big fish on Wall Street, don't forget. He doesn't take to lowly advisors questioning his judgement. If the SEC are happy, why shouldn't I be?" Then she thanked me, a little stiffly, for my concern. "Must run, much to do."

The irony of my doubt was not lost on me. Here was I worrying about the *bona fides* of an ex-chairman of a major exchange, a man respected enough for regulators to consult him, when I was the instigator of a flagrant breach of fiduciary trust. Whatever nonsense Saul had put to Amy was nothing compared with the lies I had presented to Marie-Sainte, or the deception that I'd persuaded Mallory to perpetrate on her members. Amy was right to ignore me, whilst I would be better occupied in assisting Mallory to get it right.

But I told Mallory about it over lunch. She made light of it. "Relax. It's a bitchy industry. Anybody reading the forum on a bad day would think I was far worse than Madoff."

"Even so, I'd be much happier if Amy had her money with you."

"Thanks for the vote of confidence. But she's not an ex-Name, and I wouldn't take her now even if I could. What I'm doing is far riskier than anything Madoff could be up to."

"She was married to a Name," I persisted. "She was ruined too."

"Forget it, Clem, it's not going to happen. As for young Marie-Sainte, I'm much more interested in her computing skills than I am in her rumour-mongering." From there the conversation shifted to the interest the four viewing platforms were generating amongst the members. The forum was daily packed full of suggestions, all of which, in the spirit of Ghost Trader, required reasoned responses from Mallory. "I'm afraid I'm getting swamped."

"I'll help," I suggested. "I can identify what's urgent or tricky."

And so it was agreed. Starting that afternoon, I combed the forum for the comments that most required an answer, discussed these briefly with Mallory, then drafted the replies. As I learned more, I got better at it, and she edited me less. Mostly, it was simple stuff, with members needing reassurance that a chosen buy or sell had been properly researched. From time to time, there were useful suggestions. I developed a technique for these, along the lines of "great suggestion: but for your special knowledge we'd have missed it".

Platform 4, the shorting strategy, came in for much comment. Some members queried the need for it, until persuaded that it provided a benchmark against which to judge conventional strategies.

"These are extraordinary times financially," I wrote, "If – when? – the markets go mad, Platform 4 will show this vividly."

Members were also full of other shorting candidates. We countered that our first choices must be kept, or we'd waste time and money on unnecessary trades. Even supposedly imaginary money mattered. But as June wore into July, and as prices drifted lower, the clamour for change increased. To observers, inactivity was boring.

By the end of July, AIG was down $21, Lehman $27, and RBS by two-thirds, whilst Freddie and Fannie were approaching single figures. Forgetting it was supposed to be a game, members were screaming for us to buy back now and take our profits.

The pressure on Mallory was huge. If she capitulated, the shorting operation would net a profit not much under 100%: an amazing result as far as the members were concerned, but disappointing to her, who aimed for so much more. All my drafting skills were necessary to keep the members on side. "The great thing is," I assured Mallory, "they're starting to wish Platform 4 was for real. So why don't we dump something, just to show willing?"

We argued back and forth, until finally she cashed in Merrill Lynch, as the most likely to be taken over. "It's a better fit for Citi or Bank of America." The profit was modest, and she was despondent for days. Then, to add to the pressure, Fannie and Freddie shares started to slide, until on Friday 15th July, Mallory was on notice to hand the shares back. But on Sunday 17th, U.S. Treasury Secretary Hank Paulson announced a support package; and on Monday, their nerve steadied, the lenders recanted. "It's only a stay of execution," she bewailed.

"What would you have made if you'd sold today?"

"125% or thereabouts." She made it sound like a disaster.

"More than doubling members' money. I don't see a problem."

"We ought to do better." She shrugged petulantly. "If it were only Freddie and Fannie… I'll go spare if they want the others back."

"They've sat it out this long," I reasoned. "They won't want to lock in a big loss; not now Paulson's given them hope."

Long-haul investors, I was coming to sense, were more like me in their attitudes than a professional of Mallory's calibre.

"What really worries me more is a market rally," she admitted. "Sometimes they happen for no good reason."

"So it'll soon go down again. What's your problem?"

"Precisely that. Even if it's a dead cat bounce, my lenders may decide to cut their losses before the rally dies."

"So what can you do?"

"Sit and sweat. It's my nerve against theirs."

I squeezed her shoulder. "I'll back you every time." But my words were bolder than I felt. At the beginning, Mallory had aimed at least to double her members' money, but now she wanted more. I could only hope that her judgement was right: that her victims really were heading for ruin. In the meantime, she needed distraction, or the tension of inactivity, of constantly being on the alert whilst not actually doing anything, would sap her judgement and her willpower. "Now the members are coming round, why not do some shorting in Platform 1?" This being what members believed was the real platform.

She managed a tired laugh. "We'll make a trader of you yet."

The next morning, over breakfast, she announced that she'd "bought" a bit of AIG and Lehman on Platform 1. "I've just been looking in the forum to see the reaction."

"I trust they approve."

She nodded thoughtfully. "But there was nothing from *L'Esprit*. There's never been so much chat in the forum, but not a word of it from him. Don't you find that strange?"

I was only too grateful for his silence. "Perhaps he's on holiday."

Throughout August, our shorted shares continued to slide but refused to plunge. "It's the holiday season," I suggested. "September will see the real action." She nodded curtly.

There were now prominent rings round her eyes, and her cheeks were hollow and pale. I tried to coax her to exercise, but she wasn't interested. Her world shrank to the confines of her work-station and the price movements on her screens. I rarely left her now, except to sleep. As she weakened, I became stronger, and when the day of Marie-Sainte's wedding arrived, she was far from wanting me to go. "You could come, too," I suggested.

"I don't know the bride. You wouldn't let me meet her. But you go, if that's what you want." As the morning wore on, her irritation increased. "Shouldn't you be off? I can manage perfectly well without you. You're only in my way. I don't know why you hang around." I ignored it all, and when the time really came for me to leave, I tried to slip away without a word. "Oh, you're leaving are you?" She managed a theatrical sigh. "Well, go if you must." But as I reached the door, she called for me to wait. Sheepishly, she emerged from the bedroom, an envelope in her hand. "Please give them this. I'm sure they'll be pleased with what's inside." As I took it, she flung her arms around me and kissed me fiercely. "I've been a complete bitch. Just go and enjoy yourself." Then she almost pushed me out of the door.

The wedding ceremony was short but suitably solemn. Marie-Sainte's dress had been carefully sculpted to minimise her swelling abdomen, and she hung on Andréa's arm with such obvious joy that none but the prickliest puritan could have wished her ill. He, for once, was resplendent in his formal suit and bow-tie, and seemed as pleased as his new wife, though he tried to hide it under a deadpan expression. Afterwards, we sailed on one of the lake's pleasure steamers, a section of which Armand had hired for our exclusive use. All my neighbours were there, as well as school and university friends of the couple.

Marie-Sainte introduced me to her professor, who hardly looked any older than Andréa. I thanked him for his help on our project, but he insisted that his contribution had been slight. "She's a brilliant student," he said. "I'm sure she will find plenty of work when she qualifies."

We discussed the financial climate, and he confirmed my belief that September would be the moment of truth. "Many banks will fail; plenty will be rescued by their Governments." His list of the most likely collapses covered all of Mallory's choices. "Look out, as well, for Iceland. A small country with debts that would cripple a France."

Sidonie circulated amongst the guests with determined jollity, but Armand could not refrain from buttonholing me to pronounce that now was no time to be bringing another child into the world. I tried to reassure him that no time was ever perfect. "At least you remembered Marie-Sainte in these hard times. You pay her generously."

"Don't thank me," I said. "Thank my client."

"Yes, indeed." Andréa had sidled up, and drew me aside. "I too have a commission. A publisher prepared to pay for my observations on the collapse of global capitalism." He smiled at my surprise. "You must understand, Monsieur Clem, I have sharp eyes and attentive ears. I'm not afraid of the bold conclusion, or the vivid analogy. From individual tales of frustration and tragedy a pattern emerges. Start with the family that borrows too much, then the salesman who feeds off them, and slowly, person by person, business by business, we arrive at the black widow of global capital, bloated amidst her miasmic web."

"I thought you were labouring. Is this in your spare time?"

He laughed. "Labouring doesn't engage the brain, but as I sweat I write. It's all here." He tapped his head. "My fellow drudges give me plenty of material. I have a tame Algerian, full of tales from Marseille, as well as an ex-peasant who can't work the land because the EU pays

149

his old farm boss more to keep it in retention than to be productive. So now my comrade builds for rich foreigners instead of helping to feed his neighbours. Even you, Monsieur Clem, have a tale to tell. Your ruination from the past, with its parallels to now. And your client, our benefactress," he smiled knowingly, "She too has her place in the story. The wrecker from within. The true revolutionary."

"Now look here," I said, "Marie-Sainte's work is strictly confidential. None of it's for publication." I wasn't as worried as I sounded. Andréa's ambition far exceeded his reach. Even if published, he wouldn't hit the shelves until the venture was over.

"A journalist has a duty to protect his sources." His smirk froze into *hauteur*. "But I must tell you about my most recent contact." My heart sank. The last thing I needed was an earful of Andréa's boasting, but I thought I had better listen to make sure he was not about to reveal some further indiscretion. He led me out onto the open deck, where we leant on the rail, fanned by a light breeze. "A strange man. Twig thin, hollow cheeks and sunken eyes. More dead than alive. The sort I'd normally avoid. But the look of a man in trouble. This *Monsieur De l'Ombre* – Shadow Man – is very cagey. So I don't press him, I let him talk.

"He was a manufacturer: a minor credit to the real economy. Packaging. The sort of stuff we all use, like it or not. His bugbear was insurance. Premiums up every year, despite the unblemished safety of his plants. Finally he'd had enough, and he shopped around until he found the perfect broker who happened also to be a perfect beauty. In short order, *De l'Ombre* obtained the insurance he needed, a wonderful wife and a delightful baby daughter. His future looked bright."

Andréa spoke as relentlessly as he did in my dreams, and I felt almost as powerless to stop him. His story had an awful ring of familiarity. "He wouldn't wear a black beret, I suppose? Even perhaps a black anorak on a cold day?" I tried my best to sound casual.

"You know him!" He looked crestfallen.

"Not at all," I replied airily. "But I've seen him around."

"All the more reason to hear his story." His confidence restored, Andréa continued. "But for Madame, marriage and touting insurance were not enough. She became an underwriter, number two to *Le Grand*, a high roller with a *château*, fast cars and a yacht. Far more successful than *De l'Ombre*. His thing was reinsurance and retrocession."

The packaging company, the wife, and baby daughter: all were a perfect fit for the man I'd convinced myself was safely dead. Now, it seemed, Ambrose was not only alive but nearby. If that were not bad enough, the man Andréa nicknamed *Le Grand* was an uncanny match for Rex Tonbridge. Which could only mean that my temporary partner in business, who had promised to be my lover, and whom I already adored, had once been Mrs Hanter. Whatever his intentions, Andréa could not have dropped a greater bombshell.

"How interesting." I fought to give nothing away. "I'd never have guessed any of that from his appearance."

"Like all high rollers," Andréa continued, "*Le Grand* needed credit, so he persuaded her husband to become a backer. 'We don't need your money, just the promise of it. In return we'll cut you in on the profits, which are all but guaranteed. Small claims never get beyond the original insurer. As for the ones that do come to me, I'm reinsured – retrocessed – too. Even Noah's Flood couldn't hurt us.' So there he was, daring God, like a damned atheist."

As a description of how Names backed Lloyd's, Andréa's version was more like a layman's interpretation than an insider's account. It wasn't yet clear, therefore, whether Andréa realised that his *De l'Ombre* had invested in the same organisation that had ruined me.

"Poor *De l'Ombre*! Don't you feel for him? Flattered by the attentions of *Le Grand*, and encouraged by the nods of his beautiful wife, the mother of the young daughter he so cherished. Not for him, mere happiness now: soon he would achieve the prosperity his hard work deserved. The capitalist dream seemed about to come true.

"What he forgot, any atheist could have told him. High rollers treat beautiful women as their right, and beautiful women soon tire of their husbands. Worse, high rollers forget that ordinary disasters – if there's enough of them – will break them as surely as divine intervention. Having already stolen *De l'Ombre*'s wife, *Le Grand* was now about to steal his money, the money he swore he'd never need. The capitalist dream was turning into nightmare."

He paused to allow a waitress to replenish our glasses. "Shall I continue, or would you prefer that we rejoin the others?" He hardly waited for an answer. "The story has its twists. *Le Grand* was not without conscience. He shot himself. *Madame de l'Ombre* was full of apparent contrition. She offered to help her now ex-husband and the rest of *Le Grand*'s backers by starting a fund on their behalf. She would accept whatever little they had left, and she would add money of her own. *De l'Ombre* was suspicious. Where had she got this money? Why had he never known of it before? At first, she was evasive. Finally, she admitted she'd stolen it. 'When I realised the risks he was taking,' she said, 'I started to put money aside.'"

The facts that confirmed my fears were piling up as inexorably as the disasters which had destroyed Rex's business. I could almost grasp the attractions of suicide. But for now, I could only parry. "I don't see how she could have," I said, with what I hoped was mildly salacious interest. "*Le Grand* would have spotted it."

Andréa laughed nastily. "Her main job wasn't underwriting, it was investing the premiums, and she was very good at it. To her, creaming some off the top was child's play."

"I don't believe a word of it." I even managed a scornful laugh.

"Poor *De l'Ombre*! Not only cheated and ruined, but now disbelieved." He gripped my arm. "Don't you want to hear the rest? It's interesting, even if you don't believe it."

Inside I could see Marie-Sainte glancing towards us anxiously, even as she chatted to Laure and Anne-Sophie, her friends since childhood. I shrugged. Of course I needed to hear him out.

"The fund was a success. The ruined backers dared to hope they'd be rich again. *De l'Ombre* began taking an interest in the markets, and the company that caught his eye was Enron. It used to be an ordinary oil and gas company, until it transformed itself from primary producer into energy exchange. The further it moved away from raw materials – the more, in other words, it became a satellite of Wall Street – the better its results. But our man thought it was all too good to be true, just like *Le Grand*. He wanted his now ex-wife to use the fund to sell Enron short. He was convinced they would make a huge killing."

"Don't tell me. She wouldn't, he did it alone and went bust."

Andréa stared at me. "I thought you said you didn't know him?"

I forced a worldly smile. "It's where your story was going."

"Ah, yes. The capitalist saga. Boom to bust in never-ending cycle."

"Where did you meet this man?" I asked, as indifferently as I could.

"In Annecy. I bump into him quite often, watching the *boules*."

"Does he still see his ex-wife? Or was Enron the end of it?"

"He's still trying to find her, but he doesn't know where to look."

"If you knew where she was, would you tell him? Or does your journalist's code prevent revelations of that nature?"

"The question doesn't arise. I don't know where she lives, do I?" His eyes bored into mine. "You seem very interested, Monsieur Clem," he continued. "So you like my story?"

"I'd be careful what you publish," I answered judiciously. "You don't want a libel suit."

Again he gave me that withering look, between hurt and *hauteur*. "I'm not using real names, nor even real nationalities. These are players merely in a Brechtian tragedy."

"Do you know this man's real name, then – or hers?"

"If I did, I'd never say. Not even to you."

"Good." I turned from the rail. "Your wife's missing you."

But Andréa was in no hurry. "He says she has a hidden agenda. A special hotel she wants to develop with the *Accor* group. He thinks she may have bought the site already, but she's going to need more money to bring the development to fruition. She stole from *Le Grand*'s investors before; now she's got a whole fund to work with."

"Enough! I don't want any more of this slanderous nonsense."

"Four viewing platforms instead of one. Platform 1 performing as normal, 2 and 3 for a bit of distraction, but Platform 4 something very different, and likely to show a huge profit quite soon. You tell me, Monsieur Clem, who gets that profit? Or has she fooled you, too?"

Chapter Fifteen : Buying Back at the Bottom

Whatever reaction Andréa had expected to his *dénouement* – bluster, if I were Mallory's accomplice; horror, if I were merely her dupe – white-faced rage was more than he'd bargained for. Andréa's cynicism was as much a front behind which to hide his insecurities as a seriously held view of the world. Though concerned that I might have engaged Marie-Sainte in something underhand, he had – I was sure – been mainly keen to boast his skill as an investigative journalist.

"How dare you discuss my business with a stranger."

I tried to keep my voice down, but the guests had already stopped their happy chatter to stare at us, prompted no doubt by the look of horror on Marie-Sainte's face. We might have been out of earshot on the open deck, but she'd been studying our body language through the plate-glass doors more than she'd been attending to Laure and Anne-Sophie's happy gossip. To her sharp eyes, there had been no mistaking my tight-lipped fury, nor Andréa's instinctive retreat.

"I assure you, Monsieur Clem..." He was right to be afraid. If it had not been his wedding day, I would have hit him.

"If you didn't discuss it with him, then the insinuation is entirely yours." My ice-cold stare would have given a boxer reason to pause. "Retract it at once, or our friendship is over."

The charge that Mallory intended to steal the profits from shorting was absolute slander. Though Andréa had not met Mallory, he had no business to assume the worst on the word of an embittered stranger. If she'd wished to cheat her members, she would have begun no later than 2006, when CDSs were still readily available. That she'd waited until the collapse of Bear Stearns, when it was almost too late, ought to have convinced the most committed sceptic.

"The idea does not come from me," he stammered.

"Your source is a bitter and ruined man. I don't want you anywhere near him. Nor do I want him anywhere near me – or her. Especially her. Do I make myself clear?" Then I clapped him on the shoulder. "As for now, I suggest you go and be nice to your wife."

After that we kept out of each other's way, and the day resumed its happy course. Now, as the guests disembarked at our ferry stop, Marie-Sainte took my arm. "Please thank Madame Stellenbourg. Her cheque was far too generous." She waved Andréa away to escort Laure and Anne-Sophie. "I'm sorry he told you that story, but you know what he's like. I hope you don't think I believe it about the stealing."

"What we're all doing, it's in a good cause," I assured her. She gazed up at me with such wide-eyed appeal that I almost confessed the real deception. She might have understood, but it was too risky to explain. "Just keep Andréa away from *De l'Ombre*. He's dangerous."

"You know him, then?"

"I used to know him, but I haven't spoken to him in years."

"He sounds pathetic more than dangerous."

"He is pathetic. But he's also ruined: not once, but twice."

She swore to keep them apart. "Don't be too hard on Andréa."

"He was right to tell me."

Continued anger might suggest there really was something to hide, and I ought to be grateful that he'd alerted me to danger. Never had it crossed my mind that Andréa and Ambrose would meet, and I cursed my lack of foresight in believing Ambrose safely dead. Marie-Sainte was conscientious and well-intentioned , but I couldn't rely on her to keep them apart. From now on I must be on maximum alert.

We walked on in silence. I was in no mood to discuss Ambrose's association with Mallory, which had been far closer than anything I could have guessed, even in my darkest nightmares. Small wonder she had kept me in the dark. Shaken by my belief that he'd faked suicide, she'd forbidden further discussion of him at New Year. After that, it had been easier to volunteer nothing, even when the subject of her husband had arisen months later. She had not directly lied to me, but she had prevented me from learning the truth.

But I had to think beyond my hurt feelings. It was anyway less stressful to consider Ambrose's state of mind, and what it meant, than my own. Even when I'd met him at our Rota induction, they were already divorced. But he had seemed resigned to it then rather than bitter. Doubtless his Lloyd's losses had changed all that.

Rex's suicide would have mollified him, and his membership of Ghost Trader would have made his future a little brighter. With confidence returning, he had begun to study the markets for himself. Through shorting Enron he had seen a chance to restore his fortunes, perhaps even to impress Mallory enough to come back to him.

Bitter indeed must have been his failure to carry the members. Small wonder that he had viewed Mallory's lack of support as betrayal. I could see it all too clearly. The only puzzle was why he had waited from 2001 until 2007 to settle scores. Revenge might be a dish best eaten cold, but a six year cooling-off period was excessive. It only hit me by my steps, as I bade Marie-Sainte goodbye and good luck.

In the aftershock of his second losses, Mallory had doubtless offered to help him out as best she could. For a while that had sufficed. But, at some point, he had become over-importunate, and she had fled to the sanctuary of the boathouse. Then finally Ambrose had snapped. One by one, he had determined to rid the world of his persecutors.

Though I had no proof, I was convinced he had successfully killed Wormsley. By whatever means, such as hacking into Mallory's emails, he must also have known that *L'Esprit* would be in Les Confins on New Year's Eve, before lunching Mallory the next day in the *Hôtel du Lac*. I understood now why he'd been standing so intently over the accident victim on New Year's Day. Like me, he'd mistaken the woman for Mallory, whilst the victim herself had been so terrified by the sight of him that she'd fled onto the main road. But it was very hard to believe that he'd also picked the wrong victim in Les Confins.

Then it struck me. I rushed to my laptop, logged onto Ghost Trader and opened the membership list. In no time I was reading such of his personal details as *L'Esprit* had disclosed: first name J-M, surname withheld, age 58, occupation withheld, city of residence Paris, marital status married, Lloyd's syndicates Tonbridge, etc. To make sure, I Googled Linberger & Cie. Sure enough, one of its brands was *Spirito di San Luigi*, just as George had told me. There was a photograph of acting chairman Jean-Marie Linberger next to one of his cousin, the late chairman Jean-Michel Linberger. I'd last seen Jean-Michel in ski gear, but the formal photo only enhanced the full mouth and haughty air. I'd been right in my original identification, Ambrose had found the right victim, and Madame Linberger had not been confused. It was the other witnesses, not looking properly, who had been wrong.

If only I'd read the news story more carefully; if only I'd appreciated the significance of *L'Esprit* being a username as soon as George had realised that's what it was. On the first occasion, I'd been only too relieved that the newspaper hadn't named the dead man as *L'Esprit*; on the second, I'd been focused entirely on proving to George, as well as myself, that Ghost Trader was a proper club. Even George had failed to spot that Jean-Michel Linberger was dead. His financial interest, it seemed, did not extend beyond failed companies.

Still unexplained was how Mallory could believe that *L'Esprit* was still alive, and why his name had not been transferred to the list of deceased members. Did that mean the family were working some tax dodge? Jean-Marie Linberger could have seamlessly appropriated the membership without any change to the website details, since he shared the initials J-M with his deceased cousin. But how could Mallory not have known? Surely his widow would have invited her to the funeral, given her late husband's role in setting up Ghost Trader?

Then I remembered the poor woman's sad observation that her husband had not been in the habit of discussing his business affairs with her. It was possible, therefore, that she was as in the dark over *L'Esprit*'s investment in Ghost Trader as the tax authorities.

But surely Mallory's financial researches would have unearthed the death of a chairman about to float on the London Stock Market, even supposing she had missed the newspaper report? Except that Mallory relied on Hope for much of her research, and Hope did not necessarily know the real names of the members. Unless Linberger & Cie were a target buy, the subject of *L'Esprit*'s death might never have arisen.

I cast my mind back to New Year. Mallory had had no idea what had happened until I told her. Then she'd insisted that she'd spoken that morning with *L'Esprit* himself. My conclusion at the time, which she'd rejected, was that the caller had been Ambrose disguising his voice. Once again, that seemed the only explanation to fit the facts.

Assuming he didn't know her address, he must have been combing the village for her. He'd begun at the *Hôtel du Lac*, perhaps imagining that she'd been staying there. Then he'd walked the shore and the Rue de la Plage to the main road. There, in front of him, he'd seen the Mallory look-alike. By the time I'd come on the scene, Ambrose had realised his mistake. Shocked to see me, he'd hurried away.

Later, when I'd almost collided with him, he'd not been peering into the wood specifically, but searching for her name on gateways. Seeing me again had been as nasty a shock for him as finding him so far ahead had been for me. He may even have feared that I planned to attack him. That would have explained his counter aggression and retreat. As for now, I reassured myself that the boathouse was not easy to find. For the next week, with Andréa on his honeymoon, it was unlikely that Ambrose would strike lucky on his own.

I showered and changed as rapidly as I could, then set out for the boathouse. In the growing twilight, every gateway and bush seemed to hide a crouching Ambrose, but the Route des Vignes was deserted, and I reached the wood without mishap. Nothing confronted me on the path nor lurked in the trees. The boathouse lay in its usual tranquillity. Should I disturb it by confronting Mallory with all I had learned? At least she owed me an apology. More importantly, she had a right to know the danger she was in, as well as the slander against her.

But her state of mind was so fragile that I was terrified what effect telling her would have. It was as much my job to protect her as it was hers to bring off the great gamble. When I opened the door, I found her as usual, hunched in front of her screens, her face pale, with rings under her eyes as dark as eye shadow. I decided to say nothing.

Locking the door quietly, I composed my face into a semblance of responsible cheerfulness. "You must lock your door. Armand tells me there've been a lot of break-ins around the lake. If they're disturbed they turn violent. In future, I'll knock three times."

She didn't even look up. "How did it go?"

"A typical wedding. Did you hear what I said?"

"Lock the door." She shrugged. "Did they like my present?"

"Of course. Marie-Sainte says you're far too generous."

"I'm glad she's happy." She pointed to a monitor. "Listen."

"What do you think of the report that the Korean Development Bank are in talks with Lehman Brothers?" the beautifully-coiffed Bloomberg presenter in Hong Kong was asking from one half-screen, "Is this good news for Lehman shareholders, or just another rumour?"

"It's definitely more than a rumour," the invited expert from Seoul replied from the other half of the split-screen. He was a youthful-looking Korean fund manager who spoke impeccable English. "I'm told a KDB team has been in talks with Lehman all this week."

"Lehman shareholders have certainly reacted well." The presenter turned to address viewers directly. "Lehman closed up in New York: 5% on the day, 16% on the week." She turned back to the fund manager. "Is it right to be optimistic? From what you're hearing, are KDB negotiating seriously, or are these just exploratory talks?"

"That's a good question. Nobody in the KDB team is senior enough to close a deal, but it's well known that KDB would like a presence in New York, as well as an investment banking arm. I'd say Lehman shareholders are right to be optimistic, though perhaps they shouldn't get too excited just yet. I'm sure KDB won't be hurried."

"CEO Dick Fuld has been complaining of speculators unfairly targeting Lehman. Well, this week it looks like the shorts have been caught short." She then turned to other matters.

"It gets worse," said Mallory. "My Fannie and Freddie owners are getting twitchy all over again. They've put me back on notice."

If I had been in two minds before, I was now certain that this was not the time to mention Ambrose. "How long have you got?"

"I can probably hold on till Tuesday."

"You should still be up 150%. Better than last time."

"So you don't think the Lehman news will rally the market?"

"You heard the man. They're hardly going to be signing deals on Monday. Once they get into due diligence, KDB won't want to touch Lehman with a sterilised barge pole."

"Spoken like a bond salesman." She managed a tired smile. "Were you always this upbeat with clients, or do you really mean it?"

"Of course I mean it. But I don't *know* what's going to happen."

"So what should I do? Cut and run, or hang on?"

"You're the expert."

She shook her head. "This is a sheer guess. Once firms get into takeover mode, rationality goes out of the window. It's not a question of whether Lehman are worth it, it's a question of how desperately KDB wants them. Your guess is as good as mine. Maybe better."

"Then I say hang on. KDB want Lehman, but they aren't mad." She nodded, but the energy drained out of her. Standing behind her chair, I massaged her shoulders. "You should get some sleep."

Nodding dumbly, she stumbled to the bathroom. Whilst she was gone, I switched off all the screens. Silence filled the room like a balm, until the small noises of ordinary life returned to their proper focus: the hiss of the shower, the gentle suck of the lake under the jetty, even the hum of a light bulb. If Ambrose were to approach now, I'd hear him in plenty of time. When she emerged from the shower, I told her I was staying the night. "Where will you sleep?" was all she asked.

"The sofa's fine. I just need a blanket and a pillow."

She looked relieved. Not because she was fearful of prowlers, but because she found my presence comforting. I took her hand, and led her into the bedroom. She stared at the blank screens, but said nothing. I almost had to lift her into the small bed. Even before I kissed her forehead, she was asleep. I did less well on the sofa.

For all my assurances, I couldn't stretch out fully, and I was too alert for prowlers. The hoot of an owl, a gust of wind in the wood, or a sudden movement of the lake were enough to jerk me out of sleep. If I dreamed, I was haunted by nameless shapes and formless fears.

I woke at 7:30. The bedroom door was still ajar, and I gazed down on her sleeping form. All the worry lines had disappeared, and she looked happier than I'd seen her for weeks. I blew her a kiss. After a shower, I took her keys from their hook in the kitchen, and wrote her a short note. "Gone shopping, etc. Back by 9:30, latest. Don't open the door to anyone. Clem." I left it by her bedside.

Letting myself out quietly, I relocked the door and made my way up the path to the road. It was deserted. I walked quickly to the parking bay that lay just beyond the wood and let myself into her Peugeot. I had decided that it was no longer safe to pass to and fro each day with shopping. This time I was going to stock up, and I drove to the nearest supermarket in Annecy-le-Vieux, well away from the centre of Annecy itself, where Andréa had met with Ambrose. Then I drove to my apartment and filled a bag with clothes and toiletries.

As I was putting this in the car, I saw Sidonie returning from the village with our newspapers "I didn't know you had a car, Clem."

"My client's. Urgent work in hand. So don't worry about my paper next week." It also occurred to me, as I spoke, that I had been ignoring my duties to the complex. "I think the contractors are up to speed. But if not, let me know. I'm not disappearing."

"Don't worry, Clem. Armand is coping beautifully." Her expression was knowing. "I won't keep you from your duties."

Mallory was waking as I got back. "I can't believe I slept so long."

"You needed it. Besides, it's Saturday." So the markets were closed.

Pushing back her duvet, she lurched against me as she tried to stand. I held out a steadying arm for her head to rest on my shoulder.

"You really look after me, don't you?"

I stroked her cheek. "We should get away. A weekend break."

"You think I need it?" She looked up and her eyes were soft.

"Yes," I said firmly. Then I kissed her lightly on the lips.

"So I have no choice?"

"Absolutely none." I kissed her again. "We'll just drive."

I thought she was going to refuse. Then she laughed, and extracted herself gently from my embrace. "I'll take a shower." When she returned, she was rubbing her hair vigorously with a towel, and looking years younger. Sniffing the coffee on the stove, she watched me store the provisions I'd bought. "The trouble I put you to."

"It's no trouble." I pressed my lips into her wet hair. "Not for someone you love." She started. "Relax, I haven't forgotten."

"Silly me. Strictly therapy." There was wistfulness in her smile.

We set out straight after breakfast. Leading the way to the road, I looked very carefully both ways. "What are you looking for?" she demanded, but her tone was teasing rather than quizzical.

"I'd hate to give the neighbours the wrong idea."

She slipped her arm into mine. "Who cares?" With no sign of Ambrose, who indeed?

We took it in turns to drive the meandering mountain roads, and we stopped often to walk. Mallory tired quickly, and it was too hot for serious hiking, so we ambled instead, holding hands like teens on a first date. After all the tension, we did our best to be carefree. But the future hung over us like an invisible cloud.

"Something's bothering you," she said, as we sat on a grassy hilltop amidst a vista of narrow valleys and sharp snow-blanched peaks.

"So near and yet so far. The last lap is always the worst."

She put her arms around my neck. "Dearest Clem. I'd never have managed without you."

"What about afterwards? How will we manage then?"

She shook her head. "I can't think that far. Not yet."

"Win or lose, I'm there for you."

She kissed my lips. "I know you are."

But her eyes were sad, and her manner tender rather than passionate. If Rex Tonbridge had swaggered bronzed and confident up the path, he could not have come more effectively between us. As for Ambrose, somewhere on the shores of the lake, where it lay hidden in the folds of the hills, he nursed his hatred and plotted his revenge.

"I wish we could drive away forever."

"No," she answered fiercely, "we mustn't give up now."

I lay with my head on her lap. "I'm not giving up. Just wishing."

She looked down on me kindly. "Lloyd's took a lot more than your money." She was right. But it hurt to be told that I, the once successful consultant, had stagnated, whereas she had acted for her members; that I, whose ex-wife was still alive, had wallowed in self-pity, whereas she, whose lover was dead, had driven herself all the harder. Her fingers smoothed away my frown. "It happened to lots of Names."

"But not to you. Even at rock bottom, you gave them hope."

"I did it because I had to. You'd done nothing wrong."

"Nobody else in Lloyd's lifted a finger. You actually cared."

"Rex cared too, you know." She shook her head sadly. "I wanted him to help, but he said Names would never trust him again."

"He could have helped you the way I do."

She laughed. "Not Rex. He had to be the boss." She touched my face shyly. "I really admire you for never coming the all-knowing male who has to be in charge. Even though you ran your own show."

"I may have been the boss, but my clients called the tune."

"Don't run yourself down. I'm sure you were as tough with them as you are with me. Rex hated being wrong. Underwriters weren't supposed to be wrong. It was part of the mystique."

"Didn't you hate being bossed around?" Not only had Rex Tonbridge been domineering by nature, it seemed that he'd had no

161

more difficulty demanding her love than commanding her obedience. It was not yet clear to me that my egalitarian way worked better.

"I was very young. He was my hero as much as anything, but that doesn't work for ever." She frowned. "Failure's very difficult for men like Rex. The more I challenged him, the more he thought I despised him. He couldn't understand that I still loved him. In spite, even because of his faults. All I wanted was for him to get real."

"You still love him, don't you?"

"Always."

It was the answer I'd expected, yet it hurt. I tried to console myself that I would have given the same answer about Amy. Yet I knew that my love for Amy was more like the nag of an old injury that provided neither joy nor consolation, and was powerless to prevent my adoring Mallory. But Amy was alive, and lacked the power of a ghost.

It was late afternoon, and a rising breeze forced us to move on. We walked back to the car in reflective silence, yet her hand was firm in mine, and she smiled encouragement as we climbed back in. After an hour's driving, we found a *ferme-auberge* just below the snowline. It was a lonely spot above the trees, its austerity softened only by the clink of cow-bells in the high meadows. Thanks to a cancellation, they had one room left. It was up under the slope of the roof, with white roughcast walls and heavy pine furniture.

The evening meal was hearty mountain fare, provided in a low-ceilinged room with pine cladding and tiled stoves in opposite corners. The other guests were hikers, who attacked their meal with gusto and jollity. It was catching, and after a subdued study of the menu and the arrival of our *kirs*, Mallory and I laughed and chattered our way through our dinner. The inner light in her eyes, which had tantalised me on the hilltop, became softer and more pronounced as the meal wore on, and our wine bottle emptied. So much so, that I dared to hope that I was, after all, looking at a woman on the verge of loving again.

In our room, she drew me against her. "I could forget our vow."

I held her tightly for a moment, then released her. "I can wait."

She pouted teasingly. "Listen to Mr Morality."

"Not at all. It's pure superstition. Surely we can wait a bit longer?"

She hugged me again, more quickly this time. Affection not enticement. "You see, you're perfectly forceful when you like. Perhaps there is a bit of the regulator about you."

The sun's heat on the roof tiles had dissipated and the room was chilly. Washing and undressing quickly, we snuggled gratefully under the covers. We kept to our promise, though it was a close thing, and we slept in each other's arms. My sleep was contented and dreamless. But in the morning, the mountains were shrouded in mist, an ominous reminder of Monday, when markets reopened. We did our best to be cheerful, but the tension did not abate. Even the hikers were subdued, and the loudest sound at breakfast was the clatter of cutlery.

The mist extended down into the valleys, and we drove through a shapeless landscape. When we returned that evening, Mallory rebooted her screens, and we flitted between Bloomberg and CNBC, hanging on the musings of commentators as much in the dark as we.

The two banks negotiated as warily as politicians at a peace conference. As commentators will, some took the view that lengthy proceedings were hopeful signs of progress, whereas others were as certain that the talks were going nowhere. All we could do was wait, but the energy we expended in focused idleness was terrible. If nervous energy alone could have affected the outcome, the KDB negotiators would have fled back to Seoul on the instant.

Instead, not only Lehman shares but those of all the other suspects held steady for the last week of August and the first days of September. For Lehman stockholders there was some excuse, so long as the talks continued, but the others hung on tenterhooks of wishful thinking. Lehman had become the bellwether; so long as KDB considered Lehman worthy to be taken over, all the other companies that Mallory was shorting remained sound by proxy.

Crazily hopeful though that seemed, it worked even on the lenders of the Fannie and Freddie shares. On the Tuesday after we returned from our break, just as Mallory was preparing to issue her buy instructions, the calls came in. In view of the KDB talks, they would settle for taking back only half what they'd lent. It cheered her a little.

The waiting was both draining and boring. My thoughts as often wandered to where Ambrose might be lurking, as they focused on share prices and news. At times I had to go outside to do exercises on the jetty or to walk through the wood to the road. There was never any sign of Ambrose. But my tension increased in the knowledge that Andréa would now be back. I imagined them plotting on the steps of the *Palais de Justice*, or Ambrose psyching himself up by watching the *tireurs* smashing aside their opponents' well-laid *boules*.

But my main concern was Mallory. By the end of August, she was practically refusing to eat, and it was all I could do to get her on the jetty for a half hour of sun. By the first Monday of September she was more exhausted than ever. By mid-week she could hardly get out of bed, yet once she was up, it took all my coaxing to get her back there at the end of the day. Because of KDB, she wanted to watch Asian news through the night. It was only by insisting that I could watch as well as she that she got any sleep at all, though it was only fitful.

On Friday, she roused herself sufficiently to buy and hand back the outstanding Fannie and Freddie shares for a profit of around 200%, which cheered her a little. But by Saturday, she was feverish and could hardly speak. With difficulty, I persuaded her to stay in bed. Also short on sleep, I was scarcely in better shape. But I dozed fitfully.

For two weeks, I had dreamt very little, but now as the sun played through the living room window, I found myself back in the hospital. After the tension of the past weeks, it was a relief to be comatose. Yet the nurse was less cheerful than usual. Whatever was on her mind, it did not seem to be me, though she turned me over and sponged me down with her usual efficiency. She left without a word.

Time passed, and then my door opened. It was Hope. She looked as exhausted as Mallory, and she was crying. "I wish you could do something," she said brokenly. "She's slipping away." She studied my screens. "Your brain patterns are much more active than hers. I've tried talking, but she doesn't respond." She wrung her hands. "I can't be with her as much as I need to. Thank God it's the weekend. If she's going to go, now's the time to do it. She's like that. Efficient and thoughtful." Tears rolled down her cheeks, and her fingers fretted with my hand. "I was so sure she'd pull through, but over the last two weeks she's changed. It's like she doesn't care any more."

I woke with a jerk. I ran into the bedroom, half expecting to find Mallory on her back, utterly still, and wired to her terminals. To my relief, she was rolling over, and her face was flushed instead of pale. Beads of sweat glistened on her brow, as copious as Hope's tears. Fever might be better than coma, but it was bad enough. I called René. Good friend that he was, he was round within the hour.

They were both annoyed with me: he for not calling him sooner, and she for calling him at all. But she succumbed to his examination.

"You need rest," he told her sternly, "And you need to eat. Pulse, blood pressure, breathing: they're all over the place. Unless you want a heart attack – absurd for a woman like you – it's imperative you do as my friend here tells you." He prescribed a sedative, an analgesic for the fever, anti-stress tablets and glucose. "Your blood sugar's close to zero." He'd said enough for her to accept how stressed she was. "I'll come again tomorrow." At the door, he said he was counting on me to call him if I had any concerns at all. "Day or night, I don't care."

I persuaded Mallory to take her sedative on the condition that I would watch the news on a laptop in the living room. "I'm worried about the Fed," she said. "When they step in, they always choose the weekend." Her instinct was right. That Sunday, the Federal Housing Finance Agency announced it was taking both Fannie and Freddie into conservatorship, a kind of nationalisation. "You see," she croaked, when I told her. "I was right to close out when I did."

By Monday morning, though pale and emaciated, she was feeling much better. Discussions between Lehman and KDB were still taking place, and the U.S. stock market seemed to be holding its breath. But every commentator was certain that nothing would emerge until later in the week, and Mallory was inclined to believe them.

At lunchtime, we dared to open a bottle of wine, and she ate with something close to her old appetite. That night we lay on the bed to watch the first news from Asia, and actually giggled at the jokes with which Bloomberg liked to brighten their Asian *Morning Call*. By 2 a.m., I was drowsing. Hope was just telling me that her mother seemed a bit more responsive, when Mallory exploded upright with an almighty shriek. I jerked awake on a supercharge of adrenalin.

"That's definite confirmation, then," the presenter was saying. "The Korean Development Bank has suspended talks with Lehman Brothers indefinitely. A spokesman for the bank has told us that they are, quote, facing difficulties in pleasing their regulators and attracting partners to the deal, unquote. Whatever may have been hoped previously, these factors are now seen as insurmountable stumbling blocks. So, with futures already down, the big question is whether Lehman has anywhere else to go. Or is this the end of the road?"

Mallory and I ran into the living room like children, laughing and hugging each other. Then I turned back into the bedroom and switched off all the screens. "New York doesn't open until 3 p.m. here, and there's nothing you can do until then." I went to the kitchen and filled a glass of water so that she could take the sedative. "Now rest."

I let her sleep until 10 a.m. Commentators were agreed that it was going to be a rough ride for Lehman, and when the U.S. market finally opened its shares dropped 45%, with the rest of Mallory's list faring little better. Rejuvenated, she held out until it looked certain that Paulson would mount another weekend rescue.

That Friday she bought and returned Lehman shares for an 800% profit on the stock she'd shorted back in May. The rescue attempt failed, and on Monday, Lehman filed for bankruptcy under Chapter 11 of the U.S. bankruptcy code.

On Tuesday, AIG's share price collapsed, and Mallory bought back and returned AIG shares for a 700% profit. On Wednesday, AIG was taken into conservatorship. Unlike Lloyd's, it could not save itself.

The same day, Mallory bought and returned the shares she'd shorted on HBOS, for a 500% profit, just one day before the U.K. Government broke its own monopoly rules to allow a take-over by Lloyds-TSB.

By the end of that week, her overall profit from shorting was in excess of anything she'd predicted: well over 400%. She'd transformed her members' £600 million into £3 billion.

GHO$T TRAD€R
Part Three
Warnings

"Financial disasters, I need not remind you,
are as old as money itself;
the spectres that haunt the feasts of plenty,
yet predicted only by the tiny band of Cassandras
to whom nobody ever listens."

Until now my dreams had depicted an orderly reality
parallel to, but independent of, my waking existence.
In stark contrast, the last two dreams
had merged the two worlds inextricably.
Such confusion could portend one thing only:
a crisis terrible enough to turn both my worlds upside down.

Chapter Sixteen : Off Balance Sheet

Now that the shorting operation was complete, I wanted to turn the screens off, but Mallory would only allow the sound to be turned down. After depending on the whims of the market for so long, she found it difficult to believe that we could now ignore them.

So little had we dared to presume success that we didn't possess a bottle of champagne with which to celebrate, so we poured ourselves a glass of *Mondeuse* instead. A local red rather than an international bubbly. It seemed oddly appropriate. To drink it we went onto the jetty, from where we could watch the afterglow of sunset along the ridge of *Semnoz*. The only sound was the gentle slap of water. "You were amazing," I said as we touched glasses.

"I'd never have got there without you." Her eyes glowed as the dusk deepened. "Never in a million years." It was wonderful to hear. Yet even as it stirred me, she laid a restraining finger on my lips. "It's not over yet. We still have to break it to the members."

I smiled. Far more than Mallory, I had been following the forum during the final week. "Half the members are already screaming to know why we weren't shorting for real. As for the rest, who's going to complain at finding they're five times richer than they thought?"

She frowned. "They'll still be furious with me for lying to them."

"So lay it on the line. Say you'll resign if they don't like it."

"That's so easy for you to say."

"All the more reason to say it." Her determination to be gloomy in the teeth of victory grated on me. After all we'd been through, this surely was the easy part. "You're calling their bluff. They'd never get rid of you. Who else could make them money like you have?"

"I don't want to bluff them. They're my members, my friends."

It was far too late for such doubts. I had to put a stop to this pointless self-flagellation. "Look. If you wanted to cheat them, you could simply pocket the difference, and pretend nothing's changed. The fact that you're coming clean proves they can trust you."

She sipped her wine in silence. Then, with a shiver, she turned and walked back into the boathouse. "It's getting cold out here," she complained, massaging her arms.

"I'll draft something for you in the morning." I followed her in and locked the door. Then I drew her roughly into my arms. "Right now we've some serious celebrating to do."

It was obtuse of me to try to win her round with an outburst of male passion. But I was as tired and anxious as she was, and my sensitivity had deserted me. Amy would have said that I'd never had enough in the first place. Yet for a glorious moment her lips responded to mine. But her mind was still the mistress of her passion, and she stiffened.

"Please, Clem, it's not over 'til I've squared the members. I'm sorry." I released her angrily. "You said you were superstitious; well, so am I. Very." She managed a wistful smile. "It's not that I don't ache for you, but I'm not in the mood right now. Not the mood I'd like to be in for you. Can you understand?" I seethed with impotent anger. But if she would yield neither to argument nor to passion, what else could I do? "What we both need is a good night's sleep," she concluded.

"I won't get one on the sofa."

"You don't need to stay. We're finished, remember?"

"You're throwing me out! Thanks very much."

I seized my bag, which was by the sofa, marched to the bathroom, and snatched the shirt and boxers which were drying on the towel rail. I was in the act of thrusting them into the bag when Mallory came to the doorway. "I'm not throwing you out. I just thought you'd be more comfortable." There was an edge to her voice, her expression seemed disdainful. "I'm exhausted. All I need right now is sleep."

"Have it your own way. You always do."

"Meaning what exactly?"

"I do everything for you and get damn all in return."

"Your fee times five isn't exactly nothing."

It was true that my return on the operation was to be my fee plus a 400% mark-up to match the 400% profit, yet never had the truth been more wounding. We stood face to face: anger versus reason. I should have calmed down, but in the heat of the moment I took her stance for rejection, the signal that she was now free of all fetters, including me. I ignored the pain in her eyes. I mistook the defensive tightening of her lips for dismissal. Mallory seemed transformed into Amy when she'd told me she neither loved nor needed me any more. I tried to push past her, but she stood her ground. Frustration and exhaustion fuelled my anger, and I slapped her hard across the face.

Under a similar assault, Amy – the loving Amy of old – would have responded with tears. Whether cringing from me or beating my chest with her fists, her words, all but incoherent amidst her sobs, would have been "How could you? Why are you so brutal?" – which would have turned my anger into pleas for forgiveness. Her helplessness would have urged me to take her in my arms and kiss her tears away. She would not have given in immediately, of course – and if the quarrel had been very bad, there might have been an interval of sulks and sniffs – but we would have made it up in an hour or two at most.

But Mallory was not Amy. She swallowed her shock and glared in icy silence. When finally she spoke, her tone was no less glacial.

"Oh brother, have you got problems."

"My problem is I'm far too trusting."

"No! Your problem is you blame everyone else for your mistakes." She touched her cheek, which was starting to discolour. "I begin to see where Amy was coming from."

"At least Amy never kept any secrets from me."

"Evidently she's more trusting." She marched into the bathroom. "I'm getting ready for bed. I suggest you're gone by the time I come out." She closed the door firmly. Had it been Amy, I would have flung the door open, and begged forgiveness, but Mallory was not Amy, and I feared to make matters worse. Better to leave as demanded.

Though angry still, I was calming down. The quarrel had been as ridiculous as it had been rapid, flaring up, like a bushfire, out of nothing. Cursing myself for a fool, I crossed the living room and yanked open the front door. With Mallory's spare key I locked it carefully. Quarrel or no quarrel, she had to be safe.

The road was as deserted as it usually was at this time, and I made it home without incident. Already the apartment had a forlorn and neglected air, as if to reproach me for abandoning it so readily. I opened the shutters, and the French window, which helped a little.

Tired though I was, I was too overwrought for sleep. So I poured myself a shot of *marc*, and dropped into my recliner. My brain was a confusion of anger and frustration. My main target was myself, yet I couldn't yet find the perspective to forgive Mallory entirely.

I was more exhausted than I knew, and two shots of moonshine were enough to sink me into leaden torpor. Usually my dream, when it came, tapped into unchanging stasis: this time, I felt summoned from the depths of the ground. Back from his honeymoon and in his labouring clothes, Andréa sat down at my bedside in a cloud of dust.

"I bumped into *De l'Ombre* today. He saw me first, so I couldn't avoid him. I said I didn't have time to stop, until he told me he'd found out where she lived. Nothing to do with me, I assure you. He's been working his way round the lake. Checking with letting agents, poking round bars. He even tried a *mairie*, but they wouldn't tell him anything, of course. He'd thought of trying you, but he knew you'd only warn her to go away." He paused, his face a picture of agitation.

"I came right away, because he's finally struck lucky. He consulted a letting agent in Veyrier, and one property on the list caught his eye. A converted boathouse in a secluded setting." He paused again, before taking my silence for confirmation. "The agent told him it had already been taken – by a lady from Alsace. 'I used to know a lady from Alsace,' he said, all polite and innocent, 'she wouldn't be half-English, would she?' It seemed that she would, so he's planning to pay her a visit. Tonight. I thought you'd want to know."

I woke bathed in sweat and heart pounding. I'd been away from my apartment for so long that it took me a while to realise where I was. Forcing myself to be still, I concentrated on my breathing until my pulse steadied. Then I scrabbled for my mobile and called Mallory. Being the small hours, there was, of course, no answer.

It was probably all nonsense. Of all my comatose dreams, this was the first in which the worlds of waking and dreaming had merged rather than run in parallel. Andréa had come to me in my dream as if my comatose self had been party to our conversation on the pleasure steamer and was as free to act. Yet I dared not ignore the warning. Cursing myself for abandoning Mallory, I changed into running gear. Then, with my mobile in the pocket of my top, I set off.

The sky was clear and the moon near the full, so that my way along the Route des Vignes was well lit. It should have been a beautiful night, but the stars glittered with cold, impersonal fire and the reflection of the moon shimmered eerily in the jet-black lake. Save for the occasional porch-light, the houses were in darkness, and when I reached the wood, it brooded in impenetrable shadow. The thick undergrowth conspired to make my passage slow and noisy, but I reached the gateway without mishap. The night was as still as the tomb, and the wood closed in around me, its darkness no longer the impersonal absence of light, but a malign presence that clung to my limbs and sapped my will.

But I made it to the boathouse at last. The little clearing and the expanse of the lake allowed me some light. The rake of the roof stood out in sharp relief, but the walls lay in the shadow of the overhanging eaves. All seemed peaceful. Then, as I approached the door, it seemed to my straining eyes that a deeper shadow moved there. I froze. Surely a figure crouched over the lock with his hand upon the latch? Fear iced my limbs and stiffened the hairs on my neck. Yet what could Ambrose do; and why shouldn't he be more afraid of me?

171

"This is private property," I said. "Step away from the door."

He rose with a hiss of intaken breath. He was thin and wasted, as if eating were no longer part of his agenda, and by some trick of the darkness the shimmering of the lake seemed to shine through him, so that he seemed at the same time both solid and translucent. I'd never been afraid of Ambrose in the old days, but this was a new Ambrose. A man capable of murder and the feral hatred that had driven a sane woman to run heedlessly into a speeding car. He bathed me in fear as powerfully as a searchlight would have bathed me in light.

Up on the road a car engine reverberated into life. A large six cylinder engine. Surely Mallory's Peugeot. The same thought seemed to have occurred to Ambrose, and he acted on it faster. He rushed me, head down. If the interplay of light and shadow had given him an ephemeral quality, there was nothing insubstantial about the head that rammed into my solar plexus and hurled me to the ground. Winded and gulping for air, I managed to catch hold of his wrist. It was thin, bony, and horribly cold. With a snarl, he shook me off. Cutting above his blundering progress was the sound of a car driving away.

I was in no condition to give pursuit. It was as much as I could do to breathe. I reached for the door handle to help me to my feet. My fingers encountered something heavy on a chain. It was a padlock. My first reaction was relief: Ambrose had been foiled by a simple but effective padlock. It also confirmed that Mallory was gone. The car really had been hers. But I unlocked the door just in case, and pushed it open as far as the chain would allow. "Mallory! Are you in there?"

Silence. The kind that told me the place was empty. In the distance, a dog barked. I'd been making too much noise. I stood still and waited, in the futile hope that I'd hear her feet within. The only sounds were the slap of water against the jetty, and the dog's fading barks.

What had driven her away? Had some sixth sense, attuned by the weeks of watching the markets, warned her of danger, or was she simply escaping from me, the foolish man who'd demonstrated his love and gratitude by hitting her? Whatever the reason, she was for the moment safe. But, as I made clumsy progress up to the road, my relief was tempered by the realisation that she might never return. There was finality in that padlock. Sure enough, there was no sign of her Peugeot. Nor of Ambrose, the only thing for which I was thankful.

But I ought to warn her it was unsafe to return. I pulled out my phone. After a few rings I was invited to leave a message. Of course, she was driving. She was quite right not to answer. Yet it hurt, too.

"Whatever you do, don't go back to the boathouse. Call me as soon as you can." Then I ran to my apartment as fast as I could.

After a rapid shower, I huddled on the recliner in my dressing gown and tried to sleep. For the moment there was nothing more I could do. This time, I didn't even need a shot of *marc* to send me off, though I had put a glass on the coffee table just in case. After what seemed like hours of blank darkness, I found myself once more in my hospital bed. It was nearly dawn, and its grey light gave off more cold than illumination. Mist lay thickly around my window, but the morning star gleamed smudgily through it. A silent figure was approaching, wearing the shapeless shift in which hospitals dress bedridden patients.

She was very pale, and her face was flabby from lack of mobility. There was a livid bruise on her cheek, but no cut. The sort a heavy blow might have caused. Surely I'd never hit her that hard? She sat down cautiously, her back straight. Her hands dropped demurely into her lap. "I hope you can hear me." She spoke in a hoarse whisper, as though she hadn't used her voice for months. "*L'Esprit* just called. He wants to see me right away. Him and *Le Baigneur*. I think they're on to us. It's probably for the best. If I can square them, that ought to be enough for the rest of the members. I'm not sure when I'll be back. Perhaps I won't be back at all." She managed a brief shrug.

"After Rex, I got used to living quietly on my own. I never thought anybody would rouse me the way you have." Her smile was infinitely sad. "We should have met years ago. Before Rex and Amy. As it is, we've been alone for too long. You as well as me." She leaned forward, her lips caressing my cheek, just below the ear. "Whatever happens, Clem, I promise you this: I'm yours forever or I'm nobody's."

I woke to the sound of my mobile. It was on the coffee table next to the untouched tot of *marc*. It was dawn, the same cold and misty dawn of my dream. I jumped for my phone, but it rang off before I reached it. I just had time to check that it was Mallory's number, before the handset was alerting me to call voicemail. This time, at last, I heard her voice. "I couldn't sleep after our little fracas. So I decided to sort the members right away. Starting with *Le Baigneur* and *L'Esprit*. If I can square the founder members, that should be enough for the rest. Don't call me back, because I'll either be driving or in the middle of meeting them. I'll call you as soon as I have any news."

My sleep had been leaden, but I was wide awake now. If *L'Esprit* was Jean-Michel Linberger and Ambrose's second victim, it was impossible for Mallory to be meeting him. Yet that was exactly what she was proposing. In the dream, she'd even said that he had called her.

But that had been a dream. The first in which Mallory herself had risen from her hospital bed. Until now my dreams had depicted an orderly reality parallel to, but independent of, my waking existence.

In stark contrast, the last two dreams had merged the two worlds inextricably. The Mallory of my dream world could not have executed the shorting exercise any more than the Andréa of my dreams could have conversed with my waking self on the steamer. The Mallory of my dream world was as physically incapable of walking into my room as my dream self was of walking into hers; yet there she had been, declaring that she was off to see *L'Esprit* and *Le Baigneur* just as she had in her voice message. Such confusion could portend one thing only: a crisis terrible enough to turn both my worlds upside down.

But what was I to do to avert it? I had never felt so helpless nor so full of foreboding. Not only was Ambrose alive and dangerously close, but Mallory had disappeared for an appointment with a dead man.

But how could she? If she had tried to speak to *L'Esprit* she would have failed to get through; or more likely she would have spoken to his widow. If she'd spoken instead to *Le Baigneur*, he too would have told her the truth. I could only conclude that she'd set off without speaking to anyone. But driving to Paris, at least six hours away, or even to Aix, on the off-chance of busy men being available was absurd. More likely that this was an excuse to escape from me. Yet surely a brief quarrel, however violently it had ended, was insufficient reason to drive off in the night? She herself had called it no worse than a little fracas. It might have been the trigger; it could hardly have been the cause.

I determined to go to the boathouse in the hopes that she'd left some clue as to her destination. A scribbled note, perhaps. But I needed a strong metal cutter to sever the padlock's chain. Fortunately I knew just where to look. Not for nothing had I been chairman of the residents' association. Within half an hour, I'd showered, drunk some coffee and changed into jeans and a sweat shirt. Then I made my way to the basement of the complex and let myself into the storeroom, which over the years had become an Aladdin's cave for the handyman. There was a vast selection of light bulbs, fuses, wire, nails and screws, together with every conceivable tool from shears to electric drills. All were neatly arrayed on labelled shelves, and it took me no time to find a hacksaw and a long-armed metal cutter. I even found replacements for the padlock and chain I was going to cut. I placed all these in a canvas bag that hung from the door, and set off as fast as I could go.

As I made my way through the wood I wondered if I would discover Ambrose similarly armed. But I needn't have worried. The porch was deserted, and all was quiet, save for a mournful sucking of water under the jetty. As I had predicted, the chain was no match for the cutters, and I didn't even need the hacksaw. In no time I was inside.

The air was stale and slightly damp, as though the boathouse had been uninhabited for weeks rather than hours. The living room seemed not only bare but totally devoid of life. I glanced around, trying to work out what had changed. Two things only were missing – the multi-coloured throw she kept on the sofa, and the print on the wall – but their absence had drained the room of life and individuality. Unnerved, I hurried towards the bedroom. The door was closed, which was unusual, and I pushed it open with mounting trepidation.

Bed, wardrobe and dressing table were all empty, and her screens – the focus of our lives for so many months – had gone. She'd also removed the trestles, as well as all the cables. It was as if they'd never been there at all. I ran into the bathroom. All her toiletries had gone. It was the same in the kitchen. The cupboards were bare. Even the waste bin was empty. Wherever Mallory had gone, she wasn't coming back.

I wandered numbly into the living room and stared at the wall. There wasn't even a mark to show where the print had hung. This place had been my focal point for so long; now it was devoid of everything that had given joy and purpose to my life. I couldn't take it in. Beyond tears, I was as emotionless and mute as the boathouse itself.

How long I stood there, I don't know. But slowly my brain began to function again. Everything suggested that Mallory had cut and run. But why? I couldn't believe that our quarrel alone had provoked such a comprehensive departure, nor that she was so lacking in courage that she had fled rather than tell me. Could George's pessimistic assessment of her character be true: now that she'd made her profit was she making off with it? I couldn't believe it. If she'd always intended to steal the proceeds of Ghost Trader, there was no need for the elaborate ploy that she'd hired me to construct. I was sure that – like me – she'd wanted the members to see the shorting in action. Whatever George had said, he no more wanted to believe her a liar than I. Andréa's opinion did not count, coming as it did from Ambrose, who was embittered enough to believe anything of those he felt had wronged him.

I came back to my first theory, that Mallory had caught wind of Ambrose's impending approach. Perhaps the estate agent had warned her to expect an old acquaintance, and she had escaped in the nick of time. That would explain her taking all her belongings with her. In which case, it was possible she'd left a forwarding address with the estate agent. The thought had hardly entered my head before I was acting on it. It took very little time to lock up and replace the padlock and chain. Then I hurried up to the main road and into the centre of Veyrier. At this hour, the shops were opening, though it was rather early for the estate agents. But a young woman was unlocking the last one I came to. "Good morning," I said politely.

She glanced at her watch. "I'm not really open yet."

"This won't take long," I assured her. "An old friend of mine is renting a converted boathouse. I wonder if it's through you?"

She was young and anxious to please, but also wanting to open up in an unhurried manner. But she made the mistake of letting me follow her in. "I'll get the list," she conceded reluctantly.

It took her a while to find it in one of the filing cabinets, but once she'd put it in my hands, she offered to make us both an espresso. By the time this was ready it was clear that none of her rental properties fitted the boathouse. "I'm sorry, Monsieur, but one of the others may have it. We don't handle all the rentals. They should be open in the next ten minutes." I sipped my espresso impatiently.

In the next estate agent to have opened, I found an immaculate and rather superior young man at the front desk. "Rentals aren't really our thing," he explained disdainfully in answer to my request. "You should try the people across the road. More their line than ours."

I hurried in the direction of his pointing finger. Behind a window full of photos of desirable properties – *chalets de grand standing, duplexes avec vue du lac*, and *appartements avec piscine communale* – I could see a fierce-looking lady of a certain age with swept-back hair and heavily-framed spectacles, who was booting up her computer.

"You're the second person in two days to be looking for a lady who rents a boathouse." She awarded me a suspicious frown. "So I'll tell you what I told him. We do have such a property on our books, rented out to the same lady since July 2007. But the property itself has been empty since her accident. I'm surprised you haven't heard."

"Accident?" I stammered. "When did it happen?"

"New Year's Day." A suspicion of sympathy softened her features. "I can only assume that you're not from here, Monsieur, otherwise I'm sure you'd remember the terrible accident in the next village. I'm sorry to tell you that your 'friend' was one of the victims. She's still in hospital, I believe. Along with the runner who tried to save her."

My head span and I felt myself falling. The last thing I saw was the woman rising horrified to her feet. "Please, Monsieur, take a seat. The gentleman yesterday... shall we say he took the news rather more calmly than you. Then, he was half-English, I think."

The next thing I knew, I was in my hospital bed listening to Hope. "She's gone, Clem, and I don't know how to bring her back. You're her only chance." Her self-confidence shattered, she fought to keep her voice under control. "If you can't find her, they'll have to switch off her life support. They say it's permanent now: persistent vegetative state. No brain activity, just the basic reflexes to stay breathing."

She clutched my arm desperately. Her normally calm eyes were red-rimmed and bloodshot. "But I won't let them. Not yet." She spoke with the obstinacy of a young girl rather than with the calm of an adult. "I know you can do it. If it wasn't for you, I'd never have found Marie-Sainte, and I'd never have attempted the shorting. So go and tell her it's been a wonderful success. All I have to do now is tell the members…" she broke down. "I'm begging you, Clem, you're all I've got."

Her grief infected me so much that tears ran down my cheeks. I had no means of stopping them. "You understand!" She delved into her bag for tissues, her face alight with renewed optimism. I could not let her down. As I had once before, I summoned all the energy I could muster. Hard though it had been before, this time was harder still. So hard I almost gave up. But if my body was weak, my will was indomitable. With Mallory in danger, and her daughter in despair, nothing would stop me. "She says she's gone to see *L'Esprit* and *Le Baigneur*."

She recoiled in horror. "Then she really means it." The brief flame of optimism died away. "Don't you see? It's her way of saying."

I saw all too well. Going to see a dead man could be code for going away to die. It was Hope's interpretation obviously. Which could only mean that *Le Baigneur* was also dead. Mallory had not gone to plead merely for her job. But her parting words did not suggest that she had given up. In my waking world she'd driven away, which meant she had a real destination in mind; and she thought her two founder members were still alive. Which suggested that in some reality of hers, they were indeed still alive. All I had to do was break into it.

"*Madame L'Esprit*'s number," I croaked. He might be dead, but his widow was not. It was a long-shot, but the only shot I had.

Hope stared at me in disbelief. Then her eyes lit up again, and she was soon reading me the number from her mobile. She also wrote it on my wrist. "Just be quick, that's all I ask."

A moment later I was back in the estate agency. The fierce lady was bending over me, a glass of water in hand. "You fainted, Monsieur." Her voice brimmed now with kindness.

"I'm fine." I assured her as I sipped. "No idea what came over me."

My despair lifted. I had a plan of action, and nothing was going to prevent me finding Mallory and trying to bring her back. I was so energised, that I surprised the lady by jumping to my feet. "We can call a doctor, Monsieur. You've had a nasty shock."

"No, really." I glanced at my wrist. Sure enough, half hidden by my watch strap, there was the number in blue ink. Thanking her profusely, I gathered up my tools, and hurried home, rehearsing in my mind what I must say to Madame Linberger. As soon as I was inside, I called the number on my wrist. "Madame, we met in Les Confins. I was the Englishman who understood IBNR, who saw the skier in black…"

She cut me frostily short. "I do not wish to discuss the matter."

"Please, Madame, this could save a life." I held my breath, but she did not hang up. "Has Madame Stellenbourg tried to contact you?"

"Then she's recovered." The response was immediate and eager.

"That's the problem. She's discharged herself from hospital, but she's very disoriented. One of the other patients told me she was going to see the founder members of Ghost Trader: user names *L'Esprit* and *Le Baigneur*." There was a painful intake of breath. "Precisely, Madame. That's why I need to find her as quickly as possible. As I'm sure you're aware, *L'Esprit* was your husband, and *Le Baigneur*…"

A choke concussed my ear. "Poor Robert can no more see her than my late husband. He drowned in *Lac Bourget*. January seventh."

"Drowned!" It was my turn for shock. "What happened?"

"May I ask, Monsieur, what is your interest here?"

"I should have explained. I've been visiting Madame Stellenbourg every day since the accident, and I was there just after it happened."

She thawed immediately. "I'm very sorry, Monsieur. New Year appears to have been a dreadful time for accidents. The first two you know only too well. As for poor Robert, he also fell from a cliff. Much like my husband. Except he fell into icy water, not snow."

My mind raced. If *Le Baigneur* had disapproved of shorting Enron as much as *L'Esprit*, then he too would have been a target for Ambrose's revenge. "You mean he was pushed?"

She snorted. "You must draw your own conclusions. As with my husband, witnesses claimed nobody was near when he fell."

"The skier in black was there when Madame Stellenbourg was run over," I said. "He saw her being prepared for the ambulance."

"Are you sure?" Far from denying his existence, she was all ears.

"I'm not only sure, I've found out who he is, and why he pushed your husband, as well as why he almost certainly pushed *Le Baigneur*."

I outlined to her the Enron saga as rapidly as I could. "I'm desperate to find Madame Stellenbourg before he does."

"I wish I could help you." She now seemed truly anxious for me.

"She took her own car, and Aix is a lot nearer *Lac d'Annecy* than Paris. Do you happen to know Monsieur Robert's address?"

"You ought to go to the police."

"Ordinarily, I would. But I can't with this story."

"I hardly know what to think." Warmth animated her voice. "But you were understanding in Les Confins, Monsieur. Nor would I wish on her what happened to dear Robert or to my husband. Robert lived in Aix, but his family home is on the far shore of *Lac Bourget*, near St Hippocrate. I understood he was selling it to her." Her voice faltered. "It was from there that he fell – or was pushed – into the lake."

"That must be the place!" I almost shouted in my desperation.

"If you're near Veyrier, Monsieur, you should consult *Madame de Maintenant*. She knew Robert, so she'll know where to go."

Nicknamed for her punctuality, the local taxi owner was famous from Veyrier to Talloires. "Madame, I can't thank you enough."

Yet even as I rang off, I realised that if Ambrose had pushed *Le Baigneur* to his death, he must know the place better than Madame Linberger. As soon as Mallory had driven away, he must have guessed where she was most likely to go. If his sole mission were revenge, he would have had time to dispose of her by now. My one hope was that he also wanted Ghost Trader's profit. Then she might stall him until Monday, when the banks reopened.

Chapter Seventeen : Extraordinary General Meeting

A one-woman, one-vehicle enterprise that managed to be more efficient and better priced than any fleet, *Madame de Maintenant* agreed to take me, even on her day off. As *Madame L'Esprit* had predicted, she knew exactly where I wanted to go. "A wonderful setting, 50 metres above the lake on a cliff. But the building..." she shuddered. "It used to be some kind of hospital, but I shouldn't have cared to be ill there."

A stocky, energetic woman with short, dyed blonde hair, she drove with the same urgency as Mallory, tailgating the car in front and choosing the least probable spots for overtaking, whilst talking steadily from the side of her mouth. "It's lucky Monsieur Robert asked me to collect Madame Stellenbourg for *St Silvestre*, or I wouldn't know where to go. She wanted to drive herself, but *les flics*, you know, are notorious with the breathalyser, and he'd booked a large table at that hotel near the casino, where they were certain to be lurking. He insisted I stay over, all expenses paid, so I could bring Madame Stellenbourg back. After the celebrations I drove them to where we're going. She'd been wanting to buy it for years, but his family were difficult." She laughed. "You know how families are over property. There's always the cousin in Provence or the half-brother in the Languedoc who won't budge. Anyway, it was finally sorted in time for *St Silvestre*, and Madame Stellenbourg was anxious to spend her first night there. It's dilapidated, but there's a modernised apartment in the tower."

It seemed that Andréa, through Ambrose, had been right about Mallory buying a property . But it was hardly a crime; nor proof that she was about to steal the money to develop it. I might be disappointed that she'd not told me, but she'd been so preoccupied with the shorting gamble that she'd not dared to think beyond it. All the purchase did was provide another reason, on top of visiting her dying father, for her absence between New Year and March. But it was to me she'd turned for help, and it was near me that she'd stayed during the shorting. I had every right to feel flattered and none to be angry.

We were now making steady speed along the *autoroute*, and *Madame de Maintenant*'s chatter was restful. Until we arrived there was nothing I could do. I had no plan, because I had no idea what to expect. Tired as I was, I must have nodded off.

Once again, I found Hope at my bedside. "Her condition's just the same. Any luck yet?" She sounded as fretful as a small child.

"*Lac Bourget*," I rasped, "She's there… On my way."

Her smile transformed her face. "I knew I could rely on you."

I woke as the taxi slowed down for the toll-booth. "I trust Madame Stellenbourg has fully recovered from her accident," *Madame de Maintenant* observed, as we drove into the outskirts of Aix. "Such a terrible run of accidents we had around New Year! Monsieur Linberger at Les Confins, Monsieur de St Hippocrate at the old hospital, and poor Madame Stellenbourg knocked down with some runner on the corner of the Rue de la Plage." She crossed herself discreetly. "One of your neighbours saw it: the *notaire*'s wife. She said it was bad."

"I just missed seeing it, but I saw them putting the woman in the ambulance. She *did* look like Madame Stellenbourg, but it was a different person." I tried to laugh nonchalantly. "Poor Sidonie thought the runner was me at first."

She looked relieved, if not entirely convinced. "I'd not wish an accident on anyone, you understand, but if it has to be somebody, I'd rather it wasn't one of my customers."

Unnerved by her talk of accidents and death, I was wide awake again. *Lac Bourget* was much larger than *Lac d'Annecy*, and I estimated it would be an hour or more before we reached our destination. My heart beat faster, and I clenched my fists.

As if to mock my fear, the afternoon was sunny and the waters of the lake smooth and placid. The light had the wonderful limpid quality of a perfect Saturday afternoon. Once we had cleared Aix, all the beaches we passed were crowded with families out to enjoy the last of the summer, and the water was criss-crossed by wind-surfs and boats. *Lac Bourget* was said to be unfathomable, and the water was much darker than the lake I was used to, but nothing could diminish its attractions on a weekend such as this.

We turned to follow the northern shore. Hills rose to our right, but the shoreline was flat and flanked by tall bulrushes. We crossed a canal, and then we turned south again, following the further shore. Here the lake was bordered by hills and the road wound its way up and over them. "There you are, Monsieur." *Madame de Maintenant* pointed as we crested the next hill. The road dropped sharply, and there, as it briefly levelled out, was our destination. Its grounds formed the top of a promontory, thrust out into the lake on sheer cliffs. It was a setting to fire the imagination of any architect. Here the choice had been the fantastic gothic of the late 19th century, with narrow pointy windows and dizzily precipitous roofs. Despite the sunlight, it had a sullen look, as though the granite of its frames and lintels, the brickwork of its walls, and the slate of its roofs longed only for winter.

I recognised it from the print in the boathouse: the *Sanatorium de St Hippocrate*, Mallory's one decoration. The cliff tops were flanked by dense shrubbery, otherwise the grounds were laid out formally. But the pergolas were overgrown, the statues were moss-streaked and crumbling, and the fountains were dry. To a 19th century poet, inspired by the grotesqueries of gothic romance and high on laudanum, it might once have seemed beautiful, but I could well understand *Madame de Maintenant*'s reluctance to be treated here. As a setting for murder it was perfect, and my courage foundered as we drew up outside.

Its tall wrought iron gates were slightly ajar, and there were tyre tracks just visible in the weedy gravel. Parked by the steps to the entrance was Mallory's old Peugeot Six. If a car could give off welcoming vibes, this one did. I stuffed two 100 euro notes into *Madame de Maintenant*'s hand. "If that's not enough, I'll give you the rest later," I shouted, as I jumped out and ran up the drive.

On the corner closest to the cliff was a round tower with arrow-slit windows, one of which was open. I thought I saw the outline of a familiar head as I raced up the steps to the oaken door. It was huge, on scrolled hinges and reinforced with iron studs. There was no bell, but there was an iron knocker, as bulky as a cannon ball. Grasping the ball in both hands, I sent out deep hollow booms into the house beyond. For a long time there was silence. So long my heart began to sink. At last I heard bare feet hurrying down heavy wooden stairs, then pattering across a tiled floor. There was a rumble of bolts being drawn back, then she stood before me. Pale she might be, her eyes dark-rimmed and her hair a little tousled, but she was alive and unharmed. Even the bruise I had inflicted was very faint. My fears had been groundless.

Her expression was defensive for less than a moment; then her eyes lit up with such spontaneous joy that explanation and apology became superfluous. Instantly, we were in each other's arms, her kisses and caresses fighting with mine for precedence. Whatever inhibitions had held us back before, there were none now. All doubts and fears were swept away by the overwhelming reality of her presence. My senses gloried in her beauty: the warmth of her fragrance, at once floral and musky; the pliancy of her skin, as it yielded to my hands and to my lips; the taste of her tongue as it entwined with mine; the electrifying trip of her fingers along my neck and through my hair; the glorious pressure of her body against mine.

Pushing the door shut, she took my hand, and led me through a cavernous hall and up a wide dusty stair. She was giggling like a teenager, her eyes – sparkling as I'd never seen them before – bidding me on to the gallery above. Against its stone balustrade, we paused for more kissing, before she led me past rooms full of ancient hospital beds and wheelchairs on heavy spoked wheels. At last we came to the end of the gallery, and she drew me into an almost circular room. We were in the tower, and from inside the windows seemed far less narrow. Here, away from the gloom and dilapidation of the rest of the building, was a cosy living room, with her laptop on the table, and her multi-coloured throw across a comfy old sofa.

But we did not stop here. She led me up a spiral staircase to a semi-circular bedroom. The other half was a bathroom, into which she retreated, pushing me gently back with a finger to my lips. "Just give me a minute." Her first words, since I'd arrived, and prosaic enough, but their tone was rich with joy and the promise of love.

She was as good as her word. Her shift abandoned, she stood before me as beautiful as Venus rising from the sea. She helped me to unbutton my shirt, and in no time I was as naked as she was. We sank onto the bed in glorious unison. There was no reticence nor uncertainty, no ill-chosen words to be wished away. Now at last, as she lay in my arms, I whispered the endearments I had long treasured in my mind, and in return she peppered my face with kisses.

Soon followed the glory of two joined as one, made the more joyous in contrast to the fear and disappointment that had for long seemed to doom such fulfilment. Afterwards we savoured the languorous contentment of sleep, in which nothing mattered but our nearness to each other. When I awoke I gazed down on the oval of her face, bordered by the tousle of her hair. Her eyes were closed and her chest rose gently with her breathing, and for a horrible moment I was reminded of her stillness in the gutter of my early dreams.

But these cheeks glowed with contentment, these lips were parted in a secret smile. No bruise blemished her face, no blood besmirched her temple. She awoke with a smile, and we made love again, more slowly and even more wonderfully. Then, as we drifted once more towards slumber, she murmured the words of love I'd never tire of hearing.

When I next awoke, the bedroom was bright with morning sunshine, and I could hear Mallory singing. Aromas of coffee and croissants invited me to throw off my lethargy. Retrieving my boxers from the floor, I pattered down the stairs just as Mallory was emerging from a tiny kitchen with breakfast on a tray. We sat by one of the windows, bathed in glorious light, with the vastness of the lake spread below us. "How did you find me?" she asked at last.

"It's a long story." I hardly knew how or even whether to begin. There were mysteries to be cleared up, but in the joy of our reunion I felt they could wait. "Am I forgiven for slapping you?"

"Of course." She rubbed her cheek. "I'm sorry I lost my temper."

"Why did you rush off?"

"I panicked." Lashes veiled her eyes. "Commitment isn't easy."

"You cleared out everything." I tried not to sound reproachful.

"This is home now. I'd have done it sooner, but working with you was easier from the boathouse." A frown crossed her face, and she kissed my hand to hide it. "I knew I could never hide from you."

"Why would you want to?"

"I told you. I bring bad luck to relationships."

"A risk I'd run." It was my turn to frown. "I thought you knew."

"Darling Clem. I just wasn't expecting you to burst into my life."

"So seeing *Le Baigneur* and *L'Esprit* was just a smokescreen?"

"Of course not." She studied my hand in hers. "I'd never lie to you."

I smiled grimly. "You just wouldn't tell me the whole truth."

"You make me sound terrible." She looked straight at me, her eyes pleading. "I said I'd get back to you. Once I'd straightened things out. With them, and in my own mind."

"Them? You mean *Le Baigneur* and *L'Esprit*?"

She nodded. "You got my message, didn't you?"

"And you got mine?"

"Yes, and I didn't understand it." Her brow furrowed in puzzlement. "I couldn't tell if there was some kind of danger or you didn't want to see me again, but couldn't quite bring yourself to say it."

"Obviously I wanted to see you again." I pressed her hand until she smiled. "It was a warning. The thing I couldn't quite bring myself to say was who was threatening you. In case you didn't believe me." She dropped my hand in alarm. "Ambrose found the boathouse."

"We're not back to that nonsense!" All joy drained from her face.

"It's not nonsense. He attacked me. Then he ran up the path when your car started." I briefly described the confrontation.

"But that was after midnight," she exclaimed, as if the time alone must disprove me. "Don't tell me you were standing guard?"

"No. I got there just as he was trying to open the door."

"But why were you there at all?" she persisted, as if my presence needed more explaining than his. "Are you sure it wasn't a dream?"

"I did have a dream," I admitted. "But only to warn me he'd found your address. Then I rushed round. We both just missed you."

"What makes you so sure it was Ambrose, and not one of those burglars Armand warned you about?" She seemed desperate to believe any story other than mine.

I'd almost forgotten my spur-of-the-moment rationale for extra security. "There never were any burglars," I admitted. "The threat was Ambrose all along. I should have said as soon as I got back from the wedding, but I was afraid of distracting you from the shorting. That's why I stayed the whole time after that..." I tried to sound resourceful, but my words rang hollowly. "I'm sorry I lied to you."

"You're not trying to tell me Ambrose was at the wedding?" The facts seemed to worry her more than my concealment of them.

"This came from Andréa. He's writing a book about the financial crisis and its effects on ordinary people. One of the unfortunates who poured out his life story was Ambrose."

"His life story!" She could not have looked more horrified if Ambrose had walked in with murder in his eyes. "His entire life?"

"All the salient points. How he married the woman who sold him insurance, their baby daughter, her joining Lloyd's, his recruitment as a Name... Do I need to go on?"

"I wish you'd said."

"I wish you'd said he was your husband," I responded gently.

In her agitation, she bit her lip. "I didn't know how you'd react."

"Ditto." I tried to smile, to suggest that we'd acted for good reasons, that one concealment was *quid pro quo* for the other.

Mallory sat in stunned silence, as she struggled with the painful fact that the man she thought was dead had returned to haunt her. Reaching for her hand, I led her to the sofa, and enfolded her in my arms. She clung to me like a small child in fear of a bogeyman. Feeling more like a father than a lover, I stroked her hair, and kissed her forehead. "I shouldn't have lost my temper. I'll never abandon you again."

"Andréa could have made the whole thing up," she suggested.

"He couldn't have guessed every detail."

"That depends how much you've told him. Or Marie-Sainte."

"I told Marie-Sainte the barest minimum about Ghost Trader, and nothing at all about your private life. Until he told me the story, I'd never spoken with Andréa about you at all. Anyway, I couldn't have told them you and Ambrose were married. It never occurred to me."

"So he told Andréa about Ghost Trader?"

"Of course. Even about the money you and Rex put aside."

She blenched. "And Enron?"

"That too." It seemed she must check every fact in turn.

"Then you know all about me?" I'd never seen her so agitated.

"All Ambrose knows about you, perhaps." I drew her back into my arms and kissed her. "But he never got your motives right."

"Did he say how he came back from the dead?" Though she submitted to my caresses, she tensed like an animal in a trap.

"We know how. He came off as a foot passenger or he swam."

"Did he say anything at all about the ferry?" she persisted.

"No. He only said you were buying this place to develop a hotel."

"A hotel?" she asked eagerly, pouncing for an inconsistency.

"He even thought you'd use the shorting profit to pay for it."

"How could Ambrose know about the shorting?"

"Through Andréa. They put two and two together and made five."

She broke angrily from me. "I should never have hired that girl."

With the benefit of hindsight, it was difficult to disagree, even though Marie-Sainte had done an excellent job. "I'm sorry. But I couldn't have known he'd meet Ambrose." She acknowledged this with an angry shrug. "The point is, what are we going to do?"

"What can we do?"

"That depends whether he knows this is the place you bought."

"I'm not sure. He could probably work it out."

"Then we must get away immediately."

She stood up, crossed to the window and stared across the lake. "I've run from Ambrose for too long. If he comes, he comes." She squared her shoulders, and her voice grew stronger. "Besides, I'm seeing *Le Baigneur* and *L'Esprit* tomorrow."

She was struggling with the idea of Ambrose being alive; yet she seemed to have no idea that her two founder members, who'd encouraged and drummed up support for Ghost Trader, were both dead. Even if there were plausible explanations for her ignorance over *L'Esprit*, it was impossible that she did not know that *Le Baigneur* had fallen to his death from the very cliff edge she could almost see beyond the window. "Were you here January the seventh?" I asked.

"If I remember rightly, I was seeing my father." She screwed up her eyes in thought. "In fact, I'm sure I was. Why do you ask?"

"I spoke to *Madame L'Esprit*. She said you were here."

She managed a brittle laugh. "You really should be a detective."

186

"She told me about her husband, and about his friend Robert..." I paused, not sure what to expect. Mallory's smile hardly wavered. Her eyebrows rose, as they might on the expectation of interesting tittle-tattle, but she gave no further signs of distress. However incredible, it was obvious that she knew nothing about either death. I had indeed broken into her reality, just as I'd promised Hope I would. The only question was whether I could lead her out of it again.

"What about them?" Her expression only veered towards alarm as my silence lengthened. What was my best tactic: to shatter her delusion, or to go along with it? The latter was easier, but it would make it more difficult to persuade her to leave; equally, there was no guarantee she would believe the truth. But I wanted no more evasions. Just as I ought to have told her about Ambrose, I had to tell her about *L'Esprit* and *Le Baigneur*. I joined her at the window.

"*Madame L'Esprit* – Linberger – told me they're both dead."

The colour drained from her face, and she trembled in my arms. She'd reacted badly to my claim to have seen Ambrose at New Year, and worse to my dream of pushing Saul from the ferry, but I had not seen extreme shock like this since *Madame L'Esprit* had been escorted from the ridge above Les Confins. But gradually, under my soothing, she began to recover. "Are you sure it was Jean-Michel's wife?"

"Absolutely," I assured her. "It was Jean-Michel who was killed."

"Rubbish!" she retorted. "I suppose she said Robert was with him?"

"Not quite. She said he fell off that cliff." I pointed towards the lake. "That was the official verdict, but we think he was pushed."

"That's impossible." She was almost shouting.

"Not if someone had a grudge." I kept my voice quiet and reasonable. "The same grudge he had against *L'Esprit*." Her eyes widened, in horror or disbelief. "And against you."

"Giving him a plausible motive doesn't make it true."

"You said you weren't here the day it happened."

"His family would have contacted me... otherwise, the police." It was a fair point. Yet it had definitely been Madame Linberger with whom I had spoken. "Besides," Mallory continued, "I saw them both yesterday morning. Here in this room, large as life."

I'd already concluded that in her reality they were somehow still alive. But being somehow alive was a less startling idea than meeting them face to face. "What did they say?"

"They listened mainly. I laid it on the line. Why shorting was necessary. Why I couldn't consult them. I even told them about you. Everything but your name. I said Lloyd's had ruined you, so your opinion was a good proxy for the membership. I told them the decision had been mine, but if you'd disapproved, I wouldn't have done it." She smiled at last, happier to describe what had happened than to speculate on its impossibility. "I wanted them to know their new-found wealth owed as much to you as to me." I asked how they'd reacted. "They thanked me for being so frank. They said I'd given them food for thought, and they wanted to sleep on it. They might even take further soundings. They'd be back Monday with their decision."

"What's to decide? They aren't going to refuse the money, are they?" Like her, I found it much easier to concentrate on their reaction than to dwell on their being dead.

"My future, of course. They'll want to put it to a vote. What's important is what recommendation they put with it." She shrugged. "I knew it would be like this."

"Looks like I came just in time, then."

"You want to be here for them? I'm not sure they'll allow it."

"Let's not wait for them, then. Let's go while we still can."

"Are you mad? That would only confirm their suspicions."

Then it came to me like an Old Testament revelation. "Perhaps I am mad, but I've finally grasped what this is all about." I led her back to the sofa, and settled us comfortably, with my arm around her, her head on my shoulder. "I've taken it for granted this is reality, that my hospital dreams are just that. But for dreams they're too persistent, too logical. It's more like I'm living in two realities at once. But they can't both be true, however real they both seem when I'm in them." I paused to gather my thoughts, but also to see how she was taking it.

Her face was a picture of disbelief. "Go on," was all she said.

"This is the hard part. If both seem equally real, we can't easily tell which is true. So turn everything round. What if this is the dream, that reality is both of us in comas?"

She laughed nervously. "That's too extreme, even for you."

"I said we can't easily tell which is which. But there are clues. In reality, the dream world is unsustainable, however real it seems to us now. That's why *Le Baigneur* and *L'Esprit* are alive to you, but dead to me." Then I told her how Andréa in my apparent dream had warned me about Ambrose in my apparent waking world; and how Hope had begged the comatose me for my waking-world help. "She takes it for granted that both of us have an out-of-body life in which action is possible, that I can bring you back. Whatever bringing you back means, it isn't passively awaiting the arrival of a pair of ghosts."

"Why does Hope want to 'bring me back' all of a sudden?"

I hesitated, as I sought the kindest way of putting it. "She said you'd taken a turn for the worse. Until this weekend she was convinced you'd recover. Now she's not so sure."

For almost a minute she fell silent, struggling with my crazy idea. Finally, her expression grave, she put her arms around my neck. "Your analysis is so off-the-wall. But if you're right, running away won't solve anything. If I'm to wake up again, I have to face *Le Baigneur* and *L'Esprit*. Whether we like it or not, tomorrow is the day of judgement, and there's no way I can run from it. Perhaps you can, but I can't." I couldn't tell if she believed me or if she was humouring me; or worse, encouraging me to go before I showed more signs of madness.

I told her gravely that I was going nowhere without her. "Life was empty before you. Now it's full again. We'll face this together."

She awarded me a passionate kiss, then her manner became brisk. "Now that's settled, let's not waste any more of this wonderful day brooding. I could really use some exercise." I knew then that she still didn't really believe me. But at least she wasn't sending me away in disgust. Far from it. "We'll take a picnic. Make a day of it."

I agreed. I'd pushed my idea as far as she could take it in; now all I could do was wait and see what happened tomorrow. At least we would be facing it together. I went back upstairs to shower and dress, whilst Mallory packed food into a rucksack. When I returned, she helped to put my arms through the straps. Joking that men had their uses, we quit the haven of the tower arm in arm. Our feet echoed in the bare corridor as we passed the rooms full of ancient hospital equipment. Shafts of sunlight, paled by the griminess of the windows, broke the outlines of wheelchairs, commodes and other medical paraphernalia, so that their disjointed parts stuck weirdly out of deep shadow. Beyond the comfort of the tower I was overcome by the dilapidation of the rest.

"Why the fascination with this place?"

"I know it's a mess." She kissed me. "But think of the potential."

"Potential for expense. I can see that all right."

"It used to be a TB clinic in the 19th century, when the only hope was clean air and healthy diet. I'd like to bring it back into service." I suggested that TB was a problem largely solved. "I was thinking more of asbestosis and the chronic diseases brought on by pollution."

Half-way down the stairs, she stood in a pool of light that gave a golden lustre to her hair. "Names weren't the only victims. It was Rex's greatest regret that the failure of Lloyd's was a failure to help the people who really suffered. I've never forgotten that."

As I stood on that dusty stair in the grotesque ruin that had once been a house of healing, I grasped at last what I should have known from the start. The near collapse of Lloyd's had been a disaster far wider than the ruination of its Names. Whilst we had formed action groups to sue agents and syndicates, asbestos workers had been stricken by lung disease and organ failure; families living near chemical plants and storages sites had been poisoned with cancers. Just as Marie-Sainte had identified the true victims of the credit crunch, so Mallory had pinpointed the true victims of Lloyd's. Insurance might not have saved the dying, but it should have provided proper care and dignity in death, and it should have enabled polluted sites to be cleaned up.

But the claims were so huge that the response had been resistance not pay-out. Companies and their insurers had reached for their lawyers instead of their cheque books. With the rise of the class action, other lawyers were able to bring the diseased workers and poisoned citizens into the fray. But litigation is a slow and expensive process. Though asbestos manufacturers went bankrupt, though insurers were forced to bolster their reserves on an unprecedented scale, and though law firms prospered, the pay-outs to the sick and the dying had been too small or too late. To this day, outstanding claims far exceed those paid out.

I had wasted years lamenting my own problems without a thought for the greater ones of others. I had lost my fortune, not my health, nor my life. "How can I help?" I asked humbly.

She rewarded me with an amazed kiss. "You want to help?"

"It's an enterprise, isn't it? Of course I want to help."

Her laugh was full of relief. "I was afraid you'd think me mad."

I laughed too. "Not until I see your business plan."

"You shall," she promised. "But not today." She led me down the stairs, across the hall and into the sunshine beyond. The statues threw elongated shadows across our path, whilst their sightless eyes followed us resentfully to the gate. But I cared nothing for them. Far from creeping away to die, Mallory had come here to enact the next and best phase of her life, her intentions selfless beyond even what she had done for her members. My job now was to see that she would.

We crossed the road onto a steep track that wound its way up through a coppice of mountain oaks and conifers. After an hour of steady climbing, we came to a grassy and secluded plateau. The hill rose on behind us, but in front, above the tops of the trees, was a panorama of the lake, bright immediately below, but fading into haze at its southern extremity. Far beyond the opposite bank was spread the vista of the Alps. Amidst the snow-capped cones and pyramids, one ridge curved up and over like petrified waves. The *Massif des Aravis* beneath whose slopes lay the ski resort of La Clusaz.

I couldn't suppress a shudder. Though I couldn't see Les Confins, I couldn't help but think of *L'Esprit*, who had fallen or been pushed to his death there, yet who was visiting us tomorrow, along with the friend who himself had fallen or been pushed into the placid lake below.

We spread our picnic under the shade of two old and twisted oaks. An outcrop of granite provided a crude table, on which Mallory spread a check cloth. We feasted off coarse *pâté*, *crudités* and cheese, washed down by mineral water and *Mondeuse*. Then replete with food and wine, we alternately dozed and made love under the afternoon sun. We finally woke as the shadows of evening prickled our skin. Dark clouds had gathered at the far end of the lake, and wind ruffled the water. Mallory dragged me to my feet. "It's going to rain. Let's go."

We packed the remains of the picnic, and made our way back down the track. On the last slope, the clouds caught up with us. The light dimmed and the trees sighed. The Sanatorium lay immediately below us, its dark outlines embracing the sombre mood of the weather, whilst the arms of the statues seemed to command our immediate return. The gothic windows of the house were eerily blank and unwelcoming; the studded door gave the building a prison-like air. She smiled at my distaste. "It won't be scary when it's renovated."

I tried to see the place through her eyes. Perhaps if the walls were white, and the window frames painted brightly, if the gardens were filled with patients and nurses strolling amidst flowers and topiary, it could work. But the venture was going to need preparation and marketing. "Do *Le Baigneur* and *L'Esprit* know your plans?"

"All the members do. From the start, I suggested they each contribute a proportion of what I made them to the Sanatorium fund, but it was entirely voluntary. About half contributes regularly, the others from time to time. Even Ambrose until Enron. Robert would have *given* me the Sanatorium, but his family wanted market value. I've been in competition with Accor for years."

So much for Ambrose's mean-spirited lie to Andréa that she wished to develop a hotel for her own profit. I kissed her fervently.

We were interrupted by the first drops of rain, and by the sight of a stretched black DS Citroen with darkened windows advancing down the road. Its headlights came on as it reached the gateway. But instead of passing by, it slowed and turned in. The driver's door opened, and from inside an umbrella sprang open. Sheltering under it came the unmistakeably elegant figure of *L'Esprit*, agile and athletic in the act of opening the gate with one hand, whilst keeping the umbrella aloft with the other. As soon as he had created a wide enough opening, he resumed his seat and the car swept up the drive.

I glared at Mallory. "I thought they were coming tomorrow."

The rain was steady and she took my arm. "We'll be soaked."

I planted my feet firmly. "What about them?"

She shrugged. "Obviously they've decided to come today."

The Citroen parked next to the Peugeot, and *L'Esprit* climbed out. He walked to the other side and held the umbrella aloft for his front passenger, a florid patrician with a mane of white hair and an embonpoint that the elegant tailoring of his suit could not quite disguise. Presumably *Le Baigneur*. Then a rear door opened, and a big man with a pugnacious jaw heaved his bulk from the car. I had last seen him sprawled on his patio with staring, terror-filled eyes, and I had once broken his nose. The three officially dead men climbed the steps to the front door, to which *Le Baigneur* applied the knocker. The echo of it carried even to where we stood. "What are they doing with Wormsley?" If there were a moment to run, this had to be it.

But far from retreating, Mallory set off determinedly down the track. "There's only one way to find out," she said over her shoulder.

I hurried after her. Behind me, the swish of the rain was overlaid by a cacophony of wheezes and coughs. The figures who had queued outside the bank, the swimmers who had pulled Saul beneath the water, were materialising from under the trees. Only the track down was open to us, and from the steps *Le Baigneur* was gesturing for us to hurry. Far from unravelling, my dream world had become more vivid, its unreality more real, and there was nothing for it but to confront the creatures below, be they demons, ghosts or figments of dream.

Chapter Eighteen : Without Prejudice

Taking strength from the rain, the weeds in the drive already stood proud of the many and deepening puddles. If we'd been alone we'd have raced each other for the door and laughed at our sodden clothes. But under the silent scrutiny of the three on the steps, we walked with as much dignity as we could muster. As we neared the cars I gave Mallory's hand a reassuring squeeze. Although pale, she too seemed calm, and her fingers answered the pressure of mine. She even managed a smile, brief and grim though it was.

As we passed the Citroen, I saw the outlines of two more passengers through the darkened rear window, but their doors remained closed, and they showed no signs of moving. It seemed that they would not be joining us. We mounted the steps to the front door.

"I presume you have a key?" *Le Baigneur* asked sonorously.

"Of course, Robert. The door could hardly lock itself." Her humour, I was glad to see, had not deserted her. She swept past them with a toss of rain-sodden hair. As she inserted the key, I eyeballed the three, to show that I was not afraid of them. Normal men should not have been able to penetrate my bold front to the fear within. But were these normal men any longer? I'd no idea, but must act as if they were.

Le Baigneur granted me the faintest of smiles. Normal enough. I turned towards Wormsley, whose mouth was pulled down in an amused smirk: an improvement on his old truculence. "Long time, no see," I observed, before turning finally to *L'Esprit*. He stood with the same patrician aloofness he had displayed in Les Confins. I held his eye, determined not to be the one to look away. But as I stared I found that I could see straight through him to the wall behind. Like one of those visual puzzles, where one moment you see a vase, the next two faces in profile, *L'Esprit* flipped between opaque and translucent. Noting my double-take, he allowed himself a dry smile.

"You'll get used to it, Monsieur. You are the same for me."

"But I'm not..." My protest was cut short by an outbreak of coughing. In the shock of talking to three dead men, I'd almost forgotten the crowd behind. They were as indistinct as mist, so that I wondered now whether Mallory had noticed them.

"Come in, please." *Le Baigneur*'s voice was both commanding and reassuring, that of the natural chairman imposing his authority. In my confusion, I was only too ready to comply. "I'm sure you'll want to dry off. So I suggest the ballroom in fifteen minutes." He gestured towards double doors on the far side of the hall. It might be Mallory's house now, but he had not forgotten his former ownership.

"I was expecting you tomorrow, Robert."

"Monsieur Holden's arrival rather changes things," he replied gravely. "It's why I brought Monsieur Wormsley. I doubt he needs any introduction to either of you."

Wormsley's presence was as profoundly unwelcome as it was unexpected. From the moment he'd emerged from the car, my instinct had been to run, but Mallory's brave advance down the path had made that impossible. I could not believe that any verdict in which Wormsley participated would be favourable to me. However cordial his relations with Mallory in the past, he must know by now that hurting her was his best means of hurting me. "He needs no introduction," I said. "But his presence certainly needs explaining."

Mallory took my arm. "We were expecting your verdict on the shorting. He played no part in that. Nor is he a member."

"But for my support there'd have been no Ghost Trader," Wormsley replied condescendingly. "What happened to funds that arguably belonged to Lloyd's is hardly unimportant to me. Even now."

"All your questions will be answered ," said *Le Baigneur*. "But first I'm sure you'd prefer to get out of your wet clothes."

Under the scrutiny of the three ghosts, if ghosts they were, I followed Mallory upstairs and across the balcony, acutely conscious of their eyes following our every step. But once we were inside the tower, the power of their presence diminished, and it was possible to feel normal again. Yet we climbed the spiral stair to the bedroom in silence.

"Who's first for the shower?" Mallory asked finally.

"You go," I said, peeling off my shirt.

"There's some sweaters in the middle drawer. You could probably squeeze into one. Lucky you're a runner, not a rugby player." She slipped into the bathroom and threw me a towel. "There's a hair drier on the dressing table." It was as if we were back in the boathouse, she following the markets and me the forum. Instead of talking or even thinking about what was to unfold, we concentrated on our toilet.

Mallory was soon gracefully kitted out in linen trousers and a cotton top with wide sleeves gathered at the wrists. I was more eclectic, being forced to borrow whatever of hers fitted: a tee-shirt with its tightness partially hidden by draping a sweater over my shoulders, some old exercise trousers, and a pair of ski socks. But at least I was dry.

The ballroom was spectacular, with gothic windows down both sides and a wider one at the end, which offered a panoramic vista of the lake. *Trompe l'œil* gave the impression of standing in a wooded glade amidst nymphs and satyrs beneath a summer sky, where cherubs peeped from fluffy clouds. It was meant to be light-hearted in a grandiose kind of way, but the trees threw weird shadows, whilst the sky above lowered as though the outside storm was about to be repeated indoors. The faces of the satyrs leered, the nymphs were too knowing, and the eyes of the cherubs burned with more than mockery.

"I thought this used to be a hospital," I said, from the doorway.

"It was." Flanked by *L'Esprit* and Wormsley, *Le Baigneur* greeted us from a dais at the end. "Weekly balls were part of the therapy."

As he gestured for us to join them, a huge oak table on plump legs and a number of padded chairs appeared in front of him. Everything springing into focus like projections in a film. It seemed to take an age to reach the dais. My feet in their socks were silent, but Mallory's heels clicked loudly. "This is quite informal," he explained. "Hearings come later, should we need them."

"What hearings?" My voice echoed in the bare room.

"All in good time." He pulled out a chair for Mallory. "Please." She sat without a word, her face a mask. It was her way of coping. Quieter than mine, but effective. Perhaps.

As the others sat down opposite, *Le Baigneur* cleared his throat. It was enough to bring the meeting to order, and all eyes turned in his direction. He was an impressive-looking man, and the head of the table was his natural habitat. "These proceedings are unusual, if not unique," he intoned. "The reason for that being you, Monsieur Holden."

"You rather put the cat amongst the pigeons," *L'Esprit* added.

"One might almost say that you are that cat," continued *Le Baigneur*. "Had you not come, matters would be much clearer."

"So why not bog off again?" Wormsley cut in with relish.

"I'm not going anywhere without Mallory," I pronounced firmly.

"I'd be careful what you say if I was you." Wormsley laughed nastily. "Unless, of course, you want to dig your own grave. Not that I'd put that past you, on previous form."

"Let's not be hasty," *Le Baigneur* interjected smoothly. "It is true, Monsieur Holden, that you are, at least for the moment, free to leave at any time. However," he sighed, "I regret that the same cannot be said for Madame Stellenbourg here." He turned to her with a sympathetic smile. "You do understand that, don't you, my dear?"

Her eyes met mine, commanding me to silence. "Oh, come on, Robert, even if you don't approve of what I've done, even if it goes against your deepest principles, Jean-Michel, and even if you've managed to get the entire membership behind you, you can only fire me. You can't arrest me." She pointed at Wormsley. "And nor can you." She stood up. "As for going, this is my property, and I can ask you all to leave at any time." She laid a hand on my shoulder. "Not you, darling, you can stay as long as you want."

There was silence. Wormsley bit his lip, *L'Esprit* sucked in his cheeks as though he'd eaten a crab-apple, whilst *Le Baigneur* made a careful study of his hands. Despite every shock, she had responded magnificently. "You can't arrest either of us," I said, trying to match her tone. "But I'm just as implicated in Ghost Trader."

"Sadly for you, this has little to do with Ghost Trader," *Le Baigneur* said. "Your shorting activity is of tangential concern to us, to the extent only that it impinges on the matter in hand. Nor are you in a position to send us away. We are here not because we wish it, but because we have a duty to perform, that is all. Nothing personal."

Mallory sat down again "You've lost me, Robert, I'm afraid."

"Perhaps Mr Holden should explain it to you." Wormsley smiled maliciously. "But make sure you tell her the real reason you're here."

"I already have," I told him boldly. "I'm here to take her back to her daughter, and, if necessary, to protect her from Monsieur Hanter."

"Don't worry," *Le Baigneur* said. "We have him under control."

"All three of us were his victims, after all," *L'Esprit* observed.

Was it possible that this meeting was more about Ambrose than Mallory or me? Even if not, I might be able to use him to divert attention away from us. "Mallory was his intended victim on New Year's Day, when he also assaulted me. And he sent me a threatening text on New Year's Eve." I appealed to them all. "It seems to me that each of us round the table is his victim. He must be stopped."

"I'd worry more what he can say, not do," Wormsley replied.

"We're not here to judge Monsieur Hanter," *Le Baigneur* said.

"If you're here to judge me," Mallory retorted, "I'm all ears."

L'Esprit pursed his lips. "Our role is far from judgemental."

Le Baigneur nodded. "We are here only to assist *your* judgement."

Mallory threw up her hands. "You're talking riddles."

"We've made our judgement," I added. "Our consciences are clear."

"Are they indeed?" Wormsley gloated. "I wouldn't be so sure."

Ignoring him, *Le Baigneur* laid his hand on Mallory's forearm. "I see that you're confused, and we must clear up all misunderstandings." His tone was apologetic. "There are many layers to this, but let me begin by asking you what you understand to be Monsieur Hanter's situation, or perhaps I should say, his condition?"

"He feels angry and bitter," she answered sadly, "Wronged by those he trusted most. Especially me. I encouraged him to join Lloyd's," she frowned at Wormsley, who shrugged. "I left him for another man, and I didn't support him over Enron. If anyone's a victim, it's him."

"I didn't mean his frame of mind exactly," *Le Baigneur* said.

"Do you think he's still alive?" *L'Esprit* asked. "Despite the ferry."

"I thought he drowned." She glanced at me. "Clem didn't."

"He was too good a swimmer," I said. "I think he faked suicide."

Wormsley's eyes narrowed angrily "You weren't there."

"I didn't need to be there. I've seen him swim," I retorted angrily. "More to the point, I saw him only yesterday."

"You're seeing me," Wormsley said. "And you know about me."

"We read the newspaper reports," Mallory conceded. "That's all."

"You never believe what you read in the papers, is that it?"

"I don't believe in ghosts, that's for sure."

L'Esprit and *Le Baigneur* exchanged glances. "When you summoned us, we thought you knew," *Le Baigneur* began.

"It was only as you told us about the short that we began to realise." *L'Esprit* spread his arms expressively. "In similar cases, people normally understand their underlying condition."

"The fact is, my dear, the extent of your, dare I say, delusion..." *Le Baigneur* coughed awkwardly. "It took us by surprise. That's why we said we'd get back to you. We thought you needed more time."

"I always gave Names extra time," Wormsley smiled tigerishly. "Provided they co-operated."

To everyone's surprise, Mallory laughed. "You can't frighten me with Clem's dreams. He's told me all about them. According to them, we've both been in comas since New Year's Day. But I can assure you, we're solidly alive." She slapped my back hard enough to echo round the room. She hadn't believed me, and she still didn't.

The figures before us shimmered, so that I could see the long windows and the darkening evening sky beyond. Then, as they solidified again, I saw for a fraction of a second the skeletons beneath, before flesh and sinew returned. My heart lurched just as it had when the ambulances had seemed about to burst into my living room.

"So you don't accept we're ghosts?" Wormsley demanded.

"I might." I pressed Mallory's hand. "But I don't want to."

"I certainly don't," she said firmly, crushing my hand in return.

"Names were just as unrealistic, and I always found shock tactics worked best." Wormsley rapped the table for emphasis. "Kinder, too, in the long run," he added, as *Le Baigneur* frowned.

L'Esprit nodded. "I think Monsieur Wormsley may be right. We cannot properly proceed until both of them understands fully. Emotionally as well as intellectually."

"Even if you cannot accept we are deceased," *Le Baigneur* said in his gentlest voice, "there's one death you can't deny." He turned to Wormsley. "If you would be so kind, Monsieur."

Clearly enjoying himself, Wormsley rose to his feet and headed for the double doors. I reached again for Mallory's hand, and she managed a tiny smile. Then the doors reopened, and Wormsley led another man into the ballroom. His face was obscured by Wormsley's shoulders, but Mallory recognised him, and the colour drained from her face.

"Hello, Mallory. It's been a long time." The newcomer's tone was brash to cover his discomfort, and he did his best to smile. He mounted the dais and took one of the empty chairs opposite. His shirt and trousers were immaculately casual, but he looked angry and out of sorts, an important man dragged against his will to an unwelcome encounter. Because I had seen him only briefly in two photographs, it took me a moment to realise who he was.

"Rex." She was almost inaudible, but she did not let go of me.

"It's a simple choice." Rex now affected a world-weary affability, which in any other situation might have been charming. "You can come back with me, or you can go with him."

"Now just a minute," I cut in angrily. It was bad enough to see my rival in whatever passed for flesh in the afterlife, but worse to realise that he now looked the younger.

Mallory staggered to her feet. "You're not Rex, you can't be." She turned pleadingly to me. "They're phantoms, all of them."

"You, too, darling," Rex answered. "You and your boyfriend. We're all in the same boat." His smile was one of commiseration, but he could not hide the satisfaction in his voice.

"I'm alive!" Her fist pounded the table. Though she had struggled to stand, there was no doubting the spirit that burned within her.

"So am I." Whatever else confounded me, of that I was sure.

Le Baigneur smiled, but this only made his expression sadder. "I do not deny that you are alive, unlike the rest of us. Yet you are both as much out-of-body as we are." That at least was in accord with my

198

earlier revelation. "But whereas Monsieur Holden has a good chance of recovery, your own life, Madame Mallory – I regret to inform you – hangs by a thread. Had Monsieur Holden not arrived so unexpectedly today, we would have come tomorrow as planned to guide you in the process of releasing yourself from earthly life. But his arrival with the intention, in his own words, of 'bringing you back' has changed things, even if he did not fully understand what he meant. As Monsieur Tonbridge has said, you do indeed have a choice: whether to return with Monsieur Holden to living, or to take your place with us.

"To have such a choice is most unusual: it was not given to any of us. Monsieur Hanter saw to that. But on the rare occasions the choice is given, there are rules that must be followed. An application must be made to the Court of Transition, with me in this case presiding, Messieurs Linberger and Wormsley assisting. Do I take it that you both wish to proceed with such an application? Do you, Madame, seek life, and are you, Monsieur, prepared to help her?"

Mallory swayed against me. Even though our conversation had prepared her a little for what she herself had referred to as the day of judgement, she had never imagined that Rex would be part of it. There was a limit to the shocks that even a strong constitution could take, and Mallory's strength had already been sapped by the strain of the preceding months. I held her tightly. "The answer's yes."

"She must answer for herself," *Le Baigneur* commanded.

She forced herself upright. "What's the catch?"

His voice hardened. "There are conditions only. No catches."

" All right," she answered in kind, "what are the conditions?"

"Principally, that the court will take evidence." His voice became flatter, but no less authoritative. "To assist you in your decisions, pertinent aspects of your lives will be presented and discussed. The principal witnesses will be Messieurs Hanter and Tonbridge."

"I refuse to give evidence against Mallory," Rex asserted.

"Rest assured, Monsieur, that the court will present whatever is necessary, whether you co-operate or not."

Le Baigneur looked at us gravely. "Each of you must be prepared to hear and see things that you might rather not know or be known. As I have said, the final decision is yours, but the court insists that you take it in the light of everything about you that needs to be known. It may be that in possession of all the facts, Madame, you will no longer seek life; or that you, Monsieur, will no longer wish to assist her."

He paused, but we were both too stunned to answer. *L'Esprit* took up the thread. "You've both been living a dream, and it's the dream that has kept you both alive. That is why you cannot return to normal living, my dear Mallory, without Monsieur Holden. As for you, Monsieur, you retain the chance to return alone. Or else to stay."

Le Baigneur nodded. "Once we start, you live or die together."

"As to what kind of life you might have, we cannot say." Wormsley could scarcely keep the pleasure out of his voice. "You'll probably be brain-damaged or paralysed. But it's your choice."

"Let me speak to Mallory alone," said Rex. "I'll settle it now."

"If Madame Stellenbourg has no objections, I don't see why not." *Le Baigneur* raised his eyebrows to Mallory. Her legs finally gave way, and she slumped into her seat. I bent over her anxiously.

"This is all too much for her." I could have said the same for myself, but my sole aim was to be rid of them, and for that I at least must be strong. "Go away," I shouted, "and leave us alone. We'll live or die for ourselves." I seized Mallory's shoulders. "Hang on, my darling. I'm bringing you back all right. In my own way."

She did not hear. Without muscle tone, she slipped from my grasp and landed face-down on the dais with a loud thud. Hurling aside her chair, I cradled her in my arms. Even in collapse, her face retained the same intelligence and humour as when she'd first appeared to me in my earliest dream. Just as in that dream, the bruise on her cheekbone was livid, far worse than anything I had inflicted, and her forehead was bleeding. The floor of the dais was streaked with blood. Her dark eyes glittered eerily beneath the lashes of her half-opened lids. The dream had come full circle.

Chapter Nineteen : Postponement

"Who are you trying to call?" asked Rex.

"Hope," I told him. "I can't seem to get through." I had Mallory's mobile in my hand, and I'd found Hope's number in her address list, but each time I tried to call it, nothing happened.

"You won't. As far as she's concerned you're the man down the corridor from her mother." He shrugged, but he was no Frenchman. All he managed was a half-hearted flexing of the shoulder muscles. "I'm sorry, but that's the way it is. At least you're alive." He spoke without bitterness, and I realised that he was trying to cheer me up.

After Mallory's collapse, *Le Baigneur* had not only adjourned the meeting but declared that officers of the court could in no way assist us. "You will think that harsh, but what has happened is part of the transition process. But I promise you this, if the lady is alive tomorrow, you shall have your hearing." With that he and his two companions had vanished with the same rapidity as the table had appeared.

"I'm not an officer of the court," Rex had said. "I'll help you."

His cockiness had gone, and his concern for her was obviously genuine. So I had bitten back the curt rejection which was already moulding my tongue. By the time we'd reached the apartment in the tower I'd been more than glad of his assistance. It would have been a huge distance to have carried Mallory's dead weight. As for carrying her up the spiral staircase to the bedroom on my own, that would have been unthinkable. "You get her into bed, I'll find stuff to clean up her cut," he'd suggested, and I could only be grateful for his tact.

Now, in her night-things and with a plaster on her head, Mallory looked so serene it was difficult to believe she might have sunk into her last sleep. "I'll go if you like," Rex suggested, from the other side of the bed, though I could see from the anguish in his eyes that he didn't want to. I assured him that she would want him to stay, before I realised too late that our motives were opposed. I was fearful she would die: his sorrow was that she might live. But I hadn't the heart to send him away. Grief was grief, whatever its reason. "You're a lucky man," he continued, after a long silence. "Whatever happens."

"You knew her longer." Right then, I felt anything but lucky.

"But she loves you. I saw it as soon they summoned me."

"She thinks the world of you as well." I must be as fair as him.

Rex shook his head. "I was a big disappointment to her." Then he snorted, as he tried to suppress a laugh. "Can you believe this, rival lovers commiserating with each other instead of fighting? If you'd showed up all those years ago..." Again the stifled laugh. "But you didn't, and that's the end of the matter. You won, I lost."

I stroked Mallory's brow. "This doesn't feel much like victory."

"You'll have your hearing, and then you'll lead her back to life."

"You think I trust a court with Wormsley on it?"

He smiled that worldly smile of his. "OK, they'll try to talk you out of it; they'll try and make you think she's not worth it, but you don't have to listen. It's your decision not theirs."

"They've no authority over us, have they?" I demanded. "There's nothing to stop me putting Mallory in the car, and driving away."

"Not if you want her to die." His delivery was deadpan, like the punch-line to a joke.

"So what are they," I asked despairingly, "angels or devils?"

"You tell me, it's your dream. Yours and hers." He sounded again like the jocular man of the world, the populist savant with whom it would be pleasant to share drinks and reminiscences in a city bar. "If you want to live, you will; if you don't, you won't."

"If it's my dream, I don't seem to have any control over it."

"When it comes to dreams, who does?" He had me there, and I could only shrug, a proper Gallic inflexion of the upper body and arms. "There's two of you, both in two minds. You're trying to tell me you don't want to hear any evidence about each other. All those guilty secrets out in the open! But it's what you want, too. You can't deny it, can you?" He gave me a knowing smile. "I could always give you a sneak preview. To prepare you for the worst." His voice was warm with reassurance, and I understood now why Names had flocked to his syndicate. "If you didn't like it, there'd still be time to slip away..."

I seized Mallory's hand. "I'd never do that."

He stood up. We must have made a strange tableau in that tower room with its long, narrow window: the ghost confronting the dreamer over their sleeping beauty. "Then all I can do is wish you luck." He gestured shyly towards her. "Would you mind if I said goodbye?"

I stood, too. "Be my guest."

He kissed her softly and decorously on the forehead. "Good luck, my darling. You found yourself a good man. Don't lose him."

As he was straightening, Mallory opened her eyes. Then she struggled to sit up, and we both gave her a supporting hand. "Thank you." She blinked uncertainly. "What happened?" She was still pale, but colour was returning to her cheeks. We explained that she'd fainted, that the court would convene tomorrow. "So we're going ahead?"

"Of course you're going ahead," said Rex. "It's what you both want. And I must take my leave. You've got a big day ahead of you."

"Please don't." She held out her hand.

"Mallory's right," I agreed, "You don't have to."

"I know when I'm not wanted. I'm the past, you two are the future." Then, like the other ghosts before him, he was gone.

I put my arms around her. "You've had a rough day."

"Alas, poor Rex. But I understand everything now." She was crying and laughing at the same time, and even as she brushed away her tears, she managed a joyful smile. "I've been in the hospital, and I saw Hope. Jake, too. He's such a wonderful young man. Apparently my monitors went crazy, and she said she knew you'd send me back, and she was refusing to let them switch off my life support..." She poured out her words with mounting enthusiasm. But she was still weak, and her head sank onto my shoulder. "I'd honestly no idea about the accident. Your insight wasn't crazy at all. You really did save my life, and you've kept me going in your dream ever since."

I stroked her hair until she was calmer. "Your dream too. Our joint dream. We've kept each other alive." I told her of the moment she was lifted into the ambulance. "I was already out-of-body, as Robert would say, but when you looked at me, it was like some great pulse of energy arced between us. That's when our dreams came together." I kissed her encouragingly. "So let's get this trial nonsense over with."

"It's down to that logical subconscious of yours." To my delight, she almost laughed. "I'll have to accept mine is just as crazy."

"The whole world's been living an illusion," I observed. "At least when we wake up we'll be as real as before. The illusory wealth will be gone. But not Ghost Trader's."

"In reality, the illusion of wealth: in dream, the illusion of reality. It makes for a savage kind of symmetry, doesn't it?" Her tone saddened as the irony of our situation struck home. "All that stress, when it was never really us that pulled off the short. It was Hope all along."

"You were her inspiration," I reminded her, "and she checked all her trades with us, even if you don't remember. When she begged me to bring you back, she said the success was all thanks to you."

"Thanks to you, more like."

"It was a team effort. You, me, Hope… and Marie-Sainte." Then I added, with a sudden flash of inspiration, "Just think what the four of us could do with this place once we get started."

"Oh, yes." She flung her arms around me and her eyes shone with enthusiasm. My flash of inspiration had worked: she was over the shock which the Court had provoked, and she could see the prospect of life beyond. Now I had something positive on which to build.

"All we have to do is keep faith, whatever Wormsley insinuates."

Her face clouded. "It's not Wormsley I'm worried about."

"Rex isn't going to say anything bad about you." I tweaked her nose in an attempt to maintain her good humour. "As for Ambrose, what can he tell me that I don't already know?"

She shivered, her face a picture of misery once more, but she said nothing. Her old secretiveness was not going to go away all at once. "Just don't let him make you hate me," she said at last.

These jumps from happiness to guilt, and from joy to despair were all too clear signs of her weakened condition, and I cursed Ambrose and all his intrusions into our lives yet again. "I'd never hate you." I forced myself to smile, and she responded with the tiniest up-turn of the lips. "If there's one person I ought to hate, it's Amy, and you know how I feel about her."

"Do I?" she asked humbly, but understanding dawned.

"Exactly the way you feel about Rex." At this, her smile strengthened. "I don't even hate Wormsley or Ambrose any more. So long as they behave tomorrow." I was rewarded with a nervous laugh. "We ought to get some sleep. We've a long day ahead of us."

She fingered her nightdress. "I hope you didn't both undress me."

Then I knew she was returning to her old self, and I fell back against the pillow and shook with relieved laughter. She snuggled beside me. "My darling Clem, you're the most amazing man I've ever met." Then she pulled at my clothes. "You look ridiculous in this stuff." In no time, she had me undressed, and shivering. The tower may have been picturesque, but at night it was chilly. She drew the duvet over us, and held me tightly. "I feel so safe with you." I felt the stirring of desire, but – exhausted as I was – I was asleep before I could act on it.

When I woke there was grey light seeping under the blind. But the window was rectangular, almost square, and filled that side of the room almost wall to wall. As for the room, it too was rectangular. My bed was narrow, and instead of Mallory I was embraced by tubes and wires.

I was back in the hospital, taking in more detail of my surroundings. I took that as a promising sign. There was also a young man studying my monitors. "Hello, you're with us again." Jake's voice. "Hi, Dad. I always know when you're alert. You can't keep anything from the screens." Tired and dishevelled, with a stubble worthy of René, he was nevertheless smiling. "I'll get Hope." In what seemed like no time, he was back with her. "Look at the monitors. Lots of activity."

She sat beside me without so much as a glance at my screens. "Thank you." She peered at me in that intimate way of her father's, but with all her mother's warmth. "I knew you'd bring her back. And now you're awake," she smiled as she took my hand, "I mean now you're registering again, I'll tell you what I've just been telling her."

Jake took the other chair. He didn't take my hand, that wasn't his way, but he gave my shoulder a manly squeeze. Despite the stubble, he reminded me very much at that moment of Amy. "We're doing battle on your behalf," he said fiercely. "Against medical bureaucracy." He sounded just like me, and I felt a surge of parental pride.

"You two are the longest surviving coma victims this hospital has ever seen," said Hope. That most hospitals have ever seen..."

"If you're not careful, you'll make the *Guinness Book of Records*," Jake added. Strange how I'd never noticed that he had my sense of humour. But I'd seen so little of him in the past ten years.

"They've been pressing us, in the nicest possible way, to let them switch off both your life supports," Hope said earnestly.

"Hers even more than yours, in fact," Jake added. I wasn't sure if he'd said this to make me feel better, or out of fairness to Hope.

"As I told you," Hope continued, "We honestly thought she was slipping away. Even me. But I knew you wouldn't let us down. This evening her brain activity went crazy. Not for long, but it was enough to make me postpone any talk of switching off."

"Yours was good, too, and it's been more consistent," said Jake. "But that hasn't stopped the hospital going on about false positives and sub-threshold responses. All the usual guff to brain-wash us into doing what they want." This was vintage me, and I wished I could have cheered. "But from talking to Hope I wasn't having any."

"French law doesn't allow active euthanasia, but it does allow the withdrawal of treatment if the patient asks for it. If the patient's not in a fit state to give permission, then it's a battle between the next of kin and the doctors. But the doctors would never act without our consent." This was more like Mallory: clear in content, focused in anger.

"So we've got them over a barrel," said Jake.

"We're not trying to be unreasonable," Hope assured me. "But Jake and I have been comparing notes. We're convinced that you two are

keeping each other alive, so we've put a proposition to the hospital."
She smiled at Jake. "You explain. It's your idea."

"If Hope's right about you two communicating in some way, then
that communication ought to work more strongly if we put you together
in the same room." Jake coughed self-consciously. "Let's assume
psychic exchange is a form of energy exchange, then its strength ought
to be proportional to how far you're apart: halve the distance, and the
psychic exchange increases by the square root of two, or whatever." It
was a wonderful combination of my logic with Amy's intuition.

"So Jake and I have put it to the hospital that they should put you
and my mother in the same room. If we're right, you'll soon recover. If
we're wrong…" She bit her lip.

"If we're wrong," Jake continued bravely, "We'll give permission
for life support to be switched off." He patted my shoulder again. "But
we aren't going to be wrong, are we, Dad?"

Hope glanced at the monitors. "You see! He's nearly off the graph.
He understands, just like he always does." She took my hand again.
"I've been telling Mum, and she was just as enthusiastic." Her laughter
was delightful. "I mean, her monitors were."

"Not that we're there yet," Jake warned. "Right now it's a stand-off.
The doctors don't buy our analysis. They think we're being emotional
instead of rational. I put it to them: what's there to lose? If it works, two
lives have been saved, and medical knowledge has been added to; if it
doesn't, at least we can give permission to switch off with a clear
conscience. Sadly, bureaucracy doesn't do lateral thinking."

"But we're not giving up," said Hope determinedly. "Not by a long
way. We're getting up a petition. All your visitors are on side.
Armand's going to get the local lawyers on it; René's doing the same
with GPs. Sidonie and Céline are canvassing customers."

"I'm working on the architects back home," Jake said. "Plenty of
them have French contacts. As for Mum, she's getting Saul to work on
his clients. He's really excited about it. Doing something that's more
than just money, as he puts it."

"It's the same with my contacts," said Hope, with mounting
enthusiasm. "With the financial doom and gloom, they're keen to be
seen as caring. Then there's Ghost Trader. Any flak from the members
will fall on me. So they'll want Mum back all the more."

"Hang in there, Dad," Jake said, "We'll have you up in no time."

They chattered on for some time, but I wasn't really listening. I'd
got the gist of what was going on, and that was all that mattered. All the

support was wonderful, but the detail of who was doing what was too much for my tired brain. In the end I fell asleep on them.

When I opened my eyes, I was back with Mallory, who rewarded me with her most beautiful smile. Her loose hair hid the plaster, and the bruise on her cheek was fading. "I'm guessing they'll be here by 9:30," she said. "I thought we ought to be up and ready."

She drew the blind on the long window and the room was filled with the pale light of morning. It even softened the dark stone of the frame. The clouds of yesterday had passed on, and the sky was clear.

"I know what you've been dreaming," she said. "Jake and Hope came to see you." I nodded. "They told you about putting us in the same room?" I nodded again. "And the petition?"

I laughed. Yesterday, I'd tried to telephone Hope, when all I'd needed was to fall asleep. Now Mallory's words were wonderful confirmation of the otherwise crazy idea that we were leading a dual existence. No ordinary dreams could have matched so well.

"How long do you think for the hospital to agree? Days, weeks?"

"Hope didn't tell you?" She frowned. "She thought months."

"Months! If they want the beds, they ought to settle on the spot."

"That's not how they work, is it?" She smiled at my *naïveté*.

"What's the harm, even if they think Hope and Jake are mad?"

"The fear of setting a precedent: every bureaucrat's nightmare."

I threw up my hands in disgust. But, as I showered, I consoled myself that, in the interim, we would at least be kept alive, giving us plenty of time to see the hearing through to its conclusion. So by the time we were dressed – me in my dry clothes again, and Mallory in a formal skirt and blouse – I was feeling upbeat, and no more than mildly apprehensive. The sun was now well above the horizon, and the living room was once more bathed in glorious light. In such a setting it was hard to believe in ghosts, still harder to fear their powers.

"We ought to exploit the delay," said Mallory, pouring coffee.

"How do you mean? The sooner we're shot of the court, the better."

"I've been looking at it another way. It seems to me that whatever we've been dreaming always links back to the real world, mostly through Hope, but also through your friends and neighbours." She smiled expectantly, but I was still unsure what she was driving at. "It'll be the same with the court. What we experience as a trial in our out-of-body world must have its parallel in the hospital. It's only when the hospital agrees to put us together that the real trial can begin."

"You mean *Le Baigneur* and his friends won't come until then?"

"No, they'll come. But we should ask for a postponement."

"But what's the point? If it's a hurdle, let's get over it."

She grinned. "It's our dream. High time we took control of it."

"I thought we tried that yesterday."

"You were too confrontational. We need to work *with* them." Before I could answer there was a dull boom from the hall. "They're here." She held out her hand. "We'll let them in together."

Beyond the sanctuary of the apartment, the light was harsher and the shadows deeper. The equipment in the former wards looked more threatening in its disjointedness, and the echoes of our footsteps made the building seem full of invisible shades hurrying to and fro. "Just go along with me," she said as we reached the stairs. "If they say no, we're no worse off. If they say yes..." she grinned enigmatically.

Because of Mallory's collapse, the front door was neither bolted nor locked, but its iron handle was stiff, and its massive woodwork heavy. Fortunately its hinges had been well-oiled, and the door swung obediently open as I pulled on it. The three officers of the court shimmered disconcertingly on the step as the sunlight seemed to cut through them, but they seemed more solid as they stepped into the shade of the hall. They had the solemn expressions of men who had a duty to perform. Behind them, and now more distinct, were the serried ranks of the queue, coughing discreetly, but watching us eagerly. I noticed that the old Citroen was sunk right down on its suspension, which meant that it had been parked there since yesterday. The ghosts must have stood all night on the steps to prevent our escape.

"This is a public hearing." *Le Baigneur* pointed at the figures behind. Paling only for a moment, Mallory nodded our acceptance.

"I take it we're in the ballroom again," she said formally. Then she led us to the double doors and drew them open. "After you," she said politely. These were small gestures, but she had reminded them that this was her property, and had shown them that she was fully recovered. As we followed the three to the dais, the crowd surged in behind us.

Now that we were to begin, I was beyond fear, in some no-man's land of the emotions. Physically present, but emotionally detached. I had felt much the same at my divorce hearing. But then I had, in some degree, known what I was in for: now, I'd no idea what to expect. But at least this time I and the woman I loved were in it together.

Nothing more was said until we had taken our places round the table. Then, as *Le Baigneur* was opening his lips, Mallory smiled. "I didn't want to impose a wasted journey on you," she said brightly, "but I collapsed before I could answer your question about the hearing."

Le Baigneur cleared his throat awkwardly. "Since Monsieur Holden wished to proceed, we gave you the benefit of the doubt."

"We always act with scrupulous fairness," Wormsley added.

"Doubtless you know the situation at the hospital," Mallory continued. "Until the argument is resolved, our next of kin will not give permission for life support to be switched off. So we'll be alive in the interim." She paused, but the three remained silent. Even the crowd subsided into uneasy quiet. "As Monsieur Wormsley rightly pointed out yesterday, when we wake up – assuming we do – there's no guarantee that we'll be fit and well. Under the circumstances, I was wondering if the court would postpone the hearing until the hospital's decision." She lowered her eyes coyly. "Then Clem and I can be certain of a little happiness at least. I hope that's not too much to ask."

I had to hand it to her. One glance told me that *Le Baigneur* and *L'Esprit* were on side; even Wormsley shook his head admiringly. If only I'd been more accommodating over my losses, I might have escaped more lightly. Even as the three huddled in consultation, and as I held Mallory's hand, I cursed myself for a fool.

"We sacrificed ourselves once," she murmured. "I won't again."

Le Baigneur rapped the table, as the three of them straightened, their expressions even more solemn than when they arrived.

"This case is unique. The court may prefer to act on precedent, but here there are none to guide us. Under those circumstances, we must act on our own judgement, and it is this. If it is the wish of you both to postpone the hearing until such time as the hospital agrees to or rejects the application of your offspring, then the court has no objection. You must, however, remain within the grounds of the Sanatorium. Any attempt to pass beyond the gates will be treated as the withdrawal of your application, and your lives will be terminated."

"We'll need to shop for food," Mallory pointed out sweetly.

Again the three heads bowed together, before *Le Baigneur* delivered the ruling. "We agree to shopping, once a week by no more than one of you per time. Straight there and back: no delays nor excursions."

On that we agreed.

Chapter Twenty : House Arrest

House arrest was strange. Freedom within a tightly defined space. Compared with many under similar restraint, we were lucky. House and grounds were large by any standards, and we found plenty to explore. We toured every room from the kitchens and sculleries in the basement to the attics in the roofs. The ground floor had been devoted to the grand rooms, though some of these had been partitioned into wards, consulting rooms, dispensaries and offices. Each contained vestiges of such former usage, whether beds, cupboards or desks. Some of the latter were grand with inlaid leather tops, now scuffed and faded, for consultants and managers; others were the stand-up variety for clerks and almoners. Eating had taken place in the ballroom.

Outside the ballroom was a grand terrace, its flags cracked by weeds, from which it would once have been possible to enjoy uninterrupted views of the lake, though now the shrubbery at the cliff-edge, beyond what had once been formal gardens, was too high and dense to reveal much below the level of the distant Alps.

The first floor, on which I had spotted the ancient wheelchairs, seemed to have been given over entirely to wards. There was even a manually-operated lift, like a giant dumb waiter, behind the main staircase, which must have been used to bring wheelchair-bound patients from the wards to the terrace and the ballroom.

As I came to understand the layout better, I found the building less sinister. Though it had fallen into decay, this had been the result of nothing worse than neglect. Now as Mallory and I explored it together, it seemed to respond to our interest, and to exude some portion of the benign air it must have had in its active days.

Mallory explained that Robert de St Hippocrate's several times great grandfather had built the Sanatorium in the 1870s, and it had operated successfully as part home part hospice until the 1930s, when the Great Depression had led to the collapse of the charitable trust fund which had until then supported it. It had then reverted entirely to being the family home, until the Second World War had forced its members into living more modestly in Aix. Now finally it had been sold and lay waiting to be restored for something akin to its former purpose.

This I learned gradually over the first week of our incarceration. That it really was incarceration became apparent as soon as we toured the grounds. Whenever we approached the gate the figures from the queue would start to materialise. At twenty metres, they were no more than a blur, like eddies of warm air; at ten metres, their outlines were clear but we could see through them, as though they were sketches on a giant curtain of gauze; at five metres they were solid and impenetrable. Wheezing, but otherwise silent, they stood shoulder to shoulder, their faces grim and their eyes intent. The first time, this was as close as we could stomach. As we retreated the figures faded from sight, and the noise of their breathing ceased.

Plucking up our courage, we repeated the approach the next day, a beautiful autumn afternoon that was almost as hot as mid-summer. It made no difference to the icy disdain of the queue. Mallory was all for pulling me back once more, but I wanted to try and communicate. I got as far as opening my mouth, but utterance was beyond me.

"This is ridiculous," I said, as we retreated once more.

She pressed my arm comfortingly. "They're meant to be scary."

"They don't scare me, exactly. But they certainly get to me."

"You're right. What they really make me feel is guilty."

Their laboured breathing, their sunken eyes and imploded cheeks, their pallid skin and wasted bodies had made me desperate to look away. But looking away had not helped. Their resentment had flowed over me still like an icy wind. "You've no need to feel guilty. You're helping people like them. I'm the one who's done nothing."

"There's guilt and there's guilt." Shivering despite the sunshine, she hurried me towards the stable yard at the side of the house. As we skirted the corner, I forced myself to look back. The gate languished undisturbed. Not even hot air broke the lines of its ironwork.

Guilt and guilt. She was right. Walking towards the materialising figures had provoked far more than the urge to look away that illness and emaciation normally arouse. Their growing presence accused me of living for more than a decade in an angry and self-centred limbo. Not once had I accepted my share of the blame for what had happened, and never until now had I thought at all about victims other than myself. Was it any wonder that Amy had deserted me, when I had given so little thought to how joining Lloyd's threatened her and Jake? Worse, I had belittled her prescience as though she were a simpleton.

How unsurprising that all her sympathy had been for a man more self-effacing and self-critical than me. Never until now had it crossed my mind that I, who had indulged myself with Sidonie, had long ago sapped the moral high ground from which I had wished to look down on Amy. I'd justified the lapse with Sidonie as an act of sympathy, but it had never occurred to me that Amy might have been similarly driven. My folly I had excused, hers I had punished with the ferocity of a caveman. Worse, it had happened in front of my son.

"It's their eyes." Mallory had to shake my arm to break my reverie. "It's as if they can see right through you to your guilty soul."

"My first dreams," I reminded her. "They were the judging chorus."

"I might have known it was you." She smiled reproachfully.

"Not me," I protested. "Them."

We were now walking between the house and the stables, and our footsteps echoed off the cobbles. To our left was the house, with steps down to the old kitchens, and to our right were the stalls and carriage houses, into which Mallory now led me. Abandoned though they were, there still hung over the dim stalls, with their empty and rusting feed boxes, an odour of horse sweat and straw. She drew me into a kiss. "You've always judged me. Right from the start."

"Judge you!" I protested, "I worship you."

"So much you had to check me out with George Wiseman."

"It was my accountant who was insinuating, not me. I was desperate to prove him wrong." My explanation rang hollowly in my ears. "Whatever you did once, you've more than made up for it with Ghost Trader. Not to mention your plans for this place."

"You see. Every utterance is a judgement." Then, before I could reply, she led me to the coach house at the far end. Here on the cobbles stood an old carriage, elegant in its curves, and delicately perched on huge springs between its spoked wheels. The brass of its lamps was now almost black, its windows were grimy and its coachwork no longer shone, yet it retained vestiges of its former charms. Mallory pulled open the door, and peered inside. The leather of its seating was green with mildew. She wrinkled her nose. "Perhaps not."

She scrambled up onto the driving board and reached for my hand. I was beside her in a second, and she drew me into a sudden and passionate embrace. But before I could really respond, she stiffened and pushed me away. "I'm not a judge," I protested.

She toyed fretfully with my hands. "You will be."

"Wormsley can insinuate all he likes, I won't listen to a word."

"So you think I've atoned enough, do you?"

"More than." I pulled her towards me. "I don't see the problem."

"Dear Clem. Always so certain. It's one of the things I really admire about you. But it scares me too. You're so all or nothing. That's why I hesitated for so long... why I panicked the other day. I knew from the start there could no half measures. Either I'm yours for ever or I'm nobody's. Can you begin to understand how scary that is?"

"That's what you said in my dream," I exclaimed. She could only look startled. "I had a lot of dreams after our quarrel."

"You've had a lot of dreams, period. And they all involve me."

"Of course they involve you. I love you."

"So long as you can control me." Her lips smiled, her eyes did not.

"That's hardly fair," I protested.

"You'd rather have me in a coma." She spoke lightly, but the words lost none of their sting. "Admit it, you're a control freak."

"I like to know where I stand, but that's all," I replied stiffly.

"In your heyday, you had your clients in the palm of your hand..."

"If only," I countered.

"You tried to control Amy, but she was too much of a free spirit..."

"Now who's being judgemental?" I demanded.

"Your one mistake was Lloyd's..."

"They cheated me," I reminded her. "Along with all your members."

"You were more than willing to join. All of you."

"That's no excuse. Any more than leaving your front door unlocked absolves the burglar."

"Meaning I cheated you, too."

As always, she ended up blaming herself, except that now, even her self-criticism was laid at my door. Controlling my irritation, I tried to pick my words carefully. "Meaning nothing of the kind. I meant what I said about Rex when we first met. What Rex did was too drastic, too negative, but it was honourable. As for you, what you did, what you're still doing, is absolutely positive and right. I admit I've been selfish. You've taught me that. You've even taught me to be humble." I drew her into my arms, and this time she offered no resistance. "I want to love you, not control you. There is a difference."

She returned my kisses, and warmth returned to her eyes. But she wasn't finished yet. "Are you sure you don't blame me for Amy?" Her tone was caressing but the underlay of challenge remained.

"Why on earth would I blame you for Amy?"

"If I'd been the dutiful wife, Ambrose wouldn't have strayed."

I threw up my hands. "To hell with Ambrose. If anyone was to blame it was me. You had nothing to do with it."

"That's very noble of you." She ran a finger reflectively over my cheek, before settling it on my lips. As a means of being kept silent, it had its merits. "But I do blame myself. Somehow I failed Ambrose at every opportunity. No, don't say anything." For a moment she pinched my lips shut, then, with a relenting smile, she kissed them.

"The truth is I should never have married him. But he was an attractive man. Not the way you're attractive, not the way Rex was attractive. But he was good and kind and attentive, everything a woman ought to want in a husband. My parents, of course, adored him, and blamed me entirely for the divorce. He was that kind of man."

The note of bitterness that mention of her parents had invoked once before had crept into her voice. My mother had blamed Amy, partly out of maternal loyalty to me, but also because in her eyes Amy was the one who had strayed. Yet she had loved Amy, too. The other way about, it would have been me in the doghouse. "He was that kind of man," I agreed. "He was my good friend, remember."

"Then you'll understand why I ignored the whispers of doubt."

"I didn't even listen to Amy's shouts against Lloyd's. Of course, I understand." Indeed, I understood all too well. Ambrose had always been likeable and infuriating in equal measure, so that I had as often wanted to strangle him as clap a friendly hand upon his shoulder. He'd had an uncomfortable knack of admiring me and disagreeing with me at the same time. It was as though I had appalled him as much as I had mesmerised him. He had been envious of my self-confidence, yet prepared to bask in its reflected glory; he had admired my incisiveness, but been repelled by where it often seemed to be leading him.

"We were perfectly happy at first," Mallory continued. "At least he was, and I was so busy I didn't stop to think whether I was happy or not. He told me we were, so I believed him."

"Until you met Rex."

"Until I got to know Rex," she corrected me. Then her tone hardened with self-reproach. "My parents were right. I'm the ultimate tabloid bitch. Heartless mother abandons kind and loving husband for boss's millions. That's why I persuaded him to join Lloyd's – against his better judgement – as if that would compensate him, even if it had worked the way Rex had me believe. Oh, yes," she lowered her voice as if to hide her shame even from the walls, "I still believed Rex was magical in those days. Then, having screwed up Ambrose's happiness and almost bankrupted him, I refused to listen over Enron."

"Because you didn't think he was right," I reminded her gently.

"I should have done. Ambrose was usually right about things he'd really looked into." She shrugged in disgust. "From start to finish, it was me that turned him into an avenging ghost."

214

Ghost! The word stood out luridly from the catalogue of self-recrimination. It was impossible that Mallory, so careful with her choice of words, had not meant it, and it disturbed me as much as her pain. It explained why witnesses had seen *L'Esprit* and *Le Baigneur* fall of their own accord, not Ambrose pushing them; why an apparently healthy Wormsley had suffered an unpredicted heart attack; and why Ambrose had been able to stay ahead of me on New Year's Day even though he'd been walking and I'd been running. It explained his wasted appearance and the coldness of his wrist, and why *Le Baigneur* had asserted that they had him under control.

But if Ambrose were a ghost, I must accept that ghosts also stalked the waking reality to which we hoped to return. Creating ghosts in what Mallory called my logical subconscious was one thing, it was another to accept their independent existence. *Le Baigneur* and his fellow judges, the figures from the queue, even Rex Tonbridge were acceptable, just, as figments of dream. But I had seen Ambrose in Les Confins before the accident on New Year's Day; I was uninjured when I'd listened to Madame Linberger's description of the skier in black shouting "IBNR" as he'd pushed her husband to his death.

"I know how angry you feel about Ambrose," she sat up, her voice calm and brave, "but you must listen to what he says at the hearing, and you must judge me fairly. That's all I ask."

"I don't care what happened between you and Ambrose. If you ruined him, I did the same to Amy. Our marriages broke up, and when that happens, anything goes. I'm in no position to judge you." I spoke urgently, desperate to stem the endless flow of self-excoriation. "In fact, if you must know, I'm horribly jealous of Rex."

Her eyes sparkled with something like their usual wit. "You and he seemed to be getting on well enough when I came round."

"That's the trouble. I like him. I can see the attraction. All too well."

. "How do you think I feel about Amy?" She stroked my cheek. And I felt curiously pleased that even Mallory could be jealous. "We're too old not to have pasts, Clem. I won't deny Rex was everything to me once, any more than I want you to deny Amy. But we're not the people we used to be. As I am now, you're the only man I could imagine loving for the rest of my life. I hope you can accept me on those terms, because they're the best I can give you."

"I can accept you on almost any terms," I conceded with a relieved laugh. "For my part, I promise that I won't be a control-freak. As for now, we've won this respite. We shouldn't waste our time quarrelling or beating our breasts, we should be enjoying ourselves."

She awarded me a playful smile. Then, with a dramatic frown, she straightened and sat very prim and proper with her hands in her lap. "In that case, I would remind you, good sir, that I am the mistress of this house, and that everything in it is mine to do with as I choose." She raised an imperious chin. "And that includes you." Her mood change was so sudden I almost missed the twinkle in her eye.

I rose precariously. "Your servant is yours to command."

She pointed imperiously. "Take me for a drive, good coachman."

It was the first time she had ever indulged in make-believe with me, and I was won over immediately. "We shall drive into Aix, my lady. If we hurry, we shall be there by nightfall."

"And what, pray, shall we do there?" She kissed me wickedly.

"I have secured us rooms at the finest hotel, my lady."

"You forget yourself. I am a married woman." She looked shocked.

"Your husband, my lady, set forth for Paris this morning."

"Without his coach? Without his coachman?"

"He rides to his friend's, *Le Vicomte L'Esprit*, who stays nearby. They shall make for Paris together in *Monsieur Le Vicomte's* carriage."

"Then I have you to myself. We have no need of Aix." She fell laughing into my arms and kissed me. "If I can't have you inside, my lad, I'll take you on the roof."

It was a precarious place. Its curvature threatened to roll us onto the cobbles below, whilst the wood itself creaked and cracked beneath us. I tried to protest that we would be safer and more comfortable in the tower, but Mallory was implacable. All her previous restraint had gone, and she clung to me as though her life depended on it. Her mood was irresistible, and I was in no time as abandoned as she. But afterwards, as we recovered our breath, my eye was caught by the empty shafts of the carriage. Overcome by foreboding, I fumbled in my pocket for my phone. "Who are you calling?" Mallory asked.

"Sidonie."

Mallory covered my neck in kisses. "Bored with me already?"

My phone was silent. No ring tone, nothing. Just as it had been with Hope. With mounting panic, I tried number after number. Same result. "They've cut us off from the outside world."

"I thought you'd be happy…" Her lip trembled.

I felt immediately contrite. This interlude had been Mallory's idea, and for good reason. She'd taken all too seriously Wormsley's warning of brain-damage or paralysis. Curtailed as we were, this might be the last physical freedom we would have together. "All I want is clothes. I

216

was hoping Sidonie could send *Madame de Maintenant* with some. I'll just have to wait until they let us go to the village."

"It's only small. It doesn't run to clothes."

"Fine," I joked. "I'll go round naked. Perhaps you'd like that."

"Until the hearing you're free to go," she said. "I won't keep you against your will."

"And leave you to Rex? No way." It was a tactless joke, but humour was preferable to brooding over the uncertainties of our situation. It drew a wan smile from Mallory.

"You'll have to borrow stuff from me and do a lot of washing." Then at last she laughed. "The mistress of the house seduces her handsome coachman in the old stables. Isn't that more exciting than worrying about laundry?" I had to agree that it was no contest.

The next day I determined to confront the queue. "They're under court orders," I explained over breakfast. "All we have to do is tell them one of us is going to the village. This time I'm determined."

"My hero," she grinned. "Do you want me to come with you?"

"Better still. Why don't we drive up to the gate?"

"They'll think we're both trying to get out."

"OK. Stop five metres back. Then I'll get out. If all goes well, I'll open the gate, and you can drive out. How far is it, by the way?"

"It's about 20 minutes on foot."

"Worth driving then, if there's a lot of shopping to carry."

Approaching the solidifying crowd at the gate was less unnerving from the comfort of the car. At five metres Mallory duly stopped. "Wish me luck." Now we'd come this far, there was no point in hanging around: like the *couloir* above Les Confins, the queue would only look more forbidding the longer I stared at it. Pushing open the door, I thrust my feet out of the car and down onto the gravel. Only as I straightened did I allow myself to look directly at the figures in front of me. Grim-faced, they were clustered three deep across the gateway.

"Madame Stellenbourg needs to drive to the village for provisions, as was agreed. I'm going to open the gate."

My words were greeted with a stony hush. Not so much as a cough disturbed the hard focus of their eyes, as they bored into me. The intensity of the interrogation was only heightened by the utter silence in which it was carried out. I felt the sweat trickling down my neck, but this time I was determined not to be outfaced. With my arms at my sides, I did my best to look calm, whilst returning their hostile stares with what I hoped was blank indifference. It was far from easy, and as the seconds ticked into the first minute, and then the second, my will began to crumble. Worse, I was sure that they knew it.

"This was agreed by the court," Mallory shouted from behind me. "You were all there."

They wavered, and as they did so, my courage returned. "I'm going to open the gate," I said, forcing myself forward. For a moment, it seemed as though the crowd would yet resist me. They stood taller and closer, so that their shoulders overlapped and interlocked. Then, all of a sudden, their resistance relaxed. As they drew back, they retreated like smoke between the bars of the gate, to regroup across the road. Fighting to control my trembling hands, I fumbled the gate open.

With a wave, Mallory sped down the road towards St Hippocrate. In a moment she was over the crest of the next hill and out of sight. The crowd surged back towards me. Summoning the last shreds of my dignity, I turned my back on them and stumbled towards the front door. Behind me, I heard the clang of the gate being pulled shut.

It was sunny with the soft chill of autumn in the air, and I was damned if the watchers would drive me indoors, so I skirted the tower and made my way across the ruined gardens towards the thickets that bordered the cliff. Closer to, they were less dense than they appeared from the tower, and I soon found what I was looking for: a gap large enough to walk through. Beyond was a clearing of springy grass.

In three paces, I came within centimetres of the granite lip that marked the top of the cliff. The drop to the dark, unruffled water below was all of 50 metres. Not as long as the plunge that killed *L'Esprit*, but enough. Even if *Le Baigneur* had survived the fall, the icy January water would have finished him. However good a swimmer he may have been, there was neither beach nor bank within 100 metres.

I retreated from the edge and studied the clearing. From where I was standing, I could see no more than the roofs of the Sanatorium. Only somebody in the clearing could have seen the push. Even if Mallory were wrong, and Ambrose were alive, it was unlikely that any boatman would have seen anything other than a man falling.

With nothing to do now but wait for Mallory, I returned to the house. Without her comforting presence I felt alienated by all around me. Yet as I made my way up the grand stair, I realised that this gloom did not spring from me. The watchers were testing my resolve, urging me to renounce at the hearing not only my own life but Mallory's. Wherever I went the invisible watchers followed, their voices dripping poison. "Nobody will listen to brain-damaged cripples. Anyway, you're too late. Those you could have helped are dead. Which only leaves the pair of you to be a burden on your families. Ask yourself: will you want to look after her; or she you?"

Ugly though it was, their resentment was understandable. They had suffered and wasted away, and nobody had cared. Me least of all. So long as I was alive, my existence, however tenuous, rubbed salt in their bitterness. Whatever good will there might be towards Mallory from *Le Baigneur* and *L'Esprit*, the watchers wished only to deprive us of the life they had already lost. But with that realisation came renewed determination. The future was more than Mallory and me, and for it we must endure even the worst. To bolster my resolve, I seized the push-bar of an ancient wheelchair. "I was thoughtless," I cried. "But now I'll help her. It's never too late. There'll always be victims."

Nothing moved, but the stifling hostility wavered. Then it was broken by two short blasts of a car horn. Mallory was back. Sure enough, when I opened the front door, she was opening the gate. The watchers had already formed a semi-circle behind the car. I ran up the drive towards her, and she pulled up beside me. "Thank God you're back," I said, jumping into the passenger seat.

"I was as quick as I could be," she protested with a smile.

I embraced her fiercely. "The watchers had a real go at me while you were gone." Then, as we unloaded the shopping, I described my experiences. "Perhaps I'm just silly, but that's the way it felt."

"You weren't being silly." She glanced back at the gate, but the watchers had disappeared. Not only that, I had no sense of their presence. "They whisper to me as I'm waking up."

Five of her bags held provisions, to restock our diminishing supplies. The last contained clothes for me: two shirts, a sweater and several pairs of socks and shorts. There was even a pair of tennis shoes. "I thought you said they didn't stock clothes," I exclaimed gratefully.

She grinned. "They know me quite well now, and they know I was a friend of Robert's. It's amazing what a little local knowledge will achieve." She paused to allow me to hug her. "Next week, I've told them to expect you. You need a break from this place as much as me. By then, they'll have some running gear for you, and a warm *blouson*. You can collect them from the bar-café. Opposite the church."

"You're amazing," I said. "Nothing fazes you." I felt like rushing to the gate and waving my new clothes at the watchers. "Look at this," I wanted to tell them, "Clothes from a village without a clothes shop. This woman can achieve anything she puts her mind to."

Instead, I made us a pot of tea, and we sat in the window of the living room to drink it. Clouds were gathering around the hills but the sky was clear over the lake. "You ought to take me through your plans for this place," I suggested. A small furrow darkened her brow.

"There's plenty of time for that."

"I don't meant now this minute. But soon. It would put our time before the hearing to good use. Then we can be up and running the moment we wake." She sipped her tea and didn't answer. She didn't even look at me. "What's the matter?"

She shook her head. "Nothing."

I supposed at first that her reluctance was simply part of her usual reticence. "I can't help you if I don't know what we're doing."

"You're right of course." She toyed fretfully with her teaspoon. "But telling you now seems like tempting fate. If the worst came to the worst, you could carry on without me."

"That would be the absolute worst," I answered as gently as I could. "But at least I could carry the task on for you."

She flinched as though I had threatened her. Too late, I realised why. She understood only too well that her injuries were more severe than mine and that her life hung by the narrowest of threads. For survival, she relied on sustaining the tenuous dream world she shared with me; a world now reduced to the boundaries of the Sanatorium.

Until the hearing, I retained a chance of survival on my own, but Mallory depended entirely on me. Small wonder that she feared how I would react to Ambrose's evidence; and no wonder that she had mistaken my demand to know how the Sanatorium development should proceed as a tacit declaration that even I, her lover and would-be rescuer, no longer believed that she could win through.

I put my arms around her and held her tightly. At first, she accepted my caresses only passively. But slowly her courage returned, and she gripped me tightly. "Don't let the watchers get to you," I said at last. "We're in this together, and we're going to win." She didn't answer, but she kissed me warmly, and her eyes shone. "Thanks to our friends and relations we'll soon have overwhelming support. What hospital can resist the combined will of all the signatories to Hope and Jake's petition? Even the financial world wants to help."

After that, we became acclimatised to our reduced existence. As the mellow of autumn turned to the cold of winter, we learned to live for the joy of the moment, neither to think ahead to the hearing, nor to let the watchers wear us down. With only ourselves for company, we learned to rely on each other as never before. The unspoken uncertainties that lay ahead served only to intensify our love, and we truly lived each day as though it might be our last.

Hope or Jake reported to us each week. "We aim to have all the signatures in by the end of October," Jake explained on his first visit. "If everything goes according to plan, I'm hoping for over 1,000 architects and surveyors. It's amazing how the thing is snowballing. Everyone I know wants to recruit their contacts, and so on. That's why it takes time, of course, but it's worth it."

René was somewhat less sanguine about the medical profession. "I'm getting about half of them on side, but the rest think the plan is totally unscientific. The good news is that the half who believe in the plan are enthusiastic enough to canvass their colleagues in the profession. With luck, I'll have 500 signatures by the end of the month. And that includes at least 30 senior consultants and surgeons."

Marie-Sainte described the strong interest at her university. "Even the professors want to help. They won't all sign, of course, but I'm making sure mine writes a letter as well. As for Andréa, he's already had two articles published, and he's chatting up *Canal plus* News. They've almost promised to film the petition being delivered.

"Papa Armand's networking the legal profession hard, and he's working up a human rights argument, to show that the hospital would be in breach if they refuse. As for Mama and Céline, they've got hundreds of signatures already. Clients as well as friends."

Amy arrived mid-October to show me the ring that Saul had bought her. It flashed expensively under my nose, but I was glad to see that its design was elegant and tasteful. I also noticed the exquisite cut of her coat and her suit. "But I really came to tell you how well everything's going for you. We've got the petition on display in all six restaurants, that's including the new one in Windsor, and we're collecting between 10 and 20 signatures every single day. As for Saul, well! He's back in the States at the moment, getting all his customers lined up, not to mention half of Wall Street. They're not all bad, you know.

"As for Mallory, I trust you'll do the decent thing when you're both *compos mentis*." She smiled knowingly. "From what Jake and Hope tell me, there's plenty going on between you. She sounds perfect, and I absolutely adore Hope. As for the Sanatorium, I think it's a wonderful idea, and I'm sure you'll be invaluable to it. I've made a start with your old clients, by the way: to sign the petition, of course, but I've also warned them you'll be expecting a contribution next year. And I know Jake's dying to help with the renovation work, though he's too modest to mention it to you. You won't forget him, will you?"

Soon after, a newspaper reporter managed to get his camera through the door and flash off a couple of pictures before the duty nurse shooed

221

him away. "You're becoming famous, Monsieur," she told me on her return. She tried to look disapproving, but spoilt it by smiling.

Early November, Jake and Hope came together. "The petition's been delivered, with full TV coverage. Armand served his legal opinion at the same time. It's not as formal as an injunction, but it shows the hospital what they're up against. All we can do now is wait."

Early in December, the hospital capitulated. Mallory and I would be moved into one room at 10 a.m., Thursday, the 11th of December. The experiment would then run for one week. If in that time, our condition had not improved, the experiment would be suspended. After that, they would be at liberty to switch off life support. "They've got us over a barrel," Jake explained. "In return for the experiment, we've had to agree to the switch-off. If we'd said no, so would they."

"I'm sorry," Hope said, "But it's the best we could do."

"Anyway," Jake said, with forced cheer, "A week's plenty."

GHO$T TRAD€R

Part Four
Crisis

AIG was bailed out by American taxpayers.
The insureds had to rescue their own insurer.
An Insurance Act of today would have to stand
the wise, old principle on its head:
'the loss lighteth rather heavily upon the many,
to the greater profit of the few.'

"With financial loss, tempers run high.
Just yesterday, Bernie Madoff was assaulted
prior to his arrest."
"Madoff arrested! Why?"
"His fund was a Ponzi. The biggest ever."
"Has the money all gone?"
"That would appear to be the case."
"Then Amy's lost all her savings."

Chapter Twenty-One : Before the Court

And so it was that our court hearing opened on the same day and at the same time as the hospital procedure began. It was a brooding kind of day, with dark clouds stacked around the hills, and the temperature just above zero. Ideal conditions for snow, though it was rather early to expect it at lake level. Outside the apartment, the rest of the Sanatorium was bitterly cold, and I was grateful for the sweater and *blouson* which Mallory had acquired for me in St Hippocrate.

The black Citroen arrived at 9:40, but this time our visitors were as sombre as the weather, and their greetings were curt and formal. "We need a little time to prepare ourselves," *Le Baigneur* explained. "We will begin at 10. Be so good as to join us then."

Followed by *L'Esprit* and Wormsley, he swept across the hall and into the ballroom. They closed its doors firmly behind them. The front door they had left ajar and I went to close it. "The cold may mean nothing to them," I said, "But that's no reason for us to freeze."

Outside, the watchers had formed a semi-circle around the Citroen. Through is darkened windows, I made out the shadowy outlines of two men in the rear seats. I supposed they must be Rex and Ambrose. I shut the door hurriedly. Mallory was already mounting the stair, and I followed her back to the tower. Her face was pale, but there was a steeliness about her that showed her determination to win through if she possibly could. She sat down by the window and gazed out across the gardens to the lake. "I've never seen the water so dark."

I laid my hands on her shoulders, wishing with all my heart that we were back in the boathouse and facing nothing worse than a day of market volatility. Though I had become used to this lake and this view, I missed the softer and friendlier atmosphere of my own. Despite Mallory's presence, I felt alone and isolated. The dereliction of the Sanatorium and the gloominess of its stonework weighed on me. I caught the eye of one of the watchers outside, and – as he stared at me – the others looked up as well. Their faces were gloating and I turned away. I would not let them undermine me even before we started.

Mallory reached for my hands, and her strength seemed to course through me from her fingertips. Neither of us spoke, but in those minutes before we were due in the ballroom below we felt united as never before, and we descended the stair hand in hand. The watchers were already forming up in the hall, but they did not impede our progress. Rather, they bowed their heads in mocking respect, waiting until we reached the dais before lining the walls behind us, where they stood almost as mute as the statues in the gardens outside.

On the dais the oak table and chairs were arranged as before. The three officials, who had been seated, rose upon our entrance. A new chair had been added since our last visit. An ornate and uncomfortable seat, moulded like a bishop's throne, had been placed at the end opposite to where *Le Baigneur* had been sitting. It was empty, yet it drew the eye, as though it contained an invisible and sentient presence.

Two figures materialised beside the high seat. My brain wanted to believe they had stepped from behind it, but that was not how it happened. They simply sprang into focus as if they had always been there, but only now had chosen to reveal themselves. They wore simple black robes, akin to academic gowns, over dark suits, and they stood so still that it was difficult to say whether they even breathed. They spoke not a word, either now or throughout what followed, but there was no doubt that their eyes were alert and missed nothing.

"Please be seated," *Le Baigneur* pointed graciously to the chairs we had occupied before, whilst Wormsley and *L'Esprit* took their places across the table from us. The latter acknowledged us with a patrician nod, but Wormsley simply stared through us. I took it as a new variant on his usual aggression. *Le Baigneur* shuffled papers that had materialised in his hands. "Before I declare the hearing formally open, I must ask you both whether you are still willing to have the case for life considered, or whether you have changed your minds, and are happy to enter the state of deceasement immediately."

"Do I take it," Mallory asked, "that Monsieur Holden's right to leave has lapsed, or may he still take his own chance?"

"It doesn't matter," I said firmly, "we live or die together."

"Does your question mean you wish for immediate deceasement?" *L'Esprit* laid his immaculately manicured hands upon the table.

"No. But I didn't want Clem to be deprived of any last chance."

"Too late for that." Wormsley's tone was not without respect.

"May we take it that you wish to proceed?" *Le Baigneur* asked.

I took Mallory's hand. "We do," we said in unison.

"I therefore declare the court now in session," *Le Baigneur* intoned. "To be heard jointly before the Court of Transition, two questions of Life and Death: the life or the decease of Mallory Mai Stellenbourg

225

and the life or the decease of Clem Holden. I shall preside, but the hearing will be presented by my two colleagues, Monsieur Linberger making the case for life, Monsieur Wormsley that for death."

"But the decision remains ours, does it not?" I cut in.

Le Baigneur allowed himself a judicious smile. "You are perfectly correct, Monsieur. Unlike the courts with which you are familiar, there is neither judge nor jury here. As you can see." His gesturing hand took in the ballroom, before indicating the empty throne. The sense of its containing an invisible presence increased ominously at his words. "What each of you senses there is your conscience. The one judge you can never deceive. We are here merely to assist you. But the decision will be entirely yours. To live or to die."

"But we already have decided," I pointed out.

"That may be. But the court stipulates that your decision must be made in the light of such evidence as the court chooses to present. You may feel this to be unnecessary, but I can assure you, Monsieur, that such choice is never easy. I enjoin you to remain of an open mind."

"Or to put it bluntly," Wormsley interposed, "You can hear the evidence or you can give up right now. Those are your only choices, and you're lucky to have them."

"The court has no discretion here. What stands between each of you and death is the will of the other," *L'Esprit* observed.

Drawing a slim spectacle case from a suit pocket, *Le Baigneur* fitted half-moon reading glasses to his nose, and scrutinised his papers. "It is now my duty to set out the timetable to be followed. At your request, to which the court acceded, this hearing is timed to run concurrently with the hospital procedure, and we will ensure that you are in a position to make your final choice within the limit allotted by the hospital. Today will be devoted to preliminary matters; tomorrow and Saturday, the court will present evidence concerning Monsieur Holden's life which we believe to be unknown to Madame Stellenbourg, but pertinent to her decision; on Sunday and Monday, the court will, on the same basis, present evidence concerning Madame Stellenbourg which we believe to be unknown to Monsieur Holden. On Tuesday, Messieurs Wormsley and Linberger will summarise for you, and on Wednesday you will each give your final decision to the court. I trust that is clear so far?"

"Isn't that cutting it fine?" I blenched at the idea of four days devoted to what was undoubtedly intended to be unflattering evidence, plus a final day to rub salt in our wounds.

"I shall see to it that the timetable will be strictly adhered to." He frowned benignly at Wormsley and *L'Esprit*. "How much of

226

Wednesday you need to formulate your judgements will be up to you, but so long as you are at the hospital before 10 a.m. next Thursday, you will be in time. The court will have played its part, the rest is up to you." He re-adjusted his spectacles. "Do you have any questions?"

"When evidence is presented, can we speak?" Mallory asked.

"We are less formal than the courts with which you may be familiar. Provided decorum is observed, feel free to speak as necessary. I only stipulate that such interventions as I need to make will be final."

Wormsley cleared his throat. "What about the periods between court sessions, Mr Chairman? I move that Mr Holden and Ms Stellenbourg should not be permitted to confer."

"On the contrary, *Monsieur Le Maitre*," countered *L'Esprit*, "If the court is to mirror the hospital procedure, it must allow them full contact at all times. The very purpose of the procedure is to bring the two patients together in order to enhance their communication."

"That is irrelevant," Wormsley protested. "We are a court. It is only out of courtesy to the supplicants that this hearing runs at the same time as the hospital procedure. The hospital undoubtedly has its rules, but they are not the rules of the court."

"We have few if any precedents for this hearing," said *L'Esprit*. "That provides the court with considerable latitude, as has already been exercised in the matter of the postponement."

"Precisely," Wormsley said. "We've indulged them enough."

"Perhaps we should hear from them first." *Le Baigneur* turned to us. "The court is prepared to hear your views, though I must point out that the spirit of the court is that each supplicant must reach his or her own decision aided only by the input of the court. However, most hearings involve one supplicant only, and in none that the court can recall have the fates of two hung so inextricably together."

"It's up to Mallory." Being forcibly separated from her between sessions filled me with dread, yet it was only fair that she, who so feared the evidence against her, should decide.

"There's only one furnished apartment here," she said, focusing to my surprise on the practicalities rather than the principle. "I don't see that you can ask me to vacate my own property; nor can I ask Clem to camp in the unfurnished parts. He needs food, and heat."

Le Baigneur held up his hand to forestall a further outburst from Wormsley. "I see no easy solution, and I shall ponder the matter. In the meantime, I suggest we continue." He peered at *L'Esprit* over his half-moon spectacles. "I believe we start with you."

L'Esprit explained that he would provide a brief catalogue of our earlier lives. To me, it seemed unnecessary, but it was a relief to begin now with an unthreatening run-through of childhood, university and first jobs. Since *L'Esprit* was making the case for life, he was careful to paint our earlier selves in a good light. With little opportunity for challenge, Wormsley chose to look bored throughout.

Mallory's father had devoted his working life to one company, a multinational convenience food and beverages manufacturer, headquartered in Switzerland. As a result, her schooldays had been spent in several countries, as her father's climb up the corporate ladder had sent him from place to place. By the time she was ready for university, the family was based in South London, and she had chosen to take her engineering degree at Imperial College. Her first employer was an insurance company in Colmar, where she worked as a junior actuary, before setting up her own outfit, *Risque Alsacien*, where she soon came to the notice of Gen-Va Re, from whom she was later headhunted by the Tonbridge Syndicate.

My own history was not so different. After a degree in accountancy and law at L.S.E., I did time (or so it had felt) at one of the big City accountants, before escaping into advertising, first in London then New York, from where I was headhunted by a multinational in need of a marketing director in Paris. There I polished my command of the language and developed my love of the country. It amused Mallory to learn that my boss, an *énarque* and a resolute anglophile, had thought me too independent for the corporate treadmill.

"If you want to tell us how to run our business you had better become a consultant. Boards will pay to be told what they don't want to hear from their staff." It was a civilised way of being fired. Thereafter Covent Garden beckoned. Amy was p.a. to my first client, and I owed much of my start to her. How poorly had she been repaid.

By the time *L'Esprit* was through, it was nearly 12:45, and *Le Baigneur* adjourned for lunch. "Not that we ourselves are in need of sustenance," he explained with a brief twinkle of humour, "but we have no intention of starving you." A plate of sandwiches materialised on the table as he spoke, quickly followed by crockery and a thermos of coffee. He gestured that we should help ourselves.

Then he leaned towards Wormsley and *L'Esprit*, and the three of them began a whispered but animated consultation, of which it was impossible to catch a word. But if they ceased to look at us, the two silent court officials, standing either side of us, banished all thought of conversation. We were painfully conscious too of the myriad eyes of the watchers, as they shuffled and muttered amongst themselves.

Precisely one hour later, the conferral ceased. *Le Baigneur* cleared his throat, the gowned ushers retreated once more behind the big chair, and the remains of our repast disappeared.

"We appreciate that neither of you remembers the accident in which you were involved," he said gravely, "the event that by slow degrees has brought you before the court. For the avoidance of doubt, you must now be shown what happened. Please, if you would turn your chairs." He pointed towards the centre of the ballroom floor.

For a moment nothing happened. Then the air shimmered, the contours of the ballroom faded, and the darkening weather beyond its windows was replaced by the crisp blue of a winter morning. Instead of the imprint of our footmarks in the dusty floor, I saw quite clearly before me the path that led from my apartment complex to the main road. At the end of the path, and seemingly blocking it, was an ambulance, which almost immediately drove away to reveal a second on the other side of the road.

Everything replayed as I remembered it: the car skewed across the road, the three policemen directing traffic, the driver sitting on the kerb with a blanket over his shoulders, and Ambrose bending over Mallory as the paramedics prepared her for the stretcher. It included my anguished conversation with Sidonie, and the flash of recognition that passed between Mallory and me as the stretcher was lifted. The energy exchange between us was every bit as powerful.

Then, just as the ambulance drove away, the scene jumped. I now seemed to be walking along the Rue de la Plage towards the main road, and I realised that I was seeing things through Mallory's eyes as she'd walked home from her aborted lunch with *L'Esprit*. I was about to experience the accident that had condemned her to living death.

I wanted to shout out to warn her, but the words stuck in my throat: I was watching an unalterable past. I wanted to look away. The thought of seeing my darling walk into disaster was sickening. But in mockery of my will, my senses remained on high alert. I forgot the court, forgot even that Mallory was sitting beside me, with her hand clenching mine. I was now part of the unfolding scene, guilty in my powerlessness, and ashamed of my fear. The one about to suffer was not me, but Mallory, yet I cringed and shrank like a coward.

She – or I as it seemed – was nearly at the main road. A voice called her name. I swung round. There was Ambrose. Shrunken, disjointed, yet all too real. His once long and elegant hand, with which he reached for me, was thin and claw-like. His now sunken eyes smouldered in dark sockets. Fear and revulsion went through me, but also – and more forcibly – terrible and crushing guilt. My one thought was to put as much distance between him and me as I could.

The blind corner was forgotten. All I saw was a patch of empty road and the pavement beyond. On which a runner was jittering on the spot. I recognised him immediately. The stranger whose recent appearances had aroused and intrigued me, and whom I would be meeting again tomorrow. I called to him, knowing he would help me.

His eyes dilated with horror. He waved me back, then, as he realised I was coming anyway, he leapt towards me. We ought to have met in happy embrace. Instead, he seized my shoulders and threw me back the way I had come. There was a shriek of skidding rubber…

But before there was any impact, the scene jumped backwards to the moment when Mallory called to the runner. This time the perspective was from behind her, the scene as Ambrose must have experienced it. As before, she ran heedlessly across the road, whilst the runner – not some look-alike stranger, but clearly me – rushed out to push her back. For a moment all seemed well. Then a car bonnet appeared, sliding and pitching, as the driver braked. I heard the thump of our two bodies against the bonnet, and the crack of her skull against the windscreen, before I heard the scream of the tyres as the brakes locked the wheels. The car had undoubtedly been travelling far too fast.

Mallory's head struck the windscreen with the force of a cannonball, whipping and twisting her neck. Then as the car slewed to a halt, she was pitched into the gutter amidst a sleet of glass beads and drops of blood. As for me, my ankle caught the wing mirror, flipping me into the air, before depositing me back whence I had jumped. Face down, my head jerked as it struck the kerbstone. Pain seared through me.

As the scene faded, silence fell on the court, and none of the three officials would look us in the eye. Though I'd long accepted something of what had happened, I was unprepared for the sheer violence of the accident. It was a miracle that either of us had survived. I turned to Mallory. "I'm sorry I failed." But she could only shake her head.

Wormsley rose to his feet. "If I may summarise, Mr Chairman. What we have just seen is the complete picture of what happened from every perspective. To see it must have been shocking to both its victims, who even now remember nothing. Indeed, as we first saw, Mr Holden believed he had arrived after the accident happened."

His tone was strange, and it took me a moment to realise that he was trying to sound sympathetic. "Now perhaps they will understand the severity of their injuries, and why recovery is unlikely to be complete. The chances of brain damage and physical impairment are very high." He turned to Mallory. "You are at liberty to continue with the hearing, with all that that entails, but I must ask you whether you wouldn't rather save yourselves further pain?"

"Monsieur Wormsley makes a fair point, Mallory," *L'Esprit* added. "On the other hand…" He studied his elegant nails, as though they held the solution. "You have come this far, it would seem a shame to give up now." He managed a thin smile. "Perhaps you and Clem would like a moment or two to reflect amongst yourselves."

"You were right first off," I cut in. "It's crazy to give up now."

"The question was put to Ms Stellenbourg," Wormsley said, in his familiar manner. "She has the most to lose if she chooses badly."

"I gave up one chance for the sake of this hearing," I answered hotly. "I have no intention of giving up the last chance now."

Wormsley shook his head. "You never change do you?" As I frowned, I noticed with guilty satisfaction that his nose was still misshapen from when I'd hit him all those years ago.

"You must be unanimous," *Le Baigneur* pronounced, "and I have yet to hear from you, Madame." But he continued before she could answer. "Monsieur Linberger's advice is sound. I suggest we adjourn until tomorrow, so that you can consider the matter. But first, you ought to see yourselves as you really have been since New Year."

The room that now materialised was plain, dominated by the bed and its surrounding equipment. Mallory lay expressionless in the centre of it, her dark hair neatly brushed and tied, contrasting with the pale contours of her face. Tubes led from her nose and mouth, and there was a drip to her arm. Screens showed the pulse of her heart, and the residual activity of her brain. Beside me, the out-of-body Mallory paled, and a short sigh escaped her lips.

Then her room faded, to be replaced by another, identical in every detail except that the figure in the bed, wired to the various drips and monitors, was me. A scar above my right eye ran up into my recently shaven hair, and the cheek below was misshapen. The main thing I noted as the scene faded was the foolish droop of my mouth, which mocked any idea that my brain might still function.

"Whilst you were enjoying your luncheon," *Le Baigneur* explained, "the court further considered the matter of whether you should spend the evening and night hours together or apart. Under advisement, I have concluded that, with the exception of tonight, you are not permitted to confer. At the same time, the court understands your living conditions.

231

Therefore, you may both use the apartment, provided you eat and sleep separately. The two ushers will accompany you to ensure compliance. That is my decision, and it is final."

He paused, but there was nothing we could usefully say.

"The court makes an exception of this evening and tonight. The visual evidence so far relates solely to your physical condition, it does not bear upon your characters. The court is happy for you to confer jointly on your physical prospects, should you choose to wake from your comas; but the court will not countenance either of you seeking to influence the other on their interpretation of past behaviour. On what you did in the past, and how that is to affect your judgements, each must decide for him- or herself. I hope that is clear."

I reached for Mallory's arm. If this was to be our last night together during the trial – especially if it was to be the last night we would ever spend together – the sooner it started the better.

Mallory looked as shaken as I felt, but she took my arm and we walked slowly out of the ballroom. The silent ushers overtook us, and opened the doors for us. "They will come no further than the door of the apartment," *Le Baigneur* assured us. "They will not go in with you until tomorrow evening, should you decide to proceed that far."

The hallway was dim and shadowy. Our footsteps echoed on the tiled floor, and then boomed on the wooden stair, and it seemed to take us an age to reach the sanctuary of the apartment. As promised, the two ushers took up their vigil outside the door.

The clouds of the morning had thickened until they filled the sky, rain beat steadily against the windows, and the lake was impenetrably grey. Mallory shuddered and I held her close.

"We mustn't let Wormsley scare us," I said resolutely. Seeing the accident and our comatose slumber had shaken me, just as Wormsley had intended, but I was almost sure that he'd exaggerated the risks of paralysis and brain damage, and I wasn't about to admit any doubt. "If we were brain-damaged we wouldn't be here. Wormsley can call it fantasy, but brain-damaged minds couldn't create this detail."

"You can't know that," she answered sharply. "Brain damage can stop us walking or talking without affecting our imaginations." She gazed straight and hard into my eyes. "Put it this way: are you prepared to look after me if I'm seriously impaired?"

"Of course." I kissed her to stiffen her resolve. "What about you?"

"One way or another I've been looking after people since I started Ghost Trader." She managed a brave shrug. "Anyway, once this place is up and running, we'll have experts on tap."

232

"It's not just about us any more. This place needs us."

She pounced immediately. "What if we're both useless?"

"Then the world's no worse off than it is now," I replied resolutely. "We have to play the odds as they fall. Like with the shorting."

"Think what we might be inflicting on Hope and Jake."

"After all their hard work, we can't give up on them now."

"They haven't seen the accident. We understand the risk better."

"Surely you want to see this place developed? Especially after their petition. We'll have such a groundswell of support, the project's bound to take off. Even if we can't lift a finger."

It was strange, sitting in that gloom as the rain pounded the windows, with me pleading intuitively like Amy, and Mallory arguing logically like me. It was even stranger to think that, to the rest of the world, we weren't really here at all. But my last point got home.

"I suppose it's this place that's kept me going, until you came along." She managed to smile. "I hope you know what you're letting yourself in for. Long-term nursing is no picnic, even with help."

"I'll never know, unless I have to. But we're committed to each other come what may. That's the risk we take for love."

The rest of the evening we passed largely in silence, as we prepared, ate and cleared away a small meal of *charcuterie* and salad, more for form's sake than because we felt hungry. The court's ability to replay past events in holographic detail would dramatise the evidence to come and make it far more damning. "If we're this quiet tomorrow, the ushers are in for a boring night," I said, as we prepared for bed. "Look, I don't care a toss about the evidence, even Ambrose's. But if it worries you, I'd rather hear it from your side first."

She went horribly pale, and I feared she would break down. But she mastered it and pressed my hands to her face. "Of course I want to love you forever, and I want to fulfil this project with you. But you're entitled to see me as I really am. Not from me. From them. I've played God too often with other people's lives. I won't with yours."

However much she scared me, she had put her future in my hands. "I nearly saved you from the accident. Now I'm going to finish it."

"It's the skeletons in your cupboard first," she reminded me, with something of her old humour. I laughed as I was meant to, but she was right. Whatever Wormsley would present from my life was going to be anything but flattering. But I had been so concerned to reassure Mallory that I hadn't given a thought to what was in store for me.

But it was too late now. We were both mentally drained, and we fell asleep almost immediately. No dreams rewarded us. Although the hospital procedure had begun, Jake and Hope seemingly had nothing to report. We were truly in limbo, and at the mercy of the court.

By morning the rain had abated, but a thick mist now enveloped the Sanatorium, as if the Court of Transition were already sucking us into the black hole of death. We prepared and ate breakfast in gloomy silence, but as we were starting to make our way downstairs, Mallory smiled. "I'm glad you were a thorn in the corporate flesh."

"We both were in our different ways. But you were always far more diplomatic, and Wormsley's going to play on that."

"That's why we're a good team." She couldn't have lifted my spirits better. "Just promise you won't try to confer."

"I shan't utter a word beyond please, thanks and good night, and I'll sleep down here. It's your place, so you get the bedroom."

"There's a bed in the study above. If you don't mind the screens."

Curiously, the study was the only room in the building I had never explored, despite its proximity. It was also strange that I could have forgotten the screens which had so occupied us formerly. But to realise that I would have a bed after all cheered me considerably, and we made our way across the hall almost with equanimity.

Despite the chandeliers, the gloom outside had invaded the ballroom and enveloped the watchers in shadow. As we reached the dais, *L'Esprit* offered Mallory a hand and fussed her into her chair.

"May we take it that you have reached a decision?" he asked.

"We'll see the evidence," she said strongly. I simply nodded.

Chapter Twenty-Two : Assault & Battery

Friday began, not with evidence, but with a wrangle over what precisely was entailed by the embargo on our conferring each evening. Wormsley argued that we ought never to be in the same room together, whilst *L'Esprit* saw no harm in our speaking to each other, provided we did not broach forbidden topics. Neither I nor Mallory was permitted to participate, since the points to be taken were entirely legal.

It was practically noon before *Le Baigneur* finally ruled. We would be separately escorted to the apartment, with the first to be in their bedroom with their meal before the other would be allowed to enter. Should we bump into each other, we were expressly forbidden to speak beyond an exchange of pleasantries. He then adjourned for another silent and cheerless lunch, so that it was almost with relief that we resumed for the afternoon. This time, it was *L'Esprit* who began.

"The court applauds the bravery of your decision. As for me, I also believe that it was the right one. It cannot have been easy to discover that you no longer live normal lives, that instead you are acting out an extended dream, whilst physically you lie hospital. Yet, far from being driven to despair or madness, you have chosen to live again, if you can. Even more extraordinarily, you have chosen to do so without any guarantee as to the likely quality of your future lives.

"Near-death experiences are rare, but they are not unheard of. The court often assists individuals. But here we have not one individual in suspended animation, but two. Two people whose minds are active whilst their bodies are inert, so active that they have created an out-of-body dream-world which is so real to them that it is indistinguishable from the physical world their bodies still inhabit; a dual dream, in which Eurydice is every bit as active and participating as Orpheus. You have both been brave and selfless thus far; all I can ask is that you be similarly brave in the face of the evidence. The choice is yours, and I trust that you will make the right one."

He ended with a slight bow. Then Wormsley rose brusquely.

"I will not waste time reviewing all your lives. Two events each will suffice. The first of these, as it happens, concerns myself as debt collector for Lloyd's. In which capacity I was known to you both." He turned to Mallory. "Would you describe our dealings as cordial?"

"They were perfectly proper and professional."

"Would you say that I was a reasonable man to deal with?"

She laughed. "Put it this way, I never had any problems, but my members were not always so complimentary."

"You know, of course, that Mr Holden was once a Name?"

"Of course. It was one of the first things he told me."

"Has he described to you any of his dealings with me?"

"Not in detail, no."

"Has he given you any indication of what he thought of me?"

"Of you specifically, no."

"What about his attitude towards Lloyd's in general?"

"Thieves, liars or incompetents." She grinned. "Take your pick."

"You remember the meeting we attended?" Wormsley asked me.

"You didn't just 'attend', you were the guest speaker." I'd grasped immediately where Wormsley's questions were leading, and I cursed my lack of foresight. My one hope was pre-emptive damage limitation before he could show her my violent assault on him.

Trying to ignore Wormsley, I turned to Mallory. "The Wu action group committee seemed to think that the members ought to hear from the enemy. So Mr Wormsley was allowed to make a tough speech about how we could do it the hard way or the easy way."

"I promised to be sympathetic to those prepared to deal sensibly with me," Wormsley protested. "People like you chose not to listen."

"The promise meant nothing, and the threat was much clearer," I retorted. "You told us in no uncertain terms that you would pursue objectors implacably." I turned again to Mallory. "You probably heard something of what happened."

"The fracas they hushed up, you mean? I didn't know you were involved, but I can't say I'm surprised." Her expression hovered uneasily between smile and frown. "What I don't understand is why, Monsieur Wormsley, you agreed to address an action group. Surely you must have known you were going into the lion's den?"

"I go where duty leads," Wormsley asserted loftily.

"Ostensibly, the committee wanted to sound responsible," L'Esprit said. "Their real aim, as I heard it, was to rouse the members."

"An uncompromising speech played into their hands," she said.

"One might say that you brought it on yourself," L'Esprit added.

"I said what I always said. It was Mr Holden who was provocative."

"I merely asked a question," I countered. "You made a meal of it."

"I heard it was a noisy meeting from the start," L'Esprit said.

"It was certainly noisy," I agreed. "Lots of anger and shouting."

"Was the anger and shouting started by you?" *L'Esprit* asked.

"Certainly not." So far, Wormsley was getting the worst of it.

"Monsieur Wormsley was rather brave to attend, then," *Le Baigneur* observed. Like any good chairman, he knew how to calm an argument before it got out of hand. I laughed.

The intervention might have given Wormsley temporary respite, but it had not let him off the hook. "I think he revelled in it, *Monsieur Le Maitre*," I said firmly. "If the Wu committee hoped he would enrage us members, he played his part to perfection."

I remembered that boulder-like jaw, those fleshy cheeks and the narrowed eyes with which he'd dared us to do our worst. "It was pure theatre. Posturing on all sides. Perhaps the more timid Names felt like settling, but those the group could do without. It was the real rebels they wanted Lloyd's to see, to show that we meant business."

"So your part was pre-planned, was it?" *Le Baigneur* asked sharply.

"I planned to ask a question, but nobody told me what to ask."

"Then you're responsible. You alone," Wormsley asserted.

"You attacked me," I retorted.

"Perhaps we can see what happened, and judge for ourselves," *L'Esprit* suggested soothingly. With ill grace, Wormsley directed our attention to the floor of the ballroom. The venue that swiftly sharpened into focus was some dusty hall near St Paul's, its dark panelling and inlaid woodwork as faded as its grandeur. I was on the centre aisle, a few rows from the front, with Ambrose next to me. The speeches were over, and the meeting was now open to the floor. The microphone passed from questioner to questioner, until it was my turn.

As Ambrose gave me a thumbs up, I rose slowly and let my gaze sweep the room, before fixing on Wormsley. He glared back. A real mean machine. But there was no retreating now.

"Will Lloyd's confirm they will not come after spouses' assets?"

There was a hiss of intaken breath. Flushing, Wormsley gripped the lectern hard. His eyes narrowed with real hatred, and I had to fight to hold his gaze. But I was determined to hold my ground.

"Answer the question," Ambrose said quietly but audibly.

Wormsley stabbed the air with his finger as if he hoped it would fly off like a bullet to strike me dead. "I think I know this gentleman." His voice dripped contempt. "So let me tell you all what I told him." His eyes swept the room, as his other hand rapped the lectern. "We only seek what is owed in order to settle a Name's outstanding losses, losses which were incurred as part of that Name's underwriting, and in accordance with the agreement he signed with his members' agent and with each of the syndicates which he supports."

"That doesn't answer my question," I retorted.

Wormsley glared. "What the Name owes the Name must pay."

"But not with his wife's assets!" I was shouting now.

"Those assets were transferred to your wife as a deliberate ploy." Wormsley had forgotten the rest of the meeting. "Those assets were part of the wealth you pledged to Lloyd's."

"If Lloyd's intend to rob us, why shouldn't we protect our property? Or is Mr Wormsley suggesting we leave our houses unlocked so that any thief can walk in and help himself?"

"If we did that, think of all the insurance claims Lloyd's would face," Ambrose called out, more loudly this time.

I clapped him on the shoulder, delighted with his steel.

"He wouldn't care, Mr Chairman, because the syndicates simply pass the losses to us Names. No pain to them."

Names began shouting, a few telling me to sit down, most chanting *Thief! Thief!* It was pure theatre, and Wormsley was hating it.

"Mr Chairman, I insist that gentleman retracts his insinuation."

"You're not even a thief, Wormsley, you're a thief's pimp."

"You're a wicked man, Clem Holden. That was a crass metaphor and totally out of order." Mallory wagged a finger at me, but her eyes sparkled with amusement. So far at least, Wormsley had failed to turn her against me. But the worst was yet to come.

Wormsley jumped off the platform. "You'll take that back!" His face was puce, there was spittle on his chin and he loomed in front of me. He might have been blustering, but I wasn't. Stepping smartly forward, I fired my fist at the point of his nose. There was a horrible crack, as the impact ran up my arm like electricity, and blood sprayed.

Wormsley doubled over, clutching his nose, and my memory told me that I'd done nothing further, that Ambrose had taken my arm as stewards raced down the aisle. But as I watched now, I lunged for Wormsley anew. But for Ambrose's prompt intervention, I would have gone on punching a defenceless man.

The stewards threw us out, along with several other Names who had jumped up to join in. The scene cut. We, the ejected Names, were in a bar getting happily drunk. I'd been too wound up to do anything else, and now I was basking in the admiration of the others, especially Ambrose, who hung on every fatuous word, even my threat to castrate all those on the Lloyd's trading floor, the Room, with a chainsaw.

When the bar closed, he bundled me into a taxi, and came along to see me home safely. As well as to meet Amy.

Wormsley looked down on me now, as though daring me to another fight. "If I may say so, Ms Stellenbourg, your boyfriend has quite a temper. I wonder if you're prepared for it?"

Thoroughly ashamed, I hung my head. Then I felt the reassuring pressure of Mallory's hand upon my knee. "Clem may have a quick temper, and he is liable to over-react. But I've never known him act without provocation." I mouthed her a silent thank you.

"A quick temper, you say, and liable to over-react." Wormsley nodded, as though these were the answers he'd hoped for. "May we take it, then, that you speak from experience?"

"I'm perfectly happy with Clem the way he is."

"With financial loss, tempers run high," said *L'Esprit*. "When Lehman Brothers collapsed, their CEO Richard Fuld was attacked; just yesterday, Bernie Madoff was assaulted prior to his arrest."

This jolted me from introspection. "Madoff arrested! Why?"

"His fund was a Ponzi," *L'Esprit* replied. "The biggest ever."

I was too stunned to speak, almost to grasp what it meant. It was Mallory who put the question. "Has the money all gone?"

L'Esprit nodded. "That would appear to be the case."

"Then Amy's lost all her savings," I groaned.

"I'm surprised you still care," Wormsley observed acidly.

I jumped up angrily, and if Mallory had not grabbed my arm, I might have rushed round the table and broken his nose all over again. Mallory told him angrily that his remark was uncalled for.

"Clem has always been concerned for Amy," she pronounced.

"I knew there was something wrong about Madoff." I sank down into my chair again. "I tried to warn her, but she seemed to know what she was doing." I appealed to *L'Esprit*. "What about the feeder funds? Were they in on it, too?" *L'Esprit* shook his head.

"It seems he took everybody in. Including the SEC."

If only the SEC had been as astute as Marie-Sainte and her professor, they would have listened to the few whistle-blowers, instead of treating Madoff as their old buddy, the clever man who founded the NASDAQ and who pioneered automated trading. I thought of Amy proudly displaying her ring to me on her last hospital visit. Surely Saul could not knowingly have deceived her? Amy's intuition, so sound over Lloyd's, could surely not have failed to spot a real crook.

If Saul himself had been deceived, he was as ruined as Amy. Even if he had not personally invested heavily, which I hoped for her sake he had not, he faced ruinous lawsuits from the pension funds and charities he had fed to Madoff. Whichever way I looked at it, Amy was in for a rough ride. Worse, there was nothing I could do to help. Even moral support was beyond me. I choked with frustration, but for once the focus of my anger was me. My failure to heed Amy over Lloyd's had not only wrecked her life, it had put her in permanent peril. If she'd been taken in by Saul's smooth talk, it was because of me.

"I can see that you are disturbed," said *Le Baigneur*. "I propose that we adjourn. We have in any case completed the allotted part of the timetable, and we remain on schedule."

He was right. The Madoff news had floored me, and I was in no position to keep pace with Wormsley's machinations.

"Thank you," I said humbly.

Mallory pressed my hand again. "Why don't you go first?"

I nodded, and allowed the ushers to lead me back to the apartment. One waited outside as before, but the other followed me inside. Though he kept his distance, his silent presence was unnerving. Being unable to call Amy, if only to tell her I was thinking about her, was unbearable, and after sitting all day I was desperate for something to do.

Food was the last thing on my mind, but I prepared a simple meal for Mallory, which allowed me to feel a tiny bit useful. Then I changed into sweats and told the usher I was going for a run around the grounds. He followed me silently to the front door. The Citroen seemed to have sunk even lower on its suspension, and the sky was so overcast that it was impossible to see whether there was anybody still inside it.

At a brisk pace, I started a circuit of the grounds. The usher made his way to the gate, to ensure that I did not try to escape. The watchers were nowhere to be seen, and I supposed that they were now permanently encamped in the ballroom. I felt sluggish and out of condition, but the effort nevertheless cleared my brain.

After several circuits, I returned to the apartment, where the meal had been removed. The other usher stood guard on the stairs.

"I need a shower," I told him.

He pointed me into the kitchen, and once I was inside his companion blocked the doorway, whilst he went upstairs to fetch Mallory. Only once he had escorted her to the dining room and sat her at the table, was I released to go up to the bathroom. The ushers placed themselves between us, so that we couldn't even exchange glances.

There was a chair by the bedroom window, angled as though just vacated, and an impression on the bed, where Mallory had lain. Hints of her wildflower scent tantalised my nostrils, as my guard opened the bathroom door. At least he had the decency to stay outside. Her aura permeated everything in the bathroom, from her hairbrush by the basin, to yesterday's clothes draped over the clothes basket. I wrote "I love you" on the mirror in toothpaste. Then I allowed myself to be led upstairs to the study. My guard took up his post outside the door. With its narrow bed and screens, it reminded me of the boathouse.

The exercise had worked off my restless energy, and as soon as I lay down I sank into heavy and dreamless sleep. It was only Mallory's call up the stairs next morning, Saturday, that woke me. "I'm going down now, the coast's clear." My guard was waiting for me by the doorway, but he let me pass into the bathroom. My toothpaste message had been replaced. "I love you too. Supper was great."

My guard had already made his way down to the living room, where coffee and bread waited on the table by the window. Sky and water were the colour of slate, but the pines in the higher hills were dusted with snow. I ate a little bread and drank two cups of coffee, then I was ready. I followed my guard across the gallery and down the main stairs. Inside the ballroom, everybody was waiting. Wormsley looked grim, but Mallory greeted me with a sympathetic smile.

"I trust that the troubles of your ex-wife did not disturb your sleep too much," *Le Baigneur* said, as I took my seat. "May we take it that you are ready to continue?"

"Quite ready, thank you. The best way I can help Amy is to get this trial over with as quickly as possible. So let's get on with it." Mallory's hand slipped unobtrusively into mine.

Le Baigneur nodded to Wormsley. "You may continue."

He needed no urging. "I need to know, Ms Stellenbourg, whether Mr Holden has ever been violent to you?" Her hand twitched in mine, and she did not answer. "Specifically: has he ever hit you?"

I cut in quickly. "If you must know, I slapped her once."

"I see." Wormsley frowned theatrically. "When was this?"

"Just before I came here," she said. "It wasn't a big deal."

Wormsley simulated puzzlement. "If it was no big deal, why did you pack up all your belongings, and drive off in the small hours?"

She shrugged helplessly. "I don't know. I just did."

"That's not like you, Ms Stellenbourg. I put it to you that you panicked, because Mr Holden had bruised your cheek."

"Don't put words in my mouth!" Mallory banged the table. "You have to understand. We were exhausted and fraught. Clem wanted to

241

celebrate, but I couldn't stop thinking about how I was going to break it to the members. That's why I texted Robert and Jean-Michel."

"Surely that could have waited until morning?"

"Perhaps I had a premonition that Ambrose was coming."

Wormsley shook his head. "You're not given to premonitions."

"She was tired and confused," *L'Esprit* cut in. "Isn't that enough?"

"If she was tired, she'd have gone to bed. Instead, she packed up all her things, carried them to her car, requiring several journeys, then drove all the way here, well over a hundred miles away." Wormsley leaned across the table to Mallory. "I put it to you again that it was Mr Holden's violence that made you do what you did."

"You've got it all wrong!" She wrung her hands agonisingly.

"You mean the escape was premeditated? That once you no longer needed Mr Holden's assistance, you dumped him? Is that it?"

"Of course not," she retorted scornfully. "Why do you think I asked to delay the hearing?" She turned to me. "Please, Clem, this is all nonsense. You know how I feel about you."

I jumped up to stand reassuringly behind her, hands on her shoulders. "This has gone on long enough. There's no secret about what happened. I was tired, I lost my temper, and I've apologised. Our state of mind at the time is no longer relevant. If you're trying to sow doubts, you won't achieve it by hectoring us. Quite the reverse."

I spoke forcefully not only for Mallory's sake, but also to expunge from my mind the niggle of doubt that Wormsley's cross-examination had been so cunningly designed to implant.

"I won't be bullied into thinking Clem more violent than he is."

"But you admit he has a propensity for violence?"

"I've known Clem for the best part of a year," Mallory replied dismissively: "Slapping me once hardly constitutes a propensity."

"That seems quite clear," *L'Esprit* interjected. "One slap in a period of nearly 12 months, meted out at a time of great stress to both parties, means very little. I suggest we move on."

Wormsley glanced reluctantly at *Le Baigneur*, who nodded his agreement. "Very well. I shall turn our attention to the more distant past. When Mr Holden was still married." He glowered at me with all his old truculence. "Did you and your then wife ever quarrel?"

I sat down again. "Of course." I knew now where he was going, and my one hope was to blunt his questions with prompt answers.

"During those quarrels, did you ever hit her?"

"Yes, and she usually slapped me back."

"All part and parcel of the ups and downs of married life?"

242

"Mostly we were quite happy. We only quarrelled occasionally."

"Then why did you get divorced?" Wormsley demanded.

"She was angry with me over Lloyd's. So angry, she had an affair."

"So the affair caused the divorce?"

"I think it proved to us that our marriage had broken down."

"The decision was mutual, then, was it?"

"More or less. But Amy was the one who started proceedings."

"What about the divorce itself: was it amicable?"

"No way. As you well know." It had degenerated into a three-way fight between Lloyd's, Amy and myself. Lloyd's tactic had been to argue that our divorce was merely a ploy to move as many of my assets as possible to Amy. To disabuse them, Amy's lawyers had gone to unpleasant lengths to prove that our differences were real, making a meal of my angry reaction to her affair. Though this tactic had secured a modest portion for her, her legal fees had eaten into it, to her bitter disappointment. I had been caught hopelessly in the middle.

The romantic part of me hadn't wanted a divorce at all; the generous part had conceded that divorce could give Amy and Jake their fair share of our assets; but the jealous part had feared that Amy's victory would enrich Ambrose at my expense. Jealousy had overridden my better feelings, and antagonised the judge.

"Divorce is divorce," said Mallory. "I've been there too. If you're going to present divorce proceedings as evidence, I shan't even listen." She put her fingers in her ears for emphasis.

Wormsley managed a consoling smile. "It's what preceded the divorce that interests me more." Then he turned to me again. "How did you find out Amy was having an affair?"

"Amy could never hide her feelings. As for then, she didn't care."

"She *wanted* you to know?" He aped profound disbelief.

"It was her way of preparing me for the worst."

"So you confronted her?" He was suddenly back to reasonableness.

"I asked her if she was seeing someone else, yes."

"Were you alone together when you asked this?"

I shook my head. "No, my son was there, too."

"You challenged your wife in front of your child?"

"He was hardly a small boy," I protested. "He was a legal adult."

"Was this to punish him, or to make Amy look bad to him?"

"I wasn't thinking. The question just came out."

He released a theatrical sigh. "What did she say?"

"She said she deserved some consolation for being ruined." I pressed on before he could interrupt. "I demanded to know who was the lucky man, and she said Ambrose. I'd half-guessed anyway. For a while he'd been a regular visitor, and I'd been glad, because Amy was always in a better mood when he was there. Then he stopped coming; he became cagey and elusive. But hearing her say it was still a shock. I asked Jake if he'd realised what his mother was up to. Not a pleasant question, I'll admit, but I wasn't in a pleasant frame of mind."

"What did Jake say?" He was back to the matter-of-fact tone.

"Nothing. But he wouldn't look me in the eye. It seemed they were both against me. Laughing at me behind my back, for all I knew."

"Is Jake a young man who would laugh at his father like that?"

"No. Nor Amy that kind of woman. I'm just explaining how I felt at the time. I wasn't in a fit state to think clearly. I asked her what was so special about Ambrose. She said he was more attentive than me."

I would have found it impossible to continue if Mallory hadn't just then replaced her hand on my knee. Until then I'd felt alone under the baleful scrutiny of the watchers. Her renewed support boosted me enough to forestall Wormsley.

"I said I'd be comforting if she'd let me, but she laughed. 'You don't have it in you any more.' I said I had too many things on my mind to be truly loving, and she said Ambrose didn't seem to have any problems in that department. Even Jake found that funny."

"Did you confront Monsieur Hanter as well?" *L'Esprit* cut in.

I shook my head. "As I just said, he kept out of my way."

"What made you think you had any right to lose your temper?"

"I told you, I wasn't thinking at all."

"Nor remembering," Wormsley countered coldly. "Or was your one-night stand with Sidonie, when you were happily married, so unimportant?" There was nothing I could say, but my face spoke for me. It seemed that the court knew everything about me that was to my disadvantage. "You presumed to lose your temper with Amy, as though you were a wronged innocent instead of a proven philanderer."

"Once!" I shouted. "Just the once." Wormsley threw up his hands. I glanced despairingly at Mallory. "Only because she was upset."

Mallory responded with a tiny shrug, though whether dismissing me or the incident I could not tell.

"Not once. You and Sidonie shared apartments for months."

"That was after Amy and I split up." I turned again to Mallory. "Long before I met you." Her shrug was more eloquent this time, yet still I could not interpret it for sure.

"That's clear," *L'Esprit* interposed. "Monsieur Holden does not deny that he was unfaithful once during his marriage. Nor does he deny that he lost his temper with Madame Holden. But it could be argued that by indulging in an affair with Monsieur Hanter, and by making no effort to hide the matter, she brought her husband's anger on herself."

"And I put it to you," Wormsley answered remorselessly, "that Mr Holden's anger was totally disproportionate." He pointed dramatically to the centre of the ballroom. "Just watch."

The living room in Primrose Hill seemed even bigger than I remembered it. Acres of wood flooring and a scattering of Persian rugs. Amy's choosing, not mine. I was standing in front of the fireplace – a confection of white marble shot with greys and pinks – Amy and Jake were on the big white sofa, with a small, loose rug between us. Her blue eyes seared like ice.

"At the very least, you owe me an apology," I was saying.

She laughed bitterly. "No, Clem, you're the one who owes me."

"You could at least apologise to your son."

Jake shifted uncomfortably. "It's OK, Dad."

"No, it's not OK. It's shameful."

"You're pathetic." Amy sprang to her feet. "A useless non-husband who can't even manage the basics for either of us. In any department. You explain that to Jake, unless you'd prefer me to spell it out for him." She turned dismissively. "I'm going to bed." Seizing her arm, I spun her round to face me. "Take your hands off me."

"All right for Ambrose to run his dirty little hands all over you, but not for your husband." Instead of letting go, I shook her.

"Dad, stop it." Jake jumped up anxiously.

His intervention galvanised Amy, who beat her fists on my chest. "At least Ambrose knows what he's doing. At least he's gentle."

This was too much. As in my first recurring dream, when I'd confronted the commanding woman in the queue, the stranger who'd morphed into Amy and Mallory – the two victims of my loving fury – my head boiled with a rage that threatened to tear me apart. I closed my eyes to contain it and to shut them out. Amy especially. When I opened my eyes again, she was sprawled on the floor, with the rug tangled around her feet, and I was standing over her.

"Get up, you stupid bitch. You only slipped on the rug."

Jake pinned my arms to my sides, and wrenched me away. "Are you OK, mum?" She sat up and wiped her lip, which was split and bleeding. Then she nodded slowly. Releasing me, Jake pushed me away. "Out! We don't want to see you until you've calmed down."

"We don't want to see him, period," Amy mumbled, fiddling some more with her mouth. "He's only gone and loosened a tooth."

The scene cut out. The watchers were abuzz with outrage, whilst those on the dais stood or sat in shocked silence. Mallory's hand slipped from my knee, and she wouldn't look at me. Once again my memory had proved a false friend. Until I'd seen my fist smack into Amy's face, I'd been convinced that I'd pushed her, at worst slapped her, that it was the loose rug which had done the damage. Now it seemed that Wormsley's assessment of my character was far better than mine, whilst his cunning questions had enabled him to show only the final moments of the scene, to reveal my anger in all its violence.

Chapter Twenty-Three : Assisted Death

Wormsley's last words before the court adjourned, which were endorsed by *Le Baigneur* and unchallenged by *L'Esprit*, forbade us to communicate that night in any way. Even goodwill messages in toothpaste were outlawed. Despite another punitive run, I passed a wretched, almost sleepless night. Why had I not foreseen this? Why had I smugly assumed that my past was nothing to fear?

On its own, the spat with Wormsley might not amount to much, but as part of a pattern of violence, which Wormsley had skilfully painted, it not only highlighted the ferocity of my attack on Amy, it warned Mallory that the slap she had excused could be repeated, that my temper was to be feared, that my love was less joy than threat.

Her first reaction had been to flee, and Wormsley had shown that her first reaction had been right. I was too dangerous to be trusted. Little wonder that I entered the ballroom on Sunday, another dull, snow-threatening morning, on leaden feet, or that I sat down without looking at Mallory, though I was all too aware of how tense she was.

"You have seen how evidence is presented to the court. I'm sure you both understand now my warning that your decisions would never be easy," *Le Baigneur* began sombrely. "The spotlight now turns on you, Madame. Are you still prepared to go on?"

She stared down at the table, her lips moving wordlessly. "If you've changed your mind," I said, desperate to spare her the agony of denouncing me, "I don't blame you."

She looked at me at last. "I've seen the worst of you." She choked, before her voice steadied. "It's only fair you see the worst of me."

She could hardly have put it any clearer. We were both on a fiendish probation, waiting to see which of us had the worse character, and whether the less bad could stomach the more. If that took heroism, it was of the twisted kind. "You've stood up for me as much as you can," I said contritely. "I'll do the same for you, I promise."

"Why not spare the lady?" Wormsley asked, as though he had nothing but Mallory's interests at heart. "Are you at least gallant enough to spare her the pain of hurting you?"

It was the worst question he could have asked, but it had to be answered. "We want no more secrets between us," I said.

L'Esprit gave a dignified nod of understanding. "This has been hard for you both, and it will get harder, I promise you. But the ultimate decision remains yours and yours alone. Just be strong for a little longer, and I believe you will yet deserve a lasting future."

Le Baigneur interlocked fingers. "Monsieur Wormsley?"

"I call Mr Tonbridge as a witness, Mr Chairman." Immediately the two ushers, our erstwhile gaolers, made their way in lockstep to the double doors. Moments later we heard the front door open, and then the slam of a car door. Soon after, marching ahead of his escorts, Rex Tonbridge made his entrance. With a brusque nod to *Le Baigneur*, he mounted the dais and sat in one of the chairs opposite. On his last appearance he had looked angry: this time he sprawled with studied nonchalance, one arm over the back of the chair, the other resting lightly on his knee. "Thank you, Rex. Just a few questions."

"No problem, Jarvis." Rex was all bonhomie, offering Mallory a brief smile, and me the tiniest of waves. "You know my rules."

"Some facts only." Wormsley studied the notes which had just appeared in his hand. "Ms Stellenbourg was your junior underwriter, but underwriting was not her main task, was it?"

"Not once I realised what a good investor she was," Rex beamed.

"Would that be before or after she became your lover?"

"I don't remember." He grinned knowingly. "Does it matter?"

"Which of you commissioned the risk assessment reports?" Rex conceded that, of course, he had. "Do you think they were worth the £100,000 which the syndicate paid for them?"

"They were invaluable."

"I'd be happy to settle for £90,000 each year," Wormsley observed drily, "given that's what was paid to *Risque Alsacien*, to which company the work of preparing the reports was sub-contracted, and given that Ms Stellenbourg – your lover – was its proprietor."

"I won't deny what we did," Rex answered candidly. "Nor, before you ask, will I deny that there was a similar arrangement between *Risque Alsacien* and Gen-Va Re, from whom the syndicate commissioned a certain amount of reinsurance and retrocession."

"Whose idea was it to appropriate syndicate money for yourselves?"

"Mallory acted on my instructions."

"That wasn't what I asked. Was it your idea or hers?"

"Who's to say?" A shadow of irritation clouded Rex's brow. "It was an evolving conversation. I suppose it began when I complained about the cost of reinsurance and Mallory pointed out we were tarred with the risk exposure of other syndicates; then I predicted that syndicates would soon find it impossible to buy Errors & Omissions insurance. But the clincher was when Mallory noted that Names could buy Stop Loss more cheaply than we could reinsure."

"So you decided to 'reinsure' yourselves directly?"

"We also encouraged Names to take Stop Loss," he countered.

"On which Names could claim only in the event of losses. Your little arrangement guaranteed you extra profit at their expense." It was the first time I'd ever heard Wormsley stand up for Names, and the surprise of it added to the sense of conviction. Rex's body language lost its easy nonchalance. "Did either of you think of that?"

"A small loss of profit in good times, and not much added to their losses in bad," Rex blustered, before he caught the hard stares of *Le Baigneur* and *L'Esprit*, and before he sensed the palpable disapproval of the watchers. "I suppose, of the two of us, she was more conscious of the downside than I was." If he thought this remark would soften the disapproval, he was disappointed. Even my opinion of him sank, though I'd heard most of it before. He seemed unaware how easily Wormsley was manoeuvring him into bad-mouthing Mallory.

"I thought we were avoiding stuff we know already," I cut in.

"Yes, indeed. So, when things went bad, is it true you asked Mallory to give back the money you'd taken: to return it to your Names?"

Rex nodded enthusiastically. "I told her not to forget Names."

To my delight, Mallory's hand stole into mine under the table, and I pressed it reassuringly. She was as tense as a coiled spring, and I guessed we must be coming at last to whatever it was she'd feared to tell me. I threw her a brief smile, but her face remained rigid.

"What was her answer?"

"That they had Stop Loss. We were the ones needing help." He threw her a quick glance. "Sorry, darling, but that's how it was."

"She told me," I assured him, angry that he'd made her response so heartless. Of all people, she would have known that Rex's losses had become so huge that Stop Loss reinsurance would have covered them no better than sticking plaster would staunch a severed artery.

"She didn't see how she could return the money to them without making it obvious where it had come from." This time he dared to look at her directly. "But I knew she'd find a way."

"If you hadn't died, would she still have done it?"

Rex hesitated, which was answer enough, but Mallory pitched in bravely for him. "That's not a fair question for Rex. I don't know if I would or not. Probably not, unless he'd really insisted." She turned fiercely to me. "You understand that, don't you?"

"Of course I do." Her sole focus had been Rex's happiness. As a motive, it fired my jealously, but it could not make me doubt her.

"Thank you both." Wormsley smiled cunningly. "So, Rex, is that why you shot yourself: to force her to help the Names?"

"What do you take me for?" Rex demanded with a brittle laugh. "I'm not that much of a philanthropist. It was me I couldn't face." The self-assurance drained from his face, and he looked suddenly older, almost frail. "Failure's hard. Having to accept you're rubbish instead of the best. Knowing the people who loved and admired you couldn't look you in the face. Even you, darling, not that you'd admit it."

Mallory's hand flew to her mouth. He turned to me, his eyes full of sadness, as though my welfare meant everything to him. "Whatever you do, Clem, don't let her see you as a failure."

"Come on," I said, "She was rescuing failures long before we met."

"Oh, she'll forgive you being a Name. My fault, not yours."

"I wasn't even on your syndicate," I reminded him.

He laughed, a harsh rather than a happy sound. "I belonged to the rotten tribe of working underwriters, all to blame for each and every failure. But don't expect me to apologise. I've done my bit. It's the rest of the rotten bunch that owes you, not me. Not any more."

"I'm not expecting an apology." I couldn't allow him to project his guilt onto Mallory, whose hand now trembled in mine. "In my book, taking your life was honourable. But it was your decision, not hers. Afterwards, she did everything you asked, and more. She didn't simply help your Names, she rescued them, and many more as well. All for your sake, in honour of your memory and her love for you."

"I was only thinking of you, old boy." Rex hung his head to hide the tears welling in his eyes. "I can see you're her big hero right now. Just don't do an Enron, that's all I'm saying."

"I've no intention of being like Ambrose, in any shape or form," I assured him. "But I will say this: Mallory has never thought badly of you, and she never will. As for me," I forced myself to smile, "I'll always do my best to be fair to your memory."

Mallory buried her face in her hands, and for a time there was silence, since she sobbed soundlessly to herself. Even Wormsley seemed moved enough to sink quietly into his chair.

Rex was the first to recover. "I've said everything I'm going to say." He lurched to his feet, pushed his chair roughly under the table and – his confidence returning – he came to our side of the table. He laid a manly hand on my shoulder, his other stole towards Mallory.

"Good luck to you." Then, without even touching her, he jumped off the stage and swaggered to the doors. Nobody called him back.

"I don't need Mr Tonbridge again." Wormsley pronounced. "What I must show now is the manner of his death, which – for understandable reasons – he did not wish to revisit."

"In your case, we had to show you your accident," *L'Esprit* amplified apologetically. "And before you ask, Monsieur Holden, it is necessary, I'm afraid, to show exactly how Monsieur Tonbridge met his end." His measured tone made my heart sink. Mallory's face was stony, unreadable. But it was enough to tell me that a new horror must be endured. With deep foreboding, I turned to watch.

A car drew up outside a large country house, a rambling brick pile, Elizabethan at its heart, but with 19th century accretions. The bricks were a mixture of oranges, browns and reds, with flights of Victorian purple. The oldest window frames were stone, and the oldest chimneys tall corkscrew stacks. The remains of a moat, now no more than an elongated pond, lay between the car and the house. A drawbridge gave access to the entrance: a heavy double gate leading to a courtyard. It was flanked by two stone lions. What was it about lions, I thought inconsequentially, reminded of the lions on Wormsley's terrace. Except that they had supposedly been part of a dream.

It was a pleasant summer's evening, fading into twilight, and when the car's engine stopped, a great quiet descended upon the scene. The house was on its own, surrounded by woodland. Few lights burned in its windows. The sound of the car door opening was oddly loud.

I recognised the two motorists as soon as they emerged, though the contrast between then and now was striking. This was Ambrose as Amy would first have known him, in all his handsome diffidence. As for Mallory, she took my breath away. As young as her daughter, yet entirely herself. Age since had only chiselled her features more finely. But she was as tense as I'd ever seen her, and in a hurry.

She was in work clothes, a formal skirt and blouse, and her heels clacked impatiently over the paving stones, but Ambrose, in a rumpled linen jacket, seemed cautious, glancing around him as if expecting to be accused of trespass at any moment. "The place looks deserted." Even his quiet voice broke the hush as harshly as a rook's caw.

Mallory strode across the drawbridge. At the gate, she hurriedly selected a key from the fob in her hand. "His car's here." Her voice was strong, but edged with anxiety. She pushed the unlocked gate wide to reveal a silver Bentley, hood down and slewed around, almost filling the courtyard, as though its driver had arrived in such a hurry he hadn't cared how it was parked. Mallory stared into its interior as if the pale leather seats might hold some clue, as Ambrose caught up with her. "He left the top down," she said. It seemed to worry her.

"He's planning to drive off again," Ambrose suggested.

Mallory frowned, but gave no answer. Instead, she made for the house door on the other side of the car. It was ajar. She pushed it right open. "Rex!" she called. Her voice resonated through the building, but there was no answer. "Rex!" Anxiety was turning to fear.

Silence fell again. A menacing silence that even subdued the occasional coughing of the watchers around the ballroom. "Come on." Mallory gestured impatiently to Ambrose, who seemed rooted to the cobbles of the courtyard. Then without waiting, she turned into the house, her shoes tapping on the polished wood flooring.

For its size, the house was low-ceilinged. I had a brief impression of dark oak panelling, of William Morris upholstery, and of walls hung with framed photographs of Rex Tonbridge in all his careless arrogance: Rex outside the Lloyd's building, shaking hands with the Lord Mayor; Rex at his box in the Room, negotiating with brokers; Rex in a rakish trilby leading his horse into the winner's enclosure; and just one of Rex with Mallory in the midst of a staff montage.

They weren't even looking at each other, yet their body language was redolent of love and tenderness. His wife must have hated it, and I could hardly bear to look. Of all the horrors I had endured at the trial so far, this was the worst. To see Mallory so blissfully yet so unconsciously in love with another man. Not for the first time, it occurred to me that she had another motive for dying, that Rex still had a power over her to which I could never aspire, and to which – I now realised all too well – my violence had relinquished the right.

A shot shook me from introspection, a deep percussion ripping through the silence like a firecracker. Blood drained from Mallory's face, and she cast agonised eyes to the ceiling. For a moment her body seemed to be in freeze frame. Then she sprinted for the stairs. Wide and shallow, in the same dark oak as the panelling, they creaked under the thunder of her feet. She flew up them, stumbling on the topmost step, before rushing along a wide corridor with oak doors leading off. She seemed to know exactly where she was going. Down a half-stair and round a corner. Into one of the wings. The corridor opened out into a hallway, with heavy chairs and chests along its walls. In front was a double doorway. She hurled open the doors. The room within was lit only by a bedside lamp. Which was just as well.

Rex lay sprawled upon the counterpane, with a shotgun across his chest. His left cheek was shattered and his head lay in a dark pool of blood. But he was alive. His eyes flickered as Mallory ran to his side, and as she took hold of him his lips moved. "Mallory."

"I'll call an ambulance." Biting back sobs, she found her mobile.

"No!" His croak was strangely loud. "If you love me, finish it."

"He's right." Ambrose had joined them. "He wants to die."

The sight of a stricken underwriter had galvanised him.

"There's another pellet in the box," Rex whispered. An opened box of ammunition lay on the bedside table in front of two envelopes.

"No!" She turned to Ambrose. "He's alive. We can save him."

"You heard him, He wants to die." Ambrose prised the shotgun from Rex's grasp and slipped another cartridge into the empty chamber. His movements were precise and methodical. Ambrose the details man doing his stuff. Mallory tried to snatch the gun from him, but he turned away from her. "What's it to be, Rex?" His face was pale, and his eyes were more protuberant than ever.

"Just get it over with," Rex whispered, "Please."

Mallory thrust herself between Rex and the gun. "You'll have to shoot me first." Ambrose's lips contorted into a ghastly rictus.

"He cheated me." The quiet of his voice made his words all the more deadly. He gestured with the barrel. "You both did."

For an age, the scene seemed on hold. Except that I could see Mallory's breathing, the blood trickling from Rex's cheek, and the tremor of the shotgun in Ambrose's hands.

Finally, she shook her head. "If anyone does it, it'll be me." There was amazing command in her voice, and her hard stare into Ambrose's eyes was just as powerful "So give me the gun."

He drew back sulkily. "How do I know you'll do it?"

"I'll do it for him. Not for you." She got a hand to the barrel.

His moment of certainty passed. "Promise me."

"I promise." Her grip on the gun tightened. Slowly, reluctantly, Ambrose relinquished his hold. "Now leave us. This is private."

For a moment, Ambrose stood his ground. But when she gestured impatiently, he turned away. "Just do it," he said, as he retreated.

Mallory followed him to the doors to make sure they were closed. They were old with an iron bolt to lock them. She rammed it home. Then she ran back to Rex. Setting the gun on the counterpane, she seized his hand. "Please let me call an ambulance. For my sake." But though he continued slowly and shallowly to breathe, Rex was beyond speech. "You fool," she whispered. "You stupid fool."

Reaching inside her bag for her mobile, she noticed the envelopes behind the cartridge box. One was addressed to her. The flap had been tucked under, and in a moment she had extracted the note within.

As she read it, tears welled in her eyes and trickled down her face unchecked. Finally, she returned the note to its envelope and replaced it where she had found it. Then she picked up the shotgun and returned it to his hand. Carefully, she worked the barrels under his chin and curled his slack fingers around the triggers.

Even as I turned away, I remembered her words in the restaurant, when she'd described what she'd wanted me to believe was their final parting. "That was the last time I saw him alone." Ambrose outside the door had made this ultimate moment less private than a farewell feast in a restaurant. Truly, when it came to subtlety of meaning, Mallory was beyond compare. "Goodbye, my darling," she whispered now. I heard the shot as if it exploded in my brain rather than his.

When I could bear to look again, Mallory lay prostrate on the floor in all the agony of despair, and it took several minutes of furious knocking by Ambrose to rouse her sufficiently to unbolt the bedroom doors and allow him back in. He tried to embrace her, but she shrank from him. He advanced on the corpse instead and stared down at it in horrified fascination. "You should have let me do it." He licked his lips. This was no gallant quip; he seemed only disappointed that she had saved him from committing murder.

To save her ex-husband from folly, she herself had been forced to kill. Reaching for her hand under the table, I smiled encouragement. I wanted to show that I understood her abysmal dilemma, that I would have done the same. Now, at last, the terrible burden she had carried down the years weighed on me, and I struggled not to be crushed.

Thinking once more, Mallory pushed Ambrose at the bathroom. "Get some tissues. We must clean up everything we touched." He stared at her dumbly. "Unless you want to be an accessory to murder."

The thought of murder roused him, and he loped into the bathroom. The activity of the next half hour steadied them, and they worked with absolute thoroughness and attention to tiny detail, a degree of focus that few others would ever have managed.

"What about these?" His reached for the envelopes.

She pulled him back. "They're what he wanted to be found."

"One's for you." He pointed a long finger at the envelopes.

"I've read it." She threw up her hands. "For God's sake, Ambrose, think! When they find the notes, they'll assume it was a straightforward suicide. As far as the police are concerned we were never here, because they won't be expecting it. Can't you see?"

"I don't know why you brought me." His tone was sulky. His moment of decisiveness – the opportunity to kill the man who'd ruined him – had been taken from him, and it rankled.

Without answering, she surveyed the room carefully. Then she turned to Rex. "Goodbye, my love," she whispered.

Then she propelled Ambrose out of the bedroom. Outside, she cleaned the door handles with a tissue. His expression, as he watched her, was a mixture of adoration and revulsion.

She hurried him to the stairs. "Don't touch the banisters."

"Quite the little planner, aren't we?" I had never heard Ambrose sound sarcastic before.

"Rex is all I care about!" Her voice was so taut she could snap at any moment. "He wanted this to be a condemnation of Lloyd's." They reached the bottom of the stairs, and stood in the hallway, surrounded by the photographs of Rex in his pomp. "A murder would make *them* look like the victims. They'd love it. Is that what you want?"

Chapter Twenty-Four : Last On, First Off

Compared with the despondency of Saturday, Sunday night was almost pleasant. Mallory had not only allowed the hearing to continue, she had sought the comfort of my hand during the reliving of Rex's death. Though it had never occurred to me in my wildest imaginings that she'd been present, still less that she'd fired the *coup de grace*, I exonerated her entirely. Far from causing his death, she had merely made it quicker, in accordance with Rex's wishes, and all to save Ambrose from committing murder.

Surely, Monday's evidence, particularly if Ambrose was its source, could hold no real fears. It might be unpleasant for me to see and hear, and excruciating for her, but it could not sway me. Buoyed by these thoughts, I actually slept well, though as dreamlessly as on all the nights of the hearing, and I drank my coffee and made my way to the ballroom on Monday morning with something like composure.

"We've almost reached the end of the evidence," *Le Baigneur* announced. "We have but one more piece to show you."

We turned as the ballroom faded for the last time. One of the first cars onto the vast parking deck of the cross-Channel ferry was an old Peugeot Six with 74 licence plates. It was laden with cases and boxes on all the seats except the driver's. Mallory stepped out and locked the door. She was dressed for summer in pale trousers and a cotton shirt, belted at the waist. She carried a light linen jacket over her arm.

This was the Mallory with whom I was familiar, no longer the devastated young lover of Rex Tonbridge. She looked tired, but calm, as she walked purposefully towards the nearest staircase without a backward glance. She made her way to the Club lounge, and settled herself in a comfortable armchair that gave her a view of the harbour and the Channel beyond. It was a clear, calm evening with a big red sun sinking towards the French coastline. She produced her laptop from her bag. Financial pages flashed across the screen, and she was soon on her mobile, talking crisply. A steward brought her a glass of champagne, which she acknowledged gracefully, but scarcely touched.

The scene shifted back to the car deck, which was filling rapidly to capacity. Finally the ramp was empty, and the deck hands prepared to close the big doors. In the nick of time, a belated car drove in and was ushered grudgingly into the last available space. It was an old Vauxhall Senator, well maintained but undoubtedly with many miles on its clock. Out of it, a little flustered, stepped Ambrose.

Like Mallory, he was older than in yesterday's scene, but time had weighed more heavily upon him. His trousers and jacket were old and creased, and the envelope which he withdrew from his pocket and tucked fumblingly under a windscreen wiper was crumpled and dirty. He weaved his way around the parked cars between him and the stairs with an ungainly disregard for wing mirrors and door handles.

My heart pounded afresh. I realised now that this must be his fatal ferry ride. The beautiful autumnal dusk gathering across the Channel was all too familiar from my second recurring dream. With growing dread, I realised that the figure beside me on the promenade deck had never been Amy, and that the man sitting astride the rail had never been Saul. I sensed Wormsley's gloating eyes upon me, and I tried not to flinch. I gripped Mallory's hand all the more tightly. They would not cheat me into rejecting her. Never!

Ambrose wandered along each of the decks in turn. His gait may have looked haphazard, but he was clearly searching, casting those prominent eyes of his over every table in the bars and cafeterias, around every carousel in the shops. He came at last to the Club lounge.

"May I see your Club ticket, sir?" A steward approached him. Ambrose blinked as though the thought of tickets had never occurred to him. He patted his pockets, then shook his head. "You can get one from the purser, sir," the steward suggested helpfully. What was it about Ambrose that always made people want to help him?

In the quiet of the lounge, these exchanges were loud enough to rouse Mallory from her screen. For a moment her eyes met those of Ambrose. The equanimity drained from her face. Diffidently, he raised his hand, and opened his mouth as if to speak. But the steward mistook his actions as an attempt to evade the need for a ticket. "The purser's desk is on the deck below, sir." He pointed meaningfully at the door, and Ambrose reluctantly turned towards it. But he cast a last appealing glance in Mallory's direction. "Please, sir." The steward pointed again towards the door, and never once glanced at Mallory.

Once Ambrose had disappeared, Mallory fidgeted distractedly with her screen until she noticed her champagne glass. She drained it in one. Then she picked up her phone, and hesitated over making a call. That she was agitated by Ambrose's appearance was all too apparent. For what seemed like an age, she arranged and re-arranged her belongings, but her agitation only increased. Finally, she swept phone and laptop into her bag, pulled on her jacket, and headed for the door. Making her way down the stairs, she strode along the deck below towards the purser's counter, where Ambrose was waiting in a short queue.

As she walked past him her eyes indicated that he should follow. It was such a tiny gesture that Ambrose did not react to it immediately. By the time he had turned his head, Mallory was opening one of the doors to the outside. Muttering a pointless apology to the queue, he turned to follow. By the time he reached the door, Mallory had climbed the stairs to the promenade deck. There was a strong breeze, and she buttoned her jacket and pulled up the collar. The deck was deserted except for a couple giggling drunkenly in a dark corner. They took no notice of Mallory, as she moved as far from them as she could.

Ambrose clattered up the stairs. Then he wandered the deck. He peered at the couple, realised they were two rather than one, and turned away. If they noticed him, they gave no sign. Blinking in the fading light, Ambrose searched the rest of the deck until he found Mallory standing in the deep shadow of the ship's superstructure.

"Why are you pursuing me?" Her voice was low and angry.

He tried to smile. "You know why."

"We've been through this so often. I can't afford any more."

His big eyes saddened, as though he couldn't believe she could be so insensitive. "It's not the money. I want to be with you."

She shook her head. "It won't work, it never has. I'm sorry."

"I could help with Ghost Trader." He tried to sound as though he were giving impartial advice. "I'm a good businessman."

"Finance isn't your thing. You don't have the experience."

"I was right about Enron. As for the rest, I'd soon learn."

"That's what I pay Hope for. Apply to her if you need a job."

He bit his lip. His demeanour was that of utter hopelessness, and he could now only plead with those doggy eyes of his. But evidently their appeal had long been lost on Mallory, and she struggled not to look contemptuous. Seeing them like this, it was a wonder that they had ever been married. It was hard to remember that Ambrose had once been successful and that success had buoyed his self-confidence. Even in the early days of failure, he had retained the ability to make people feel sorry for him. Amy especially. A busy, successful Mallory must once have thought he was attractive enough.

"Sorry to be brutal. You're the last thing I need right now."

He reached for her, but his hand fell short. "We *were* happy."

"Were we? I can't remember." Her tone was more understanding than her words. "All I want is to get on with my life. And so should you. I'm not the only woman in the world."

"You are, so far as I'm concerned."

"What about Amy?" she demanded. I clenched my free fist under the table, whilst the other hand crushed Mallory's the harder. How could the bastard pretend that he had never cared for another woman, when he had robbed me of Amy? It didn't help that Wormsley was watching me smugly. It was all I could do not to hit him again.

"Go back to Amy, find yourself another Amy," the Mallory on the ferry told Ambrose. "I can't take it any more."

"I stood by you over Rex. I never said what really happened."

"What really happened!" She kept her voice low, but the venom in her words forced him to step back until the ship's rail dug into his back. "I saved you from yourself."

He held the rail to keep upright. "I hate living off hand-outs."

"That's not my fault."

"You got me into Lloyd's. You and Rex." His voice rose petulantly. "Between you, you ruined me twice over."

"Why do you think I set up Ghost Trader?" Her voice kept low.

In the distance the drunks laughed inanely, oblivious to anything beyond their blurry focus. But their noise reminded Ambrose to keep his voice down. "Not to save *me*. Anybody more than me."

"That's so unfair! You were a member. I made you money."

"Add it up," Ambrose persisted. "I was only wrong once. Shorting Enron on my own. Whereas you..." This was vintage Ambrose, full of pedantic detail, arguing point by point, as he had in those business presentations I'd made to him. Only the whining was new.

"I was a bad wife. I'm sorry. I got you into Lloyd's. I'm sorry again. But that's life, Ambrose. We've both suffered, not just you."

"I'd settle for getting back together. Or else, pay me off." He cocked his head slyly, as though he were presenting a fair offer

"All my profit is for the Sanatorium. As you well know."

"I'm begging you, Mallory." He slouched in front of her, craven and shameless. It was sickening , yet curiously moving. Even to me.

"I'm sorry." Her voice softened. "You know I won't let you starve. But you must let go of me. For your own sake, not just mine." She planted the briefest of kisses on his cheek, then she turned to walk away. Hidden from him, her expression was now one of disgust.

"There's nothing left for me then. That's it." The desperate tone made her pause, and as she hesitated, he heaved himself onto the rail.

Alarmed, she sprang towards him. "It's in your hands, Mallory." He swung a leg over the rail. "Do as I ask, or I'll jump."

They were face to face. Mallory on the deck, Ambrose perched precariously astride the rail. The last of the sun briefly reddened his face before it sank below the horizon, leaving only the faintest glitter in his eyes. Slowly she reached out to him, and it seemed that she had relented. Ambrose certainly thought so. With a smile of relief he leaned towards her. His eagerness was his undoing.

As his face neared hers, the movement became a parody of his intimate way of conversing. If she had suffered it before, she stiffened now. Instead of supporting him, and helping him back onto the deck, her hands thrust hard against his shoulder and pushed. For a moment he resisted, then – as eagerness turned to resignation – he accepted his fate with a sad smile as he tumbled towards the water below. He struck it head first, and sank from sight.

Immediately the scene cut, and the dusty floor and shadowy outlines of the ballroom returned. In the shock of what I had just seen, all I could think was that, even in the dream with which he had haunted me, Ambrose had lied. Not even to himself, and therefore never to me, could he admit that the love of his life had killed him.

Chapter Twenty-Five : Closing Arguments

After another dispiriting meal under the unmoving scrutiny of my guard and for which I had little appetite, I retired to the small bed by the computer screens. The snow for so long threatened was falling steadily to crown the statues in white and to bow the thickets around the cliff under a growing burden of cold, soggy flakes.

At last I understood why Mallory had been so reluctant to talk about Ambrose. Firing the *coup de grace* on Rex had been an act of mercy for the lover who did not want to prolong the agony of death; an act of mercy too for the man who would otherwise have carried the stain of murder. But pushing Ambrose off the ferry, when he had pleaded for his life and believed he had been reprieved: that was murder plain and simple. No jury would have been happy to convict her of murdering Rex: any jury would have condemned her of murdering Ambrose.

But the Court of Transition did not have a jury, and the only judges were Mallory and myself. It could be said that the evidence showed no more than another similarity in our characters: we knew now that we matched not only in intelligence and humour, that we were compatible in everything we had done together from the workplace to the bedroom, but that we also shared a propensity to violence.

We now knew that we were as capable of hatred as of love; that our hatred was most likely to turn on those whom we'd once loved. But had we learned from our secrets, or would we finally kill each other?

With such thoughts raging in my head, I fell asleep, and, for the first time since the hearing began, I found myself in a vivid dream. I was standing on the edge of the cliff beyond snow-laden foliage. Fifty metres below lay the lake, dark and still. "Tempting, isn't it?" said Mallory, who had appeared at my side, or been there all along.

"Simpler," I agreed. "I'm sure Hope and Jake can manage."

"She knows what's required, that's true," Mallory replied, though her tone was more doubtful than her words. "There's a pilot scheme in the UK she can use as a model."

The pilot scheme was news to me, but I was inured to Mallory's secrecy. I took her hand, which hung unresponsively in mine. "Just one step, a rush of wind. The cold will do the rest."

She turned to face me. Her face was deathly pale, with the bruise I had inflicted just visible in ghostly outline on her cheek. Her dark eyes reflected the moonlight, making them glitter with an unearthly and unreadable intensity. "Kiss me goodbye," she said.

Releasing her hand, I took her in my arms. We embraced, like old friends about to go our separate ways. As she drew back, her face was full of sadness and compassion, but her eyes were hidden in shadow. Her hands rested lightly on my chest. "I'm sorry, Clem, I hope you understand. But it has to be this way." My back was now to the cliff. Her mouth firmed, her arms straightened and her hands pushed my shoulders hard. I toppled backwards into the void.

I seemed to fall forever, and just as I was sure I must hit the water, I found myself in a tangle of sheet and duvet. The only moisture was cold sweat. I lay in the darkness, not sure if I were still alive, let alone awake. I could hear Rex talking urgently into my ear, though I couldn't see him, however much I turned my head. "Like I said, Clem, don't ever let her think you're a failure. I was the love of her life long before you, and you saw what she did to me." Then I sank into sleep so heavy that it might as well have been death.

When I woke, the room was bathed in ghostly grey. It had been so dark when I went to bed that I'd forgotten to pull down the blind. It was almost dawn, and the snow had finally stopped. The lake was a dark gash amidst endless shades of white. As in the mist on the morning of the second day, we seemed marooned in nothingness.

The apartment was profoundly silent. Mallory, normally the first to wake, must still be asleep. I dressed slowly and made my way down the spiral stair to the kitchen. My guard followed me down, and watched my every move with the coffee pot, but I had become used to his presence and ignored him. Fortified by coffee, I made my way to the hall and out the front door. Under a deep layer of snow, the Peugeot and the Citroen were indistinguishable mounds, and the snow was deep enough on the drive to be above the first few steps.

Without boots, it was no weather for a stroll, but I enjoyed the still, sharp cold on my face, and I watched as a snow plough made its brisk way up the road from the village. Its speed and raw power as it cast the snow aside were proof of the living world beyond the gates, as well as a reminder that it remained within reach. In the meantime, it was eight o'clock, with two hours to wait until the hearing re-opened.

Shivering, I made my way back inside. With nothing else to do for the next two hours, I toured the building, trying to see it through Jake's eyes. The renovation now looked less daunting, and the more I examined the basic structure the more solid it seemed. Even the topmost floors, under the roofs, were dry. The tiling remained sound. I yearned for ordinary life again, and I chafed at the idea of sitting through another day. At least there would be nothing to do other than listen to the closing arguments of Wormsley and *L'Esprit*.

At 9:30, I made my way slowly to the ballroom. It seemed empty, though I had a subliminal sense of the watchers and the court officials, present but choosing not to be visible. My guard stationed himself by the door, to prevent Mallory arriving too early and, as the minutes ticked away, I stood beyond the dais by the long window.

The sun was well up, and the Alpine peaks on the far side of the lake stood out sharply against the deepening blue of the sky. No footprints disturbed the snow that carpeted the garden. Last night's dream had been a proper dream, not a window onto another reality. But whether it signified nothing more than the anxieties of an overwrought brain or whether it had the prophetic qualities of my first recurring nightmares I had no idea, and I preferred not to think about it too deeply.

"Good morning, Monsieur."

I turned to find *Le Baigneur* seated at the head of the table. Wormsley and *L'Esprit* slowly solidified next to him, their backs to where I was standing. After them, with their usual shuffling and snuffling, came the watchers around the walls. All we awaited now was Mallory. Acknowledging *Le Baigneur*'s greeting, I walked round the table to my usual place. As I did so, the double doors were pushed open, and Mallory entered next to her guard. One look at her gaunt face told me that her night had been as disturbing as my own.

"Good morning, Madame."

She acknowledged the court with a curt nod. Only then did she look at me. A smile animated the corners of her mouth, and she managed a tiny hello. Then she sat down stiffly. "Today is for these gentlemen to sum up everything we have seen, is it not?" Her voice strengthened as she addressed *Le Baigneur*. "Could I ask that we waste as little time as possible on these summaries?"

"I agree," I said, finding her hand under the table. Her response was no more than a brief tremor of the fingers, depressingly reminiscent of last night's dream. I tried to reassure myself that she was as worn down by the hearing as I was, and that she was not rejecting me.

"The process is what it is." *Le Baigneur*'s shrug was impatient. "Rest assured that I will not allow proceedings to over-run." He then turned to *L'Esprit*. "I believe we are to hear first from you, Monsieur Linberger. I'm sure you will bear the supplicants' wishes in mind."

263

Gathering copious notes into his hands, *L'Esprit* sprang elegantly to his feet, and stood almost to attention before us.

"I don't ask either of you, Monsieur or Madame, to ignore the negative aspects of your lives, but I urge you to dwell most on the positives. You are intelligent, thoughtful people with much still to contribute to society. The development of this place, for a start." He spread his arms to encompass the building and its grounds. "Your intentions for the future are selfless and admirable. You have plenty of friends and supporters able and willing to assist you. Thanks to the efforts of your daughter, Madame, and to those of your son, Monsieur, you have considerable public support. It would be a tragedy to throw away everything now, when the achievement lies within reach."

He expatiated on our accomplishments. He spelt out how successful we had been, and how adaptable we were in the face of challenges. Then he reminded us how well our characters dovetailed, and how well we had worked together over the shorting. Our combined strength, he assured us, was yet greater than the sum of our separate parts.

"I know, Monsieur Holden, that you feel that you have wasted ten years, but those days are over. Since Madame Stellenbourg came into your life, you have been inspired. As for you, Madame, you have faced many tragedies in your life, and since the death of your lover and the fall from the ferry of your ex-husband your life has been an act of expiation. Monsieur Holden has at last given you the chance and the inspiration to live positively again."

He outlined the aims we sought to achieve with the Sanatorium, and he reminded us in some detail how many of our friends were eager to lend their many and varied skills to our cause. "To live for others need not exclude your own happiness. Indeed, it should not. You are likely to work harder and more productively when you are secure in your private lives, just as your happiness will increase knowing that you are working together in a good cause."

He laid his notes upon the table and leaned towards us, his expression sombre. "You have both done bad things." He reprised our misdeeds briefly and factually. "But in your different ways you have atoned." He reminded us that by hitting Wormsley I had lost more of my fortune than might otherwise have been the case; that by hitting Amy I had forfeited my marriage; whilst Mallory had devoted all of her life since the deaths of Ambrose and Rex to the benefit of others.

"I urge you now not to be defeated by your mistakes, but to learn from them. Vow to yourself, Monsieur, that you will never be violent again; believe, Madame, that he means it because he loves and respects you as he has never loved or respected anyone else. Trust, Monsieur, that Mallory loves and honours you too much ever to hurt you; trust, too, that you will never jeopardise her respect in the manner of poor Monsieur Hanter. Nor, I am sure, are you ever likely to be suicidal, and not therefore in need of euthanasia by her hand. Accept, both of you, that you are what you are: perfectly compatible without being perfect. Do not, I implore you, pass up the singular opportunity that only together you have made possible."

If a little preachy for my liking, it had been an uplifting speech, and Mallory's hand finally responded to mine with an exhilarating clasp. More heartening still was the smile that kindled a spark of warmth in her eyes and brought a touch of colour to her cheek. In my euphoria, I even forgave him for taking up the whole of the morning. Indeed, the time had passed so quickly that I was surprised when *Le Baigneur* called the mid-day adjournment.

As usual we picked at our food in silence, knowing that we had Wormsley's closing argument yet to endure. He sat quietly enough, but with an expression of unnerving certainty on his face, as he doubtless practised the most damning phraseology in his mind. He was ready promptly, and scarcely waited for the lunch things to clear, or for *Le Baigneur*'s nod, before he was launched into his opening arguments. Just as *L'Esprit* had done, he began with our early careers, but with a view to showing us the developing flaws in our characters.

It seemed that I had felt constrained by the precision of accounting, and the rigour of the law. Far from seeking liberation and lateral thinking, I had sought advertising only to learn how best to manipulate my peers. Far from applying myself to the marketing tasks that my Paris job required, I had annoyed my board by telling them their business. In short, I was a control freak, whose self-appointed mission was to order the lives of others. Like so many, I'd joined Lloyd's because I'd thought it was easy money; but unlike those who had met their obligations, I had used devious tricks to evade paying.

On the personal side, I'd been lucky enough to marry a loving and intelligent wife. Indeed, it was thanks to her that my consultancy business had got off to such a flying start. In return I had belittled her, ignoring her warnings over Lloyd's and sleeping with Sidonie at the first opportunity. "Only to comfort her," he added sarcastically.

"Yet it was to Sidonie that Clem turned as soon as he moved to France. Fortunately for her, Sidonie understood his true nature, and put aside any ideas of marrying him, despite both being now divorced, and despite the fact that Marie-Sainte was very likely his child."

"You can't possibly know that," I yelled.

"Look at the facts," he replied. "You occupied adjacent apartments, which you treated as one. You installed an intercom, so Marie-Sainte could be safely asleep in hers, whilst you and Sidonie cavorted in the other. Marie-Sainte even asked if you were to be her new father…"

"As in step-father. She knew I wasn't her real father."

"She knew only what her mother was prepared to tell her."

"This is hearsay, not evidence." I appealed to *Le Baigneur*. "Surely you can't allow this innuendo?" Yet even as I protested, I was torn by opposing emotions: joy at the idea of Marie-Sainte being perhaps much more than a friend; dismay at the effect these revelations must be having on Mallory. How often had I bemoaned her secrecy without once grasping that I had scarcely been more candid with her.

"Plausible hypothesis, Mr Chairman," Wormsley answered. "Sidonie even put their apartment sharing onto a permanent footing. She did everything, in fact, to ensure that Marie-Sainte was close to her father throughout her childhood: everything that is except marry him."

Le Baigneur nodded thoughtfully. "The court allows plausible hypothesis where relevant, and it seems to me that your relationship to your neighbour's daughter is a relevant factor." He turned to Mallory. "May we take it, Madame, that this is news to you?"

Mallory was a picture of confusion, as her scrutiny darted from one of us to the other. "If it's as relevant as Monsieur Wormsley seems to think, I'd like to hear the story from Clem." She threw me a contorted smile. "I think you owe me that, at least."

Wormsley promptly objected that any explanation from me would constitute conferring. "If I have to hear it from you, I don't want to hear it at all," she retorted. "If you thought this was important you ought to have introduced it earlier, instead of sneaking it into your closing argument." She appealed to *Le Baigneur*. "Please support me."

"Madame Stellenbourg is right," *L'Esprit* agreed. "New evidence about Monsieur Holden must come in his own words."

"Do you have a replay we could see?" *Le Baigneur* asked Wormsley. Shamefacedly, he admitted that he did not. "Then I will grant Madame Stellenbourg's request." He turned to me. "Please tell us succinctly about your relations with your neighbour and her daughter."

I did my best, but I felt anything but comfortable. Wormsley's scepticism I could manage, and I had become inured to the subliminal whispering of the watchers; what was dreadful was trying in public to make Mallory understand my strange relations with Sidonie.

"Sidonie is one of my closest friends, but we both knew we could never live together permanently. I can't explain how we knew, but we did. I'm glad she married Armand, because I know they're happy together, and he's a great step-father. For what it's worth, I like him for himself. He's been a good friend and an excellent neighbour."

"So if you're Marie-Sainte's father, it must have been the result of that one night?" Mallory shook her head in bemusement. "Surely Sidonie would have said, wouldn't she?"

"I honestly don't know. Sidonie's never been a great one for revelations. She might have felt it was best if I didn't know." I shrugged carefully. "It's equally possible she doesn't know for certain herself. She was still married to her first husband at the time."

"Would you like to be Marie-Sainte's father?" Mallory asked, as she struggled to decide which answer would disturb her less.

"If she wanted it too, I'd be very happy. She means a lot to me."

"What about Sidonie? Does she also mean a lot to you?"

The rest of the ballroom was forgotten. All I cared was that Mallory should understand the way it was. Those dark eyes of hers were sharp and penetrating, yet they were sorrowful rather than angry. It seemed that she wanted to understand. "As a friend, absolutely. As a lover, no." I sighed. "I should have told you before. I'm sorry I didn't."

A spasm of pain clouded her brow, and her eyes took on their familiar shuttered look. "I'm the last person…" she began, then trailed into silence. But before I could speak, she turned abruptly to *Le Baigneur*. "I think we should move on, *Monsieur Le Maitre*."

"Fine by me," I concurred thankfully.

"Monsieur Wormsley, I suggest you proceed," *Le Baigneur* instructed coldly. "I trust there will be no more new evidence."

Wormsley leaned on the table, with eyes only for Mallory. "I want you to consider now the darker side of Clem's character. Whenever he's thwarted – by Lloyd's, by Amy, even by you – he resorts to violence. Don't fool yourself that he'd be any different in future."

He stroked his misshapen nose. "Imagine what he'd be like if he were paralysed. So long as he could lift an arm, you'd be in physical danger. Even if he were powerless, the psychological damage he could wreak would be immense. Being married to Ambrose was bad enough for you, but at least Ambrose was gentle and understanding. Ambrose may have been a lamb ripe for shearing, but Clem is a ravening wolf. You'd do well to fear him. By comparison, death is nothing."

He paused, milking the silence that followed. I wanted to take Mallory's hand again, but found that I couldn't. If she'd been swayed by Wormsley's speech, no amount of caressing on my part would help. I sat rigidly and wretchedly, lost in a tangle of conflicting thoughts. Next to me, Mallory seemed to be faring no better.

Wormsley resumed in a quieter voice. The soft voice of reason. "If I've been hard on you, Clem, it's only for your own good. The good of you both. It's all too easy to take a romantic decision that you will only live to regret. Either or both of you. It's the same reason I was hard on Names. In the end, realism is the only approach that pays." He sighed. "Which is why, Clem, I must now be hard on Mallory."

He then began his review of her earlier career. By his reckoning, she was ambitious, quick to learn, and capable of brilliant insights, that rare person who made sure of the details of an operation without losing sight of the goal. "An uncommon gift," he conceded, "but dangerous when the one thing Mallory lacks is a moral compass. Cheating her investors or rescuing them, it's all one to her. What matters is the difficulty and danger of the challenge, not its moral direction.

"To her, investing was more exciting than underwriting, and embezzlement through bogus trusts and unclaimable reinsurance was more exciting still. As for the great shorting exercise, what could be better than ruining the financial world at the same time as keeping it hidden from her members? One has to ask how setting up and running the Sanatorium could possibly match up. At what point in the future will she become simply bored with the whole thing, and run off with what's left in the kitty? She's good at running off, as we know.

"As with business, so with her personal life. When she met Ambrose, he seemed successful enough. But Rex was far more of a challenge. Already married, already more successful, and already in need of her skills. So Ambrose was abandoned, even though her daughter was small and in need of a stable home. Small wonder Mallory's parents never forgave her. To salve her conscience, perhaps, she persuaded him to join Lloyd's. He – poor fool – accepted her advice, because he assumed that when it came to risk, she was the expert. But she was careful only over the risks to which she herself was exposed. Ambrose could take his chance with the other Names, whilst she and Rex plundered the syndicate's reserves.

"Then when the losses finally came home to roost, it was Rex not Mallory who had an attack of conscience. It was Rex not Mallory who wanted the money returned to Names; it was Rex not Mallory who committed suicide out of shame for what had been done. And it was only Rex's death in all its peculiar circumstances – and, I submit, the scrutiny to which the syndicate's financial affairs were subjected as a result – that shook her into setting up Ghost Trader. Yes, she undoubtedly helped loss-making Names to restore their fortunes, but she also kept herself out of gaol, as well as earning good fees.

"Mallory is a fascinating woman, and she has ensnared you, Clem, just as surely as she ensnared Ambrose and Rex. Never forget what happened to them. Doubtless you'd like to believe that she killed Rex as an act of mercy. But had her intentions been truly merciful, she would have called an ambulance. Who knows, Rex might be alive today. Had she acted purely to put a dying man out of his misery, she would have admitted what happened to the police. Instead, she covered the crime with all the care of which she is so capable. I put it to you that she was just as strongly motivated to be rid of him. As he warned you only the other day, she does not tolerate failure.

"Of all Ghost Trader's member, who was the only loser? Ambrose. Her ex-husband, the man whom she had already wronged. Not only did she ignore his Enron recommendation, which would have earned him and all the other members a huge profit, she allowed him to quit and to ruin himself. She had the trading clout which he lacked, but because he'd had the temerity to spot an opportunity she missed, she abandoned him, to ruin himself anew by shorting Enron on his own.

"Finally, years later, when he was at his wit's end, pleading with her to take him back, she pushed him off the ferry, as we've seen. For that callous act there can be no extenuating circumstance."

He pointed an accusing finger at Mallory. Her face was a mask, yet she managed to outstare him, forcing him to turn again to me.

"If she lives, she'll give you no more love than she gave to Ambrose or even to Rex. Forget your fantasy relationship. She is incapable of the personal love for which you crave. She is an unscrupulous manipulator who stops short of nothing to achieve her goals. You say you came here to bring her back, but after all you've seen I urge you to change your mind. You have lived a brief fantasy together, and that should be enough. For the real world, this heartbreaker, this speculator is not a woman that any sensible man would restore to life. As for this place, your son and her daughter will serve it better."

He sat down to an outburst of whispering from the watchers, who were not brought to order until *Le Baigneur* threatened to eject them. He then addressed himself to Mallory and myself.

"The court has presented its evidence, and my colleagues have put their closing arguments to you. We shall adjourn for today to give you time to consider your final judgements. When we reassemble in the morning, you may each present your judgement in as much detail as you choose. We shall toss a coin to decide which of you speaks first. In the meantime, you are – as before – forbidden to confer."

Mallory may have out-stared Wormsley during the climax of his peroration, but now her face was shrouded in misery. It came to me that Wormsley's ruthless bad-mouthing of us was more cunning than malevolent. He had sought not only to sow doubts in our minds about the other's true worth, but also – perhaps primarily – to play on our guilt. By painting us as heartless dissemblers, whose preferred solution to every problem was dishonesty, and whose likely answer to setback was violence, he wished to convince us that we deserved nothing more than the deaths to which we had come so close.

Now, as I watched her mounting despair, I grasped why Wormsley had pressed so vociferously for the embargo on conferring. Far from believing her to be a heartless destroyer, he knew how vulnerable she was to the poison of guilt. The hair-shirted existence in the boathouse now made perfect sense. Her inability for so long to accept my love, and her ambivalence even after she had given way to her feelings, had never been any reflection on me, but driven by her own self-disgust. I quailed at the thought of her brooding alone on her judgement.

Even the first day's replay of the accident had been designed to weaken our resolve, but hers especially. How carefully had Wormsley rubbed in that she was the more seriously injured, and how brilliantly had his warnings been tuned to her acute sense of risk. The full import of his argument, which none would understand better than she, was that even if she deserved to survive – which she did not; even if she chose to survive for my sake – which I did not merit; our happiness together would yet be thwarted by brain-damage or paralysis.

My yearning for her intensified even as my hopes of a future together ebbed away. My one chance of conquering her scruples was to speak first tomorrow, but the chance of that was 50% at best, zero if Wormsley were able to rig the odds. I had to speak out now.

"The court wishes our judgements to be independent when they can't be. As Monsieur Linberger has argued, and as the court has accepted, we are here because our dreams are entwined. But if we've been keeping each other alive all this time, we have the right to decide together whether we live or die. That is not only just, it is embedded in the logic of our situation. If the first speaker tomorrow is me, I don't want to make a choice at odds with Mallory's. There are no precedents, *Monsieur Le Maitre*. I appeal to you to use your just discretion."

"Too late," Wormsley said. "The ruling must stand."

"Monsieur Holden's right, there is no precedent," said *L'Esprit*.

"Not quite," pronounced *Le Baigneur*. "You yourself cited Orpheus and Eurydice. You will remember, therefore, that he was forbidden to look back as he led her to the surface. Whether legend or history, the story shows the existence of a right and a power to impose constraints. Orpheus was forbidden to look back; in these more enlightened times, the constraint of the court is more balanced, in that it applies equally to both parties." He turned to me. "The court hears what you say, Monsieur, but its ruling will not be lifted. You may not confer."

Desperate measures were called for, and I finally lost my temper. "That's ridiculous," I shouted. "If I'm living in a dream world, at least it's my dream. You're all dead. But for me, you don't exist. It's my dream and from now on you'll play by my rules."

The watchers growled, *L'Esprit* looked horrified, even Wormsley seemed lost for words. Not so *Le Baigneur*. Like any chairman, he reacted robustly to challenge. "Have a care, Monsieur Holden," he answered sternly, "unless you wish your lives to be terminated this instant." The awfulness of his tone as much as his words made me pause. For all my brash outburst, I could never put Mallory at risk. "There will be consequences for your contempt, on which I shall have more to say tomorrow. Until then, I suggest you remain silent."

"It's my dream, too." Mallory marched for the doors. "I'll give you my judgement when I'm good and ready."

Chapter Twenty-Six : Judgement & Ruling

That Tuesday night was one of the worst I'd ever lived through. The more I reviewed what had happened and what had been said during the day, the more convinced I became that Mallory would choose to end it all. My final outburst, and the rebuke it had earned, confirmed the violent and controlling character that Wormsley had attributed to me. The court was part of my dream, but it was not solely my dream, and I had no more right to control it than Mallory. I should have remembered Rex's warning, on the night of our first encounter with the Court of Transition, that dreams were always out of our control.

I saw everything now through Mallory's eyes. I understood only too well the revulsion she felt against herself. Though she might have connived in embezzlement, she was ruthlessly honest when it came to self-appraisal. She understood that I forgave her for Rex's death, she suspected that I would also forgive her for pushing Ambrose off the ferry, but she could never absolve herself. Only the urge for penitence had kept her going since. But now that the task of rescuing her members had been fulfilled; now that the Sanatorium had been acquired, and the blueprint for its development had been drawn up, the task of running it could be left to others. Knowing that she was close to death, she was inevitably tempted to let go.

Ordinarily, she would have excused my temper and my urge to control, sure that I loved her enough to refrain from either, and that she was strong enough to curb any lapse. But in her current mood, the doubtful aspects of my character would only reinforce the self-destructive judgement she was predisposed to make.

If anything, loving me only made matters worse. If hers must be a life of expiation, it held no place for the joys of love. If she still toyed with the idea of a future with me, she did so for my sake rather than for her own. She might pretend to be happy to please me; she would struggle to be happy for herself. If this really were what she thought, there was no way I could plead for her to live for my sake alone. I must release her with good grace, to prove my love by dying alongside her. If there was to be any hope of a future together, I had to convince her that she was far from worthless, that forgiveness was always achievable,

272

and that personal happiness was not only compatible with serving the Sanatorium, but would strengthen her in the task.

I would not only have to make the speech of my life, I would have to make it first. By midnight, I had made little progress in either direction. For my judgement I knew what had to be said, but I struggled for the right words to express it, just as I lacked the clinching argument to ensure that I could speak first if Mallory won the coin toss.

The last thing I wanted was to fall asleep with matters unresolved, yet that is what happened. Just when sleep was the last thing I needed, when my brain was in sufficient ferment to make it impossible, I sank into exhausted and dispiriting oblivion. Such dreams as there were came in sporadic fragments: happy moments with Mallory and with Marie-Sainte, trivial in themselves, made significant only by the doubt that hung over their ever being repeated.

I awoke in the pale darkness of a cloudless night. I felt as though I were floating weightlessly under the great canopy of the Milky Way, so clear that the visible stars were without number, from those as huge as gemstones to mere specks, noticeable only in their unchanging lustre. I drew strength from their unearthly and ageless presence, until slowly their fire re-ignited the dying embers of my courage. By the time dawn blushed the peaks of the distant Alps, I knew what I had to say. Finally, I fell properly asleep, and when I next woke, the sun was bright upon the snow outside and I felt refreshed and hopeful.

Faint sounds from below told me that Mallory was taking her breakfast. Sure enough, when I opened the door with my towel across my shoulder, my guard turned down the stairs, indicating that the bathroom was free. I showered deliberately under cold water to wake me up, and then I towelled myself vigorously dry. By the time I was dressed and making coffee, I felt ready for anything. My euphoria carried me through breakfast and into the ballroom. But the grim whisperings of the watchers and the stony faces of the officials immediately had my stomach churning anew. Nevertheless, I made my way to the dais with a show of dignity. Mallory had her back to me, but I could see that she too was apprehensive.

"Good morning," I said pleasantly, glancing quickly at each of the three officials before offering Mallory a hesitant smile. "Our turn at last." She managed a quick smile in return. It was almost her old grin, except that her face was pale and her eyes solemn.

Before sitting down, I addressed myself to *Le Baigneur*. "I must apologise, *Monsieur Le Maitre*, for my outburst yesterday. It was quite uncalled for, and I can only offer the strain of the past week as its cause. I accept whatever punishment you feel to be appropriate."

He acknowledged me with an almost imperceptible nod. "Thank you, Monsieur. I shall, of course, return to the matter, but for the moment I wish us to proceed with your judgements. Does either of you have a desire to go first, or are you happy for us to toss a coin?"

"I think Clem should speak first," said Mallory in a quiet but clear voice. "He came here to find me, and he insisted on placing himself under the jurisdiction of the court, when he didn't have to do either. I think that earns him the right to speak first."

Delighted at this sudden turn for the better, I thanked her for her understanding, before deferring once more to *Le Baigneur*. "I should be happy to go first, *Monsieur Le Maitre*, but I shall, of course, be governed by your decision in the matter."

Le Baigneur raised a quizzical eyebrow to *L'Esprit*, who signalled his acquiescence. "What about you, Monsieur Wormsley?"

"I believe, *Mr Chairman*, that Ms Stellenbourg, as the more injured, has more right to speak first. Mr Holden is a persuasive man, particularly where she is concerned, and I would hate for her to be talked into a decision she may live to regret."

"I'm not a fool," Mallory said with some heat. "Of course I intend to listen to what Clem has to say, but my decision will be my own." She appealed to *Le Baigneur*. "Monsieur Wormsley said more than enough yesterday, and I don't think he has any right to influence matters further. Even if I won the toss, I'd prefer Clem to speak first."

Le Baigneur did not hide a smile. "The court is all ears, Monsieur."

"Monsieur Wormsley is right about one thing, Mallory," I began, "the final choice should be yours. I want you to listen to what I have to say, but I don't want to persuade you to anything against your better judgement. Whatever you finally decide, I'll happily go along with it. Because the one thing I'm sure we agree on is that we're in this together. We both choose life, or neither of us does. Whichever way we choose, we won't be parted from each other." I turned to *Le Baigneur*. "It's what I meant, *Monsieur Le Maitre*, when I said that our decisions could never be independent." He remained impassive.

"The case for life has been eloquently put by *Monsieur L'Esprit*," I continued. "We work well together; we've proved it the hard way. Our temperaments match and complement each other perfectly. Developing this place will need inspiration, not just hard work. Together we can bring that extra ingredient to make the difference between success and failure. Of course, Hope and Jake could do it, but they have their own careers. They'll be happier contributing than masterminding. As for the final direction, this is your brainchild, and I've no intention of trying to take over. Sometimes I'll disagree with you, but I'll never go against you, any more than I did over the shorting. I've been accused of being a control freak, but I'm not mad.

"That may not sound very romantic, but Monsieur Wormsley has warned against taking romantic decisions, and I know how important the Sanatorium is to you. I'm sure you know just as well how much you mean to me. Before you came into my life, I was a selfish loser. You've taught me that I'm not the only victim in the world, that most of the others have suffered more. In doing so, you've given me a cause to believe in. I won't deny my temper, nor the violence it can lead to, even against you. I can't promise I'll never lose my temper again, but I promise to keep the lid on it. My feelings are as strong as ever.

"But I don't love you blindly. I know what you've done, and I'm not asking you to forget those things or pretend they never happened. All I ask is that you put them in perspective. You've more than paid back your Names. The slate there is clean. As for Rex, he was already dying from his own hand. You couldn't have saved him, but you spared his suffering, and you saved Ambrose from committing murder.

"Knowing you, I'm sure you feel worst over Ambrose. You've told me often enough, even though you couldn't bring yourself to go into detail. So I'll do it for you now. You feel bad about not loving him. But not loving your husband is regrettable – for you both; it's not a crime. You feel bad about falling for someone else. Join the club. Ambrose and I are already members, and he doesn't even have the excuse of loving Amy, nor I of loving Sidonie. Feel bad if you must, but don't feel unique. Rest assured that when I first met Ambrose he wasn't bitter about the divorce, nor did he blame you. Nor does your daughter, who's steadfastly refused to let the hospital switch off your life support. Hope loves you, and she wants you back.

"Ambrose was right over Enron, and you were wrong, but not morally wrong, and you had your other members to think about. Ambrose was foolish to resign from Ghost Trader, and he was stupid to short on his own. At least kept him afloat afterwards."

I had spoken exclusively to Mallory, and the rest of the ballroom had fallen so completely silent that they had almost faded from view. For her part, her eyes never left me, and her expression had gradually softened. But now, her brow clouded once more.

"I still pushed him from the ferry. I don't know what you're going to say, but there's no excuse that I can see."

Le Baigneur sprang back into sharp focus. "You shall have your turn, Madame, but you must refrain from interrupting Monsieur Holden." She hung her head in apology.

"No matter, *Monsieur Le Maitre*," I assured him. "Mallory was only drawing attention to the importance of my next point." I appealed to her again. "When we first learned of the court, we were told that the only witnesses would be Ambrose and Rex. We've heard plenty from Rex, but Ambrose has only appeared in the replays, not as a direct witness. There can be one reason only for that: Monsieur Wormsley knew he'd never say anything against you under cross-examination."

Wormsley opened his mouth to protest, but *Le Baigneur* frowned him into silence. I pressed on. "Not just because he loves you, but because the Ambrose I knew as a friend was always scrupulously fair. He knows, better than I've described, that there's nothing really bad he could say about you, and he would never lie simply to satisfy Monsieur Wormsley. Even about his last ferry ride."

She looked up again now, her face a battlefield of emotions. She wanted to believe me, yet she feared still that she wouldn't be able to. But she was listening intently to every word.

"If he'd testified, he'd have had to admit that when he drove onto the ferry he was planning to commit suicide. We all saw him leave his note under the windscreen wiper. It was for the captain, apologising for any inconvenience, explaining he had nothing left to live on or to live for. I know that because it was in all the newspaper reports. I've no doubt he hoped that he might convince you to take him back, but he knew it was unlikely. He pleaded with you nonetheless, not because he really expected you to change your mind, but because he was desperate.

"When you told him it wouldn't work, you told him nothing he wasn't expecting. When he perched himself on the rail, he was only doing what he'd intended all along. But he couldn't resist one last desperate piece of moral blackmail. 'Take me back or I'll jump.'

"It was never going to work, and you did what you'd done for Rex; you administered the *coup de grace* because he couldn't manage it himself. Of course you feel remorse, of course it'll haunt you, but you needn't let it defeat you. What you did was understandable. It was the opposite of unpardonable. I'd have done the same myself.

"That's important, because it's me you're going to have to live with, and there's no way I'll ever point an accusing finger. Once Ambrose knew his affair with Amy was out in the open, he was wise to keep away from me. Otherwise, who knows what I might have done to him. For me, there's no moral high ground from which to condemn you.

"The past can't be undone. But the future is open. I don't know what it holds, but I'm certain restoring the Sanatorium is a worthy project, and always will be. There are always victims, though I gave them too little thought until now. I'm just as certain you deserve the rest of your natural life. For better or for worse, for richer or for poorer, in sickness probably, in health perhaps, I want us to live together, to do the best for ourselves and for the victims of disasters not of their making."

There was an excited buzz from the watchers, who seemed to have set aside their normal hostility. It was an encouraging sign. But it was not them I needed to convince. I tried to smile at Mallory, but I was too tense. The decision was now out of my hands.

Slowly I sat down, and waited for her to speak. For some time, she simply stared into her lap. But just as *Le Baigneur* was commanding her to begin, she stood and faced me, her eyes bright with tears.

"Thank you," she said in a low voice. "You understand me all too well, and I think you got most of it right." With this promising start, her voice strengthened, and I dared to hope. "Of course I should never have embezzled, but I know I've repaid Names in full through Ghost Trader. There at least my conscience is clear. As for Rex, I try to think what I did was right, though I hated having to do it." She couldn't suppress a shudder. "I hope you can understand why I never told you. I couldn't bear you thinking badly of me. You were so implacable over Lloyd's, I was afraid everything with you was absolutely black or white.

"It took me a long time to appreciate your tolerant side, you hide it so well." She managed a nervous laugh. "Admittedly, you were always generous about Amy, but that only reminded me that I must live up to her to win your approval. Yesterday, you showed great understanding for Sidonie, and I'm delighted you aren't ashamed of Marie-Sainte. But the clincher was what you said to Rex.

"Not many men in your shoes would have paid my ex-lover the tributes you did even though he exemplifies the part of Lloyd's that ruined you. So I wasn't surprised by your judgement. The generous words of a loving man." Her voice shook, and she paused to compose herself. Then her brow darkened, and her next sentence was short and uncompromising. "But you got it wrong over Ambrose."

Until this moment I had scarcely been able to breathe. Now a terrible calm came over me. She was letting me down gently. As I'd known she would all along, she was about to elect for death. I felt like Ambrose, smiling as he resigned himself headfirst to his fate.

"Yes, Ambrose had an issue with fairness," she continued, "but only because it played to his vindictive streak. He resented you as much as he admired you, and shagging Amy was his way of paying you back. Yes, he helped me cover up how Rex died, but he blackmailed me ever after. Insidiously, like he did on the ferry. I came to France when I could stand no more. I thought the boathouse would be hard to find, but he managed to track down the right ferry. As for suicide, I think your original guess was right. He meant to fake it, so he could hunt down his persecutors. The reason he wasn't cross-examined here is that he's still alive. Either way, I'm sure he *wanted* me to push him.

"Do I regret it? Of course. But, if I'm brutally honest, more for what it made me than for what it did to him. Yet it was only when Clem came to find me that I learnt what I'd done to you gentlemen." She bowed her head to Wormsley, *L'Esprit* and *Le Baigneur*. "If I'd spared Ambrose, you'd all be alive. You said you weren't here to judge me, but I think you must. I defer my judgement to you."

For a moment or two there was absolute silence, as the entire courtroom struggled to make sense of what she had just said. It was broken first by *L'Esprit*. "It was Ambrose who killed me," he said even as she was sitting down again, and long before I could take in the import of what she'd just decided. "That was his vindictiveness at work, not yours. I think from everything that has been said, you remain free to judge for yourself. As for my opinion as to how you should judge, you have that already." He even smiled.

Le Baigneur nodded solemnly. "As chief officer of the court, I have no power to take your decision for you. But if you want my opinion as a private individual, I agree entirely with Monsieur Linberger. You retain the right to choose, and you are free to choose life."

All eyes now fell on Wormsley, who surprised us all by throwing back his head and laughing. "You never cease to amaze me, Mallory. You've sat here enduring my diatribes against you and Clem for the past five days, yet you pass your decision back to me." He learned forwards again, and his demeanour was now stern. "I've said all along that I too have an issue with fairness, though Names did not always choose to believe me. But, unlike Ambrose, I do not have a vindictive streak. I never sought more than Names owed, and I took no pleasure in their suffering. My colleagues are quite right. Ambrose is responsible for his own actions. He chose to kill us, you did not. So of course you must judge for yourself. As for how you should judge, I am not in a position to advise you. Ball back in your court, I'm afraid."

Care and guilt faded, and she gave me a smile that not even Rex could have hoped to see. Then she took my hand, and we stood side by side. "We choose life." A ragged cheer broke from the watchers.

Le Baigneur rapped the table with the gavel which appeared in his hand. "Let the record show that the choice of both Mallory Mai Stellenbourg and Clem Holden before the Court of Transition is life." He also stood, and he extended a hand to each of us. "As to health and happiness, I make no promises, but I certainly wish you luck." Releasing our hands, he resumed his seat, and his formal manner.

"Before I close the hearing, there remains the matter of Monsieur Holden's contempt. Throughout this hearing he has demonstrated that he is both independent and resourceful. He came here with the intention of taking Madam Mallory back to her daughter. Normally, this would have been achieved by your returning to your beds in the tower and falling asleep. Then, instead of dreaming of your hospital room, you would have woken there in physical reality.

"Instead, I rule that Monsieur Holden fulfil another task. He must return you both safely to the hospital by physical means." He consulted his watch. "It is now just the lunch hour, and you probably wish to feed yourselves. Your actions from now on are your own. You have your car, and you have until 10 a.m. tomorrow before your life supports are switched off." He smiled. "I trust the task is not too onerous."

I looked at Mallory, and she threw her arms around me, her expression full of happiness and laughter. "It's not onerous at all. Especially not for you. I'll be driving."

Le Baigneur turned to his colleagues, who were also smiling. I had never seen Wormsley so benign. "I believe we're done. Madame Stellenbourg, perhaps soon to be Madame Holden, should be left in possession of her property." As he spoke the crowd of onlookers faded slowly away until we could not see or hear them. Next went our gaolers and all the physical paraphernalia of the court. "After you," *Le Baigneur* continued, ushering us to precede him to the doors. "We shall return to the car." Our footsteps echoed in the empty room.

As we saw them off, *L'Esprit* glanced up at the sky, which was darkening with cloud. "It's going to snow. I suggest you get moving as soon as you can. Traffic can be very bad when it's snowing." He used the word *méchant*, which seemed a trifle excessive, though I wasn't about to argue with him. The sooner we got to the hospital the better.

The snow on the drive had been largely cleared away, presumably by the watchers, so that the Citroen made easy progress to the gate and onto the snow-ploughed road. "Why don't we go right away?" I suggested. "We don't want to risk getting stuck on the drive."

Mallory nodded. "I'll just throw some food in a bag."

"You start the car, I'll get the food."

In fact, her keys were still in the apartment, so she took my hand and led me back into the hall and up the stairs. As we passed the various rooms, the old hospital equipment no longer threatened. Without the presence of our gaolers, the apartment in the tower seemed once more welcoming and homelike. We fell gratefully into each other's arms. "Thank you, my darling, for believing in me when I'd almost lost faith in myself," she said between ever more passionate kisses.

"We rescued each other. What could be fairer than that?" After the agony of being separated within sight of each other, yet forbidden to speak, it was inevitable that we should make up for lost time. "It won't snow for another hour at least," I assured her.

"I've got winter tyres anyway. Besides, we don't know what state we'll be in. This could be the last time for a long time."

It was a sombre thought, and it drove us all the more determinedly to take our pleasure whilst we still could. What we forgot, of course, was how heavily we would sleep afterwards. By the time we woke it was pitch dark and snowing hard. We showered and dressed quickly. Then, as Mallory went down to start the car, I threw cheese, biscuits and mineral water into the back-pack. Despite the loss of four hours, I wasn't worried. It would take three hours, four at worst, to reach Annecy, and there were more than sixteen before 10 a.m.

By the time I reached the front door, we'd hit the first snag. The car wouldn't start. The battery was completely flat. "It can happen when you've been parked for days in cold weather." She sighed angrily. "I'm sorry. I should have parked in the stables."

"What about jump leads? Then we could flag down a car."

Mallory pointed at the front tyres. "I don't think so," she said.

I followed her finger. Because of the snow and the dark, it was not obvious at first, but the nearer front tyre was completely flat. Yet the car was even in its stance. I brushed snow from the adjacent rear tyre. It too was flat. I rushed to other side. All the tyres were flat.

Chapter Twenty-Seven : Mercy Dash

"This is sabotage," I shouted. Yet it seemed impossible to believe that *Le Baigneur* and *L'Esprit*, who had throughout acted so properly and been so sincere in their good wishes, would stoop to anything like this. Nor could I believe it of Wormsley. If he'd intended to stop us, he would have said so. But if not them, who?

Ignoring my expostulations, Mallory was opening the bonnet. As soon as it was up, we saw, even in the darkness, why the car wouldn't start. The leads hung uselessly into the basket in which the battery normally sat. My heart sank, but Mallory refused to panic. "I've got summer wheels in the stables, there's a garage beyond the village."

"We can't call them," I pointed out, "Our phones don't work."

"I can ski there. Robert left a whole pile of cross-country stuff. You be changing the tyres while I fetch the garage." She showed me where the wheels were to be found. Luckily the tyres were still inflated. The saboteurs hadn't thought to check for spare sets of tyres.

Mallory was soon in her ski-gear, and pushing off towards the gate. One look told me she was an experienced skier *de fond* who would have no difficulty getting to the garage. But I'd reckoned without the saboteurs. If they'd overlooked the summer wheels, they hadn't forgotten the gate. Already Mallory was double-polling back. "The gate's been padlocked. There's a spare key in the apartment."

Extricating herself from her skis, she ran into the house. I hurried after her. "I need an extension cable and a light." Cable and lantern were soon found, but Mallory couldn't find the key. She looked in every conceivable place before we had to accept that it had been stolen. But she had a hacksaw in her hand.

Together we raced to the gate, Mallory on her skis, me stumping through the deepening snow. The chain was so tough we had to take it in turns to saw at it, and it took nearly a quarter hour of painful effort before the chain finally snapped. Then at last Mallory hurtled down the side of the deserted road towards the village.

Changing the wheels was slow work. Each time, I had to loosen the nuts on the existing wheel, jack up the car, remove the wheel, put on the new one, release the jack and tighten the nuts. By the time I'd finished my body was dripping and my hands freezing. It was only afterwards that I thought of snow chains, essential with summer tyres. I found a set in the boot, and I spread them out ready. A task for the garage man when he arrived with the new battery.

The exercise so far had taken me over an hour, and I was beginning to worry that she should be back by now. But it was another 20 minutes before she returned, not with a garage truck, but alone. "The place was closed," she cursed. "I pressed on to the next village, but there was nothing doing." She did her best to remain optimistic, despite the further setback. "The snow's perfect. I'm sure I've got boots that'll fit you. We can make it to Aix easily. For a taxi or a train."

Tired and frustrated as I was by the wasted effort, I agreed. "This isn't the court's doing. Wormsley wouldn't pull a trick like this."

She nodded grimly. "There's only one person I can think of."

She was right. Everything fitted Ambrose's style. Carefully planned but indirect. He might not dare to confront us, but he could impede our progress. I said nothing, but I determined to keep vigilant. We still had nearly 14 hours, and it would take five at most to reach Aix. The snow was easing, so there was little danger of roads or railways becoming impassable. But we fetched the skis in sombre mood.

Just outside the apartment door was a heavy old *armoire*, in which there was a good selection of skis, poles and boots, somewhat old-fashioned, but perfectly usable. "Robert thought I might find a use for them," Mallory explained. "How right he was."

I was soon kitted out. The boots were too large, but an extra pair of socks was all that was required to make them snug, and I soon found skis and poles to suit my height. We were off in no time. Mallory was the better cross-country skier, but I was the fitter, so we kept pace with each other easily. We had decided in any case to take it steadily.

There was little hope of skiing all the way to Annecy in the time, even assuming we could manage the distance, but Aix was a plausible target. She was right about the snow, and we made better progress than I'd anticipated. In an hour and three-quarters we reached the northern end of the lake where the land was flat, and forty-five minutes later we reached the farther bank. There was little traffic to impede us.

By this time we were both hungry and thirsty, so we skied off the road and into the shelter of some lakeside trees to nibble biscuits and to sip water. "How are you feeling?" I asked.

She smiled. "Tired. But I'm fine. We're going to make it."

As we prepared to set off again, I noticed a car edging slowly towards us along the road. It had stopped snowing some time ago, and the clouds were clearing, so that there was no need for excessive caution. It was more as if the driver were searching for something, and some sixth sense warned me to stay within the shelter of the trees. I laid a restraining hand on Mallory's arm, but she was way ahead of me.

"It's the Peugeot," she hissed.

The car edged past us at scarcely more than walking pace, just as a bright three-quarter moon broke from behind cloud. We could now see clearly that the car was indeed an old Peugeot Six, and the driver's beret could not disguise Ambrose's gaunt profile. He was hunched over the wheel, peering intently at the verge, rather in the way he had long ago peered into the wood by the boathouse. A few metres down the road he stopped the car, and climbed out, dressed in his familiar anorak. Leaving the engine running, he carefully inspected the snow on the verge, then he walked slowly round the back of the car. After a moment's contemplation, he climbed back in and reversed past us. We huddled together, thankful for the protection of the trees. "He's been following our ski tracks," I whispered.

Sure enough, Ambrose stopped again. Then he switched the headlights to full beam. He could easily see where our tracks turned away from the verge and into the wood. He cut the lights immediately, and for a while he sat in the car debating what to do. "He must have put the battery back in," Mallory murmured in my ear.

"All that time changing the tyres!" I bemoaned. "Just for him."

That Ambrose should benefit from my industry was appalling. My only consolation was that fitting the chains had seriously delayed him. But not enough. I'd judged that he wouldn't dare to confront us; certainly he had not followed Mallory to the garage, but presumably he didn't have skis; nor had he interfered with my exertions. But he must have enjoyed them. I wondered what he was going to do now.

We didn't have long to wait. Once more he emerged from the car, and walked slowly towards us, peering cautiously, ahead of him. When he reached the first tree, he stopped with one hand on the trunk. The other hung at his side, weighed down by whatever he was carrying.

"Mallory," he called, "I know you're in there."

"There's nothing to say, Ambrose," she called back.

"You'll never make it to the hospital, unless you let me help you."

"Keep him talking," I breathed. We'd unclipped our boots from the skis when we stopped, so it was easy to circle through the closely-packed trees. Another cloud had passed in front of the moon, to keep me hidden, but Ambrose was silhouetted against the snow.

"How are you going to help me?" Her hands gripped a ski pole.

"Come out where I can see you, and I'll explain."

She moved noisily away from him, then stopped to see what he would do. I used the distraction to close in on him from the side. "It's all right, Ambrose, I won't bite." She was handling him beautifully.

"Where's Clem?" he asked suspiciously. He shuffled forward a pace swinging his burden. It was a claw hammer.

"He's down by the lake," she said. "Having a pee."

He lumbered towards her, and she retreated, holding her ski pole in front of her, its metal tip pointing towards him. But she was going backwards. Suddenly her foot caught in a fallen branch. Dropping her pole, she threw out her hands to break her fall. He rushed towards her, and I leapt on him from behind. Instinct must have warned him.

He turned as I charged, and although I half-tackled him, he caught me a sharp blow on the shoulder. It was enough to give him the advantage, and he was on top of me as we fell. One hand snatched at my throat. The other raised the hammer. I parried the blow with my arm. Then Mallory was upon him, jabbing her stick into his back. He screamed, and I managed to kick him off me. He stumbled to his feet, the hammer still in his hand. But he was no match for both of us.

With an angry snort, he turned and ran back towards the car. I tried to follow, but my shoulder and arm were numb, and my legs were shaky. Mallory sprang past me, wielding her ski pole, but Ambrose was too far ahead. He jumped into the car, and the engine roared into life. As we stood on the verge, he drove straight at us. We jumped aside only just in time. The car started to slew as one wheel flailed in deep snow and the other gripped the road. For a moment, it looked as though he would be stuck, but at the last moment the chains regained their grip and the car lurched across the road. He drove on towards Aix.

"Are you OK?" Mallory asked anxiously.

I flexed my shoulder, then my arm; neither appeared to be broken. Moving them was painful, but not impossible. "What about you?"

"I'm fine." She stared down the road. "He's effectively cut us off from Aix." Then she pointed to the hills. "There's a village at the top, so there must be a road. We can telephone there for a taxi."

"Assuming the phones there work for us."

"Have you got a better idea?"

I shook my head. With more than ten hours remaining, there was enough time to take even a wasted detour to the village, and there was always the hope that Ambrose would give up in the interim. We retrieved our skis and continued on our way. Steep hills rose in front of us, but the road clung to the shore. It was like skiing beside the *Roc de*

Chère. Soon the road forked. One prong continued beside the lake, the other climbed steeply up the side of the cliff. "If Ambrose had any sense he'd be waiting here," said Mallory, as we reached the fork.

"He's sure we'll head for Aix. He knows we'd never make it across country." Perhaps he also knew the village would have nothing.

The road hadn't been cleared since the morning, so its snow cover was quite deep, though there were a few tyre tracks. We kept to the deep snow at the edge to maintain grip. It wasn't far to the top, but it steepened all the way. We were soon at the limit of adhesion, not to mention strength. Our speed slowed to a snail's pace.

Mallory had the technique to keep going, but for every metre forward I seemed to slip back half of it. But under her guidance, by side-stepping and herring-boning, I kept going. Just ahead, the road narrowed and swung sharply to the left. We were on the steepest section, and the soft snow had been blown away. Yet, centimetre by slippery centimetre, we made it to the start of the bend. At the top there was a stone arch over the road: the village entrance. Through a roadside mirror, we saw that the road levelled beyond. At most 50 metres.

At 25 metres there was a movement in the mirror. A car without lights was coming through the arch, and coming fast. With uncanny intuition, Ambrose had worked out what we would do, and had been waiting for us. Now, it seemed, his one intention was to run us down. The car jumped forwards, but in his anxiety not to miss us, he was going too fast. The car skidded, swayed and rammed the crash barrier on the edge of the cliff, throwing the car back across the road. By this time, the tail was coming round, and the car was careering straight at us, picking up speed as the wheels lost all grip.

Mallory seized my arm and flattened me against the nearside cliff wall. Here we had the protection of a slight buttress, and it was this which took the force of the car's rear wing, throwing it round once more. Desperately spinning the steering wheel, Ambrose took his foot off the brake in the hope that the wheels would regain traction. All he succeeded in doing was ramming the crash barrier again, and this time, as the car once more spun across the road, it rolled onto its side. Now it hurtled down the slope like a loose ski, until another collision with the cliff threw it onto its roof. It slid upside down most of the way to the bottom, until a final swipe from the cliff flipped it back onto its wheels. It finally came to rest on the far side of the lake-side road.

We waited for Ambrose to emerge. But there was no movement from the car at all. "We can't just leave him," said Mallory. "If he's badly injured, he needs help." I was tempted to say he'd brought it on himself, but the words died in my throat. Whatever his faults, and however hard he had tried to imperil us, he was a fellow human being, and there was no way we could simply abandon him.

"Try and rouse somebody in the village," Mallory continued. "I'll go down and see how he is." She pointed up the hill. "Go on. I'll get to him faster." She was right. Only a better cross-country skier than me would volunteer to ski fast to the bottom on narrow *skis de fond*.

"Don't go too near," I warned her. "He may be bluffing."

I watched as she headed down the road in a scarifying mixture of jump-, stem- and step-turns. Then I pressed on up the last of the hill. The village beyond the arch was in darkness save for a couple of street lamps. The one restaurant and the sole bar were both closed. Hardly surprising, as it was now after midnight. The houses too were all silent. But this was an emergency. I turned to the nearest front door, which faced directly onto the pavement, and I rang the bell loudly. Nothing happened. They must be asleep. I tried again. Still nothing. I moved to the next house, and the next. It was as if the entire village were in hibernation. Finally, at the seventh house I tried, an upstairs window was flung open. A tousled and angry head appeared over the sill just above me. "I'm sorry to trouble you, Monsieur, but there's been an accident. I wonder if you would telephone for an ambulance?"

He looked down on me as if I wasn't there. Then he leaned out precariously. "Who's there?" asked a woman's voice behind him.

"Nobody. It's that damned bell. Same every winter."

"I told you to get it fixed." Then the window banged shut.

I tried one more time, shouting for good measure, but to no avail. Then it struck me. Ever since we'd been imprisoned in the Sanatorium, we had been unable to communicate with the outside world, with the exception of our once a week visits to St Hippocrate. Trying to raise help was a waste of time. Until we made it to the hospital, we really were as good as ghosts, entirely reliant on our own resources. What should have been a simple matter of driving from the Sanatorium to Annecy, an ordinarily trivial journey, had been frustrated by Ambrose. For a moment or two, despair threatened to overwhelm me.

It was the thought of the car that saved me. *Le Baigneur* had intended us to use the car, and but for Ambrose we would have reached our destination by now. The car might be seriously damaged, but it had not ceased to exist. So long as it was drivable, we could at least get as far as Aix and drop Ambrose at the nearest hospital. Then, our humanitarian duty done, we could either drive on to our final destination, or, if the car was breaking down, we could take the train, as we'd been planning to. Ghosts wouldn't even need a ticket.

I skied back to the arch, and edged carefully under it. The road was far steeper than any cross-country trail I had ever encountered, as well as a lot icier. It reminded me of the *couloir* in Les Confins on New Year's Eve, which had been even steeper and narrower. But it had also been many orders of magnitude shorter, and I'd had the benefit of wider alpine skis, firmer bindings and steel edges. But it had to be done. In great trepidation, I set off in wide, ungainly snowplough turns. The first 50 metres were the worst. As I got lower, the snow became softer. It was slow going, and my thighs burned from the strain of being far too defensive, but at last I was back at Mallory's side. Breathlessly, I explained the problem. "So we have to get the car going."

It was a mess, and so was Ambrose. If the car hadn't turned over, his seatbelt might have saved him from injury. But the roof and door on the driver's side were badly crumpled. His head was gashed in two places and there was a jagged wound in his right leg. Mallory had patched him up as best she could with torn lengths of his shirt and her blouse, and she'd managed to lie him down on the back seat. "I'm glad I keep a blanket in the boot, or he'd have shivered to death by now. As it is, he needs a hospital urgently." It was no overstatement.

We inspected the car. It looked as though it had completed a season of stock car racing, but amazingly the tyres were still intact and the chains still in place. From the passenger side, Mallory crawled into what was left of the driving space and turned the ignition. It fired. "It's pretty flat all the way to Aix. We'll drop him at the hospital."

She had to crouch to avoid bumping her head on the stoven-in roof, but the engine sounded healthy enough. The gear shift was stiff, but she could select second and third without too much difficulty. She edged forward cautiously, and tested the brakes. They still worked. "The steering's all over the place, but I can manage if we take it slowly."

Within ten kilometres, the engine was over-heating. We stopped to check the radiator. Hot water was dripping into the snow with an angry hiss. We topped up with our remaining mineral water, and continued for another few kilometres. From then on we had to rely on snow. At last we limped into Aix. We parked by a waste-bin, tipped out its contents and filled the removable container with snow. We now had water to spare. Late though it was, there was still traffic about, and our battered car earned funny looks from passing motorists.

When we next stopped to top up the radiator, a police car pulled up ahead. Before we had time to react, two policemen had jumped out and

287

were pulling on our doors. Mine flew open, but Mallory's was stuck fast. The car rocked with their efforts, and Ambrose uttered a low moan. The policemen looked straight through us, as though we didn't exist. "Scarpered," exclaimed the one who had opened my door.

"So fast we didn't even seen him," agreed his companion.

Ambrose groaned, this time more loudly, and the policeman on my side turned his attention to the back seats. "We've got one in the back. In a bad way, too." He pulled open the rear door and peered in at the stricken man. "Left his mate behind. That's nice, that is."

His companion opened the other door. "He needs an ambulance."

The first spoke into his handset. "Hurry. He's losing blood."

Signalling to Mallory to follow, I jumped out of the door which the police had so conveniently left open. "Let's run for it."

She needed no second invitation. The policemen didn't even look up. As we passed their car, she paused. "The key's in the ignition."

Our eyes met, and we laughed. Then we jumped into the vacated police car and drove off at speed. Behind us, the two policemen stared after their retreating car, as if they couldn't believe their eyes. Police cars were full of wonderful gadgetry, but they were not known to drive off of their own volition.

"The joys of being a ghost," I grinned. "How far's the station?"

"Five minutes, max."

The dashboard radio was already spluttering instructions, and a minute later there were blue lights flashing towards us, and sirens screaming. "They can't see us, remember. Drive until they force us to stop." I shouted, feeling like the hero of a Hollywood film.

Two police cars swerved across the road in front of us. Mallory braked hard, narrowly avoiding collision. Then we jumped out and ran.

"We don't even need a ticket," I said, as we jogged along.

It was uncomfortable in our cross-country boots, but at least the pavements here in the town centre had been cleared of snow.

On foot, it took us half an hour to find the station, and we were both breathing hard. We needn't have hurried. The next train wasn't until 6:00 a.m., but it would reach Annecy at 7:15. Two and three-quarter hours should be plenty of time to walk to the hospital, even though it had been moved to the outskirts. Our problem in the meantime was to stay warm. So far we had been exercising hard, and neither of us was dressed to withstand more than four hours of inactivity in a temperature which the station's electronic clock informed us was minus one Celsius. Clouds were filling the sky once more, and it seemed certain there were would be more snow before the train arrived.

The station building was locked and the platforms were bleak and without shelter. Even the underpass beneath the tracks was sealed off. Despite my two pairs of socks, my toes were feeling the cold, and Mallory was already shivering, having shed one of her garments to staunch Ambrose's bleeding. "There must be a big hotel somewhere. The kind that keeps its doors open all night," I suggested.

"By the casino." She brightened. "I was there for *St Silvestre*."

"Can you find it?"

"It's near the lake. There must be a map somewhere."

"There was one on the station wall, which gave us the right general direction. Then we followed brown hotel signs. "Walk fast," I instructed, " And swing your arms. Generate as much energy as you can." I broke into a slow jog to make my point. It was painful in our boots, and we both began to blister. But by alternately walking fast and jogging, we managed to stay warm until we arrived at the casino.

It formed one side of an ornate square. Opposite was the lakeside boulevard. The other sides were occupied by the kind of grandiose hotels that had been popular in late 19th century France. But this was not the high season, and most of them were closed. But right next to the casino there was one, even grander than the rest, whose marble hall was still lit. But its resplendent revolving doors were locked. We tried the bell. A bored-looking porter glance up from the reception desk across the hall. He gave no signs of wishing to answer our ring.

"He can't see us," I said. "He thinks it's an electrical fault."

Mallory pressed again. "He'll have to come, if only to shut us up."

The porter hid defiantly behind his newspaper, but we kept pressing. Eventually he put down the paper and stood up. Then he turned into the office behind, and disappeared. A moment later the bell stopped. The porter reappeared, and picked up his newspaper again. Rather than come to the door, he had resorted to a simpler expedient.

"If that's the way he wants it, we'll kick the door in," I shouted.

We attacked the glass with the hard toecaps of our boots. The doors shook under the onslaught, but their reinforced plate glass neither broke not gave. But the noise echoed round the square and through the hall of the hotel, so that we had the porter's full attention. His response was to seize the desk telephone. Soon he was shouting into it. "He's calling the police. He'll have to open the doors when they arrive."

Thanks perhaps to our earlier brush with the police, two cars arrived within minutes. We stood aside as four *policiers* raced towards the entrance. They banged on the doors with their fists almost as loudly as we had struck them with our boots. The porter released the doors immediately, and three of the policemen rushed inside, whilst the fourth mounted guard. None of them took any notice of us.

Inside, we heard angry voices, as the porter defended his actions, and the police berated him for wasting their time. The one outside reported into his intercom that this looked like a false alarm, but after the incident with the police car it was as well to be sure. Whilst they were all engaged, we pushed our way in. They all gaped at the sight of doors revolving by themselves. "You see!" the porter shouted.

One of the policemen strode to the door, and pushed it several times to see if it was loose. "Must be the wind," he concluded.

The porter protested that it wasn't windy tonight, to which the police retorted that he was hardly in a position to know from the reception desk. Whilst they argued, we crept down the hall, its marble pillars and barrel ceiling reminiscent of a baroque church. We found a seating area behind the pillars and snuggled into a capacious leather armchair.

Like the decor, the heat was over the top, and I soon discarded my blouson, whilst Mallory unzipped her anorak. "We mustn't oversleep," I whispered, just as the police were leaving.

The porter returned to his desk, and all was quiet once more. We dozed rather than slept, but nothing could take away the joy of being warm. Even if we had overslept, the arrival of the cleaners at 5 a.m. would have woken us. Outside it was snowing hard.

There was a snowplough already out on the boulevard. Snow clearing was also underway in the rest of the town, though sometimes our boots squeaked over deep snow. We made it to the station in plenty of time, but our train was delayed by half an hour, and we guessed that our journey would be slower still. But the waiting room was open, and we could shelter from the snow.

Don't worry," I assured Mallory, "We're going to make it."

"I don't suppose they'll switch off our life supports on the dot of ten," she said hopefully. "So it won't matter if we're a bit late."

"We wouldn't peg out on the spot, anyway." Or so I hoped.

Stopping trains are never fast at the best of times, and we seemed to crawl between stations, and wait too long at each. There also seemed to be too many intervening stops for the distance we had to travel, due to the roundabout route by which the railway threaded its way between the ridges and high hills that lay between Aix and Annecy. We finally arrived just after 8 a.m. But two hours should suffice.

"It's straight up the Avenue de Genève," I explained, as we hurried out of the station. Both of us were exhausted, and our feet were badly blistered. But there was nothing for it, but to make progress as best we could. "At least we'll keep warm," I said, as we hobbled through the driving snow. Mallory said nothing.

Her cheeks were very pale, and I realised with horror that she was close to collapse. Neither of us had eaten much for days, and I guessed that she was out of blood sugar. Sure enough, her pace grew slower and slower. "You've hit the wall," I explained. "It happens to marathon runners quite often. You're burning fat instead of glycogen."

"My stomach feels like jelly, and my calves are cramping."

I assured her that these were the symptoms to expect. Then I put my arm around her and half-supported her. The Avenue de Genève runs from the town centre to the ring roads on the very outskirts of the town. I reckoned it was about 10 kilometres to the hospital, 12 at the outside. Not far, compared with the distance we had already covered, but for Mallory it was almost unthinkable. But we crawled on as best we could. By 9 a.m., we had covered less than half the distance, but in theory we were only slightly behind schedule.

But even as I was looking at my watch, Mallory sank to her knees. She pushed feebly at my legs. "Go on. Save yourself."

"No way I'm leaving you." I hauled her to her feet and over my shoulders in a fireman's lift. "From now on I'm carrying you."

I set off before she could protest. Every step was agony. Pain stabbed through my bruised shoulder, my spine felt as though it would snap, and the extra weight was too much for my blisters. Telling myself sternly that Mallory was far from heavy, I progressed in five minute bursts, with a minute between each to rest my aching limbs.

Everything now was a blur, but I was vaguely aware of passing a giant hypermarket. Two kilometres to go. Or was it 20? The snow was as thick as sand, and when I looked down, it seemed that it was sand, that I was staggering up a deserted beach towards a line of white bathing huts. The snow was blinding, and I was no longer sure if I was moving at all, still less of my direction.

A black shape loomed alongside. At first I thought it was a boat drawn up on the beach. But, as I sank to my knees, it sharpened into the familiar outlines of a stretched DS with darkened windows. Strong hands lifted Mallory from my shoulders and supported me into the car. *L'Esprit* pressed a silver flask to Mallory's lips and then to mine.

"You said you had Ambrose under control," I spluttered.

"He'd agreed to abide by the court's decision," Wormsley said.

"He was more cunning than we thought," *L'Esprit* continued. "He took the ruling that you must make your own way to the hospital as *carte blanche* for him to prevent you."

"It shouldn't have happened," said Wormsley. "We'd have got to you sooner, except we had to fast-track Ambrose first. He's chosen to die. But he thanks you for trying to save him."

We'd been driving during theses exchanges, and *L'Esprit* now turned the car off the ring road towards the hospital, a long modern building with clean, simple lines. *Le Baigneur* was waiting by the entrance, and he opened Mallory's door for her. Revived a little by the brandy, she was able to take his arm and walk shakily under her own steam. I took position the other side of her, and the five of us passed the reception area to the lifts. Nobody took any notice of us.

"You're on the second floor," *Le Baigneur* explained. "Your monitors have been active since you set out, but they flagged in the last hour. Yet I am pleased to inform you that you are not too late."

At the door to our room, where the experimental procedure had been in play for the past week, each of them shook us by the hand. "I misjudged you," I said to Wormsley.

He slapped me on the back. "Good luck. You deserve it."

"You may now rejoin your material selves," said *Le Baigneur*.

L'Esprit opened the door and ushered us inside. It was 9:59.

GHO$T TRAD€R

Part Five
Aftermath

"The markets could be dead for decades,
with inflation, currency collapse,
government defaults,
you name it."

"At best, in aiding others,
we also fuel our own prosperity.
The economics of altruism
instead of the feeding-frenzy of greed."

Chapter Twenty-Eight : Return to Reality

The room beyond the door was crowded with people, standing and sitting around two beds arranged side by side and almost touching. Nobody took any notice of our entry, but we were accustomed by now to being invisible. More than anything, we were exhausted, and we collapsed gratefully onto the beds. Twisting as I fell, I lost my hold on Mallory's hand, and landed on my back. The mattress beneath swayed and heaved, as if it had sprung to life. I opened my eyes in panic.

I was alone. The walls had disappeared, and the ceiling had receded into a dark, cloudy sky. Lights bobbed dimly beyond my feet. As I rolled over, a wave slapped me in the face. The lights blurred, not many straight ahead, for that was the beach, but there were more beyond the dunes, and in the port. The shock broke my lethargy. I was perhaps 200 metres from shore, and the waves were beginning to crest.

So near and yet so far. I resumed my swimming, and as I swam a little strength returned. Nearer and nearer came the beach, until at last I could stand. I dragged myself out of the water, becoming heavier as more of me lost its support. But the bathing hut was almost in front of me, and I stumbled towards it, the sand clinging to my icy feet. At last I reached the door, and fumbled in the wetsuit pocket for the key.

The swim had been almost fatally more tiring than anticipated, but everything else had gone to plan. I'd half-hoped she'd have taken pity, but in my heart I'd known she would not. Otherwise I needn't have worn the wet suit under my clothes, or put weights in the pockets of my trousers and jacket so they'd sink to the bottom when removed.

They'd have found my note under the windscreen wiper hours ago. As far as the world was concerned I was dead by now. So, of course, there was nobody on *Calais* beach to greet me in the strange pre-dawn grey, its flatness exactly matching the gloom of the sea.

Yet if I wasn't dead, my fingers were so stiff and I was shivering so hard that I could hardly get the key in the lock. I forced myself to stay calm. Everything came to him who waited. The hut was dry and smelled pleasantly of creosote. I fumbled open the strong box I'd hidden under the beach umbrella and chair, the wrapped towels and blankets, and took out the torch. I slipped it out of its wrapper, and it worked perfectly. When it came to keeping things waterproof, I was the expert: the former packs and wraps entrepreneur. I pulled the door shut and locked it. Now I was safely out of sight. As fast as my whitened fingers would allow I lit the butane stove to boil the soup I'd stored on the bench, along with a multi-pack of bottled water. I stripped off the wet-suit – far from easy in the confined space – and broke one of the beach towels out of its protective plastic. It was as dry as new.

As I waited for the soup, I inspected the other contents of the box. Everything was just as I'd left it: my American Express card, still valid though I hadn't used it for ages; the money belt with €10,000, the final extent of my liquid wealth; my French driving licence and French passport. None of the things in my name were known to Hope, my about-to-be executrix. She knew that my father had been the son of French *émigrés*, escaping Nazi occupation, and that I'd been partly educated in France. But she didn't know that I had a French passport and driving licence. Any more than her mother.

I liked to have alternatives to fall back on. On that score, I'd had a good teacher in my father: a man who'd always thought of himself as equally British and French. When his business faltered, he'd returned to France, and when I was ready he'd sent me back to sort things out. He died before he knew for certain that I had.

The only time I'd forgotten his rule and mine was when I married Mai. But then how can you have a back-up for the woman you love? Mallory Mai Stellenbourg: the love and the curse of my life. Her beauty and her charm were always so perfect, it seemed to follow that everything else about her was perfect, too. She had always been so certain of everything that she'd seemed sure enough for both of us. It was the same with Lloyd's. I trusted her because she was convinced that Rex could do no wrong. I forgot she too was blinded by love.

I was beginning to have doubts when it came to the Rota, but there I met Clem Holden, and he disarmed me enough to allay my doubts. Of course I should have sussed him for an arrogant know-all, but his sense of destiny was as absolute as Mai's. They'd make a perfect pair.

Back then he seemed like the kind of strong character I could look up to. So I trusted his judgement. It was only later, when he made all those unacceptable recommendations for my business that I realised he was not always right. His reasoning was plausible enough, but he never considered what *I* might want for the business. Not to put too fine a point on it, he patronised me; just the same as Rex.

I suppose she did, too. Yet I know she loved me at first, when she thought I was the kind of successful entrepreneur an ambitious woman needed to have behind her. In those days she was still prepared to listen, and I taught her the importance of detail, and how vital it was always to have a back-up strategy. Even the best plans can be ruined by the unexpected. Mind you, she was a good pupil.

But I gave her the proper grounding to become such an excellent investor, even if she had to learn the nuts and bolts for herself. That was nothing to do with me, any more than embezzling the syndicate's funds. I've always been rigidly honest in my dealings.

She understood the difference between right and wrong, but only in the way colour-blind people understand that there are subtle shades of red, obvious only to others. Her thinking was also wonderfully flexible. There was always a greater good which outweighed the current little difficulty. Her deep love for Rex, which was real enough, was far nobler than her duty to her husband and to her daughter.

With the soup nearly ready, it was time for dry clothes. I had two sets hanging from hooks on the side wall. I unzipped one of the covers and extracted flannels, a lumberjack shirt and a black anorak, which dated back to the happier days of cross-country skiing with Mai. Once dressed, I gulped the soup hungrily. It gave me warmth and strength, and cleansed my mouth of oil and salt. Afterwards I rinsed my teeth in mineral water, unwrapped the blankets and curled up on the floor.

As soon as I closed my eyes I seemed to be back in the sea. From the vantage of the ferry, the water was calm, but for a swimmer the swell was prodigious. Only one thought drove me on: that I was the chosen instrument of justice: an executioner, not an avenger. I consoled myself that without Mai's push, I'd never have jumped. The drop from the upper deck to the sea had at the moment of truth seemed dizzyingly long. In her own way she had played her part in the reckoning.

I drifted at last into deep sleep. After what seemed like an eternity of nothingness, I became slowly aware that I was no longer curled up on the floor of the bathing hut, but lying on a hospital bed, hooked up to wires and drips. I opened my eyes. The light was dazzling, and my surroundings were so blurred I thought I was back in the snow.

I seemed to be alone, but that was the blurry effect of seeing for the first time in months. Slowly a young woman emerged from the snowstorm: a seated Madonna to the left of my bed, patiently suckling a baby under a halo of unbearable light. Smiling down at the baby, she seemed utterly absorbed in her task, yet as I struggled to bring her into focus, she glanced at me. Our eyes met, and though her face was blurred, her delighted smile was unmistakeable. Her smiles to the baby had been small and private, to mark the simple joy of an habitual task, but the response to me was radiant and public, and was directed at the indistinct figures standing beside her as much as to me. Immediately, more faces loomed above white uniforms: a doctor and a nurse.

"Are you with us again, Monsieur Holden?"

Before I could answer, there was a tug on my right hand. Somebody had been holding my hand all along, and was now summoning my attention. I turned my head. This time, the act of focusing was easier and quicker. Next to me was another bed, with standing and seated figures on its far side. They looked familiar, but I couldn't quite make them out. Another yank on my arm drew me back to the occupant of the other bed. I focused on our clasped hands until they were sharp, then I followed the arm to its shoulder, and to the face beyond. I saw dark hair glossily brushed back and dark eyes shining at me.

"Hello, Clem," she whispered.

"Mallory!" That's when they knew we were both conscious.

I tried to squeeze her hand, but my fingers were reluctant to move. With great difficulty, I managed to lift my left hand and wave. She raised her own free hand, and wiggled the fingers. I blew her a kiss, and her lips rounded into a reasonable 'o' in return.

They told us later that we both fell asleep after that. But we were no longer comatose, our brain patterns those of normal sleep.

"It's been a crazy week," Hope explained as soon as we were awake again. "Your monitors yo-yoed up and down all week, but last night they went crazy. Jake and I were convinced you were going to come round any minute." Jake nodded, and pressed my shoulder for good measure. "Then they sank, and we thought we'd lost you."

"All except Marie-Sainte," he said. "She's hardly left your side."

I opened my eyes. Since I'd woken up at around 10:15, I'd found the lights far too bright, and focusing on anything tiring.

"I'm a patient, too," said the Madonna, as she transfigured into Marie-Sainte. She laughed. "Not a patient, exactly. I'm in the Maternity wing, but they let us come and see you." She held up the tiny bundle in her arms, and I had a brief vision of dark hair, a snub nose and a perfect little mouth. "This is Clémentine. We named her after you."

She laid the tiny creature beside me, and guided my arm around her. Clémentine snuffled contentedly, but otherwise took no notice of me. She smelled fresh and warm: the scent of renewal and regeneration.

"I prayed for you, Monsieur Clem. Andréa, too. He said to remind you of Pascal's wager." Joyfully, she raised my hand to her lips and kissed it. With an effort, I touched her cheek, and I did my best to smile, though she told me later that it was rather twisted.

Recovery was slow, but after all we'd been through, we vowed that nothing would defeat us. We had the support of every kind of therapist, and they kept us at it as if we were elite athletes in training rather than middle-aged accident victims. Our visitors now had to be fitted round physiotherapy and speech therapy, writing practice and computer skills. At first, we were almost as helpless as Wormsley had warned.

But he had reckoned without the skill and goodwill of our support team. The hospital were proud of our recovery, and as resolute that we should restore our motor and intellectual skills as they had once been sceptical that we would even regain consciousness; and there were enough of them to maintain a constantly cheerful front.

It helped, too, that Mallory and I were so competitive. Where one was ahead, the other would be determined to catch up. Yet our rivalry was as loving as it was fierce. Whenever one of us stole a march, it was a point of honour to help the other. Being ahead was wonderful, but helping to close the gap was better.

There was no escaping the extent of our injuries. Mallory had a plate in her skull, I was partially blind in one eye, and I had a pin in one ankle. But the main damage was to our brains. When we awoke we were almost like babies again. We had to teach our brains to use new neural pathways where the old ones were too damaged.

My first attempts at talking made me sound like a drunk; until, like a hardened alcoholic, I learned to enunciate my words with exaggerated care. But after weeks of intensive therapy, I was almost back to my old manner of speaking. Mallory joked that I was most natural when I was angry. I hadn't lost my old impatience, but I focused it better.

At first we could barely shuffle to the bathroom, but slowly we came to manage the corridor, and finally the gymnasium and the swimming pool. Even if we'd really been Olympians in training we could not have put in more effort, nor had better or more intensive support. But it paid off. Not in time for Christmas, which fell only a week after our recovery, not yet for *St Silvestre*, though the hospital did their best for us, and all our friends came to toast our health. But by mid-February, it was certain that neither of us would be confined to wheelchairs, even if I would retain a permanent limp and Mallory would stoop when she was tired, her stride degenerating into a shuffle.

Our brains functioned more or less as before, except that both of us sometimes struggled for the right word, or to remember a name, even of the person we were talking to. But our thoughts flowed as smoothly as ever. The most curious outcome for me was that English now seemed like a foreign language. Before the accident I'd been bilingual, and it was always difficult to remember whether any particular conversation with Mallory had been in English or French. She told me English, but I seemed to remember word for word in both languages. Now we spoke only in French, and even with Jake I found it easier to reply in French. He took it well. "I need to brush up my French anyway."

His need for fluent French was driven not only by his wish to communicate with our doctors, but by his determination to make a critical assessment of the Sanatorium. He made several visits with Hope, and also with Sidonie and Armand. "How committed is Mallory to the Sanatorium, Dad?" he asked me one day in February as we walked to the swimming pool. Mallory had already gone ahead with Hope. "I mean is it absolutely vital to your plans?"

It was not an easy question, and I had to halt my limping walk to consider it. The Sanatorium was not only a magic castle where we'd become lovers, it had been a haunted ruin where the dead had set up their implacable court before whom all secrets had been exposed.

"I can't answer for Mallory." I shuffled on. "Why do you ask?"

"*Accor* want to develop it as a destination hotel. They were about to make an offer before. The publicity's reignited their interest."

"How much?"

"At least 15% more than she paid. Probably 20." As far as I was concerned it was more than tempting. But I wasn't sure if Mallory would brook further delay whilst we searched for another site. But Jake had anticipated this objection. "Sidonie will happily let you have her site above Talloires. She's never found enough buyers to get it started. She blames the credit crunch, but in my opinion she over-extended herself. The site's too large for a small developer, but it's ideal for you. Armand says the *Mairie* would rather have a going concern than a building site. You'd be up and running in no time."

"How much does she want for it?"

"For a good cause, she'll be happy if she breaks even."

To make sure, I checked with Sidonie before I said anything to Mallory. With her usual calm, she confirmed her willingness to sell. "You'd be doing me a favour, Clem. That site's been a millstone round my neck. There are other sites I'd love to develop, but I need the cash. The banks are nothing like as helpful as they used to be."

I knew her well enough to grasp that she was in more need than her calm suggested, and I promised to speak to Mallory right away. After a good day of exercises, Mallory was in a receptive mood that evening. Far from cutting me off, she plied me with searching questions, a sure sign that she was interested. Once I'd satisfied her there would be no delays, she was all enthusiasm.

"To be honest, I'd happily be shot of the Sanatorium. Too many harsh memories. If it helps Sidonie as well, that's perfect."

Despite her injuries, Mallory had lost none of her decisiveness. Not that it was a difficult decision. The ordeal of the trial had weighed far more heavily on her than on me, and had overshadowed the ambiguous happiness of the postponement period, where pleasure had been counter-balanced by our confinement amidst the watchers.

Hope had ensured that we lost none of the detail of our dreams by suggesting that we wrote our experiences down whilst they were still fresh. At first, the therapists had been unsure that dwelling on our dreams was helpful, but Hope had argued that writing them up was more motivating than meaningless exercises. "Your minds blend very closely," they took to saying, as the unfolding tale intrigued them. "No wonder you're such a good couple." Mallory reminded them that it was in our dreams we had fallen in love. To which physio and speech therapist would only smile, as though our dreams were cover for an affair that we preferred to keep secret for reasons into which they, as professionals, would never probe. Hope accepted it all. "It must be real, or I wouldn't have hired Marie-Sainte."

In one respect, the physio and the speech therapist were correct. We sanitised the narrative, reducing my role from co-conspirator to co-executive: the provider of the moral support that enabled Mallory to bear the burden of sustained exposure to risk; and the finder of Marie-Sainte, whom I recommended with the aim not of hoodwinking the members but of showing them all sensible strategies in action. As for the trial, we kept details to a minimum. We revealed the principles under which the court had operated, but we did not elaborate on the unflattering features of our past lives which had been presented as evidence. We never at any point referred to Ambrose – or *Monsieur De l'Ombre* – so that he played no part in our struggle to return to the hospital. We wrote only that the car had been sabotaged, perhaps by vandals, and that we had crashed it ourselves.

At first, we had both written something each evening, then after comparing and discussing, we had agreed the final version for the others to read. Sometimes this was based more on Mallory's draft, sometimes more on mine. But when it came to writing up the trial, she sat in agonised silence in front of her computer. When I'd finished, she accepted what I'd written after a cursory reading. A stickler for detail, she was usually the one to spot inconsistencies and errors in my draft, and to have caught some dramatic detail I'd forgotten in hers. "This isn't like you," I said. "There must be something to tweak."

"You're much better at this." She waved at the text. "It's good."

"It's supposed to be therapy. You need to be typing."

"What's the point if we aren't going to tell the truth?"

"We are telling the truth. More or less. Just not all of it."

"The trial doesn't make sense." She threw up her hands awkwardly. Many of our gestures had become clumsier in the aftermath of waking. "The shorting was real enough, except Hope did it. And Marie-Sainte really did create the viewing platforms, even if you didn't literally brief her. But the trial took place entirely in our heads."

"Hope begged me to find you, and I actually came out of my coma to promise I'd bring you back from the Sanatorium. For her sake, we can't say nothing. We just don't need to go into the full detail."

"If Hope needs an explanation, she has a right to the full one. You've seen the worst of me, and she needs to see it as well."

"She won't thank you. She'd rather cherish her illusions."

"Illusions!" She grimaced. "I doubt she has any about me."

"She loves you," I protested. "Why else did she beg me to go and find you? If she didn't love you, she certainly wouldn't have fought the hospital to keep your life support going."

She smiled, if doubtfully. "The experiment was Jake's idea."

I bent down and kissed her head. In my new clumsiness, I also pushed her sweat band over her eyes. "That's how I realised Jake loved me, despite what I did to his mother." Pushing the band back into place, she smiled unambiguously and I sensed acquiescence. "At the very least, Hope's memory of her father should rest in peace."

"She isn't his, she's Rex's. She and Ambrose never really got on. He was too pedantic for a lively child, and absurdly over-protective." So much so that he'd imparted to her his mannerism of coming up close and wide-eyed to those he talked to. "Not that I told her until she grew up. It didn't seem fair."

"How did she respond?" I asked gently. "Not too angrily, I trust."

"If anything, she was relieved. She'd always felt guilty for not loving Ambrose, and now she knew why."

I thought back to the time Ambrose and I met after our Lloyd's Rota induction, when he'd agreed that his daughter was a consolation for his divorce, even though he didn't have time to devote to full-time fatherhood. Perhaps that had been an admission of sorts.

"It's not just about telling her," I persisted. "Think what the trial would look like to the hospital. You can't expect doctor-patient confidentiality to cover confessions. The last thing Hope needs to endure is the agony of you being arrested for Ambrose's murder."

She read through my narrative again in silence, making sure it was anodyne. "You're right," she agreed with finality. "We must put the past behind us. It's the future that matters."

At the mention of the future, our hospital surroundings, which until now had felt safe and protective, seemed stark and confining. "Where shall we live? My place or the boathouse?"

"I think it had better be your place." She smiled enigmatically. "There never was any boathouse, Clem, just a dilapidated ruin at the bottom of the path. The jetty's completely rotted away."

I was about to protest, until I remembered being unable to find it, when I'd wanted to show George Wiseman how humble it was. Though our dreams had generally meshed, reality had sometimes intruded.

"How did it get into the dream?" I felt bereft of an old friend.

"It was where I could be undisturbed." Her guardedness returned, before it was diffused by a blush. "Then after we met, I dreamt it was our trysting place." She grinned sheepishly. "Don't look so surprised. You intrigued me from the first moment I saw you."

"No, I didn't," I retorted. "You called me a stalker and a prat."

"Defensive reflex, I'm afraid. I didn't want a relationship."

"You should never have kissed me, then." I stroked the place on my cheek that would tingle still at the memory. "Till you did, I was more than prepared to dislike you."

"I should have gone skiing with you," she bewailed, as the enormity of her refusal hit home. "I was in two minds, believe me."

We sank to the floor, and embraced on our knees. "Ambrose was up there, remember? It might have been you he pushed off the ridge."

She shuddered, and we held each other tightly like frightened children. Then she shook her head. "I don't know about that. Remember the replay of the accident? Ambrose didn't threaten me, or push me. If I hadn't panicked..." She buried her head once more in my shoulder. Then we fell silent, as we tried to imagine how life might have been. But it was too huge an idea to grasp without going mad.

"We survived," I said at last. "That's all that matters."

She raised her head, and her dark eyes pierced me, even as a tear glittered in the corner of each. "We can't alter the past," she agreed solemnly, "but the future is all ours."

We might be past our prime, mentally and physically depleted, but after what she had said, with all the boldness she had shown in our dream, but one question remained: the simplest and most momentous. "In that case, will you marry me?"

For a full minute she stared gravely into my eyes, her hands resting on my shoulders. Then slowly her face radiated a broad smile of pure pleasure. "Of course I will." Our embrace was as electric as that moment in the boathouse when her inspection of my scalded hand had triggered our first explosion of passion. Then our feelings had been raw and new: now we came together as old lovers in joyous affirmation of what had long gone unspoken. Finally drawing a little away, she let forth a roguish laugh. "It's nice to know the key reflexes remain in full working order." She kissed me again. "Not that I ever doubted them."

Laughing too, I asked her to name the day.

Chapter Twenty-Nine : Crime & Punishment

Hope had, of course, known Mallory's plans all along, and she had shown Jake a copy of them on her BlackBerry, whilst in the early days of therapy Mallory had painfully typed out a summary for me. Reminding me, as she had done over the shorting, that it was impossible to achieve everything for everybody, she explained that her aims were strictly practical. The Sanatorium was not to be a permanent rest home, a final hospice for the dying; rather it was a place to which the seriously impaired and their families could come for a recuperative break: anything from a week to two months. During that time, the victims would not only be looked after physically, they would also have access to the best advice on how to pursue their claims for compensation from the firms which had injured and incapacitated them, or else from their insurers. Prior to the accident she had already begun fruitful discussions with Lloyd's.

Keeping the project moving was demanding, but the hospital soon realised that its importance reinforced our therapy. Armand became our invaluable legal advisor, who smoothed away all obstacles to the rapid development of the new site. Jake split his time between his London clients and the new Sanatorium, on which he went into temporary partnership with a local architect, introduced to him through Sidonie. She and Céline were always dropping into the site to offer advice and moral support, though their main activity was acquiring two small development sites with the cash we had released to them.

René helped to find and choose the right staff, as well as promising to be our chief medical advisor. Hope was confirmed as Ghost Trader's new active trader. As I had anticipated, the members forgave the subterfuge once they realised what it had achieved for them.

Marie-Sainte took on all our computing, including the design of an online booking procedure, which she turned into a register of all industrial accident victims, not just those insured by Lloyd's. Our aim was fair and speedy settlement, and we hoped to become the focal point for both plaintiffs and defendants. How well we succeed remains to be seen, but at least we have all the infrastructure in place.

The greatest revelation was Andréa. Fulfilled as a husband and as a father, he became a different man. Neither his humour nor his cynicism deserted him, but he now had a cause, as he explained when he came to see me one morning, in late January. It was a cold, blustery day, and the physio had been delayed by a fallen tree outside her house. Mallory had gone to the pool, and for once I had time on my hands.

"I hope I'm not disturbing you." Andréa looked curiously diffident, and I reassured him that I was at his disposal. "I've been wanting to catch you alone." He lowered himself into my one easy chair, and I returned to the desk, and fingered my keyboard: useful idle-time therapy, as the physio had taught me. "I've freelanced for you so far. What I'm after now is to run your press office, with full responsibility for your P.R." He watched me from under lowered lids, and I gestured for him to continue. "Believe me, I'm a changed man.

"What you and Madame Mallory are doing... you've inspired me, and I want to be a member of the team. I'll even work for free, until I've proved myself." At least he had not lost his self-confidence. "Just to show that I mean it," he continued earnestly, "I'm adapting the book, to show there's hope for the world after all, thanks to you two. As for *Monsieur De l'Ombre*, he's out. His values are too negative."

"I thought you were the fearless investigative journalist."

"You're family," he said, "and Madame about to be."

"I know you've talked about me being Clémentine's godfather. But that's not family exactly, is it?" Not that I wished to dissuade him, but I was nonplussed by this change of heart, and I wanted to be sure he meant it. "Perhaps this is your wife's suggestion?"

"I suppose she hasn't said, has she?" He shrugged, to show that the real answer was more complicated. "About you being her father." So it was true. Wormsley had not simply been stirring it. I was almost too overcome to speak, but I managed to ask him if she was sure.

"Absolutely." His smile was almost that of his old self, except that there was warmth not mischief in his eyes. "She persuaded the hospital to do a DNA test. With you both here, it was simplicity itself."

Now it was my turn to smile. Marie-Sainte might be too shy to tell me the truth herself, yet she was persuasive enough with the hospital authorities. "Does Sidonie know this?"

"Of course. And Papa Armand. They're both rather happy."

This was almost too good to be true, and I did my best to keep my feelings under control. "What about Marie-Sainte?" Her not telling me might be a sign that she had reservations, despite naming her daughter after me, and despite her vigil at my bedside. Parentage was no trivial matter, and Marie-Sainte was a woman of delicate sensibilities.

"She's overjoyed." Andréa laughed, which told me that he felt the same. We both rose to our feet, though I needed his steadying hand, and indulged in a fulsome embrace. "She's been wanting to tell you, but she didn't know how you'd feel... or Madame Mallory."

"You can tell Marie-Sainte from me that I couldn't be happier." Then, fighting the tears of joy that prickled my eyes, I told him something of what we had not included in our narrative of the trial. "So you can tell her that Mallory understands everything."

"We asked your permission to marry. You won't remember."

"Not exactly." Then I described how in my dream he had told me about the pregnancy, how she had later invited me to the wedding, and something of my attendance there. He confirmed that the reception had indeed taken place on one of the lake steamers.

"So you came in spirit. I'm glad." He seemed so genuinely pleased that I did not tell him of our quarrel over *Monsieur De l'Ombre*. He had, after all, redeemed himself by warning me of Ambrose's discovery of the boathouse. "So shall I call you Papa Clem from now on?"

I clapped him on the shoulder. Whatever my old reservations about him, his love for my newly-established daughter was undeniable. Of his abilities I had few doubts, and now I knew that he meant well, I was eager to help him. "I'll speak to Mallory," I assured him.

To my pleasant surprise, she was entirely supportive. "I know I was rude about him in the dream, but now that I've met him and seen how he works, I like him. We need a man who'll tell it straight, who won't indulge in corporate-speak. In fact, darling, he's just like you."

I could only laugh. "Shall I tell him, or will you?"

"We'll both tell him. Then he'll know he's part of the team."

All that remained was for the hospital to declare us fit enough to leave. But despite our progress, doctors and therapists were unanimous in their caution. Perhaps they were right, perhaps they were over-protective of their famous charges; either way, Mallory persuaded me to go along with them. "Whatever you think, they're the experts," she told me in tones that would not be over-ruled.

As a result, our first unsupervised venture beyond the hospital was to attend Sidonie and Armand's tenth wedding anniversary party, where we felt it was appropriate to announce our intention to be married mid June. By one of those symbolic strokes of Fate, the day of the party turned out also to be the day that Bernie Madoff pleaded guilty to all eleven charges against him: March 12th 2009.

"Where will you live?" asked Amy, as the party began.

She and Saul had just returned from New Jersey, glad of a respite from the anger of investors and the more calculated outrage of their lawyers. She had already inspected my apartment, and declared it too small for anything other than emergency accommodation. "Not that I'm saying we won't be needing something similar in the end," she'd announced bravely. She had then spent the early part of the evening inspecting Sidonie's adaptations to her old apartment. Whether she approved the new decor, with its mixed trappings of showroom and *salon*, I doubted, but she had always been capable of tact, as well as an admirer of Sidonie's acumen.

Now, she had young Clémentine in her arms, and was intent on making her laugh. "Fancy calling you after my old husband," she cooed. "But why not? He'll be a good god-father, yes he will. And if he isn't, he'll answer to me."

We all laughed at that, with the exception of Clémentine, who nevertheless furrowed her brow in a fervour of concentration, her clear eyes following Amy's lips intently. Needless to say, I had not told Amy about Marie-Sainte, though she may well have guessed. She had always had the most acute antennae.

"We're going to live on the new site," Mallory explained. "We move in on our wedding day. Two weeks before the place opens for its first guests." We'd long ago decided that we would never call those we tried to help patients. "We have a whole corner to ourselves."

"I'm not sure I'd want to live over the shop," Amy declared.

"We're very hands on," I reminded her. "*Over* the shop is right, but Mallory's too modest. It's more tower than corner." Amy smiled, but I could see from the tiny wrinkle of her nose that she couldn't understand why we'd want to exchange one hospital for another. "Think of it as living in your own hotel in the best suite, with everything on tap."

Now that the conversation had veered away from her, Clémentine began to fret for the more familiar embrace of her mother, to whom Amy graciously but rapidly relinquished her. Then she took Mallory's arm, and drew her into a corner. I'd warned Mallory to expect a catechism, though I was sure she could fend for herself.

They looked well together, the one fair and vivacious, the other calm and dark. The simplicity of Amy's ensemble – blue shot silk, full length but neither too full in the skirt nor too figure-hugging, offset by single diamonds at ears and throat, and a wrist watch as narrow as a bracelet – could not disguise the fact that she was the most expensively dressed woman in the room. Her hair too was fuller and longer in the American style. Yet I preferred the clean lines of Mallory's trouser suit, and her relaxed manner. Amy was gushing and condescending, Mallory reserved and amused. Amy would tell me later how well they had got on, and how much she liked my wife-to-be, yet I knew that Mallory had found the encounter a strain. Nor could Amy have known how taxing it was for Mallory never once to reveal her stoop.

As for my friends, they could not have been more natural. Armand made a little speech in which he spent as much time congratulating us on the progress of our recovery as he did on the joys of his ten years of marriage, and he wished me and my wonderful partner-to-be as much good health and happiness as he wished on their own future.

Sidonie, in her quiet way, was no less emphatic. "She's right for you, Clem." I sensed too that she was more than happy about my fathering Marie-Sainte, though she never once alluded to the matter.

René did his best to entertain Saul, who was the only person there who looked uncomfortable. Not attuned to René's sardonic wit, he did his best to seem entertained. He got on better with Marie-Sainte, who could charm anybody, and well enough at first with Andréa, until his criticism of the financial world became too pointed.

"Not that I'm entirely disagreeing with you, young sir, but let me say, as one more familiar with the ways of Wall Street, that political interference never cured anything." His voice carried through the room. "I'll grant the banks, etc have a lot to answer for, but the free market will cripple the rogues better than anything they cook up on the Hill. The best you'll get from those assholes is hot air and horseshit."

With some signs of his new tactfulness, Andréa assured him that politicians in Europe were not to be outclassed in either department. But the suggestion that Europeans could outperform their American counterparts, even in ineptitude, seemed too like a challenge to Saul. Reckoning it was time to intervene, I explained to Céline, with whom I had been enjoying a civilised conversation about the property market, that Saul was in need of rescue.

"Of course. It must be difficult for him not speaking French."

That was not my point, as she well understood, but she maintained the pretence. Which was ironic now that English was the language in which I found conversation harder. It was Céline, therefore, who did her best to give Saul the benefit of her English small talk, whilst I reminded Andréa in French that Saul too was a victim.

"He told me," Andréa said. "I'm putting him in my story. The victim of a real crook." His smile was almost benign, but he could not suppress the cynical slant to his brow. "Though Madoff is more honest than the rest. What was it Brecht said: robbing a bank is nothing to the crime of founding one?" Andréa might be acquitting himself well as our press officer, but he had not lost his revolutionary zeal.

"That's too extreme," I objected. "Banks doing their normal thing is fine. It's all the other nonsense they now get up to that puts them in the Madoff league. And it's not just banks. I wasn't screwed by a bank, and nor were Mallory's clients. It's not even confined to the financial sector. No con man could operate without his willing marks."

"Sharks need prey: prey don't need sharks."

"Sharks are sharks: that's how they're made. Humans don't have to be con men or bankers; bankers don't have to be sharks."

"And you, Papa Clem, prove that Anglo-Saxons don't have to act like Anglo-Saxons. Truly, I have the best of fathers-in-law!"

The wine was going to his head, and I laid a calming hand on his arm. "Hone your philosophy on Céline. I must speak to Saul."

He grinned wickedly. "To see he's good enough for your ex?"

"Too late for that. I lost all responsibility for Amy long ago."

With that we turned again to the others, and after a few minutes of awkward conversation, I managed to draw Saul to one side. However I might have blustered, Andréa was right. I *was* anxious about Amy. Saul sensed it immediately, and his heartiness during our opening exchanges could not mask his wariness. I got straight to the point.

"Great party or not, Saul, are you two going to be OK?"

"Way back, when we came to the hospital, I promised you I'd look after her." Resplendent in mohair suit and perma-tan, he exuded sincerity. "Maybe you don't remember."

"I remember. Some things you do, even in a coma."

"Amy said you'd registered." He nodded wisely. "I meant it."

"I'm sure you did. But that was before the shit hit the fan." Maybe the wine was getting to my head, too, but I found that the English part of my brain was now functioning perfectly.

"I warned her it'll be rough." He looked me straight in the eye, man to man. "But she insists we see it through together."

"I ruined her once. I don't want her going through it again."

"Don't think I'm not feeling bad about all this. Blame me if you have to. But Amy – God bless her – 100% does not." Leaning closer, he lowered his voice. "Truth is she feels bad about quitting on you the last time." He nodded emphatically. "It's true, I swear to God."

Amy having regrets was music to my ears, if I could believe it.

"I was the one who never listened to her warnings."

His face saddened. "She said *you* warned her against *me*."

"Not you," I corrected him, "Madoff. But I had nothing to go on."

"You and the rest. He absolutely suckered us all. But if you'd met the guy you'd understand. The way he spoke, the way he'd take your arm and level with you. He was like 'Saul, when have I ever let you down, when have I ever failed to deliver? Trust me.'" He punched fist into palm. "Jail's too good for guys like him. Pity he never cheated on the mob. They'd have whacked him by now. No question."

"That wouldn't get your money back," I countered sharply. "You all relied on his bedside manner instead of challenging his data."

"Regular printouts for fund managers, same for every goddamned client." Saul's tone turned petulant. "What was to challenge?"

"The data was bullshit," I snapped, my anger rising with his.

"I'm no number-cruncher." He made it sound like a commendation. "But if the SEC saw zilch to question, how was I out of line?"

I remembered all too vividly Marie-Sainte telling me how the SEC had brushed aside the few whistle-blowers, so I could hardly blame Saul for not being one of the astute few. But I said nothing.

"OK, OK! I goofed big-time!" He spread his palms in a show of contrition. "To make amends, I want to help you guys."

"You've helped already," I conceded, "and we appreciate it."

"That was for openers. I mean on a lasting basis." He took my arm in his best confidential manner. "I'm a salesman, and I'm darned good at it." That at least wasn't difficult to accept. "But I'm no originator. That's where guys like you and Mallory come in. You have the ideas, then you hand them over to guys like me to make the pitch. Symbiosis, right?" His eyes sparkled in supplication. "Fact is, I'd kill for the chance. What you're aiming for is so right on. Getting the rich to part with a piece of their hard-earned in a just cause. That's so feel-good, it's win-win all the way. Even young Andréa would approve."

After that, we both relaxed, whilst Armand, ever the attentive host, replenished our glasses. "You know, Saul," I said loudly as the wine mellowed my tongue, "Bernie Madoff was more honest than any of Wall Street." He stared at me as though I were crazy. "He knew there was a risk of going to jail, and he took it. Whereas all the rest keep their ill-gotten bonuses, and their organisations get rescued by governments into the bargain. Supposing Madoff had been too big to fail?"

"What are you telling me here? The Street were doing a Ponzi?"

"Worse than that. A legal Ponzi."

"Holy shit!" Only Saul could be both non-committal and emphatic.

If I were to push the point further, I needed the leavening of humour. "Do you know the one about the professor and the socialite?"

Only then did I notice that the room had been silent for a minute. Or more. Saul and I had been talking far too loudly. René raised his glass with a wicked smile. "Don't keep it to yourselves. Tell us all."

The entire party gathered eagerly around me, just as they had in the days of my prime. But this wasn't the old days, this was now, and my powers were as diminished as my wealth. I looked desperately for rescue, but Mallory only grinned. There was nothing else for it, and I launched into the joke, with René translating *sotto voce*.

"An economics professor and a beautiful socialite get talking at a cocktail party, and they discover they've both seen the film in which Robert Redford offers a woman a million dollars to sleep with him." Once I was started the words came easily. "They debate whether the film is true to life. 'For example, if I offered you a million dollars,' he asks her earnestly, 'would you sleep with me?'

"She laughs. 'I was wondering the same thing. The answer's yes, I suppose I would. There's a lot you can do with a million dollars. Plenty for good causes as well as for yourself.'

"The prof smiles. 'So how about sleeping with me for a $100?'

"Taken aback, she decides he's joking. 'You're not serious?'

"He smiles one of those superior academic smiles. 'I'm perfectly serious. Would you sleep with me for $100?'

"Now she's affronted. 'What do you take me for, a hooker?'

"He nods. 'That we've established. Now we're negotiating price.'"

The Frenchmen laughed loudly. Céline, inured to René's humour, was almost as appreciative, but Marie-Sainte, though she smiled, could not prevent her cheeks reddening. Sidonie merely shrugged, whilst Amy and Mallory exchanged rueful smiles. "Not bad as financial jokes go," Mallory observed. "Shame about the sexism,".

Only Saul looked puzzled. "So what's your point here?"

"Duh!" said Amy. "Wall Street don't think they're whores either."

"It's worse than that," said Marie-Sainte, unable to contain herself, yet blushing all the harder. "Because they all do so much better than a million dollars, Wall Street and the City have convinced themselves they're saints who can do no wrong."

Chapter Thirty : Wedding Bells & Warnings

We were finally released from hospital at the end of April. But, as our development would not be ready for six weeks, we moved into my apartment, where we remained as busy and active as ever. Waking each morning with a list of tasks to complete, calls to make, and progress to check, I felt rejuvenated. As for Mallory, she never stopped.

If she had a problem, it was the need to delegate so much more than she'd been used to. But, she was as quick as ever to learn, and we soon developed an infallible routine, in which she would cajole and I would bully. Not that we needed too much of either tactic.

The triumvirate of Jake, Sidonie and Céline kept building work on schedule, whilst Armand cleared all legal and bureaucratic hurdles. Andréa's publicity, in which he worked the internet as much as the traditional media, ensured that we were booked solid for our first year, whilst Marie-Sainte's system guaranteed that everyone was fitted in as efficiently as possible. Saul more than lived up to his promise, keeping our cash flow healthily positive. So positive that Mallory and Hope now had two funds to run: Ghost Trader I, for the existing membership of ex-Names, and Ghost Trader II for the new venture.

With an eye to tradition more than faith, we married in the village church. Andréa teased me about it, until I reminded him of Pascal's wager. "You prayed for our recovery despite your lack of belief, and now we want to give thanks in a proper place of worship. And never forget that some of our guests will feel a need for spiritual consolation. It's not for us to tell them what to believe or not to believe."

As a result he participated in the service with enthusiasm, and afterwards he conversed for some time with the *curé*. He told me later that he was cementing our *concordat*. If dictators made accommodation with the church why shouldn't we in a good cause?

After the ceremony, *Madame de Maintenant* drove us, whilst the convoy of cars behind endlessly sounded their horns, in the French tradition. Under contract to ferry our guests from Annecy station or Geneva airport, she had invested in two new people carriers, and hired her son-in-law and his brother as drivers. Delighted with her expanded business, and intrigued that I should have dreamt of her taking me to the Sanatorium, she felt personally responsible for our success.

In just over two weeks, the last Monday in June, we would open our doors to our first guests, and now the all-but-completed site made an ideal setting for our wedding reception. Situated on a plateau, half-way up the hillside above Talloires, the building took the form of a shallow arc, with all guest rooms facing the village and its bay. Its clean pastel lines were a long way from the brooding Gothic of the Sanatorium, though Jake had topped one end with a square tower to provide us with an apartment and an office suite. With balconies front and back, and a roof terrace, we had everything we needed. It was state of the art and easy to use, without encumbering the building proper.

For the reception, the site was open for scrutiny, and the wedding guests enjoyed exploring and testing everything. It was a beautiful day, and we had the long windows on the ground floor open, so that indoors and out made a harmonious whole. We kept things informal, allowing everyone to mingle at will. As Mallory and I walked hand-in-hand amongst our guests, I felt wonderfully fulfilled.

Despite our brush with death, we were now close to achieving everything. Far from being crippled and useless, we had most of our faculties in working order. After years of self-centred and miserable inertia, I once more had a business to run and a life to lead.

"Thank you, my darling, my love, for coming into my life."

She said nothing, but her eyes shone with a deep lustre.

"I'm so happy for you both." We were so lost in ourselves that we'd failed to see Madame Linberger's approach. Her normally hard features were softened by a rare smile. Yet, in her unadorned black dress, she cut an austere figure amongst the other guests, and the pain of her loss was apparent still in her eyes. "It was kind of you to think of me."

"Jean-Michel was my rock," Mallory said. "I really miss him."

"But you have Monsieur Holden." *Madame L'Esprit* laughed thinly. "I'm sure he's less brusque than my husband, God rest his soul."

Mallory smiled pleasantly. "I wouldn't be so sure of that."

Before I could say anything in my defence, the catering manager was at Mallory's elbow. "I'm sorry, Madame, if I might trouble you?"

Mallory excused herself, and I was left alone with *Madame L'Esprit*. "I want to thank you, Monsieur, for your kindness at the time of my husband's accident." Her voice faltered, but she managed to steady herself. "I'm sorry that I caused such a fuss."

"Your reactions were entirely reasonable, Madame," I assured her.

313

"You may not know it, but they made me retract what I said about the skier in black." Her hands fretted with the clasp of her bag. "There were other witnesses who saw things differently." Her voice was controlled, but there was no mistaking her anger and despair. I almost forgot that we'd spoken since only in my dream.

"I believed you then, Madame," I assured her, "and I still believe you." Her eyebrows shot up, but she did not contradict me.

I ought to have left it at that, but her anguish was too palpable to ignore. "I didn't say anything at the time, because I wasn't sure. But I am now. The skier in black was an ex-Lloyd's Name, with a grudge against your husband... and against Robert de St Hippocrate."

Her lip trembled. "Then it *was* murder."

"In both cases. Not that I can prove it, but I'm sure I'm right."

She cast anxious glances around her, as though she feared that Ambrose might be amongst the guests. "Have you told anybody?"

"Only Mallory, and she agrees with me."

Her eyes narrowed. "Then what are we to do about it?"

Far from consoling her, I had succeeded only in whetting her desire for justice. "There's nothing we can do. He's already dead."

"How do you know?"

Ambrose had died only in our dream, yet I was almost convinced that it had happened in fact. As for Mallory, on the one occasion we'd talked about it since, she'd agreed even more strongly. "The detail may have differed from reality, but the substance of the dreams was always true," she'd assured me. "Briefing Marie-Sainte, the shorting, the trial: they all had their parallels in reality." I'd agreed that the car crash had been too vivid to mean nothing, and then we'd dropped the subject, all too anxious to banish Ambrose from our thoughts.

My dream at the point of recovery had been a sharp reminder of Ambrose's ability, in my pre-accident nightmares, to climb inside my head. Fortunately, the demands of therapy and of the development since then had ensured that I slept too soundly for dreams of any kind. Until now, Ambrose seemed to have perished with my coma.

"Officially he committed suicide, jumping off a Channel ferry," I began, choosing my words carefully. The last thing I wanted was her asking awkward questions of the authorities. "We think he faked it, so he could carry out his revenge unsuspected. The last I heard, and I hope it's true, he was killed in a car crash in December."

"You don't seem very sure."

I shrugged apologetically. "I've had other things on my mind."

"I quite understand, Monsieur." She hesitated. "But if you could find out for certain, I would be grateful. It would give me some kind of closure. I'm sure you understand. Then, of course, I should be in a frame of mind to make a contribution to your cause."

"I'll do my best. As for contributions, that would be most generous."

"My husband would have wanted it." She composed herself once more. "Meanwhile, am I permitted to know this man's name?"

"When I have all the facts, Madame, I will tell you as much about him as I can. But I must crave your discretion. I would not wish to hurt the feelings of people dear to me." I could only hope that she would understand how important it was to keep her mouth shut.

She stiffened. "Monsieur, that goes without saying."

Before either of us could say more, a cluster of guests approached, and in the swirl of greetings we were separated.

"Clem, it's so wonderful to see you up and doing." Max Carstairs pushed through the throng. Just behind him came the diminutive figure of George Wiseman, wedding-smart, with his wife on his arm.

"George came to see you when you were in hospital." She laughed self-consciously. "It was so kind of you to invite us."

His eyes twinkled agreement. "I was in Geneva at the time."

"Winding up a collapsed hedge fund." I grinned at his surprise. "My visitors always talked to me, and I wasn't quite as asleep as I seemed. In fact, you told me so much, I look on you as an old friend."

"The hospital encouraged it," he concurred. "It seems they really knew what they were talking about."

"As for Mallory, she wants to thank you for being understanding over the collapse of the Tonbridge syndicate, and to show you that everything she did after Rex's death was in a good cause."

"*Two* causes, if all I hear is true. I gather you're booked solid."

"Yes," I agreed. "Thanks to all the support we've had."

"International from the off, I see, though we're surprised the locals let you put the English part of the name first, aren't we darling?"

His wife nodded. "Haven *L'Abri* is a bit of a mouthful."

"Naming by committee, I'm afraid. The idea is you use whichever name you're more familiar with. As for the word order, there was quite a debate over that." Opinion had split about equally between those who thought French should come first as we were based in France, and those who thought that we should start with the more internationally recognisable name. "Mallory had the casting vote, of course."

"Your wife's a remarkable woman," he agreed. Then he lowered his voice, and his eye lost its twinkle. "A word in your ear." He drew me aside, a pre-arranged action, judging from the acquiescence of his companions. "I've a friend in the Serious Fraud Office, and he told me an odd story about Ghost Trader. Last September he had an anonymous letter alleging that the members were being defrauded. Far from being safely invested, as they were led to believe, the fund had been used for a massive and very risky short."

Last September! The month the short had paid off, and not long after Andréa, at his wedding, had denounced the four investment platforms as a cover for fraud, based on his chats with *De l'Ombre*. As always, my dreams had been a distorting mirror on reality, and I fought to keep my tone nonchalant. "What did your friend do?"

George frowned, yet his eyes regained their twinkle, as if he were torn two ways. "He put out feelers naturally, just to see if there was anything in it, and he satisfied himself that the fund *had* been used for a massive shorting operation, which had been very successful."

"So it was a success," I parried. "What's his problem?"

"It depends who got the distributable profit. Did it all go to the members, or was any creamed off the top?" He glanced meaningfully around him. "Even for the benefit of this place, that's fraud."

"Is that an accusation?" In my alarm, I felt my temper rising.

He pursed his lips. "Therein lies my friend's difficulty. At the time of the shorting, the fund was being managed by your new daughter-in-law, Hope. Yet the letter puts the blame on you and Mallory."

The protest died in my throat. Our comas provided Mallory and me with the perfect alibi, yet I could hardly shift the blame onto Hope. George smiled as he read the dilemma in my face.

"You and Mallory could have planned it before the accident, then you could have passed it on to Hope in an interlude of lucidity. That's how the writer explained it anyway. He claimed you'd briefly come out of your coma, and told Hope how to bring off the deception."

The brief recovery was certainly how Hope had explained to Marie-Sainte how I had been the one to recommend her.

"Alternative on-line viewing platforms," he continued, "one of them showing the shorting, but ostensibly only as an exercise." More or less exactly what Andréa had said to me in my dream. "Ingenious and simple. Just like recycling Tonbridge syndicate money through *Risque Alsacien* was ingenious and simple." His voice hardened. "I trust your wife's told you all about the Tonbridge syndicate?"

"You certainly did. Like I said, I wasn't entirely asleep."

I had the brief satisfaction of seeing his double-take. So often had my visitors proved to be the conduit between reality and dream, that it

316

was unlikely that my encounter with George could have stemmed entirely from my imagination. But it wasn't much of a respite.

"That would make all three of you culpable." He gazed up at me, his head cocked expectantly on one side. "If there's anything you want to tell me, I'm all ears. Off the record and without prejudice."

I did my best to assume an air of dignified affront. "I don't know there's much I can add, on or off the record." In my dream, George had let Mallory off the hook because she'd persuaded him to believe in Ghost Trader; now she had been lured away by the catering manager. But I couldn't afford to stall until she returned, I must speak out immediately. Stalling would only encourage him to dig further.

"As always, the members got the profit they were entitled to, which is virtually all of it. They know what happened and why, and they accept their good fortune. As for here, all our money is legitimately raised." He nodded encouragingly, but of course he wanted something more concrete than my uncorroborated word. "You can look at the books if you want. Ghost Trader's, too."

His manner softened immediately. "That would help a lot."

"It's got to do better than that. If the books satisfy you, I want your word that's the end of the matter." Now it was my turn to sweep my gaze over the site. "Our aims here are purely philanthropic. Any hint of scandal could jeopardise the entire project, ruin everything Mallory's worked for during the last ten years. Is that what you want?"

"I can't answer for the SFO, of course," he said carefully.

"You can do what you like with me," I added self-righteously, "but it would be the supreme irony if the only members of the financial sector to be punished for the credit crunch were two fund managers who'd succeeded in making their clients five times richer."

"That thought had crossed my friend's mind," he conceded.

"A jury would laugh it out of court."

"I will need to see the books." He was definitely weakening. "And I will need your reassurance there'll be no repeat performance."

"The past's dead," I assured him. "All we want is a future."

"So when could I drop by?" He was nothing if not persistent.

"We're back in work mode Monday. Say 10 a.m.?" We shook hands on it. "Does your friend have any idea who sent this tip-off?"

"The letter was posted in France, and it was signed Charon. My guess is that's the user name of a disaffected member."

"To the best of my knowledge, no member has or had that user-name." Being the name of the legendary ferryman who transported the dead across the River Styx into the underworld, Charon was more private and more pointed, and it confirmed the more likely of the two people who had discussed the doings of Ghost Trader last August and September. Ambrose had every reason to disapprove of a short in which he could not share, whereas Andréa had assured me that he was cutting all references to *Monsieur De l'Ombre* from his book.

With that, George took his leave, and I went in search of Mallory. I was seriously in need of her cheering presence. More importantly, I had to warn her about George coming to inspect the books. Scouring the building and grounds, I found her at last in the car park, bidding goodbye to a po-faced man, as he climbed into a mid-range Renault of nondescript colour. Similarly unremarkable, he wore his mid-brown hair *en brosse*, and his suit looked too lived-in for that of a wedding guest. Nor did I recognise him from the church. As he drove off, she watched stiffly as he passed the gate, but she did not wave.

"Who was that?" I asked, as she re-joined me. She smiled, but I knew that something was wrong. "What's the problem?"

"Nothing. I hope." Her eyes had the shuttered look that I hadn't seen since recovery, and I feared that we were back to her old secretiveness. Until she continued. "There wasn't a catering problem. Monsieur Porfirie's from the police. A judicial investigator, no less." She laughed grimly. "He claimed he didn't realise it was our wedding day."

My heart skipped several beats. George's bombshell had been bad enough, but the police were far worse. "What did he want?"

"It seems Ambrose really did kill himself in the Peugeot."

Ambrose, Ambrose! On what was supposed to be the happiest day of our lives, he was suddenly plaguing us at every turn.

"So the dream was true!" At least investigator Porfirie's news was confirmation, but it couldn't prevent my fear from kicking in. "The accident was months ago. Why now all of a sudden?"

"He needs to know how Ambrose came to have my car."

"You were in a coma. How could you possibly know?"

"I should have reported the car as lost or stolen. Or Hope should." She slipped her arm into mine. "I honestly don't think it's anything to worry about. He came to the hospital several times, apparently, but they refused to let him see me, and I told him in no uncertain terms that we've had things other than cars on our minds; nor did I wish to have our wedding disturbed. But he insists on coming back Monday."

"Monday!" I groaned. "He's not going to be our only visitor." I told her about George. "Showing the books was the only option."

As so often, Mallory faced the new crisis squarely. "You did the right thing. And don't look so worried. What can they do?"

"They could put us in jail. If Ambrose wrote to the SFO, how do we know he didn't write to the police as well? About the ferry."

She stopped dead, as this new possibility weighed on her. Then with a shake of the head, she dragged me on. "Impossible. If he had, Porfirie would have insisted on interviewing me, doctors or no."

"But he can't be coming about nothing."

"It's all red tape. He has a file to close, and he's sat on it so long his superiors are giving him grief. He needs something to put in it."

Her words were more assured than her expression. "There's no point speculating what he knows. We'll find out soon enough." She kissed me fervently. "Right now, let's enjoy the rest of our wedding."

We both did our best to cheer up. That evening none danced longer nor more spiritedly than we, and that night our passion was unbridled. But when I fell finally asleep in Mallory's arms, no blissful oblivion awaited me. Ambrose was back in my dreams. Worse, I seemed now to be Ambrose, just as I'd been in the dream of Wormsley's death, and in the minutes before recovery. Dead he might be, but his ability to invade our lives had lain only dormant.

Chapter Thirty-One : Due Diligence

I left the hut early, when the beach was deserted, and made for the station, from where I took the Eurostar to Paris. It was a long walk to the station at Sangatte, but I was determined, it seemed, not to waste money on unnecessary bus journeys. By the time I'd bought my ticket, I was glad to rest my blistered feet. I was apprehensive that the man at the ticket office would denounce me, but he was too bored in his business-like way to take any notice of me at all. To him, I was just another nondescript passenger. It was lucky that I, Ambrose that is, had always had the ability to blend invisibly with the background. I, or rather he, should have been a spy or a private detective.

Gare du Nord was vast and impersonal. I blended effortlessly into its hurrying throngs. Once outside I followed the overhead tracks of Metro line 2 in the direction of Barbès-Rochehouart, and then into the tightly-packed streets of the tenth *arrondissement*. Here there were no gardens nor courtyards, only the flat impersonal walls of terraced buildings, not high-rise, but tall enough to overshadow the narrow pavements onto which life spilled. I had constantly to step around the narrow tables of the cafés at which old men hunched in their overcoats and puffed on the stems of their hubble-bubble pipes, or the trestles on which were displayed rolls of fabric and carpet, kitchenware and plates, knick-knacks and shoes, as though the dark interiors of the establishments themselves were no place for living beings.

Even their proprietors preferred to hover in the doorways, as though daylight mattered to them so much that the wintry cold could not keep them indoors. The mist of their breath blurred and softened the scene so that I felt as if I were walking through an impressionist painting. My pace never faltered. It seemed that I knew where I was going.

Sure enough, in a few streets I arrived at the entrance to a scruffy hotel, set between a horse butcher, a golden horse head above its door, and a night club that was closed now but which promised to be both garish and noisy that night. The hotel was small and dingy, cheap only by Paris standards, and more expensive than the tiny room on its top floor deserved. It was a long climb up the narrow, uncarpeted stairs, but I consoled myself that the exercise would do me no harm, and that I would be as far from the sounds of the nightclub as possible.

Not that it mattered. I planned to spend as little time in the hotel as possible. From dawn until dusk I was pounding the streets. On my tight budget, bus and metro were out. My first call was to one of the general stores I'd passed on the way to the hotel, where I chose a small roll of plastic bags. There were several varieties to choose from, and I chose carefully, but not so slowly that I would arouse the shopkeeper's awareness. For the same reason, I bought one or two other useful items, including a black beret that was almost Basque in its capaciousness. The total was €20, but my supply was still holding up well.

My destination was the *Bois de Boulogne*, whose every pathway I combed with great care, until after nearly a week I found the man I was looking for. He was a middle-aged jogger, taking his daily exercise slowly but determinedly. Tanned and confident, and only slightly overweight, he reminded me of Rex Tonbridge. Yet there was a furtiveness about him, too. He would glance sharply around him, as though expecting to be accosted, and he kept to the narrower and less frequented paths. His confidence seemed now to be defiance.

I woke with a start. Mallory's side of the bed was empty, the duvet peeled back. The impression she had left in the mattress was cold, and the tower utterly silent. No singing nor scents of coffee and croissants greeted my senses, as they had on my first morning in the round tower of the gothic Sanatorium. The apartment was deserted, but her coat was still in the cloakroom, and she had taken none of her clothes from the bedroom. Her mobile was still beside her bedside reading lamp.

The sun was already well over the hills, and the air was warm, so I checked the roof terrace. There was no sign of her. Throwing on the first clothes I could find, I hurried down the stairs and into the main building. It took very little time to establish that it was entirely empty. I cast my eyes over the lawns that covered most of the plateau from the front of the building to the boundary wall. They were deserted. I hurried over springy turf towards the clumps of trees that broke up the vista, and shaded the seats on which our guests would be able to relax and to breathe clean air. But there was no Mallory enjoying the view from any of them. There remained only the water garden.

This was Mallory's particular favourite, tucked into the highest corner of the grounds. It was shady here, and the air was cooled by a small waterfall, splashing its way into a series of ponds, their surface covered in lily pads, their depths trammelled by sinuous carp. Alpine flowers in a riot of improbable blood reds, royal blues and butter yellows filled every fissure and crevice between the stones, fighting with the turf itself for growing space, their very scents teasing me with her aura but showing nothing of her presence.

Beside the cascade was a path leading up the wooded slope beyond the grounds. Being spring, the flow was strong, and some of the water had splashed onto the path. There in the mud I saw the imprint of bare feet. At last I had a trail to follow, and I hurried up the steepening path. It narrowed as it went. The thin cotton of her nightdress would have offered little protection for her legs against brambles and nettles.

Whatever had impelled this early morning ramble, it could not be benign, and my alarm mounted to panic the further I went. For the moment the path was small and private, but soon it would join another, more public way that led to the *Cascade d'Angon*, a huge waterfall that dropped 40 or 50 metres down a granite cliff into a rocky pool.

I joined the wider path. On a Sunday it was too early for walkers and I had it to myself. Running now, I pressed on as fast as I could go. The way narrowed again, and turned around the edge of a cliff. I could hear the rush of water long before I saw it. Then, as I rounded the buttress of rock, the path fell away steeply. I was on bare, slippery rock, but there was a rope handrail, and I was glad of its support.

I came to the bottom, then climbed again towards an iron railing, and a viewing point. The rush of water filled my ears as I reached the top. Before me was a curtain of water, shifting and eddying from the lip of the cliff above my head and down into the pool below. The water in the pool was dark and impenetrable. From here it was possible, with the aid of another rope, to scramble down behind the waterfall. Or else, I could climb up another narrow way to the very top. A muddy footprint showed the way, and I hurried upwards.

Then I saw her. She sat on a smooth granite boulder, staring down into the pool. The water slithered past her like an endless python, thick and undulating. Her perch was safe enough, provided she did not move suddenly, and she sat so quietly that there seemed little danger of that. The relief of seeing her safe was so powerful, that my legs shook as I made my way quietly up to her. She took no notice.

I was above her now, and the rock where she sat sloped downwards. I seized the branch of an overhanging birch and lowered myself down beside her. Then I took her in my arms. She lay against me, her eyes unseeing, and for a ghastly moment I thought the coma had returned. Then she stirred, and her eyes focused.

"Clem!" Smiling, she kissed me full on the mouth. Only then did she take in her surroundings, and her eyes dilated with shock.

But she recovered quickly. "I walked in my sleep! Haven't done that since I was a child." She smiled contritely. "Did I give you a terrible fright?" She inspected her ankles and shins, which were covered in scratches and nettle rash. "Ouch!" She grimaced as I ran soothing fingers over them. "I feel such a fool."

"Do you remember anything?" I asked.

Her brow furrowed. "Vaguely. I was following someone. I only ever saw his back. I think it was you, but I'm not sure. You know what dreams are like." She grinned. "Ordinary ones." Returning to the path, we walked homeward. "I don't know how I didn't wake up. The path is agony on my bare feet." She winced bravely. "I've never walked so far without waking up. It must be the shock of marriage."

"Talking of shock, I dreamt, too." I hesitated, then plunged on. This was the new era with no secrets between us. "About Ambrose."

"Ambrose?" she frowned. "I don't like the sound of that."

"No," I agreed. "But *Madame L'Esprit* was asking about him." I gave a brief account of our conversation. "I meant to tell you."

"Never mind, you handled her just fine. Tell me your dream."

"It was a follow-on from the dream I had just before we recovered." I'd described the swim to the *Calais* beach hut long ago, when neither of us had known what to make of it. "He – I – caught a train to Paris, and checked into a grotty hotel. Then I went to the *Bois de Boulogne* to look for a jogger. I don't know him, but Ambrose did."

"Describe him." I did. "Could be anybody."

We were back inside our grounds now, and Mallory was grateful for the soft grass of the lawn on her sore feet. Once inside, she took a hot shower, cleaned up her cuts and soothed her stings with calamine. By the time we'd had breakfast, the phones were going. It might be the Sunday after our wedding, but there were still tasks to complete if we were to be ready for our first guests. Nothing further was said about Ambrose, or sleep-walking, but that night I double locked all the doors. In bed, my dream resumed, almost where it had left off.

The jogger was a creature of habit, and after another week I knew all his circuits. I followed them round each day, after he'd gone, until I'd picked my spot: a clump of oak trees that topped a small hill. Not only was it secluded, it featured in all his routes. In the distance I could see the roof of a restaurant and cafe, which must once have been a hunting lodge, and the gleam of an ornamental lake, but here all was lonely. From the litter, I judged it to be the haunt of prostitutes and their clients, but, at this hour, all such folk were long gone.

It was another cold morning, and I was glad of my anorak and warm shirt. Fortunately, I didn't have long to wait before I heard the jogger panting up the path. The first I saw of him was the steam of his breath; then came his head, which was tilted down so that I could see his scalp through his thinning hair. When he was no more than a metre away, I stepped in front of him. "IBNR." There was no need to speak loudly, since all was quiet, the traffic but a subliminal hum.

He stopped as though he'd hit a wall. His eyes bulged and his lips worked. "You... you're..." He spoke in English.

"Dead." I finished his sentence for him. Then, as the colour leached from his face, I kicked his legs from under him. He fell heavily, and I had one of my precious plastic bags out of my pocket and over his head in a moment. Twining my fingers round the drawstrings, I tightened the bag around his neck. It was good quality, and he stood no chance.

Each time he drew in breath, the bag tightened around his nose and mouth. Shocked and breathless as he already was, his strength soon deserted him. All I had to do was hold the bag in place for another minute or two. Finally I tied the bag tightly around his head, and left his corpse to cool under the stark branches of the oak trees.

Because the dream was long, I slept late, and our policeman arrived early. So there was time only to give Mallory the bare outlines before Porfirie was being shown into the apartment by Sylvie, our new p.a.

A brisk, dark-haired thirty-something with dramatic features, she was the daughter of a retired doctor, with whom René had once worked. "He taught me all I know," René had explained. "Not the chemistry, but the psychology of patients. How their minds affect their bodies, and how their prejudices affect what they tell you. If half of his approach to life has rubbed off on Sylvie, she'll do you proud."

Told that Porfirie was here about Mallory's stolen car being involved in a fatal accident, she treated him with a deft politeness that reached but did not cross the threshold to condescension.

It was another sunny morning, and we invited him up to the roof terrace, where Sylvie offered him coffee and croissants. Close to, his face was hard but otherwise expressionless. Like his car, his eyes were of indeterminate colour, and gave nothing away.

Small talk was beyond him, and he went through the motions of choosing how he liked his coffee as though he were talking a foreign language, in which he was prepared to communicate only what was absolutely essential. Though he did allow himself two lumps of sugar.

But he showed no signs of wishing to drink.

As soon as Sylvie left, he extracted a notebook from his pocket, as well as a tape-recorder, for which he gave no explanation, but which he switched on with a jab of his finger. "There's no need to remain, Monsieur, but I have no objections to your doing so." Thereafter he ignored me, all his attention fixed on Mallory. "When did you learn of your husband's – I should say, your ex-husband's – suicide, Madame?" Mistake and correction seemed entirely rehearsed and intended.

"About two weeks after it happened. My daughter called me."

"Why the delay?"

"He'd been looking after a friend's car whilst the friend was sailing in the Caribbean, and he borrowed it for the trip. He even booked it in his friend's name with himself as passenger. They were so busy at Dover, they didn't argue when he turned up with a valid ticket."

"He didn't have his own car." It was a statement not a question. "So the poverty described in his suicide note was real. What went wrong?"

"They went through all that at the inquest."

"Which you did not attend. Why not?"

"I wasn't up to it. His death hit me hard, and the coroner said it was unnecessary, provided I made a statement sworn before a notary that could be read out at the inquest." She allowed herself a brief shrug: clear but not too eloquent. "They thought it was a routine matter."

"You weren't recently divorced. Why was his death such a shock?"

"This wasn't just death," she protested. "He'd committed suicide, or so everybody thought. I felt responsible." She shuddered. "If you must know, and I suppose you must, he was always asking me for money. Ever since he ruined himself over Enron. In the end I couldn't stand his importuning any more. So I came back to France."

"So you were already in France when he jumped?"

"From two months before. July fourteenth." She smiled. "Bastille Day. That's how I remember it." I hid my surprise by pouring more coffee. Surely she could not be so foolish as to give him such a precise date in the hopes that he wouldn't check? Then, with the coffee's warmth, came relief. In the replay at the trial, her car had had French licence plates, which likely meant she'd bought it in France. Then she'd returned with it to collect her stuff. So long as the investigator, like the coroner, didn't know of this trip, all was well.

"Did you see him or speak to him between Bastille Day and his ferry ride two months later?" His tone remained flat, almost bored.

"No. I didn't give him my address." Impressed by her calm, I was grateful that Porfirie continued to ignore me and my tension.

"What about your mobile?" His persistence fuelled my alarm.

"He never called me." Her shrug this time meant "so what?"

"Didn't you find that surprising? If he was short when you left, he must have stayed short, unless your daughter helped out."

"He knew I wouldn't answer," she replied coldly. "As for Hope, he was far too proud to sponge off his daughter."

"Yet he tried to sponge off you. Explain that to me."

"He saw it as getting back what he was owed." Her voice tightened with anger. "He blamed me for his losses. He thought I'd inveigled him into Lloyd's and that I'd deliberately sabotaged his chance to short Enron." Then she launched into the history of her marriage. She did not spare herself, nor did she disguise her bitterness against Ambrose. It was a daring tactic. If Porfirie knew nothing, she was providing him with the perfect motive for suicide, feigned or real; but if he suspected attempted murder, her every word incriminated her.

"So you had broken all contact with him?"

"Absolutely."

Sucking on the end of his pen, Porfirie paused to study his notes. I felt the sweat trickling down the inside of my shirt. Surely he must see it, hear it even. Fear grew into certainty that he was playing with us, waiting for the right moment to denounce her. As an interrogator, he was streets ahead of Wormsley, and as the silence lengthened, even Mallory could not refrain from drumming the table.

"Were you satisfied with the coroner's verdict?"

"I don't see what other verdict they could have reached."

"Drowning is not the most efficient means of self-destruction."

"He was squeamish about blood, so he wouldn't have slit his wrists. He hated taking pills, so he'd never have tried an overdose. He didn't own a gun. As for hanging, that would have appalled him. Painful and undignified." She talked fast, conviction growing with elaboration. "He was a good swimmer, you see. I took it he would have preferred fading away in a medium he understood. I also assumed he didn't want his body to be found." She smiled sadly. "I honestly thought he wanted to spare us the pain of identifying him."

"So it never occurred to you that he wanted only to disappear?"

Now that he'd shifted to Ambrose's motives for faking suicide, I couldn't suppress a sigh of relief. Immediately, his eyes drilled into me, and I muttered that croissants didn't agree with me: too fatty.

"Did you know that he also had a French passport? Registered in the name of Hanter." He pronounced it in the French way: like Antay.

She managed to look realistically surprised, even though she knew it from my description of the beach-hut dream.

"It took us time to connect the Monsieur Etienne Ambroise Antay with Mr Ambrose Stephen Hanter." He placed special emphasis on the H. "It seems that your former husband led a double life."

"It doesn't entirely surprise me. He was that kind of man."

Shy yet forceful when he needed to be, nondescript yet curiously appealing, Ambrose had been a bundle of contradictions, and his diffidence had always masked a streak of ruthless cunning.

"Faking the suicide was obviously well planned. He'd rented a beach hut in Calais, where we found a wet suit. He seems to have rested up there for a while, recovering from his ordeal in the Channel, no doubt. Mid-October finds him in Paris, and late November in Geneva. He even returned to the UK for Christmas." In time, I realised, to terrify Wormsley into cardiac arrest. For whatever reason, it seemed that my dreams were a window into Ambrose's soul.

"Didn't passport control pick him up?" I asked.

Porfirie allowed himself a judicious smile. "Border control is merely bureaucracy. Had he presented his British passport I've no doubt the checks would have shown that he was supposedly dead. But a French passport…" He completed the sentence with a shrug. Then he resumed his narrative. "Between Christmas and New Year he arrived in Annecy, by which time, Madame, you were living in Veyrier. When you had your accident, were you still in possession of your car?"

"Yes. I took a taxi to Aix for *St Silvestre*. When I got back, my car was still outside my apartment. It's above the old cable car station," she explained, "so no parking restrictions."

"Is it possible that your ex-husband tried to contact you at any time between his jumping from the ferry and your accident?" He glanced at me. "Your accidents, I should say."

Exactly at that moment, Sylvie appeared importantly. "Monsieur Wiseman has arrived." She pointed to her watch. "It is 10 a.m."

I lumbered to my feet. Jumping or springing were now beyond me. "I'll be right with him." I turned to Mallory. "Perhaps you could show him the right books?" I smiled regretfully at Porfirie. "If you'll excuse us, Monsieur. I only need Madame Holden for a moment." I crossed to his chair, and held out my hand. "Sadly, I myself have another meeting. Perhaps I'll see you before you go?" We shook hands solemnly.

On the stairs I instructed Sylvie to keep Monsieur Wiseman happy downstairs. Delighted at the prospect, she hurried away, whilst I drew Mallory into our bedroom. "If last night's dream is as accurate as all the others, Ambrose didn't spend his time between September and New Year twiddling his thumbs. He was on a killing spree. I'll lay odds the

327

victim in the *Bois de Boulogne* was an ex-Lloyd's underwriter, and that there's at least one more in Geneva. Then he went back to England on his French passport to do away with Wormsley. You ought to tell Porfirie about Ambrose's role in our accident. Explain we didn't say anything earlier because we thought it was a dream. Then I can tell him about Les Confins: how I wasn't sure then, but I am now."

Her whispered reply was quiet but vexed. "I thought we were saying nothing about that for Hope's sake? At your insistence."

"This is getting too big to keep the lid on forever. I've already promised to tell Madame Linberger as much as I can. The poor woman's desperate for closure, to be believed. And what about the man in Paris? Doesn't his family deserve to know what happened?"

"Are you mad? The tabloids would have a field day."

"There doesn't have to be any publicity. Ambrose is dead. There's nobody to try. But at least the victims' families will have an official acknowledgment of what happened."

"Tell that to Hope."

"If there's no publicity, she doesn't have to know."

"If! If!" Her whisper was fierce with mounting anger.

"She's a grown-up. I'm sure she can cope."

"She's my daughter, not yours."

"And you're my wife," I retorted, growing angry in my turn. "This is to protect *you*. The more Porfirie focuses on Ambrose, the less he'll be interested in you. But you're not absolutely off the hook so long as he thinks you were the only person being stalked. So far he thinks he's investigating a domestic quarrel. He needs the broader picture."

"I hear what you're saying," she snapped, as she reached for the door in furious confusion. "But I'm not making any promises."

Restraining her, I drew her against me. "I understand, darling. I'll leave it to you." She stood stiff and unresponsive. "I love you." I kissed her on the forehead, then released her. "You'd better get back. Don't worry, I know where the books are. I'll get George settled, then pop back to see where you've got to. I'll take my cue from there."

"Big of you." She swept out. Her shoes clattered on the stairs.

Composing myself, I made my way down to the office, where George and Sylvie were chatting like old friends. His cheerful manner gave her no clue as to the gravity of his visit, but she was experienced enough to grasp that he was important. So she'd made sure that he was comfortably seated with coffee exactly to his liking.

"George," I greeted him. "Please don't get up." I turned to Sylvie. "I need the books for this place, and for Ghost Trader. 2007 and 2008.

They're on the bookshelf in your office." She set off briskly, as though my instruction had been unnecessary.

The tower had three floors: this one, the lowest, was devoted to offices, our personal sanctum *d'affaires* and the nerve centre of our enterprises. George was sat in one of my low-set easy chairs. I could have taken the leather-clad throne behind my desk in order to look down on him, but I chose one of the identical chairs to his, to show that I was affording him the courtesy of equality.

"I suggest you start with the books, then if you've got any questions I can't answer, I'll let you loose on the spreadsheets." I gave him my disarming smile. "We've nothing to hide or to be ashamed of."

Sylvie was soon back with everything. I thanked her, and told her to keep the rest of the Haven at bay until lunchtime at least. She smiled with anticipation. George was already absorbing columns of figures as if they were a musical score. "I'd rather go through these on my own. By lunchtime, I should have a list of questions for you."

I left him to it. Then, waving to Sylvie, who was already fending off importunate callers, I made my way with some trepidation back to the terrace. "George is buried in figures," I explained, as I emerged into the sunlight. "So I'm free, if you want me."

Talking earnestly, they both looked irritated by my intrusion. Mallory glanced at Porfirie, before she would look at me, and he permitted her to speak to me with a grudgingly minuscule lift of the palms. "I think the Haven needs you more than we do, Clem." Her thin smile gave nothing away. With a nod, Porfirie confirmed my release.

"But we will need to talk later, Monsieur." His deadpan expression gave me no clues, but this time I caught a flicker of acknowledgment in Mallory's face, and I knew that she had told him. Assuring them that I was at their disposal, I left them to it.

Back in the office, I told Sylvie to get Andréa for me. She came back to me a few minutes later to say he was out for the day, and that she'd made an appointment for him in my office for 10 a.m. tomorrow. There was nothing for it, in the meantime, but to immerse myself in the minutiae of Haven business.

Chapter Thirty-Two : Collateral Damage

George had plenty of questions, but they were all routine. By the end of the day he was fully satisfied that Ghost Trader's members had all received their due share of the profits, and that the Haven development had been funded properly. There were no fees to *Risque Alsacien* to trouble him, and no unclaimable insurance from Gen-Va Re.

"You once told me that apple pie order was a sign of trouble," I reminded him, when he'd declared himself more than satisfied, and that we would not be troubled by the SFO.

"Did I?" He laughed heartily and his eyes twinkled brightly. "I must have been referring to collapsed businesses. Whereas you have two on-going concerns. Not even the most suspicious auditor could find any material uncertainties here." He tapped the books for emphasis. Then he shook my hand and wished us every good luck for the future.

It was 16:45, and I'd seen nothing of Mallory since I'd left her with the investigator mid-morning. But now, just as George was leaving, she appeared, with Sylvie at her elbow. They were laughing, and as soon as Mallory saw that George and I were parting on good terms, she rushed to greet him. "George! I trust Clem has looked after you." He offered his hand, but she embraced him instead, to Sylvie's delight.

For the next hour, Mallory and I caught up with Haven business. Only when Sylvie had finally straightened her hair and departed for the car park was there any chance to discuss the day's events, over a glass of wine. "Did Porfirie give you a hard time?"

"Not at all." She smiled, though she was still keyed up. "But he was very thorough. He took me through all Ambrose's movements. He's got himself a watertight theory that will allow him to wrap up the case, once he's spoken to you. So he's coming again tomorrow." She raised her glass in salute. "It's nothing to worry about. As far as he's concerned you made an honest mistake in Les Confins. But he has to take your evidence for the record."

"A mistake? Didn't you tell him I'd spoken to *Madame L'Esprit*?"

"He thinks she's very confused: the only witness to think Jean-Michel was pushed." She ruffled my hair. "You weren't there. All you saw was a man in a restaurant who you didn't recognise at first."

"Nobody else but Ambrose would have shouted 'IBNR'."

"If he did shout it. The poor woman probably misheard."

"IBNR in an English accent is the last thing she'd hear by mistake."

"I'm only telling you what Porfirie said. In his official capacity."

"What about the accident, then? Doesn't he believe that either?"

She kissed me happily. "On the contrary, he's more than prepared to believe Ambrose caused the accident. It explains why I ran into the road, as the driver and other witnesses insist, and it fits his theory about Ambrose. Which is what you said: he was stalking me. Me alone."

"That doesn't explain Paris and Geneva, or why he went back to the UK," I protested. She made me sit down, choosing the old sofa from the Sanatorium. Then she perched on the arm and stroked my neck. I knew I was being soothed, but she wasn't clamming up on me.

"My father was in a care home near Paris. Reuil Malmaison. He was working there when he retired and he carried on living there to be near his sister. When mother died, he moved in with Tante Camille until his Alzheimer's got so bad she couldn't cope." I nodded. I'd already heard it from her aunt at the wedding. "Tante Camille never forgave me for Rex." A stern woman without a shred of humour: I could well believe it. "None of them. They thought it was bad for Hope."

"Was it?" I felt I had to ask, despite what she'd told me before.

"Not as much as they liked to make out."

"When did you tell Ambrose about Hope?"

"Not for a long time. I couldn't deprive him of a daughter as well as a wife." It accorded with her old secrecy, but for once I sympathised.

"When did you?"

Standing abruptly, she topped up her glass, then – almost as an afterthought – she refilled mine. "It's all water under the bridge. Do I have to go through it all again?" She dropped down heavily beside me, almost spilling her wine. "I went through it endlessly with Porfirie. He practically wanted to know how often we had sex." I couldn't help wondering whether she meant with Ambrose or with Rex. "He wanted to know precisely what happened before I came to France." She drank deeply. "His idea is that Ambrose thought I'd fled to Daddy."

I tried to help her. "You mean you got so angry at all his begging for money that you told him Hope wasn't his daughter." Her angry shrug told me I was near the mark. "But if Ambrose hoped to track you down through your father, he'd have chosen to stay in Reuil not the 10th District. Or doesn't the investigator know where he stayed?"

"Of course he knows. But he doesn't have to explain, because he's discovered Ambrose visited my father, claiming to be my cousin from

Réunion. Which was clever of him, as I do have a cousin there, and Ambrose met him once. Anyway, the nursing home didn't query."

"Didn't your father recognise him?"

"He may have done, but I doubt it. He hardly recognised *me*." She sighed wistfully. "We're talking about the last months of his life."

"Didn't the staff tell you about these visits?"

"Oh, yes." Her expression hardened. "They said my cousin wanted to meet me before he flew home, and was it all right if they gave him my address? I said no way. He was another of the family who'd lectured me on infidelity, particularly with an Anglo-Saxon. I point-blank refused to meet him or to let them give him my address."

"Let me guess. Ambrose asked your father where you lived and he said Geneva, forgetting that was long ago, as old people do, and later he said you were back in England."

"Exactly what Porfirie thought." She managed a hollow laugh. "You haven't lost your touch, have you? As to how Ambrose found me on New Year's Day, even I can tell you that. Jean-Michel confirmed our lunch via the forum. That way I was bound to see it and read it."

I sipped my wine pensively. Porfirie had certainly been thorough, and he'd accounted for Ambrose's movements until that New Year. "What about after the accident? Did Ambrose try the hospital?"

"Oh, yes. He tried the long-lost cousin ploy again, but the hospital said they had to have a name, which they could check against their approved-visitor list. Hope had an even lower opinion of the cousin from Réunion, so he wasn't down. Ambrose went off in a huff, and they only saw him again once, though he phoned a few times."

"When were these visits?"

"The first was mid-January. The last was September, just as the short was coming good. But he never got to see me."

"He didn't meet Andréa until August, and he crashed in December. Does Porfirie have any idea what he was up to otherwise?"

"He *knows* what Ambrose was up to." She had to force it, but she managed one of her endearing grins. "He was lying low with one of *his* cousins. On the French side. I don't know her well, except she's also divorced. Lives on the border with Geneva. Works for CERN. He turned up one January evening in a terrible state. His money had run out, and he was really ill. Practically at death's door."

"So he couldn't have told her what happened on the ferry?" A cousin who could report what had really happened would have had Mallory arrested. It was my turn to refill our glasses.

"He told her he'd faked suicide to avoid his creditors. With a French passport, he was effectively reborn. All he needed was somewhere to recuperate. Without doctors and without questions."

I let out a long whistle of relief. "And she went along with it?"

"She was terrified he'd die on her, so she took time off to nurse him. He was off his head for about three days, then the fever dropped, and he began to recover. But it was a slow process. It seems he hadn't eaten for a long time, and he seemed in despair over what he'd done."

"Hardly surprising. Even if he justified the killings to himself as legitimate executions," I surmised. "He didn't give you away because he didn't need to. He'd already put you in a coma."

"I don't think he meant to hurt me." She huddled in my arms. "He probably hoped I'd have to take him back to keep him quiet."

"So you want me to go along with Porfirie. 'So sorry, *milord*, I'll never humour women of a certain age again.' Will that do?"

She laughed uncertainly. "I mean it, Clem."

"I know you do." This had little to do with Hope, I now realised. However disappointed she would be to learn the truth about Ambrose, it would not shatter any childhood illusions. It was for Mallory's sake that I must keep stum. "What am I to say to Madame Linberger?"

Sure now of my compliance, Mallory kissed me gratefully. "I'm sure you'll find the right words."

It had been a long day, and now that its perils had receded, we were exhausted. After only a light supper, we retired to bed. But if I'd hoped for peaceful slumber, Ambrose, or the part of my subconscious that had ensnared or recreated him, had other plans. In mockery of Porfirie's theory, I found myself not in Reuil Malmaison to visit Mallory's dying father, but waiting on Ile St Louis for a dog-walker.

Ascetic in looks, and spare of frame, he dressed neatly, favouring the recessive tweeds and cravats of the expatriate who refused to bow to local habits. His brogues, like his jacket and trousers, were far studier than he was. Unlike the jogger, he looked neither to right nor left, so that it was difficult to say whether he even noticed the banks of the Seine along which he chose to walk. Studying him closely, I saw him as a once wealthy man keeping up appearances.

Apart from his dog-walking he seldom went out. He bought his *Daily Telegraph* each morning at the end of his walk, and for the rest of the day he could be seen reading it at his fourth floor window.

His apartment was modest, and belonged to his wife. That must have been something Ambrose knew already, because the information was never forthcoming in my dreams. Like us – it was easier to think of

Ambrose and I as a double act – the man never splashed money on taxis, but once a week, he and his wife strolled stiffly arm in arm onto Boule Miche, where they would take a modest meal in *Les Deux Magots,* or one of the other cafes made famous in the 1890s. There they would sit self-consciously under the winter awning, as though he were some louche artist and she a beautiful *demi-mondaine,* instead of an aged couple who never sparkled and hardly spoke to each other.

His other excursion was by metro to Montparnasse, where he was admitted each week to a nondescript apartment building. He stayed for an hour. After he'd returned, I waited outside to see who emerged. In the first two weeks, I saw only an elderly woman with a shopping bag, and a student with wire frame spectacles and a straggly beard. Neither seemed likely as the host to our man.

The third week, our patience was rewarded by the emergence of a youngish woman. I took her for thirty-something. Everything about her was neat and precise, and her stride had a jaunty youthfulness, which almost disguised the limp of a game leg. As a gait, it was oddly provocative in its very defiance. She made her way to a dark, narrow cafe, nothing like the monsters favoured by our man, where she sat near the counter and ordered a coffee and a small spirit. She and the waiter exchanged pleasantries like old friends.

It was early evening, and the cafe was beginning to fill, so I quickly secured the last seat at the counter, from where I could observe the woman unobtrusively. Though she carried it well, her face was older than her manner. Her so careful make-up could not quite disguise the lines around her eyes and mouth. After a while an unkempt man with dirty hair and stubble like sandpaper asked if he might join her, but she shook her head. He glanced around angrily to find another seat.

I slipped off my stool. "It's all yours, Monsieur," I offered him politely. He took it with a surly grunt. and turned his back on the woman. She smiled a brief thank you, which I took as an invitation to join her. "Stools can be uncomfortable," I explained. The waiter appeared instantly and expectantly. I offered her a drink.

"If you like." She affected boredom, but it was no rejection.

Though she sipped her drink with a primness that verged on disapproval, she made no secret of her profession. Her clients, of course, were her dear friends, she explained, fastidiously dabbing the corner of her lip with the tip of a paper serviette, but in these difficult times she had to consider her overheads. "I like to think of myself as a personal counsellor, and like any professional, I charge for my time.

Not here, of course. Back in my consulting rooms. Perhaps, Monsieur, you are in need of a little consultation?"

I could tell that Ambrose was shocked, and my enquiry as to her fees was brusque. She drew herself into the stiff pose of a housewife who must stoop to the vulgar task of arguing money with a tradesman.

"€250 per hour. But were you to become a regular, there would of course be a discount." She sucked in her cheeks, so that her lips became thin and tight. "Like you, Monsieur, I would prefer to have a brass plaque by my door, and had my dear husband been more careful with his investments, and had I not had the misfortune to suffer a childhood accident," she rubbed her leg meaningfully, "or had I been endowed with a brilliant mind, that is how I would serve you. In the meantime, we must make the best of what The Lord sees fit to provide." She lifted her shoulders and spread her hands, but there was a merry sparkle in her eye that amused me, and offended Ambrose.

But he accompanied her back to her apartment, even deigning to take her arm when she explained that such consideration would make it easier for her. It was small, and fussily decorated, yet perfectly tasteful in its old-fashioned way. Her kitchen was clean, and her bathroom was spotless, with a bidet that would have done service as a christening font. The bedroom, which she conceded must serve as her consulting room, space being these days at a premium, boasted heavy and dark furniture, and over the carved bed-head a Madonna portrait gazed down upon the tasselled covers and square pillows with melancholy disapproval. I couldn't help wondering if she expected me to pray before more carnal matters could proceed.

In fact, she was insistent only on cash up-front. With a skill worthy of Saul, she extracted enough for four weekly visits. His only stipulation, but on which he was as immoveable as she, was that he should have the same day as today, and one particular hour, which I realised was the one preceding that of her client from *Ile St Louis*.

Whether Ambrose enjoyed his visits, I cannot say, but he treated her with rigid politeness. He always brought a change of clothes in a carrier bag, though afterwards he rarely changed more than his shirt.

Her procedure was precise and unvarying. When I pressed the bell, she waited a full minute before releasing the door. She was on the fifth floor, but there was a narrow lift that moved so slowly it seemed hardly to move. She would greet me with a handshake and a formal kiss on either cheek, then we would take tea and *petits fours*, over which she would amplify on the shortcomings of her late husband, and the misfortunes of her childhood.

She had a horror of the written word. I guessed that she was very dyslexic. Then, as she cleared the tea things, she would suggest that I might like to use the bathroom. Here I was expected to disrobe and put on the silk dressing gown that hung on the back of the door. It was old and quilted with wide sleeves. "I'm in the consulting room," she would say from the bedroom, where I would find her in bed with the sheet pulled up to her chin. She was embarrassed about her bad leg, which was slightly shorter than her good one, and did not welcome inspections of it, still less comment.

If she had a repertoire of amazing tricks she did not vouchsafe them to Etienne, the name Ambrose chose to give to her, when she'd told him hers was Lisavette – and he did not suggest any. We coupled so decorously that had any teenagers been spying on us, we would have confirmed every prejudice about the older generation's lack of passion. Yet the very stateliness of these weekly sojourns was soothing, a respite from the endless tailing and watching of a doomed man.

Afterwards, she would encourage me into the bathroom again, where I would wash and dress, taking care to leave the old dressing gown upon its hook. I don't know what Lisavette did with it, but if it was used by her other customers, they left no trace of themselves behind, and it always smelled fresh and personal.

Forced to leave minutes before our man was due to arrive, I always loitered in the vicinity until he'd pressed the buzzer. He was as regular in this as in every other feature of his life. Yet I still had no idea how Ambrose planned to dispose of him. At no point in his dog-walking or his marital strolling down Boule Miche, or his soulless dining in faded cafes did he present any risk-free opportunity for his demise.

By the time we visited Lisavette for the fourth time, Ambrose was agitated and depressed. I guessed he was angry at the expense, and furious at the lack of opportunity. But it was worse than that, and he pressed the buzzer in a state that was close to despair. Abrupt with Lisavette's rituals, he paid for the next four weeks with bad grace. "What's the matter?" Her wrinkling brow aged her ten years.

"Let's get on with it," I snapped, wishing I were anywhere but here in this close, over-furnished apartment, where everything seemed a wistful and faded reminder of a time when her husband was alive and she in the money. She stared in silence, and for a horrible moment I thought she was going to burst into tears. "I'm sorry," I said in gruff apology, and she gathered up my cup of half-finished tea and my plate with its abandoned *petits fours*. Her hand shook and the cup rattled in its saucer. Once in the bedroom, we lay side by side, neither of us capable of either conversation or coitus.

Several times, she made coy attempts to arouse my interest, but each time I pushed her away. Finally, I could stand it no longer, and I seized one of the square pillows and smothered her. She struggled and kicked. Muffled though they were, her cries seemed sure to bring her neighbours rushing to her door, so I seized an onyx bedside lamp and smashed it time and again against the top of her head, where it protruded from under the pillow. When it was all over, her spotless sheets and her tasselled bed cover were soaked in blood.

There was even a long splash on the seamless blue of the Madonna's gown. Her huge eyes reproached me from under lash-less lids, and in desperation I tore the picture from the wall and stuffed it under the bed. Then I covered Lisavette's corpse with the heavy dressing gown.

My instinct was to flee, but Ambrose had other ideas. Before the murder he'd been a broken man, now he was calm and galvanised. Closing the bedroom door, he retired to the bathroom, where he cleansed himself of gore. Then he changed, this time entirely, into the extra clothing he always brought. He went so far as to put on the beret, checking in the gilt-edged mirror that it obscured his face.

In the kitchen he put the kettle on to boil and placed a bag of Yellow Label ready in one of the ornate cups. Then he found the *petits fours* and put two on a matching plate. When all was ready, he carried the tea things to the living room and set them on the table. Then, amidst the heavy furniture, he waited.

When the buzzer sounded, he patiently timed a minute on his watch before releasing the front door. Then he opened the apartment door a crack, just as Lisavette had always done. From far down, I heard the clack of the lift gates, and then the rumble of its slow passage up the building. There was a nearer clack of gates, and then a muffled tread. The door creaked, and in walked our man, very upright in his brogues and tweeds. "Lisavette?" His voice was clipped and military.

I stepped into view. "She's been taken ill."

"Who are you?" he demanded imperiously.

"Just a neighbour." I gestured for him to sit down. "It's nothing serious. She's gone to the pharmacy for her prescription." I glanced at my watch. "She should be back in ten minutes." I allowed myself a sardonic smile. "She didn't want to disappoint you."

The man frowned, suspiciously.

"I made you some tea." I gestured towards the cup.

Reluctantly, he sat down. Then, making the best of a bad job, he sipped his tea, and nibbled on *petits fours*. I crossed to the window.

"I'll let you know when I see her coming."

He had his back to the window, and – as soon as he ceased to pay me attention – I slipped a plastic bag out of my jacket pocket, and over his head. "IBNR," I whispered fiercely until he ceased to struggle. Killing him had been much easier than killing Lisavette.

Afterwards I removed the bag from his head. It seemed that Ambrose wanted there to be as little connection as possible between the deaths here and the assassination in the *Bois de Boulogne*. It had all been carefully planned. He even remembered to take his money back for the month ahead, which she'd put in a drawer in the kitchen.

The only place in which he could have cornered his true victim alone had been Lisavette's apartment. Solely for this reason had he become one of her regular customers. Poor Lisavette had been no more than a means to an end, a sad and lonely woman who'd committed no crime, who had given transient solace to other lost souls, but who had been forced to die in the furtherance of Ambrose's brand of justice. As soon as I awoke, I ignored the peacefully slumbering Mallory and staggered to the bathroom, where I was violently sick.

Chapter Thirty-Three : Lines of Enquiry

Compared with Mallory's, my time with Porfirie was brief. If he noticed that I was shaky, haunted by the horror of last night's dream, he made no comment. His questioning over the events in Les Confins was comprehensive, but it was obvious that he was going through the motions for the benefit of the record rather than gathering vital new evidence. In deference to Mallory's wishes, I allowed him to make my identification of Ambrose very uncertain. "It relies, it seems to me, on Madame Linberger's assertion, since retracted, that the skier in black shouted 'IBNR' as he allegedly pushed her husband off the piste." I agreed that this was so. "It relies, too, on your assertion, which I am unable to corroborate, that IBNR was used by Monsieur Hanter as a rallying cry against Lloyd's of London some ten years ago."

I debated whether to show him the text I had received in the early hours of that New Year. Enraged by Ambrose's callousness, I felt it my duty to tell Porfirie everything. At the same time, I felt too weak for wearying explanations that he would not want to believe. Until I had independent evidence of Ambrose's murderous activities, it was better to keep quiet. I had no proof that the message had been from Ambrose, whilst its alternative rendering of IBNR would only confuse.

"I shall incorporate your statement into my report. You and Madame will receive a copy in due course." He switched off his recorder.

"Two questions." The interview over, I felt less fragile. "When did he steal the car, and why did he crash where he did?"

"It will all be in my report." Then, as he closed his notebook, he relented. "The car was taken sometime in March 2008. He appears to have broken into the apartment of Madame Stellenbourg, as she then was, and taken her keys. In his financial straits, he doubtless found the car useful. A 12-month rental had been paid on the apartment, so her belongings stayed there to await her recovery."

"Hope believed totally and absolutely in recovery."

"Quite so." Porfirie allowed himself a rare smile. "As to your second question, we believe that Monsieur Hanter visited the *Sanatorium de St Hippocrate*." He lowered his voice, as though he feared to be overheard in the act of indiscretion. "There's evidence, just confirmed, to suggest that he squatted there from September."

The irony was bizarre. Our occupation of the place, which had seemed so vivid and so real, had been a dream, whilst the real occupier had been officially dead. "But why that road, I wonder?" I mused out loud. "With all the snow, it was bound to be treacherous."

Porfirie nodded. "Under normal weather conditions, that road offers an excellent short-cut to Annecy. We believe Monsieur Hanter had learned of the experimental procedure in the hospital that hastened your recovery. It was in the news, after all. He may have been hurrying to the hospital, to greet Madame Stellenbourg as she woke."

"But I thought he was driving down the hill, not up it," I said without thinking whether this was something I was supposed to know.

Far from challenging me, Porfirie was delighted by my analysis. "A valid point, Monsieur. He had proceeded up the road at first, then stopped in the village for refreshment. When he was told that the road ahead was impassable unless he had winter tyres, which he did not, he drove back down the hill, where he lost control. Unfortunately he had been drinking." He rose abruptly to his feet.

"Monsieur Hanter was a very disturbed man. His cousin hardly saw him during the last months of his life, so she was unable to exert the stabilising influence she had provided earlier in the year. He was also a very determined man. Seriously injured though he was, he managed to drive the car all the way into Aix before he collapsed."

He sighed heavily. "It's a sorry tale. I trust you will ensure that Madame Holden does not try to shoulder all the blame."

"I'll make sure she doesn't shoulder any," I told him firmly.

As if on cue, with that sixth sense that is essential to the perfect p.a., Sylvie opened my door with quiet efficiency. "Your next appointment is here." Then, with a sweet but meaningful smile, she escorted Porfirie from the tower, as Andréa sauntered into my office.

"Am I early?" Then he noticed my pallor. "Are you quite well?"

"Never mind me." Gesturing for him to close the door, I pitched straight into my first question. "Why did you tell *De l'Ombre* about Ghost Trader, when you knew he wasn't a member?"

In the past, I'd always found it best to confront miscreant staff before they'd had time to sit down, let alone to construct an excuse.

My tactic was so unexpected that, for a moment, Andréa could only stand and blink. But he was not a journalist for nothing. "He knew far more about Ghost Trader and about Madame Mallory than I did." He managed one of his sardonic smiles, though it seemed a little forced. "Including how she'd got the seed money to start things off."

"You believed him?" I tried to remain stern, but he was shrewd enough to know when he'd scored a point. "You were happy to give out confidential information to a complete stranger?" I restrained myself from adding "and a murderer".

"He told me he was her cousin." His tone was sulky more than angry. "From Réunion," he added, as if the detail proved the claim.

I said nothing, clamping my lips in an uncompromising line.

"Look, I'm writing a book, as you know, about the effects of the credit crunch. This guy had the perfect hard luck story about his cousin's ex-husband, starting with Lloyd's of London, taking in Enron, right on to now. How could I not be interested?"

His eyes flashed defiantly. "I hardly said a word, until he told me this cousin – the ex-wife of the man in his story – was in hospital in a coma, *and*..." He milked the pause. "The runner who tried to save her was this man's old friend, from their days in Lloyd's."

Again he waited, perhaps for confirmation, but I merely gestured for him to continue. "I told him I also knew the runner, that Marie-Sainte and I often visited him in the hospital. He asked me if I'd seen his cousin, and I said no, but Marie-Sainte had met her daughter. Then he asked me what I thought were the chances of recovery."

He executed a shrug of persecuted innocence. "That's when I told him about you coming out of your coma long enough to give Hope the idea of briefing Marie-Sainte to set up the four viewing platforms." The words tumbled from him. "I gave him the details to show your brain was working. I wanted to give him a positive prognosis."

I had to admit it made some sense. "What did he say to that?"

"He agreed it was a good sign, and he wondered whether Hope had had the same response from her mother. I said I didn't think so, though Hope was convinced her mother's brain was active." He lowered his voice. "She had the idea, right from the start, that you and Madame Mallory communicated in your dreams. But I didn't tell that to *De l'Ombre*. It would have sounded crazy. I'm sorry, but it would."

"Of course it would." I was almost sure that Andréa could not have produced such a good story on the spur of the moment. But I wasn't yet about to let him off the hook. "You're an honest man, Andréa, so you'll understand me when I say you've always been a maverick. I even admire you for it. But there are times when I fear your discretion. From what you've just told me, my fear isn't entirely unjustified."

He sat awhile in angry thought. "I'll tell you just what happened," he said at last. "Then I think you'll judge me less harshly."

He explained that he usually saw *De l'Ombre* after work. They both liked to watch the *boules* over a beer, for which Andréa usually paid. *De l'Ombre*'s story only emerged slowly over the course of several encounters. "The time I told him you'd come out of your coma to tell Hope to brief Marie-Sainte, he seemed to be focused on the chances of recovery, particularly his cousin's, and nothing else.

"It was only later that he showed any interest in the viewing platforms. Did I know what trading was being done on each? How would the members know which was real and which was purely for comparison? Were any of them performing much better?

"I told him I didn't know the details. To me it was just an interesting job for Marie-Sainte. He wanted to know if it was well paid, too. I said no job paid enough, but it wasn't bad as things go." He couldn't resist smiling at his slick answer, then he resumed in all seriousness.

"Wasn't I surprised that she'd been hired for the job when she had so little experience? On the contrary, I told him, it dovetailed very well with her studies. Yes, but surely an established outfit like Ghost Trader would prefer someone with experience?" Andréa scowled to show the depth of his irritation. "His questions were really starting to piss me off. I told him if he was that interested he should ask his cousin's daughter. She was his relation, too. But he confessed he and Hope didn't see eye to eye. 'She's her mother's daughter. Hasn't even got me on the list of approved visitors. Me, her own flesh and blood.'

"Then he started in on Ghost Trader again. 'She's short-trading. She has to be. It's the only way to make a killing right now. When she pulls it off, all she has to do is buy the stock the members think they were invested in, pocket the difference, and nobody's any the wiser.'

"Didn't I see the pattern? Like mother, like daughter. Her mother did it with Tonbridge, now her daughter – all thanks to you, Papa Clem –was doing it with Ghost Trader. Real City boys would have seen through it, but not my fiancée. That's why you chose her. You can see why I was angry." Andréa clenched his fists, nostrils flaring.

"For starters, I didn't like him insinuating you were a crook..."

I cut across him. "We discussed that in my comatose dreams, so I'm guessing you told me about it in one of your hospital visits."

It was hardly surprising that Ambrose had managed to implant doubts in the mind of a cynic, and under his relentless probing, Andréa, in the anger of confusion, had let something slip, if only by gesture.

"He wanted me to believe Hope's a crook, too," he continued, not denying my comment, nor choosing to amplify it. "I told him I refused to believe it; that Marie-Sainte would never work for anybody she distrusted. He had the gall to repeat his opinion that she was a simple girl with no experience." He laughed scornfully "As if. She knew the Enron saga from Hope and as soon as she saw there was shorting on Platform 4, she understood what Hope was really doing, and why the members had to be kept in the dark." His fists pounded the arms of his chair. "Not to cheat them, for their greater profit."

I should have known that Marie-Sainte was too astute to be fooled for long, and had I been in Andréa's place, I would have taken more umbrage at criticism of her judgement than at charges of dishonesty on Hope's part, or mine. But his admission that Marie-Sainte knew about the shorting told me that he must have let the cat out of the bag.

"In my dreams," I said sternly, "You told me *De l'Ombre* was Mallory's ex-husband himself, not her cousin."

"That would have been impossible!" He sounded convincingly dismissive. "Her husband was dead. Jumped off a Channel ferry the previous autumn. I assumed you knew."

"But you didn't, not then." I pointed out, "He admitted he was the ex to win your sympathy."

"Too risky. Supposing I'd gone to Hope and said I'd met some man who claimed to be her father. She'd have called the police."

"Didn't you warn Hope anyway about her cousin?"

"I'm a journalist! *De l'Ombre* may have been a pain in the arse, but what he was telling me was in confidence." He shifted awkwardly under my unwavering gaze. "OK. He expressly asked me not to say anything to her." Ambrose, as always, had thought of everything.

"What did Marie-Sainte have to say?"

"She thought it best not to worry Hope. She said *De l'Ombre* was a pathetic nutcase, who only talked to me because he knew Hope would send him away with a flea in his ear. It didn't seem to matter much, because after I'd given him stick, he kept out of my way. So we forgot him, and got on with wedding preparations." Now it was his turn for the penetrating stare. "What's this about? Why the third degree?"

"I'm coming to that," I promised, as I tried to square Marie-Sainte's pathetic nutcase with the man who'd beaten Lisavette to death. In one way at least, Ambrose had judged Marie-Sainte right: she was happily ignorant of absolute wickedness. "In my dream, you warned me after your honeymoon that *De l'Ombre* was about to pay Mallory a visit. Does that mean he tried to get into the hospital?"

"That's right." He nodded. "I did see him once more. He looked terrible. Really ill. I had to ask him if he'd seen a doctor. He said he had, and he was checking into the hospital that evening. 'When I'm there, I'll be able to slip into her room and tell her everything. Then it'll be up to her to put things right when she recovers.'"

"Do you remember when this was exactly?"

"How could I forget. It was the weekend Lehman collapsed. The Friday, to be exact. And just before the short paid off. He actually got as far as her room, before the nurses chased him off. He even shouted at the door: 'We can start again. Whatever happens, I'll find you.' The nurses said he looked as much in need of hospital as her. But they couldn't compel him to stay, even if they'd wanted to."

"How do you know this?" Despite knowing he had failed, the thought of Ambrose creeping into Mallory's room as she lay helpless filled me with unreasoning panic, so that I almost forgot that he was beyond finding anyone. "Were the nurses so indiscreet?"

"They had to tell Hope, and Hope told Marie-Sainte. Hope was in despair, because she thought Madame Mallory was slipping away, even that her cousin's visit had caused it."

No wonder Mallory had fled the boathouse in my dream. Her answer to Wormsley at the trial, that perhaps she'd had a premonition of Ambrose coming for her, had been right, though nobody had believed her. In an effort to calm myself, I described to Andréa the content of my dream of that night: how I'd struggled with Ambrose at the boathouse door before we'd heard Mallory drive away; how Hope had pleaded with me to bring her mother back. Then I thanked him for being so forthright. "It all matches, you see."

"After that, *De l'Ombre* vanished for good," Andréa continued. "I hope you're about to tell me what happened to him. Something you've just heard from Monsieur Porfirie, perhaps?" He grinned innocently. "When judicial investigators come two days in a row, I'm bound to notice. Knowing what's going on is part of my job description."

"Very good," I conceded, curiously pleased by his watchfulness. "I'd like to explain, but you must understand you're an employee now. Whatever I tell you, my right to your silence is absolute."

"Papa Clem, you shouldn't need to ask."

"Thank you. I also accept you were not under contract to me when you met *De l'Ombre*, and I'm grateful you gave him so little. So now I really am going to take you into my confidence, provided you can reassure me that you never wrote to the Serious Fraud Office in London, alleging that Ghost Trader was trading fraudulently."

He could not have looked more dumbfounded if he'd tried.

"I didn't even know there was a Serious Fraud Office."

"Don't worry. I never thought it was you."

Relief surged through me. Ambrose had done his worst, and there was no way that he could reach out from beyond the grave to hurt us further. Provided only that I could be rid of his dreams.

"It has to be *De l'Ombre*," I continued. "Who wasn't Mallory's cousin, but her ex-husband himself. He faked the suicide."

I smiled at his incredulity. "This is from Porfirie, who's really checked him out." I gave him the facts as Porfirie had described them: the beach hut in Calais with its tell-tale wet suit, the French passport, the stays in Paris and Geneva, the visit to the UK, his role in the accident, the illness and convalescence with the cousin from CERN, his stealing the Peugeot, his squatting in the Sanatorium, and finally his fatal crash in the snow. "Now you know as much as Porfirie."

Even Andréa was lost for words.

"Now cast you mind back to the fatality in Les Confins," I said. "It's relevant, even though Porfirie doesn't think so."

"The widow said her husband had been pushed." He screwed up his eyes the better to search his memory. "You thought the murderer – assuming there was a murderer – was from Lloyd's, something she claimed he'd said." Then the implication hit him. "You mean the skier in black that nobody else saw was *De l'Ombre*!"

I explained the resonance that IBNR had had with Ambrose. "I didn't say too much then because I wasn't sure. Not after Amy told me about his suicide. But Porfirie's findings change everything." I told him about the death of Robert de St Hippocrate. "In *De l'Ombre*'s eyes, *L'Esprit* and *Le Baigneur* – to give them their usernames – had bullied the other Ghost Trader members against shorting Enron, and were the main cause, therefore, of his ruin."

"So the accident wasn't an accident." Andréa's thoughts raced ahead of my narrative. "He deliberately chased her into the road."

In the disgust that Ambrose had aroused in my last dream, I was all too tempted to agree. Terror he had certainly aroused, but that had been part of his *modus operandi*. It had helped in the *Bois de Boulogne*, and it had been sufficient to see off Wormsley. "It's more than possible," I conceded. "Except Mallory herself doesn't believe it."

"Let me get this straight. Porfirie's report will conclude that *De l'Ombre* was a deranged obsessive who faked suicide in the hopes of being reborn in his French identity, but who couldn't stop stalking his ex-wife. Or trying to. The one time he confronted her, she was so shocked, she ran into a speeding car. An accident which also put his old pal Clem into a coma. As a result he cracked up, alternating between illness and drunkenness. Finally, in a mad drive through the snow to greet her as she woke from her coma, he totalled himself and her car. Complete tragedy, nobody to prosecute, end of story.

"Except you don't buy it, even if she does." His eyes narrowed thoughtfully. "You want me to dig around, is that it?"

I unlocked my bottom drawer, extracted a folded sheet of paper from an unmarked file, and pushed it across my desk. "I'd like you to start with these." *These* were the four names I'd typed on the folded sheet: Brabazon, Micklewright, Pargetter, and Wu. He read them aloud, struggling with the pronunciation. "They're ex-Lloyd's underwriters whose syndicates made ruinous losses. Ambrose Hanter, alias *De l'Ombre*, was a Name on each. He was also a Name on the Tonbridge Syndicate, but we can discount Rex Tonbridge, because he was honourable enough to commit suicide, genuine suicide, as soon as he realised he'd ruined his Names. The other four did not..."

"You want me to see if they're still alive." He jumped to his feet, the light of battle in his eyes. "I'll be back by the end of the day."

He was as good as his word. At 17:30 Sylvie announced him, brought us coffee then asked if there was anything else we needed before she left. "Ask Madame Mallory to join us."

Whilst he'd been gone, I'd filled Mallory in on my session with Porfirie, then I'd started on my conversation with Andréa.

"I had to be certain it wasn't him who tipped off the SFO, as well as exactly what Ambrose had told him. With investigations virtually over, we don't want loose ends coming back to haunt us." Prepared to trust my judgement, she'd reacted with a grim nod. "He wanted to know why Porfirie had come two days running, and I thought it best to tell him." Her eyes had narrowed as her trust wavered. "He's observant, but discreet. Especially to protect his wife."

"So he knows who caused the accident?" she'd demanded.

"And he knows about IBNR, and about *Le Baigneur*."

As I'd held up my hand to forestall an outburst, I couldn't prevent it from trembling. "These dreams are driving me crazy. So I asked him to find out what's happened to Brabazon, Micklewright, Pargetter, and Wu." Even my voice had begun to shake. "I had to."

Woken by my vomiting, having mopped my pasty-white face, as she'd listened in horror to the tale of my dream, and then seeing that the revulsion was still with me, she'd taken me in her arms.

"So long as he doesn't know what happened on the ferry."

Now she walked into my office as Andréa was booting up the net-book he was carrying. He was so engrossed he didn't acknowledge her. She propped herself against my desk without a word.

"I checked the four names as you asked me to," he said as his file opened. "In their late sixties, early seventies: two British, Micklewright and Pargetter; one Australian, Brabazon; and one Hong Kong Chinese, Wu. Lead underwriters, their syndicates named after them. All wound up as part of R & R, with combined losses of £2 billion plus."

"We know all that," I said. "I was on Wu myself."

In his element, Andréa ploughed on. "Micklewright and Pargetter lived in Paris, both retired; the other two in Geneva: Brabazon also retired, Wu dabbling. Micklewright killed, probably murdered, in the *Bois de Boulogne*; Pargetter murdered, along with a prostitute, in her Montparnasse apartment." Mallory and I couldn't avoid an exchange of glances. "Why do I get the impression you knew this already?"

I ignored his question. "When?"

"Mid October and early November, 2007."

"Was anyone arrested?" Mallory asked.

"The police rounded up the whores who work that part of the *Bois*, but they all swore blind the man wasn't a customer. The police thought it was an asphyxiation game gone wrong. He had a plastic bag round his head when they found him, but nothing could be proved. It might have been the same with the other one. He was definitely asphyxiated, but the bag had gone. The woman had been battered to death with a bedside lamp. She may have had two clients, and things got out of hand. The neighbours heard noises, and one saw a man in a beret leaving the building, but couldn't describe him."

"Do the police think the murders are connected?" Mallory asked.

"I doubt it. The official line is: if you mix with prostitutes, you get what's coming to you. I don't have the impression cither investigation is being actively pursued." He laughed. "But you, Papa Clem, have other ideas about all this, I can tell."

"That depends what happened to the other two."

"Then it won't be a surprise if I tell you they're also dead. Both in November 2007. Do you need the exact dates?"

"Just tell us how they died."

"Wu jumped into the Rhone – it's very fast flowing there – Brabazon threw himself under a train." He smiled grimly. "And no, the Swiss police don't think they had a suicide pact."

"Why are they so sure it was suicide?" Mallory demanded.

"Witnesses swore they both jumped." He smiled again. "The Swiss don't do murder, especially in Geneva. It's bad for the image."

"No nondescript men in black berets in the vicinity, then?" I asked.

"None that anybody saw, no." He spoke now with complete seriousness. "But that was *De l'Ombre*'s genius, wasn't it? Nobody ever saw him unless he wanted them to."

"What about families and friends? Were they expecting suicide?"

"Brabazon had a girlfriend, who said he was a heavy drinker and a depressive. Wu lived alone, kept himself to himself. But a business associate said he was in debt, that his deals tended to unravel." He shrugged. "If you want to believe suicide, the evidence for it is there. But it's hardly conclusive. There were no notes or anything."

"What about Lloyd's?" Mallory asked. "Is there any suspicion there of a witch-hunt against underwriters?"

"These guys were the old era. Lloyd's prefers to forget them."

Chapter Thirty-Four : The Power of Speech

My hunch had proved correct. Now that I knew what had happened to the four underwriters, my dreams of Ambrose ceased. Not only did I sleep soundly each night, I was able to devote myself wholeheartedly to ensuring that the Haven would be ready for its first guests. All the staff were now in place, and trained in their routines. Everything worked as it should. Mallory and I felt in the best shape since hospital, and it was a joy simply to watch her mounting enthusiasm. Gone were the shuffle and the stoop, as if they had never been, whilst my voice was back to full strength, and my native command of English had returned.

Now at last, I was able to spend a precious hour with Marie-Sainte. It began as a business encounter, to bring me up to speed on her computer systems. She was polite and clear, but distant. I was her boss, whilst she – the perfect employee, in her sensible black skirt and her neatly trimmed hair – was conscious of her position. "Come on," I said, after ten brisk but dull minutes, "it's too nice a day to waste indoors."

It was indeed a pleasant afternoon, white cloud interspersed with clear sky, warm but not hot. I led her across the lawns to a clump of mountain ash, whose pointy leaves offered a pleasant mix of sun and shade. There, as we sat around the wooden table, with the vista of the lake spread below us, I was delighted to watch her relax. By the time she'd finished her presentation, she was almost her old self again.

"I've been meaning to talk you for some time," I said, as she closed her laptop. "Now you know exactly who I am, there must be things you want to know." Sitting back, I did my best to look relaxed and paternal, though inside I was gripped by sudden anxiety.

"I guessed long ago." A shy smile played across her lips, and she lowered her eyes. "I think you can tell when you're that closely related to someone, don't you?" I shrugged modestly. "I wanted to ask Mama, but I didn't know if I should. I didn't want to make life more difficult for her than it was. She was always so busy, and she and my father… her husband, whom I thought was my father," she frowned as she corrected herself, "they weren't getting along very well." She plucked at her skirt. "Then when you came to live here permanently, the three of us seemed so natural together. I think that's when I knew."

"You asked if I was to be your new Papa. Is that what you wanted?"

Her turn to shrug. "I did wonder why you two didn't marry."

"We were too raw. Starting again isn't easy after failure."

"Would it have been different if you'd known?" Honest, not at all accusing, she was so like her mother. Was there anything of me?

"We both knew we didn't really love each other. Perhaps that was silly. Affection and understanding count for a lot."

"Papa Armand has been a good step-father to me, and he's been wonderful for Mama." How neatly had she explained everything. Like Sidonie, she wasn't going to agonise over what might have been. "You were there for me. What more could I have wanted?" She smiled. "As for you, now you have the woman of your dreams."

"Almost literally," I agreed, impressed by her maturity. "How are you managing to balance motherhood with work and husband?" Her smile was immediate and so spontaneous it told me all I needed to know. "Personally, I don't know how you can possibly cope."

She laughed. "Anne-Sophie, Laure and I take it in turns. We all work partly from home, so we're lucky." She glanced discreetly at her watch. "I'll have to go soon. I'm on bedtime duty this evening."

"Of course. But first I want to talk to you as a father should. I'm still here for you, whatever happens. You only have to ask."

"That's why I had the test." She stared down at her hands "Just so I could hear you say something like that." It was such a charming *non sequitur*. "When you and I were both in hospital, it was an opportunity not to be missed. Particularly if you might not recover." Her face clouded. "I so wanted to talk to you about it on my visits."

"I wish you had." Her mood changes were as rapid as in my dreams.

"I knew you understood a lot of what was said. I didn't want to shock you, when there was nothing you could do about it."

"One more thing." This I had to get off my chest. "I should never have deceived you over the shorting. Can you forgive me?"

She smiled."How could you deceive me? You were asleep."

"Our dreams were more complicated than what you've read in our narrative." I described how the short had come about, and how I had briefed her. "I was convinced the cause was just, that the short would succeed. I was also certain you'd have wanted to help. But I had to protect you. In the remote chance it went wrong, and the members started suing and summoning prosecutors, I wanted you to be in the clear. But it's on my conscience that I put you in danger."

Her expression throughout was hard to interpret. Gone were the smiles, but nor was there any hardness in her eyes, nor any gesture of withdrawal. When I finished, she sat in silent thought. "Hope briefed me the way you told her to," she said finally. "You read my character very well. It was harder on Andréa, getting all that poisonous nonsense from *Monsieur De l'Ombre*. As he explained the other day." Now she frowned. "He said you gave him a hard time."

As I'd expected, he'd told her everything. "With the SFO and a judicial investigator sniffing around, I had to be sure who had said what and to whom. I hope he understood that."

"You needn't worry." She grinned at last. "He admires you."

"I don't expect secrecy between husband and wife, but there must never be a word to anybody else," I urged her. "Not to Laure, not to Anne-Sophie. Not even to your mother."

"I'd never say anything you asked me not to." Far from avoiding my gaze, her clear eyes never wavered, and I knew I could rely on her. "I was a little angry with Hope, though. I thought she didn't trust me. But I really wanted it to work. So there was no need to protect me, Papa." She let her first use of my title hang in the air. "But thank you."

"I was thinking of Clémentine-to-be, as well," I pointed out, as she readied herself to depart. "I'll walk you to the car park."

"I never believed any of that stuff from *Monsieur De l'Ombre*," she said, as we crossed the turf. "He seemed such an embittered man. Besides, Hope had told me all about the Sanatorium plans, and as soon as the shorting was over, she wrote to all the members. The forum went crazy, but of course they all came round soon enough. As Andréa said, it's very easy to forgive being made unexpectedly richer."

"It was a huge risk, even so," I reminded her, trying not to smile.

"Hope was very brave." Our feet crunched over the tarmac of the car park, and we soon reached her car, a second-hand Renault Twingo. "I'd happily have gone to jail for her," she added in a crisp, matter-of-fact voice, as she unlocked her door. "And for you, of course."

"In my dream, Mallory was the brave one," I countered, feeling more than ever that I deserved nothing. "The strain nearly killed her."

She embraced me with a warmth that took my breath away. "I didn't know her then, but now I love her nearly as much as you." With that, she drove off, leaving me with a lump in my throat, and thanking God, with none of Pascal's opportunism nor of Andréa's cynicism, that her willingness to risk prison had never been tested.

As I trudged back to my office, I longed for a similar heart-to-heart with my daughter-in-law. But Hope was back in London, and it would have to wait until next Friday, when, just before we opened the doors to our first guests, we planned to put kitchens and dining room through their final test, with a thank-you dinner for friends and helpers.

We'd intended it to be informal, but Armand soon convinced us that we must invite the mayor and the other *commune* officials who had been so helpful. Then Sylvie argued that a speech from at least one of us would be necessary, whereupon Mallory said that oratory was my department. "Besides, you're almost *Savoyard*."

"I don't know what to say that isn't known by everybody already," I protested. "After-dinner speeches are purgatory all round."

"Not if you remind them about Madame's vision," Sylvie said, "and how it kept you going despite the accident. Then thank everybody for their contribution. Nobody takes exception to being thanked."

"There's so many. Anyone left out will never forgive me."

"Just thank them all for their community spirit. They'll understand."

"I'm a foreigner, the last person to lecture them on community."

"Don't lecture them," said Mallory. "Just thank them."

So I bowed to the inevitable. But I determined to myself that my speech would go beyond platitudes. To explain the *raison d'être* of the Haven, I must spell out the grandeur of Mallory's vision, as well as the limitations necessary to its fulfilment. I must explain the inevitability of the financial crises to which the world perpetually subjects itself, and I must remind everybody that we could never rescue the entire world, but that our example might point the way to a more co-operative future. It was a tall order for a single speech, and as the day drew nearer, the enormity of the task only got worse. But I refused to shirk it.

The dining room, with its clean decor and airy spaciousness, was a far cry from the lowering grandeur of the Sanatorium ballroom. Yet, when the evening of celebration arrived, and as the guests found their places, I seemed to be looking down, from the top table, not upon the faces I knew, but on the ghosts who had haunted our trial.

Mallory sat to my right, in the central spot, with *Monsieur Le Maire* in the place of honour to her right, whilst his wife was the neighbour to my immediate left. We in turn were flanked by dignitaries from the hospital and the *Mairie*. Of our friends, only René, as our chief medical officer, and Armand, as our invaluable *notaire*, together with Sidonie and Céline, made it to the outer fringes of the top table, where they were too far away for friendly banter.

The steady chatter told me that our guests were enjoying their feast, though I scarcely noticed what passed my lips. I ate little, and I drank almost nothing but mineral water. The speech filled my mind, and my small talk was mechanical at best. But even the most elaborate meal must come to an end, and the time came at last for me to speak.

I began by thanking the mayor and his staff for their assistance, and I promised that the partners in the enterprise would do all in our power to ensure that Haven *L'Abri* would become a monument to the community they served as well as to the spirit of co-operation worldwide. "Without community," I said, "the world degenerates into chaos and greed." This was greeted with loud applause. So far, so good.

I then outlined our purpose and scope. "Small though we seem, this was, from the start, and always will be an international project. Our donors as well as those we are about to help come from around the world. We are therefore both local and global." The applause to this was more cautious, as the audience began to realise that I intended to engage their brains as well as their ears.

"When I, and then my wife more recently, came to live here, we came as strangers, neither of us a born *Savoyard*, and I cannot lay claim even to one French parent." I paused for the ripple of laughter. "Yet you forgave my outlandish ways, and took us both to your hearts.

"Throughout the ordeal of our accident and hospitalisation, we received the most dedicated and professional treatment, for which no thanks from us can ever be enough. Yet I am sure the doctors, the nurses and the management of the hospital would not deny the equal debt we owe for the kindness and support of our families and our friends, all of whom, I am delighted to say, are able to be with us tonight. To each and every one of you in this room, we owe nothing less than our lives." I raised my glass. "We salute you all."

The toast was impromptu, but the guests responded with enthusiasm. Best of all, Mallory's hand slipped into mine.

"I think none of us here would disagree that the real inspiration behind Haven *L'Abri* is the lady beside me. A man is entitled, if not expected, to say that his wife is wonderful, but I am able to say it with all my heart." Applause mingled with laughter, as Mallory looked up at me with a smile that was pitched between indulgence and alarm.

"She is, of course, being modest, and would rather I did not go on. Yet it is only fair to spell out something of her achievements. For the last ten years she has managed a fund for ruined investors in Lloyd's of London, and I can tell you that they are not ruined now, despite the credit crunch and its continuing fallout. [Applause]

"Yet all the time, she had a greater purpose in mind: to assist the real victims of that calamity and of those that follow. Thanks to her vision, to the efforts of everybody here, and to the generosity of our donors, we open our doors on Monday, to begin the task of helping those who can no longer help themselves. *Monsieur Le Maire*, Messieurs-dames, please raise your glasses to Madame Mallory."

The response was as enthusiastic as I could have wished, and even Mallory overcame her embarrassment enough to smile her thanks.

"I mentioned Lloyd's just now, because its near collapse in the nineties was the direct inspiration for Haven *L'Abri*. But in the wider context of the world at large, the Lloyd's debacle was just another financial crisis. Not the first. Not the worst. Financial disasters, I need not remind you, are as old as money itself; the spectres that haunt the feasts of plenty, yet predicted only by the tiny band of Cassandras to whom nobody ever listens. For the rest of my speech, I'd like, if I may, to analyse them a little." The room fell quiet, as the audience weighed their chance of being enlightened against their chance of being bored. "Don't worry. I promise to be brief." [Relieved laughter]

"All financial disasters are the same. First there's the new dawn, as some discovery seems to offer opportunity and wealth. Then, as the early promise seems to be justified, euphoria sets in, and experts convince us that this time it's different.

"If this were the 17th century, they'd have convinced us that demand for tulips, whose industrial production the Dutch had just mastered, could never go down. Until the market crashed in 1637. [Smiles]

"In the 18th century, they'd have assured us the South Sea Company and the Mississippi Scheme would be sources of ever-expanding trade. Until both bubbles burst in 1720. [Laughter]

"By the 19th century, it was 1840's Railway Mania, in which many more rail companies were speculated than lines built.

"Quaint and ridiculous they seem to us now. Yet today's experts are no better. ['No!'] Bulbs, exploration and railways were at the cutting edge of their times: in the 20th century, we were treated to the same nonsense over internet technology. Until the millennium crash.

"And now we're living through the 21st century credit crunch, because finance itself found its cutting-edge technology, convincing banks and hedge funds, even regulators and governments, that the instruments of securitisation had put an end to risk itself. Particularly when the risk in question – a nationwide fall in the U.S. property market – was judged to be minimal in the first place.

"Major default was impossible, we were assured, and minor defaults would be spread so thinly they would be invisible, thanks to the wizardry of mortgage-backed collateralised debt obligations, CDOs for short, not to mention their exotic spin-offs, like the Synthetic CDO squared." The audience smiled edgily. "In mumbo-jumbo lies safety, it seems." This time there was a trace of anger in the laughter.

"The Lloyd's disaster was not on the scale of the current one, but it seemed at the time very shocking. Just think for a moment about the nature of Lloyd's business. Insurance. Its whole purpose to combat risk not to create it; to be the cornerstone of prudence and security. Which indeed it was to centuries of shipping merchants whose prosperity rested precariously on the perils of wind and piracy, and who depended on Lloyd's when disaster struck. And which it still was in 1906, when San Francisco was smashed by earthquake and fire.

"Recognising the plight of its victims, Cuthbert Heath, the leading underwriter of his day, instructed his agents to pay all reasonable claims immediately. Not only did he prevent a disaster from becoming an irrevocable tragedy, he made Lloyd's a byword for probity and security. Heath, more than most, understood the farsighted lawmakers of 1601, whose preamble to the world's first Insurance Act defined insurance as the means whereby 'the loss lighteth rather easily upon many, than heavily upon few'.

"Insurance then, securitisation now. Different means, in principle, to the same end: to spread the heavy losses of the few ever so lightly upon the shoulders of the many. What's just gone wrong, and what went wrong for Lloyd's in the nineties, typifies what always goes wrong when greed, arrogance and stupidity – all bad, but none deadly on their own – combine to suppress prudence and even sanity.

"Our first guests, who arrive Monday, are the living consequences. By the time they were struck down by asbestosis and pollution, by natural catastrophe and industrial accident, there was no Cuthbert Heath, and little provision to meet their claims. Lloyd's syndicates, and insurance companies generally, were under-reserved, treating premiums as profit to the few, not provision for the many.

"How could it happen? As individuals, few of us ignore traffic lights or leave our doors unlocked; nor do we put all our eggs in one basket. Under normal circumstances, wise investors hedge their positions, forgoing some of their potential profit to insure against things going wrong. Sadly, organisations have shorter memories than individuals. Boom time blunts the memory, until the day prudence is forgotten, and hedging is for wimps. And for an obvious reason: the lag between money coming in and money having to be paid out.

Banks receive our deposits, funds receive our savings, and insurers receive our premiums before cash has to be distributed, well before capital has to be paid back, and long before insurance claims have to be met. During that lag, organisations take their profit, and pay their bonuses, so that by the time things go wrong, it's ordinary people who lose their deposits, ordinary investors whose savings are destroyed, and ordinary victims of disaster who receive no compensation.

"If it was bad then, it's worse now. Insurance has degenerated into a gambling game that any financial institution can play. They no longer cover their own risks, they bet on other people's, and every risk is gambled thousands of times over. They call it Credit Default Swapping. If that sounds like Las Vegas or Monte Carlo, it is: with one difference. Unlike casinos, financial institutions expect taxpayers to bail them out, because they're too big to fail."

Angry hands beat the tables as if they were war-drums, and I now had to shout. "And who was the highest roller of them all?"

Various banks were called out, followed by cries of "Tell us!"

"No, not a bank. The world's largest insurer, AIG, and for a time the largest issuer of swaps. The authorities forced takeovers of Bear Stearns and Merrill Lynch; they even let Lehman Brothers go bust; but AIG was bailed out by American taxpayers. The insureds had to rescue their own insurer. An Insurance Act of today would have to stand the wise, old principle on its head: 'the loss lighteth rather heavily upon the many, to the greater profit of the few'.

"The good news is we are fighting back. Right here, and right now. Some of our most generous donors work in the City and on Wall Street. The culture is rotten, not necessarily its members. We cannot save the world, that's a task too far for one community. But by providing support and guidance to some, we set an example to all. In this organisation and in this community, we work for others and for each other. At the very least, we offer an antidote to greed and arrogance; at best, in aiding others, we also fuel our own prosperity. The economics of altruism instead of the feeding-frenzy of greed. Thank you."

I sat down to cheering as well as applause. Smiling, Mallory whispered in my ear: "Rousing stuff, my darling, but you're forgetting our success was a total gamble. The only difference between us and the financial cowboys is that we were lucky enough to be right."

Chapter Thirty-Five : Closure

Somebody was shaking me by the shoulder, insistent that I woke up, and taking no notice of my grunts to be left alone. Drained by the speech and chastened by Mallory's criticism of it, I wanted only to be left alone to sleep until morning. At first, I thought it was part of some dream. Then, as I was dragged reluctantly from the deepest recesses of slumber, I thought it must be Mallory. "Not now, darling," I muttered. The shaking continued unabated. If it were Mallory, whatever she wanted must be more important than sex in the small hours. If it were Mallory she'd have said something. If it were Mallory, I'd recognise her touch. However importunate, Mallory was never rough, and there was always a hint of caress in her fingers.

I rolled onto my back and opened my eyes to thick darkness. I knew immediately that something was wrong. I turned towards Mallory's side of the bed, where the faint illumination of her bedside clock confirmed what my other senses already suspected. She wasn't there. Nor was there a crack of light under the bathroom door. I sat bolt upright. There was somebody else in the room, and it wasn't Mallory.

"You'd better come, Clem, if you want to save her."

The wasted figure at the bedside was as recognisable as his voice. Now I knew how his other victims must have felt: Micklewright, Pargetter, Wu, Brabazon, Wormsley, *L'Esprit* and *Le Baigneur*. I was only thankful that the accident had blanked Mallory's terror at the sight of a dead man come back to life. But surely Ambrose could not have cheated death again? The fall from the ferry he had planned; his cousin from CERN had saved him from fever, but no less an authority than Porfirie had pronounced him dead from a car accident, a version of which had found its way into the last of our comatose dreams. Those seven men only thought they had been confronted by a ghost: I was certain. No wonder that the hairs of my neck stood up like the quills of a porcupine, or that my heart threatened to shatter my ribcage.

I thought of Lisavette: the only victim to have accepted him as a living, breathing man, and who had been done to death more brutally than any of the others. Now anger conquered fear. Fitter than

357

Wormsley, I was not about to suffer a heart attack; angrier than the others, I was not about to give in quietly to my fate.

"What have you done with her?" I shouted.

"Nothing. But I know where she's gone." His voice was bone dry.

"If you've harmed her..."

He laughed, which had been rare enough during our friendship, and which sounded now more like a rattle of pebbles on a tin plate than a movement of throat muscles. "She's fine. She's just taken a walk in her sleep, like when she was a child." I demanded to know where she'd gone. "The same as last time. She's quite safe, if you hurry."

He switched on my bedside light. He looked terrible, even worse, I imagined, than when Andréa had seen him last. His eyes had sunk into his skull, and retained their prominence only in contrast to his wasted face, and his imploded cheeks. The veneer of flesh was so thin, and so pale, that I felt I was looking directly at his skull. The stubble on his chin seemed more like iron filings than hair. He pointed to my trouser press. "I'd get dressed, if I was you."

I did as he suggested, then I made for the door. Ambrose came right behind me, and he had no difficulty keeping up with me down the stairs, down through the main building and out the back door. A day later there would have been a night porter, but now there was nobody. Even so, the door ought to have been double-locked. Since her previous episode I had made sure to seal all exits from the building.

But I said nothing, simply hurrying across the expanse of the lawn, past the clump of mountain ash where I had sat with Marie-Sainte, and over to the water garden. It was not yet four, and the sky was overcast, adding substance to the darkness. It got worse in the garden, and under the trees. But I was immune to hindrance. My one concern was to reach Mallory as quickly as I could. I would have run, except that the ground was too uneven to risk it. Throughout the journey Ambrose said nothing, but he kept to my shoulder, emaciated though he was.

I heard the steady rush of the waterfall long before I saw it. In the stillness of the night, it roared like a hungry beast, and its impatience spurred me on. By the time I had climbed to the railed viewing point, I was panting hard. Just behind, Ambrose wheezed hoarsely. Ignoring the water, I looked up the granite outcrop, but I was too low down to see its summit. I raced up the path, until at last I saw her.

Dressed in her thin nightclothes as before, she hunched over her knees, hugging them for warmth. But she was no longer alone. Standing respectfully beside her, as he gazed down upon the cascade, was the *Le Baigneur*. He turned at my approach. "I'm sorry to disturb you like this, but there's been an appeal. It seems that one vital piece of procedure was omitted at you trial." He tapped Mallory respectfully on the shoulder. "Come, my dear, it's warmer in the car."

She roused herself immediately and allowed him to assist her to her feet. Then she scrambled up the rock to the path, taking my hand to steady herself. "Hello." She smiled at me, but at the sight of Ambrose she flinched. "This is all his doing." She took my arm.

Before I could say anything, *Le Baigneur* joined us. "If you would follow me." Such was his natural air of authority than Mallory and I fell in behind him as he led the way up the path to the very top. Breathing heavily, Ambrose shuffled in our wake.

At the top was another railing. It flanked a small car park, in which the only car was a stretched black Citroen DS with darkened windows. Standing beside it were *L'Esprit* and Wormsley. They greeted us sombrely. Then Wormsley opened the front passenger door. "If you please, Mrs Holden." He gesturing for Mallory to get into the car.

Now that I knew Mallory was unharmed, my courage returned. "Before we go anywhere, I want to know what this is all about."

"Mr Hanter claims that he was prevented from putting a proposition to you at your trial," Wormsley explained briskly. "Please get in."

"His condition at the time was ambiguous," *L'Esprit* added.

"Your wife's cold. We'll explain as we drive," said *Le Baigneur*.

"Let's just get it over with," Mallory said, through chattering teeth.

"Where are we going?" I demanded.

"We've commandeered an empty building," Wormsley said.

"It's only a few minutes away," *L'Esprit* added soothingly.

The car must once have been a diplomatic model, and there was space for two folding seats in the back, providing room for all six of us. It was also pleasantly warm, and Mallory soon stopped shivering. Taking the wheel, *L'Esprit* drove us quietly out of the car park and onto the road, which ran along a ridge of the hills. Above us, the summit of *La Tournette*, the highest mountain around the lake, brooded under a mantle of cloud. In the back, *Le Baigneur* and I had the permanent seats, with Wormsley and Ambrose facing us. Throughout the short journey Ambrose's bony knees dug painfully into mine.

"The situation is this," *Le Baigneur* explained. "Monsieur Antay," he now used the French pronunciation of Ambrose's surname, "Monsieur Hanter was himself close to death at the time of your trial. When I announced that the principal witnesses would be Monsieur Tonbridge and Monsieur Hanter, I was of the belief that Monsieur Hanter would be available to us. He nearly died in January 2008, not long after your accident. During three days of acute fever he came before the Court of Transition, but he chose to live."

"Your accident was a mistake," Ambrose cut in. "I hoped to see you recover." His knees dug more sharply into mine, but it was over his shoulder that his eyes strayed, towards her.

"He took some time to recover his strength, but he was never the same again. When Madame came to the Sanatorium last September, he was a very sick man, and he was under surveillance by the court from then on. At each appearance, he rejected a trial. But we had reasonable expectations, even so, of his being available for yours."

Mallory's supposition, which she'd articulated in the ballroom, was correct. Ambrose had not been called for cross-examination because he was alive, though he had been much closer to death than she could have guessed, or than the court had been prepared to reveal.

"How long were you squatting in the Sanatorium?" I asked.

"From mid-September," Ambrose replied.

"I'm amazed we didn't see you."

"Contact between you was forbidden," *Le Baigneur* stated.

"We're here," *L'Esprit* interposed, as he turned the car into a tall gateway. The grounds beyond were overgrown, and the driveway itself was choked with weeds, through which we made bumpy progress. The house was of a similar age to the Sanatorium, but much smaller, though it boasted one turret. Waiting on the steps of the gloomy porch were the two ushers, dressed as before. They were holding lanterns, which they held aloft as we got out of the car. Then they opened the door of the house, and we followed them inside. We passed through the hall, where their lamps cast eerie shadows on the high curve of the ceiling and on the dark wood of a wide staircase. Then we turned into what must once have been the drawing room. It was now bereft of furniture, but its lines were gracious. There was a magnificent stone hearth, with a blotched mirror over its mantel, and a huge bay, with long windows, in stone frames, pointed at their tops. Our feet echoed over oak floorboards that still retained a patina of their former polish. Behind us came the watchers, who must have been waiting in the garden, their faces hidden by thickets of bushes and trees.

As we took in our surroundings, the heavy table and chairs around which we had sat during the trial sprang once more into view, giving – as before – the sense that they had always been there. Even the heavy throne was back, so that for a horrible moment I had the sense of never having left the trial, and that all our recovery had been a tantalising dream. It was as much as I could do to take Mallory's hand, as everyone resumed their former places, whilst the watchers filled the room behind us. The only new feature was Ambrose.

The ushers set their lamps upon the table, which had the effect of throwing our faces into harsh relief. "The court is now in session," *Le Baigneur* said in a sombre voice. "As we were explaining, Monsieur Hanter was in a kind of limbo, too ill to do much for himself, yet not prepared to relinquish life. He was neither ready for a trial of his own, nor yet able to participate in yours as an active witness. That is why I told you, during your informal hearing, that we had him under control, but why you did not see him around the table as you do now."

Ambrose opened his mouth to speak, but *Le Baigneur* frowned him into maintaining silence. "As your trial progressed, Monsieur Hanter's condition deteriorated. He appears to have felt that you, Madame especially, would opt for death, and he wished to join you in that state. But when, to his surprise, you chose life he was re-galvanised. He rose from his sickbed and he did his best to hinder your return to the hospital in ways with which you are all too familiar. Since he was now active once more, we were powerless to intervene.

"Then, as a result of his car accident, Monsieur Hanter returned to our jurisdiction. Whereupon he pronounced himself ready to die. In the meantime, with some assistance, you reached the hospital in time, where you recovered as your son and daughter had intended. And there the matter might have rested." The watchers murmured eagerly.

"But on learning that we had assisted you in your journey, Monsieur Hanter felt he had been cheated. He lodged an appeal on three grounds: first, that as he was already under the partial jurisdiction of the court during his illness, he should have been allowed to participate in your trial; secondly, that as you were not yet recovered during his own trial, he should have been able to call you as witnesses; and thirdly, that the court had no authority to assist your return to hospital.

"On the third count, his appeal was dismissed, on the grounds that your return to the hospital by physical means was imposed by the court as a punishment for contempt, and that such punishment had not envisaged intervention by Monsieur Hanter; the court was therefore within its rights to restore you to the position you ought to have been in had Monsieur Hanter not intervened. On the first and second counts, however, his appeal was upheld, which is why we are here.

"Monsieur Hanter wishes to address you, and you are, of course, free to address him. As in all such trials, the decision rests with you. That is to say, Monsieur and Madame Holden, having heard *Monsieur* Hanter, you can either rescind or uphold your first choice; by the same token, Monsieur Hanter, having heard what Monsieur and Madame Holden have to say, you also may rescind or uphold your choice."

"What's Porfirie going to say if Ambrose suddenly springs back to life?" I demanded. It was an obvious question, and much easier to think about than anything else we had heard.

Wormsley answered. "When Ambrose stopped in the village, he got talking in the café to a stranger who'd recently abandoned his car in a snowdrift the other side of the village. They were both loners, about the same age, and not dissimilar in appearance. Ambrose offered to drive him into Aix. During the accident both men were injured. When the car finally broke down in Aix, the less injured of the two abandoned it. The man found in the car was carrying Ambrose's papers, so who is to say whether the dead man was Ambrose or the stranger?"

Ambrose nodded. "I simply come back as the other man."

"That's preposterous!" I protested.

"That is not an issue for the court," *Le Baigneur* asserted. "I suggest, Monsieur Hanter, that you make your statement."

"Why do we have to listen?" I demanded. "We made our decision months ago. A lot of people have worked very hard to make sure we recovered. We welcome our first guests on Monday. There's nothing Ambrose can say that ought to change any of that."

"Let's just hear what he was to say," Mallory said quietly.

"Why?" My anger was building fiercely. "He's a serial killer. I'm damned if I'm going to help him back on the rampage."

"You have no choice but to participate." *Le Baigneur* spoke ominously. "Not whilst you are under the jurisdiction of this court. If you again show contempt, I shall not be so lenient."

Mallory gripped my arm. "The sooner we start, the sooner we can get this over with. Let's just listen to what he has to say." Her eyes glowed darkly in the lamplight.

"Very well," I conceded, trying not to look at Ambrose.

"Monsieur Hanter, please." The watchers sighed expectantly.

Ambrose stumbled to his feet. Although he had followed my hurried pace to the waterfall, now he could barely stand, and his shoulders stooped. "I'm sorry about this," he said, "but I'm perfectly within my rights." He began in a hoarse whisper, but slowly his voice gathered strength. "You two have done pretty well for yourselves, all things considered, whereas I seem to have made a complete mess of my life. But I don't see how that entitles you to a happy future, and not me. I married you, Mai – Mallory, as you prefer – because I loved you and because I thought you loved me. But you cheated me at every turn. You

362

cheated on me with Rex, and, between you, you cheated me of out of a daughter. Then you cheated me over Lloyd's. I didn't want to join, but you insisted it would be a spectacular investment for me.

"It was, too. Spectacularly bad! Putting me on five of the worst losers in Lloyd's: Brabazon, Micklewright, Pargetter, Tonbridge and Wu. You must have known how bad they were. Otherwise you and Rex wouldn't have been stealing the syndicate's reserves. I should have shopped you to the authorities, but I was too kind. You told me such a wonderful story about rescuing Names that I went for it. But you did it as much to save your own skin as to rescue them. And because Rex asked you to. Putting him out of his misery must have been hard, even for you. I offered to do it, but you wouldn't hear of it.

"Then you set up Ghost Trader. You did well there, I grant you. Though whether it was all for your personal glory or to help your members, that's between you and your conscience. All I know is you made us keep the bulk of our investment in the fund. If we wanted to take out more than 10% in a year, we had to resign. Think of the control that gave you! And didn't you use it over Enron?

"It would have been a wonderful opportunity, but you wouldn't hear of it. You didn't even offer to help me do it on my own. So there I was, broke all over again, and living off your grudging charity. Is it any wonder I snapped in the end? I admit I provoked you into pushing me off the ferry, but you did it readily enough. Far more readily than I thought you would. But at least I can thank you. But for you I'd never have jumped on my own, and I'd never have fulfilled my cause.

"Your cause too is a good one, and I really hope you meant it all along. But what if I hadn't challenged you over the embezzlement; what if Rex hadn't begged you to remember Names; what if George Wiseman hadn't delved into the books; would you really have set up Ghost Trader? When it finally came to the great shorting opportunity, would you really have passed the profits on to your members, if I hadn't tipped you off, via Andréa, that I was on to you?

"The deception was Clem's idea, but you approved it, and he passed it on to Hope, the dutiful daughter. Only you can answer."

He paused to run his tongue, lizard-like, over his pale lips, and his eyes fell on Mallory. Her face was as expressionless as a mask, and she neither flinched nor looked away. Her hand, which had lain throughout in mine, pressed hard against my fingers. I smiled and blew her a silent kiss. Even *Le Baigneur* could hardly object to that.

"Since that peroration was mostly directed at you, Madame, would you care to comment?" *L'Esprit* asked quietly. "Or shall I?"

Mallory shook her head. "I have nothing to say, and nor should you. This is all old ground, well and truly picked over last time."

Le Baigneur turned to Ambrose. "Are you finished, Monsieur, or do you wish to address Monsieur Holden, perhaps?"

Once again Ambrose drew his tongue over his lips. "Yes, I certainly wish to address Monsieur Holden." His eyes glittered in the lamplight, and I was again reminded of a lizard. "We were friends once, weren't we? Good friends as these things go. I admired your get-up-and-go, your certainty over everything. It really was thanks to you that I didn't pull out of Lloyd's at our Rota induction. You were even more certain than she was, and because you were an outsider, who seemed to have done his homework, I trusted you." He held up a deprecating hand.

"It was my choice, of course, and I made it. I'm too cautious by nature, and it was only my instinct that rebelled. It wasn't until I got to know Amy that I realised how dangerous you are. Her instincts were the same as mine, but she had no chance against your granite certainty. The affair was our assertion of independence. That's all.

"I ought to apologise, but I won't. An apology from me would only patronise Amy, as though her actions were entirely dictated by me. Which they certainly were not. By the time I met her, her love was long gone. I'm only sorry I didn't tell you. That was cowardly.

"But you've more than had your revenge. You've really done a number on my ex-wife. Not that I can blame you. For all you both knew, I was already dead. But that doesn't stop the pain. Nothing can do that. Nevertheless, you probably deserve each other. She wanted to pull off the great short, but she needed you to work out the deception. How much of a deception, I leave to your consciences.

"Let me turn instead to the future. I told you that I had a cause, and that I faked suicide in order to further it. You called me a murderer just now, but I see myself only as an arm of justice. The financial world is too rich and powerful to be regulated. But not so rich or so powerful that it can cheat death. If governments refuse to bring its denizens to book, then we must do it ourselves. If they won't behave like decent humans, let them fear like animals.

"What I'm asking you, Clem, is to join my crusade against greed and corruption. You're fitter than me. With my cunning and your strength we'd be invincible. No more killing of innocents. We'd be the financial *Al Qaeda*, turning the pride of the greedy into fear.

"Remember that evening you broke Mr Wormsley's nose?" In the full flight of rhetoric, he turned on the man with a gloat of triumph. Ambrose as I'd never seen him before. "Remember how you said you'd like to go round the Room with a chainsaw? You were even angrier than me, Clem, at what they'd done to us. In your heart you must want to join me. We'd be the perfect team: Mallory healing the victims in the Haven, you and I eliminating the perpetrators. That way justice is done all round: fairness for me, happiness for you two, recompense for the victims, and, above all, retribution for the guilty."

For a moment he paused, whilst Mallory and I sat in stunned silence. Even the watchers held their breath. "I've said enough. Time now for action. I propose we return to the *Cascade d'Angon*, that the three of us stand on the granite outcrop. Then those of us who choose death should jump, and those of us who choose life should return to the path. No coercion, a free and simple choice. You two have chosen life once; give me the chance now to do the same."

The watchers could scarcely contain their excitement, and *Le Baigneur* had to rap the table several times to restore silence. "A most unusual proposition," he intoned, as he solemnly studied his knitted hands. Finally, he gave a heavy nod of his head. "Nevertheless, provided you all agree to it, I see no objection in law."

"It's a good idea," Wormsley observed. "A bit dramatic, but none the worse for that." Wormsley had always enjoyed milking the moment for its drama. He glanced now at *L'Esprit*, whose expressive mouth was already turning down to form a definitive frown.

"Perhaps, Madame and Monsieur, you would rather think about it first," said *L'Esprit* carefully. "I cannot see what purpose would be served by your being over-precipitate."

"It would save time," said Mallory decisively. "If Ambrose is happy with a quick decision, so am I. The sooner the better."

All eyes now turned on me. Yet my brain was in freefall. Ambrose sounded so mad that he had almost come full circle, back to sanity. At face value, his proposal contained a kernel of sense, as well as the smack of decisiveness. Only the stark drama of his proposition betrayed his preference for the mindlessness of Russian roulette to the wisdom of rational thought. Yet his purpose was cunning.

Here in the semi-darkness of this deserted house, where our faces floated disembodied in the light of the lamps, when our faculties were dulled by lack of sleep, he hoped to beguile us into a Faustian pact that we would not even contemplate in the sunlight of office hours. By choosing to live, we would be granting life to him, however little we relished the prospect, and by granting him life, we would be complicit in his crazy revenge. By choosing death, our lives would end up as curtailed and wasted as his.

Yet the thought of endless and arid debate, with Wormsley urging one way and *L'Esprit* another, of having to listen to the constant whine of self-pitying justification from Ambrose, filled me with weariness. He might hope to have us at his mercy on that sloping outcrop of granite, with nothing between us and the rock-toothed pool far beneath our feet, but there were two of us to one of him. Since *Le Baigneur* forbade us simply to walk away, it was better to get the matter settled at once. "All right," I said. "Let's get on with it."

In no time, the lamps had been raised, and we had been ushered back into the hall, and out onto the drive. As we climbed once more into the car, the watchers surged around us, so that *L'Esprit* could only edge the car towards the gate. He made up for it once we were on the deserted road, so that we were back in the car park above the waterfall in a matter of minutes. Throughout the entire journey, Ambrose's eyes burned from within their sunken sockets, but I ignored him, concentrating all my thoughts on Mallory, who sat once more in the front, gazing straight ahead of her all the way.

From the car park we followed the court officials down the path, with *Le Baigneur* in the lead. Dawn was approaching, but it would be another hour and a half before the sun cleared the mountain behind us and brought any warmth to the air. I peeled off my sweater and draped it around Mallory's shoulders, before hugging her to me. Smiling bravely, she did her best not to shiver. Ambrose stumped behind us in the rear. Throughout the journey not a word had been spoken.

When we reached the outcrop, we came to an unbidden halt and stood in a loose semi-circle on the path. "In the interests of fairness," *Le Baigneur* raised his voice above the steady rush of water, "I propose that each supplicant be assisted onto the rock by one of us. I shall assist Madame Holden, Monsieur Linberger will assist Monsieur Hanter, and Monsieur Wormsley will assist Monsieur Holden. When you are ready, we shall release you. According to your choice, you should each then take a pace forward or a pace back. Is that clear?"

Le Baigneur stepped carefully onto the rock, before reaching out to Mallory. Squeezing her hand, I released her with reluctance, fearful that she might be overcome by madness when the time came and step forward. But it was too late now. "I love you," I whispered, but I doubt she heard above the noise of the water. Gingerly she stepped onto the rock, wincing at its coldness upon her bare feet. She placed herself to *Le Baigneur*'s right, in the centre of the outcrop. Agile as always, *L'Esprit* was soon in position on *Le Baigneur*'s left, and then Ambrose worked his way clumsily down between them.

Until he was steady, I feared that he might try to push Mallory into the abyss, whilst telling myself that his target for dirty tricks was more likely to be me. Once he was in position, *Le Baigneur*'s bulk stood between him and any direct contact with Mallory. Now it was my turn. The task looked easy enough, but in the dim greyness it was difficult to secure a footing, but at last we were all in a line, with Mallory in the middle, Ambrose to her left and me to her right.

"Are you all ready?" *Le Baigneur* called out. "I shall count to three and then we will release you. One… two… three."

Wormsley's hand slipped from my arm, and he stepped backwards. *L'Esprit* and *Le Baigneur* did likewise. The three of us were now alone, swaying as we realised how precariously we were poised. I turned to Mallory to find that Ambrose had done the same. It seemed that we would take our lead from her, in my case because I feared what reaction my stepping back would provoke from Ambrose. What ran through his mind I'd no idea, but I was alert for any lunges.

"Whenever you are ready," *Le Baigneur* called again.

Mallory stepped smartly back. Watching her, Ambrose smiled, and it seemed like a leer of triumph. Instead of stepping back, he reached for her. Perhaps he only intended that she should help him to ascend, but I couldn't take the risk. Stepping quickly towards her, I shoved her backwards towards safely. She almost lost her footing, before *Le Baigneur*'s arms enveloped her. At the same time, Ambrose made a grab for me. I staggered, but managed to right myself. I was above him now, and he had his back to the abyss as he tried to rush me. I seized his wrists. Then I threw my weight forward and released him. His feet slipped, as he flailed his arms in a vain effort to restore his balance. But he was too close to the edge, and suddenly he was gone. His wailing shriek was cut off by the crack of his skull on the rocks below.

I would certainly have followed him if Mallory had not grabbed my arm. Then it was touch and go whether we would both fall, until she managed to grab hold of the very birch tree that I'd used the last time we were here. With arm-wrenching slowness she hauled me towards her until we collapsed shaking into each other's embrace. The next minutes were a blur, and by the time we'd dragged ourselves painfully upright, it had grown much lighter, and we were alone on the path. *Le Baigneur*, *L'Esprit* and Wormsley had disappeared.

"I'm sorry, I'm so sorry," Mallory repeated, as she kissed me with an intensity that was close to anger. It took her time to calm down. "I must have walked in my sleep again. You must have slipped. If I hadn't woken up, you'd have been over." She shuddered. "I thought you locked the doors so this couldn't happen."

I stared at her in amazement. "You don't remember?"

"Of course I don't. But I've never unlocked doors. Ever!"

I took her hand and led her up to the car park. It was empty. Was it possible they had simply driven away without my hearing the engine? Even if that were possible, why would they have retreated so quickly? I was expecting *Le Baigneur* to rule my pushing Ambrose as the most outrageous contempt, even for him to order Wormsley to push me over as well. I hurried down the path again.

"Clem, what is it?" she demanded, as she scrambled after me.

"I need to check something." I was soon down by the railing, with its clear view of the pool. If the events of the night had really happened, Ambrose's bloody corpse ought to be bobbing in the water, and I blenched at the prospect of it. Yet I had to know. I leaned over the rail and looked down. Below me the pool was disturbed only by the indifferent and endless flow of the waterfall. The events of the night, that were seared into my brain with such sickening clarity, had been another of my dreams. A dream in which Mallory had not shared.

Tears rolled down my face. The joy at discovering that I was not a murderer was tempered by the realisation that I had lacked only the opportunity, not the intent. As I replayed in my mind those last terrible moments on the rock, I understood all too vividly that Ambrose had reached for Mallory's assistance only; he had not intended to drag her to the edge, neither to push her over, nor to take her with him in a lovers' leap. I had pushed him to his death not to save her, but because I couldn't bear the thought of his being alive a moment longer.

The lesson of my dreams was all too clear. Better luck not better judgement nor loftier morals had prevented me from being the killer. In dream I'd experienced what Ambrose had done because I could have been the one to have carried out his murders, even of Lisavette.

"I thought I was going to lose you all over again," I said. "Instead I lost myself." She slipped a comforting arm around mine, and on the long walk back I told her the whole story. Back in our apartment, Mallory took a hot shower whilst I prepared coffee, which we sipped in the comforting warmth of our bed. "That dream was closure," she said at last, "You've finally got Ambrose out of your system."

"He'll never be out of my system," I answered gloomily. "For all I know he's still out there, and it's the stranger in the morgue."

"I'm sure Andréa could find out if there's any missing person from that night. But if you want my opinion, the idea of Ambrose swapping with the stranger came from that over-logical subconscious of yours. If Ambrose came to our bedroom, you assumed he had to be alive."

"Which means I killed him."

"A dream is a dream. Nobody's punished for their dreams." She kissed me softly. "I'm the one who actually pushed him, and you've forgiven me. Don't be so hard on yourself."

"Ever since his thing with Amy," I fretted, "I've always hated him."

"Yes, and it's eaten you up. Lord knows, I've hated him too. Whatever he's done, I have to take responsibility for driving him to it." She sighed heavily. "He's a scapegoat, really. All the ills of the world heaped on him. At least he had the courage to hit back." She kissed me decisively. "I think he deserves finally to rest in peace."

She curled up in my arms, and was soon fast asleep. But, exhausted though I was, I could not join her: my mind was still in ferment. Finally, I slipped quietly from the bed. Then I went downstairs to my office, from where I texted Andréa. He called me right back.

"Sorry to disturb you," I answered, "But there's something I'd like you to check for me." I gave him a brief outline of my dream. "Mallory has a history of sleepwalking, but I don't. So you can see my concern." Then I explained what I wanted him to do.

He promised to get onto it right away. As good as his word, he was back to me within the hour, whilst Mallory was still asleep. "I can set your mind at rest," he said. "There *was* an abandoned car the other side of the village, and the driver collected it the next day, once the road had been ploughed. He and *De l'Ombre* did chat in the bar, and he was offered a lift. But he refused the offer, probably because he thought Ambrose had drunk too much. According to the barman they didn't look that alike anyway. Porfirio would never have been fooled."

I was so relieved by his news, that my thanks were almost incoherent in their effusion. Patiently, he accepted that he was the best son-in-law that an undeserving man could possibly have, and promised to tell Marie-Sainte and Clémentine that I would love them for the rest of my life. Finally, he suggested that I pull myself together so that I could give the good news to my wife, who deserved to be told, and whom he loved and respected more than any woman of my generation.

I rang off, and raced up the stairs to the bedroom, where Mallory was just waking. I poured out Andréa's news in a breathless stream, before collapsing into the consoling warmth of her arms.

"That's wonderful!" She said when finally I calmed down. "Now we can concentrate on making sure this place is ready for Monday."

There was indeed plenty to occupy us that weekend, though we were fussier than we might otherwise have been, double- and triple-checking every last detail, and testing the patience of the staff to breaking point. But by Monday morning we were ready and waiting on the front steps, as *Madame de Maintenant*, her son-in-law and his brother drove up with the first of our guests.

It was June 29th 2009, and later that day, when the guests were all comfortably settled in, we learned that Bernie Madoff had been sentenced to 135 years. With Ambrose already committed to eternity, all that remained to us was the future.

The end